# DARK ANGEL

## THE LASSITER/MARTINEZ CASE FILES #2

## JOSEPH BADAL

SUSPENSE PUBLISHING

DARK ANGEL
by
Joseph Badal

PAPERBACK EDITION
* * * * *
PUBLISHED BY:
Suspense Publishing

Joseph Badal
COPYRIGHT
2017 Joseph Badal

PUBLISHING HISTORY:
Suspense Publishing, Paperback and Digital Copy, January 2017

Cover Design: Shannon Raab
Cover Photographer: iStockphoto.com/Derno
Cover Photographer: iStockphoto.com/Blake David Taylor
Cover Photographer: Studio Background/Danish Abbasi

# JOSEPH BADAL'S BOOKS & SHORT STORIES

## THE DANFORTH SAGA
EVIL DEEDS (#1)
TERROR CELL (#2)
THE NOSTRADAMUS SECRET (#3)
THE LONE WOLF AGENDA (#4)
DEATH SHIP (#5)
SINS OF THE FATHERS (#6) (To Be Released in 2017)

## THE CURTIS CHRONICLES
#1: THE MOTIVE
#2: OBSESSED (To Be Released in 2017)

## STAND-ALONE THRILLERS
THE PYTHAGOREAN SOLUTION
SHELL GAME
ULTIMATE BETRAYAL

## LASSITER/MARTINEZ CASE FILES
#1: BORDERLINE
#2: DARK ANGEL

## SHORT STORIES
FIRE & ICE (UNCOMMON ASSASSINS ANTHOLOGY)
ULTIMATE BETRAYAL (SOMEONE WICKED ANTHOLOGY)
THE ROCK (INSIDIOUS ASSASSINS ANTHOLOGY)

# DEDICATION

"Dark Angel" is dedicated to Heather Elizabeth Badal, a wonderful daughter-in-law who has brightened and enriched our lives in so many ways.

# ACKNOWLEDGEMENTS

To all my readers, thank you for your loyal support. You virtually keep alive my passion for writing. Your kind feedback and suggestions are invaluable.

I have been fortunate to have had reviews and blurbs for my novels written by many successful and prolific authors, including Mark Adduci, Tom Avitabile, Parris Afton Bonds, Steve Brewer, Catherine Coulter, Philip Donlay, Steve Havill, Anne Hillerman, Tony Hillerman, Paul Kemprecos, Robert Kresge, Jon Land, Mark Leggatt, Michael McGarrity, David Morrell, Michael Palmer, Andrew Peterson, Mark Rubinstein, Meryl Sawyer, and Sheldon Siegel. I know how busy these men and women are and it always humbles me when they graciously take time to read and praise my work.

Thanks to Tim Thackaberry for his invaluable assistance with IT issues. As technology becomes more and more complex, this writer would be lost in the electronic woods were it not for friends like Tim.

Thanks to John Badal for his assistance with Spanish language matters.

Deirdre Badal was extremely helpful with anecdotes that became an important part of this story.

Anne Carstensen contributed in a significant way by recommending changes to "Dark Angel" in the areas of forensics and police procedure. Her advice has been invaluable.

I am grateful for the assistance of Jim Coad in Albuquerque. Jim owns one of the premiere coin shops in New Mexico, which I have patronized for decades. He was an immense help in providing background about coin collecting. On January 30, 2016, just as I finished the first draft of "Dark Angel," two men entered Jim's shop, attacked him with a hammer and a taser gun, and robbed him. Jim courageously fought back and shot and killed one of the robbers. I am pleased to report that, despite being hospitalized after the robbery, Jim's injuries were not life-threatening and he is back running his business.

Many thanks to Sara Badal's expert editing. You contributed in a meaningful way in making "Dark Angel" a better read.

As always, I appreciate the continued support of John & Shannon Raab and of all the staff members at Suspense Publishing. You have all made the publishing process easier, more rewarding, and most enjoyable.

# PRAISE FOR 'DARK ANGEL'

" 'Dark Angel' is another thrill ride by acclaimed suspense author Joseph Badal. The second book in his *Lassiter/Martinez Case Files* series, this one finds them hunting a vengeance-crazed vigilante, who forces them to question their idea of justice. It's relentless from start to finish. Badal just gets better and better."
—David Morrell, *New York Times* Bestselling Author of "Murder As a Fine Art"

"Great characters, action and plotting. 'Dark Angel' is a real winner!"
—Paul Kemprecos, *#1 New York Times* Bestselling Author of "The Minoan Cipher"

"Tense, tight action drives you to 'Dark Angel's' pulse pounder ending. Badal's best yet and a thriller that keeps you up all night breathlessly turning the pages."
—Parris Afton Bonds, *New York Times* Bestselling Author of "The Calling of the Clan"

"The uniquely original 'Dark Angel' is a riveting, on-point thriller that reads like Brian Garfield's 'Death Wish' on steroids. The second in Joseph Badal's series featuring detectives Barbara Lassiter and Susan Martinez offers up a dark world of murder and madness where just enough light manages to push its way through. The pacing is crisp and the plot twists constant, as Badal plants himself firmly on the hallowed ground of Tess Gerritsen and John Sandford. 'Dark Angel' is crime-thriller writing at its absolute best."
—Jon Land, *USA Today* Bestselling Author of "Strong Cold Dead"

"From the first page to last, if you have a pulse, you're hooked! Badal delivers a gripping story that never gives up, never quits until all accounts are settled."
—Tom Avitabile, Author and #1 Bestseller of "Give Us This Day"

"Lassiter and Martinez chase from one end of New Mexico—and one end of the country—to the other, drawn deeper and deeper into a deadly game against killers who stand to lose millions. Badal just gets better and better."
　　—Steven Havill, Award-Winning Author of "Come Dark"

" 'Dark Angel' is an adrenaline junkie's delight. It serves up an addictive fix of high-voltage tension in a tightly-woven tale of spine-tingling intensity."
　　—Mark Rubinstein, Award-Winning Author

"In 'Dark Angel,' Badal masterfully weaves a plot which begs the question, follow the law or seek justice? Detectives Lassiter & Martinez refuse to back down from peer-pressure as they walk the tightrope between law and justice, proving they are one of the best crime-fighting duos in modern literature."
　　—J.M. LeDuc, Amazon # 1 Bestselling Author of "Painted Beauty"

"When renowned thriller author Joseph Badal picked up a different pen to write a police procedural mystery featuring two female cops, he hit the mark the first time out of the chute. Now he returns with Detectives Lassiter and Martinez pursuing a thankless case no one else will touch. Joe's thriller roots show through in this exciting mystery that features multiple points of view and disagreements between law enforcement agencies. Hang on for a mystery with thriller elements penned by an author who could teach a Master Class in suspense."
　　—Rob Kresge, Award-Winning Author of the *Warbonnet Mystery Series*

# DARK ANGEL

## JOSEPH BADAL

# PROLOGUE

*Three Years, Three Months Ago*

Robert Thornton barely suppressed a groan as he turned his head toward the hospital room door. The slight movement shot shards of pain from the top of his head to his ribs.

"Mr. Thornton. I'm Doctor Sheila Washington. Your surgeon, Doctor Crombie, suggested I come by."

"You . . . the shrink?" he muttered through his clenched, wired jaw.

Washington nodded and smiled. "I prefer psychiatrist, but shrink will do."

"You're . . . wasting time . . . here, Doctor."

"Hmm. Perhaps we could talk for a little bit."

Thornton shrugged and grimaced when even that little movement painfully racked his body.

"How are you feeling today?"

He pointed at his bandaged face and wired jaw. "What do you think?"

"Of course." She paused a second, and then asked, "How do you feel about what happened?"

"I promised Doctor Crombie . . . I'd speak with you. I always . . . keep my promises. But don't ask . . . stupid questions."

Thornton adjusted the oxygen tube in his nostrils and tried to catch his breath.

"Keeping a promise you made to someone else isn't the ideal motivation to meet with a psychiatrist. You should want to talk with me for your own personal reasons, not because you promised Dr. Crombie."

Thornton scoffed.

"What would you like to accomplish today?"

"To tell Crombie . . . I kept my promise."

Washington sighed. "That's it?"

"Yeah."

"Can I call you Robert, or do you prefer Bob?"

"Race."

"Race?"

"Yeah. Father called me that. Always racing around . . . as a kid."

"Okay, Race. Answer a question for me."

Thornton nodded once.

"What's the first thing you think about when you wake in the morning?"

Race closed his eyes and exhaled. "Same thing every day. In my dreams . . . and in nightmares."

"Uh hmm."

"The bastards who murdered . . . wife and daughters."

"What about them?"

"Finding them."

"And what if you find them?"

"I'll make them suffer. The way they made . . . Mary . . . Sara . . . Elizabeth suffer."

"So, you want revenge?"

Thornton stared at the doctor. "Whatever. Justice. Revenge. Payback."

The doctor's professional mask cracked momentarily, then she asked, "What other goals do you have?"

"None."

"We all should have a purpose in life. That purpose should be grounded in the mores and rules of one's society."

Thornton scoffed again. "I've always obeyed rules. Assumed most . . . members of society followed them. I was wrong."

"We don't get to change the rules if we expect a society to survive."

"Wrong, Doc."

The doctor shook her head. "You know what Confucius said about revenge?"

Thornton, expressionless, continued to stare back.

" 'Before you embark on a journey of revenge, dig two graves.' "

"I plan to dig more than two."

# PRESENT
# DAY 1

# CHAPTER 1

Robert "Race" Thornton checked the time as his burner phone chirped: 7 a.m. "Yeah, go ahead," he answered.

"You in the city?" Eric Matus said.

"Room 113. Corner of Tenth and Central."

"Ten minutes."

Matus sat across a tiny, round table from Race in an Albuquerque motel room. He watched a cockroach in a corner wriggle its antennae and then scurry under the bed. "You know, you can afford a lot better than this."

"You sound like a wife. I only stay at places without security cameras and that aren't picky about ID. We've been over it before."

"Yeah, Race, I know. But it's not much of a life...I didn't think it would come to this."

"If you gauge life by luxury hotel rooms and expensive restaurants, you're correct. I use a different metric today."

"I understand. It's just that I hate how our lives have changed. Three years of this shit."

"Eric, remember you called me. It was your idea in the first place. We'd both lost our families."

"Yeah, and you came through for me. You took out that drunk who killed Suzy and Andy after the bastard had been sentenced to probation. But we haven't gotten any closer to the men who killed

17

your family. Maybe we should . . . get on with our lives."

Race sniffed. "When they murdered Mary and the girls, I could have gone back to running my company, but that wouldn't have given me the time to do what I do now. I could have felt sorry for myself, been a perpetual victim. That's not me. I'll find the bastards one of these days. In the meantime, we're doing good."

"The law won't look at it that way."

"When the law brings justice to innocent people, I'll stop."

"You ever count how many ways you've . . . you know?"

Race shot an ice-cold look across the table, which caused Matus to look at everything in the room but him.

He squinted. "Strange question." Despite the time they'd known one another, worked together, Matus had never seemed to relax in his presence. He looked like a small-town shop keeper—always wore plaid sport jackets, a tie, permanent press khakis that probably came from Sam's or Costco, and comfortable lace-up shoes. Horn rim glasses and a crew cut completed the image. No resemblance at all to the Army-trained killer he'd once been. "Most people would want to know how many *times* I've killed. But I guess you already know that."

"So, how many ways have you"—Matus dropped his voice to a whisper—"killed?"

"Read the newspapers."

"I was just . . . you know, making conversation."

Race glanced around the room. He never met in a place picked by someone else, including Matus. He'd already checked the room for listening devices and cameras. He had been confident there would be none in this dive-of-a-room. He was just paranoid-careful.

"I'm not here for conversation. You hand over the information and then you leave. Just like always." Race softened his tone a bit. "You're exposed enough as it is."

Matus bobbed his head as though it was attached to his neck by a Slinky. "Yeah, yeah, I understand. Just like always."

"That's right."

Race sat up in the straight-backed chair and crossed one leg over the other. He looked at Matus and waited.

"Oh, right."

Matus slid a large manila envelope across the table. "The information's in there." After a pause, he said, "You know you could charge a lotta money for what we do?"

Race grimaced at Matus as though he were a slow child. "Jeez, Eric, you know it's not about the money. Are you telling me I'm not paying you enough?"

"No, no. I understand. It's just that . . . I guess I just saw an opportunity."

"You start thinking like that and you could get us in trouble. Money breeds distrust."

"I shouldn't have said anything. I hope you don't think I'd—"

"Eric, we've known each other for . . . what? Over twenty years. We were in Basic, AIT, and SF training together. We served together in Iraq. We saved one another's lives. You're the only person in the world who I truly trust."

Matus blurted an uneasy laugh and swallowed.

Race continued to shoot his squint-eyed stare until Matus finally seemed to understand it was time for him to leave. He stood and moved toward the exit. He grabbed the knob, but before he opened the door, he looked back over his shoulder. "Las Vegas. Wednesday."

Race said, "I'll be there."

"Okay."

"You forgot something."

Matus's expression turned uneasy. Then he threw his hands in the air. "Oh, yeah. The burner phone. Damn. Sorry. You have it?"

"Of course." Race tossed a burner phone to Matus, who juggled it and dropped it to the floor. He quickly retrieved it and held the phone in a two-handed grip.

"You know, we could do all this electronically," Matus said. "No face-to-face meetings."

"Yeah, I know. But even with all the safeguards I've put in place, most electronic communications can leave a trail. That's why I use IDs bought through the TOR browser on the Dark Web. I also opened a new email account there. The next message you get from me will have the words *two graves* in the sender name."

"Two graves? How'd you come up with that?"

"Took it from someone I talked to a few years ago."

"You sure about that TOR site?"

"Hell, Eric, even the NSA can't hack it. It bounces traffic off encrypted proxy servers. It involves over six thousand relays. And the software I downloaded is encrypted, as well."

Matus shot Race a sour look. "I just don't understand all that stuff, so I get nervous."

Race pointed at his Mac Book Pro. "Between the Dark Web, TOR, the burner phones we use, and that baby over there, you've got nothing to worry about."

"Forget I mentioned it," Matus said and left the room.

Race exhaled as the door closed. He used the next fifteen minutes to pack his bags and to stow his computer and the envelope Matus brought him in his briefcase. Then he left the room, walked three blocks north along 10th Street, to where it transitioned to Luna, turned right onto a residential street, and went to his two-year-old Chevrolet Impala.

The ride from downtown Albuquerque to the Old Town Plaza took five minutes. He parked on the plaza, in front of a small shop with a sign that read *Treasure House Books* and gazed around. This early in the morning on a cold February day, the plaza was almost empty of people. There was a gaggle of elderly women who had just exited the San Felipe Church on the north side of the plaza, and a delivery truck of some sort circled the square.

He sat in the car for a minute and thought about the private investigator out of Dallas who he'd hired to track down the men who'd murdered Mary, Sara, and Elizabeth. He felt a sharp pain in his chest. Heartburn had become a part of his daily existence. It seemed to occur every time he thought about how little progress the investigator had made. So far, the guy had found nothing. Three years and two hundred fifty thousand dollars. The three men who had invaded his home and murdered his family had certainly not stopped robbing and killing. The crew had invaded at least six homes since they'd broken into Race's Amarillo home over three years ago. He made a mental note to call the investigator and fire the guy.

Then Race thought about the conversation he'd just had with Eric. Warning vibes ran through him. He paid Eric two hundred thousand dollars, plus expenses, each year to do his research, to identify targets who had not been punished by the judicial system, to vet the families whose loved ones had been injured or killed. That was more than twice as much as Eric had ever earned in any single year. And now his old friend had again brought up the subject of charging their clients for their services.

The heartburn pain became worse. Race pulled a pill case from the Impala's console and popped two antacid pills. He'd have to be especially observant about Eric's actions. It wasn't about money for Race. Not just because he didn't need to charge for what he did. The insurance proceeds he'd received for his stolen goods and the cash from the sale of his house and the sale of his business had brought him enough money to live in almost any manner he chose for the rest of his life. But he didn't want it to be about money for Eric, either. He wanted their mission to be all about doing right, about making bad people pay for hurting good people.

Race took the envelope from his briefcase and pulled a folder from it. He stared at a photograph paper-clipped to several sheets of paper. The face in the photo was smooth and pinkish, almost child-like. He wondered if the man ever had to shave. The guy wore his blond hair short, in a sort of brush cut. His eyes were languid-blue; his lips slightly purplish. The nose small, almost feminine.

Race lasered in on the eyes in the photo. A shudder shook his body.

He considered Eric's question: How many ways have you killed? He'd never thought about it. A minute passed as he ran his assignments through his head. He could tick off each murder in chronological order. Could remember each one as though it had occurred yesterday. Thirteen in all over three years. Five different methods: Gunshot, fall from a roof, hanging, explosives, and drug overdose. One guy had even died of a heart attack when he realized he was about to be shot.

But Race's favorite method was to administer a liquid heroin overdose. It allowed him to talk to the target for a while before he passed out. To tell him why he was about to die. And, finally, to watch the scumbag suffocate. He never shared any of this information with Eric. The less his friend knew, the better. But there was another reason. He didn't want Eric to know about the conversations he had with his victims. He guessed Eric would find that weird . . . sick even. Those conversations satisfied Race's appetite for justice. When he first began on the path of vigilantism, he never imagined he could do what he now did. Sure, he'd killed in the Army, but that was different. His first assassination was only about payback, about giving the loved ones of an innocent crime victim some degree of satisfaction, of closure. And ridding the world of evil, too. But the more scumbags he confronted, the more disgusted he became, and the more he wanted them to suffer. Their pain seemed to ease his own suffering over the deaths of his wife and daughters.

He flicked a finger against the photo. "What will I do with you, Mr. O'Brien?"

# DAY 2

# CHAPTER 2

Detective Barbara Lassiter smiled at the reaction of the four male detectives to Detective Susan Martinez's entry into the Bernalillo County Sheriff's Department Violent Crimes/Homicide Squad. The men were seated at four desks that formed a square on the other side of the squad room from hers and Susan's desks. Since they were promoted to Detective Sergeant rank about six months ago, after they'd solved the Victoria Comstock and Nathan Stein murders, Susan had toned down her appearance. She'd swapped her skirts and blouses for conservative suits. She now wore low heeled shoes instead of spiked heels. But there wasn't much she could do to hide her long black hair, mahogany-colored eyes, sensual mouth, and perfect figure. Barbara suspected that Susan would still turn heads even if she came to work in a burlap bag.

Susan wasn't just gorgeous, she was bright, gutsy, and one of the most intuitive detectives Barbara had ever known. Barbara glanced down at her own outfit and wondered for the thousandth time whether she could ever turn heads the way Susan did. She was tall and statuesque, and now that she'd lost twenty-five pounds, she figured she could get away with wearing clothes that were sexier. But that had never been her style. She looked severe compared to Susan.

Susan moved to her desk. "Thanks for covering for me this morning. I'd put off taking my car into the shop for too long."

"What's wrong with it now?"

"Apparently, it needs a new transmission."

Barbara frowned at her. There was no point in telling Susan to sell the damned car. She was nuts about the vintage Corvette.

"What'd you do last night?" Susan asked.

"Henry and I went to the movies."

"I can't believe you. Henry, Henry, Henry. It's always Henry."

Barbara blurted a laugh. "You've got to get over my relationship with Henry. He's a—"

"—nerd. A stone-cold, anemic-looking, bore-me-to-death nerd. Look at you." She shot Barbara a toothy smile. "Next to me, you're the hottest woman in the BCSD. There are hunks that want to take you out, but you won't give them the time of day. Because you've hooked up with nerdy Henry."

Barbara smiled. She and Susan had had this conversation a hundred times since she'd first started dating Henry Simpson. She knew Susan actually liked and admired Henry. He was a full professor in the Geology Department at the University of New Mexico. He came across as a little geeky, and his wire-rimmed glasses only accentuated that impression. Susan was correct that there were a number of good-looking men in the Bernalillo County Sheriff's Department who had hit on her, now that she had gone on the wagon, slimmed down, and toned up. But Henry had followed her around like a puppy dog when she was out of shape, when some of the cops she worked with had referred to her as "Big Babs." From the first time they'd met, Henry had looked at her as though she was the most beautiful, fascinating woman on the planet. They'd met when he stopped to help her change a blown tire. From that minute, Henry'd acted like a love-sick teenager around her.

And Henry had turned out to be a selfless, attentive, energetic lover. There was nothing nerdy about him when he took off his clothes.

"You're just jealous," Barbara said. "Compared to Leno Sanchez—"

"Oh, that's got to be it." Susan made scales of her hands and moved them up and down. "Henry Simpson, Leno Sanchez; Henry Simpson, Leno Sanchez. How could I be so screwed up? I could have had Henry instead of Leno. What a fool I am."

"Leno Sanchez is all brawn and no brains. What the hell do you two talk about?"

Susan sneered. "You're supposed to talk?"

Barbara shook her head. Susan's expression suddenly went sad. She suspected Leno did nothing more for Susan than satisfy her libido. Ever since her husband, Manny, had shot her and then been shot and killed by Shawn Navarro, Susan had avoided emotional attachments with men. Leno Sanchez served a purpose, but it was a shallow purpose.

Susan's expression changed. She smiled and her eyes narrowed. "I don't get it. Your husband, Jim, was tall and handsome, a real hunk. Henry's like the anti-Jim."

Barbara slowly nodded her head. The conversation had suddenly gone in a direction that made her uncomfortable. Susan wasn't just her partner at work; she was her best friend. But she hadn't shared something with anyone, even Susan. She took in a big breath, held it, and then let it out.

"Yeah, Jim was wonderful. But what he looked like wasn't what I loved about him. It was the way he brushed an errant strand of hair away from my face. The way I'd catch him staring at me with a look of amazement on his face. How he'd bring me a cup of coffee in the morning, kiss my forehead, and walk away without a word. Jim loved everything about me. When cancer took him, I thought I would never get over his loss."

Susan's eyes glistened. "You don't have to talk about—"

Barbara held up a hand. "You need to understand something. Henry is nothing like Jim in the looks department. But he's everything that Jim was in almost every other way. I won the lottery when I married Jim. I won it again when I met Henry. How lucky can one woman be?"

Susan smiled again. "Henry's still a nerd."

"Yeah, maybe he is. But remember something—he's *my* nerd." She slung her purse over a shoulder and picked up a file from her desk. "Can we please drop the subject of my personal life and get to work?"

Susan pointed at the file. "We got a case?"

"Yeah. Let's go."

They took the elevator down to the underground parking garage and crossed the concrete expanse to their department-issued Crown Victoria. Barbara opened the driver side door and slid behind the wheel, while Susan got in on the other side. After she cranked the engine, Barbara handed the file to Susan. "We're going south on I-25 to Rio Bravo. Got a cold one. Been dead a while."

"Oh, damn. That means it's foul by now. It'll be a half-jar-of-Vicks day."

Barbara had never gotten used to dead bodies, which she knew was a disadvantage for a homicide detective. Susan somehow compartmentalized the victims in a non-emotional part of her brain. She could talk about homicides as though they were nothing more unusual than shopping or going to the movies. Barbara just couldn't make that happen. To change the subject, she said, "What did you do last night?"

"Nothing."

Barbara glanced over at Susan and knew from her body language and sour expression she'd done far more than 'nothing' last night. "Come on, fess up. What did you do?" She glanced at her again, and added, "Were you with Leno?"

"No. One night with Leno goes a long way."

"You mean you can only stand the asshole once or twice a month."

"Something like that."

"Hey, I remember. Didn't you have that hot yoga thing last night?"

"Yeah."

"You usually talk my ear off after you've been to your yoga class. All the hot bodies and great workouts. What happ—"

"Geez. Can't you stop bugging me?"

"Now you've got me worried," Barbara said. "What happened?"

"You really want to know?"

"Of course."

"Promise you won't say anything if I tell you?"

"Cross my heart."

Susan sighed. "You say one word to anyone and I'll make you pay big-time."

Barbara waited.

"I'm forty-five minutes into my class and the place has gotten real raunchy. I mean, there are maybe forty people in the room sweating their asses off." She scoffed, and said, "You know, that locker room smell that makes you wish there were a thousand Febreze Plug Ins in the room. That's all bad enough, but the guy on the next mat smells like he's been soaked in pickle juice. He reeks as though he hasn't bathed in a month. Got nothing on but a pair of short-shorts. No shirt. No socks. He's been spraying me with sweat every time he swings an arm. Then, like I said, we've been there forty-five minutes; he stands up, rolls up his mat, and announces to the class he has to leave."

"That should have made you happy."

"Thrilled. Absolutely thrilled. I was thinking I'd be able to breathe again."

"He didn't leave?"

"Oh, he left all right. He took the shortest route to the door and stepped right over me. Right over my head. Showed me his junk. Dribbled sweat right on my face. Came out of the bottom of his shorts."

Barbara said, "I hope that's the end of the story."

"It gets worse. Musta been a gallon of sweat on his yoga mat. He tipped the damned thing as he crossed over me and drained it right on my face. It was like being water-boarded."

Barbara stared at the highway ahead and tried not to laugh. She tried with all her might. To no avail.

"You promised me you wouldn't say anything," Susan said.

"I'm not saying a thing. I'm laughing. There's a big difference."

"It's not funny."

Barbara pulled a tissue from her jacket pocket and blotted her eyes. She attempted to control her laughter but failed. She laughed even harder when she looked over at Susan and saw her expression.

"I told you it's not funny," Susan said. But then she broke out in raucous laughs. It took them ten minutes to control themselves.

A BCSD cruiser was parked cantilevered to the four-foot-tall chain link fence that separated the street from a well-tended front lawn, backed by a tidy, blue bungalow with white window trim. The vehicle's roof rack lights flashed red, white, and blue in a hypnotic cadence that would have, Barbara thought, triggered a grand mal seizure in an epileptic.

She pulled up next to the cruiser while Susan radioed their location to the dispatcher. Then they exited the vehicle and moved through an open gate to the bungalow's small, blue-painted, concrete porch where a deputy waited.

"Hey, Patterson," Susan greeted the man.

"Good to see you, Detective."

"Where's your partner?"

Patterson pointed at the far end of the porch. "I'm breaking in a rookie. He's around the side fertilizing the lawn with his breakfast."

"His first stiff?" Barbara asked.

"Yep. And it's a rank one. Somebody turned up the heat to max level after they killed him."

Susan tilted up her head and took in a big breath through her nose. "Boy, I can smell it from here."

"Bring us up to date," Barbara said.

"9-1-1 got a call from a neighbor. Old lady in her eighties. Said the man who lived here would come over every morning and have coffee with her. When he didn't show this morning, she walked over to see him."

Patterson turned and pointed at the window on the front of the house. "Said she looked through the window and saw the occupant lying on the couch. Stark ass naked. When she knocked on the window and the guy didn't move, she called it in. We caught the call and found the front door unlocked. Just like the old woman said, he was naked on the couch. And deader than dead."

"Cause of death?" Susan asked.

The deputy raised his eyebrows. "There's a tent peg in the guy's chest."

"A what?" Susan asked.

"A tent peg. You know, for anchoring a tent rope to the ground."

"Huh," Barbara said. "Did you call OMI?"

"Yeah. Wulfie's on his way."

Barbara thought that was good news. Martin Wulfe, the Chief

Field Investigator for the Office of Medical Investigation, was the best the department had.

"Why don't you and your partner tape off the property."

"Sure," Patterson said. "By the way, the victim's name is Sylvester O'Neil. He's—"

"You're shitting me?" Susan said. "The guy who killed that kid, then got off because the chain of evidence was corrupted?"

"One and the same."

# DAY 3

# CHAPTER 3

Barbara and Susan drove to the Office of Medical Investigation on the University of New Mexico campus at 9:30 in the morning, after they'd gone to the Sylvester O'Neil crime scene. They sat in a glass-fronted observation room and watched a pathologist and morphologist work on O'Neil's corpse.

"What do you think about all this?" Barbara asked as she pointed at the body on a metal table.

"I think this case will be a bear to solve," Susan said. "O'Neil had a long history of child molestations, with two stints in the state pen. The guy was an unrepentant pedophile. I went through the computer database last night. There were seven complaints brought against him over the last ten years for everything from indecent exposure, to fondling little boys, to Adam Graves's murder."

Barbara shook her head. "I could kick the ass of the cop who screwed up the Graves case. I mean, how hard is it to log in evidence and follow the chain of evidence rules?"

"There's that," Susan said. "But remember, Adam Graves had asthma. OMI could never prove that O'Neil's assault of the kid caused his death."

"Bull. The assault is what probably brought on the kid's asthma attack."

"I agree, partner. But the wheels of justice and all that."

"I recall that O'Neil had somehow talked his way into a scout troop as a volunteer. No one checked his background. He went along on camping trips with the boys. Can you imagine? Talk about inviting a wolf to protect the lambs. I'll bet there were a lot more assaults than were ever reported."

"No bet," Susan said.

"Detectives," a voice blared over the speaker system. "We're done."

"Anything?" Barbara asked.

The pathologist said, "Nothing really. No fingerprints; nothing under his nails; no body fluids other than those of the victim. No hairs or anything else at the crime scene, other than the victim's."

"What about the tent peg?"

"Someone hammered a fourteen-inch tent peg into the victim's chest."

"Is that what killed him?" Susan asked.

"I'm pretty sure he died of a myocardial infarction," the pathologist said.

"He had a heart attack?"

"That's right."

Susan said, "I guess a tent peg inserted in your chest can do that."

"I'll tell you for certain after the lab tests are done. Give us twenty-four hours."

Back at the Violent Crimes/Homicide Unit in downtown Albuquerque, Barbara and Susan joined the other four unit detectives in a meeting with their boss, Lieutenant Rudy Salas.

Barbara glanced at Susan when Salas said, "All right, people, let's get this show on the road." That's how Salas began every meeting. That was irritating enough. But his voice squeaked, his ears were too large for his head, his body was thin to the point of emaciation, and his smiles were like grimaces. The lieutenant had earned the nickname "Sniffles" after the old cartoon character, *Sniffles the Mouse*. Barbara had always thought that "Gargoyle" would have been a better nickname. But, all in all, she was glad to work for Salas. He was a fair, experienced, gutsy boss who shielded his people from politicians. And he'd been responsible for promoting Susan and her.

After the meeting ended, the six detectives drifted to their desks. Barbara pulled a wheeled white-board over to her side of the office and wrote across the top, three headings: Date. Crime. Victim.

"Let's look more closely at O'Neil's victims."

"You thinking one of his victims killed him?"

"Or a family member of a victim."

"That will only give us the names of local victims," Susan said. "There may be a whole lot more around New Mexico, even out of state."

Barbara nodded. "After we pull what we can from his jacket, we'll access the Interstate Identification Index in the NCIC system."

"We should probably check the National Sex Offenders Database, as well."

After an hour, Barbara had written seven entries on the white-board. O'Neil's earliest arrest was for Indecent Exposure with a Minor fifteen years earlier, when O'Neil was twenty-two years old.

"You notice something about the date of the offense?" Susan asked.

Barbara looked at the first line entry on the board. "February 12. What about it?"

"That's O'Neil's birthday."

Barbara cleared her throat. "So, he went out and flashed a little boy as a birthday present to himself?"

"Could be."

Barbara scanned down the board. "Notice how his offenses escalated from indecent exposure all the way to murder."

"Not an unusual progression. This guy should have been put away for life a long time ago."

"Someone just put him away for life."

"Yeah, Barb, but how many kids were traumatized in the meantime?"

"Probably more than show in his jacket. Let's check the NCIC."

Susan accessed the National Crime Information Center database, input Sylvester O'Neil's name, and exclaimed, "Holy cow."

"What?"

"I got"—she counted out loud—"one, two, three, four . . . fourteen arrests, including the seven in his jacket. He committed seven other crimes outside New Mexico. In three different states." She hesitated for a moment. "This gets curiouser and curiouser."

"How so?"

"The notes in the file raise the possibility that O'Neil committed dozens more assaults over the years. There's an entry here that says the FBI assigned a team of agents to investigate child molestation cases. Based on M.O., O'Neil was one of the suspects in those cases. But there was no forensic evidence to ID the perps."

"How'd all that information wind up in O'Neil's file?"

Susan shrugged. "Maybe we should call the Bureau and ask if they'll share with us."

"Don't hold your breath."

"You have a friend at the Bureau. Why don't you call her?"

"I wouldn't call Sophia Otero-Hansen a friend. She was a little aloof when we worked together at APD. Now that she's a federal agent, she'll probably be insufferable."

"Worth a try."

Barbara nodded. "You know there's something else we should ask. If there have been any other murdered pedophiles who had tent pegs hammered into their chests."

"Or other unusual items stuck in ungodly places."

Barbara stood, stretched her back, and walked back and forth in front of the white-board. After a while, she said, "I guess we'll have to talk to the families of the local victims. They would have the best motive for murdering O'Neil."

"Yeah," Susan said. "Let's start with the Graves family."

# DAY 4

# CHAPTER 4

The nightmare never varied. It recycled itself in Race Thornton's brain in the same detail, with identical sameness, almost every night. The only nights that were nightmare-free followed bouts of binge drinking capped by an Ambien. But those booze/drug reprieves were few and far between. Race didn't like the fuzzy feeling that followed in the wake of scotch and sleeping pills.

He awoke with a start, drenched in sweat, a phantom drummer beating a violent riff against the inside of his skull. Screams seemed to echo off the room walls. That's how the nightmare wreaked its worst on him. He wiped tears from his eyes and moved to the side of the hotel room bed. Involuntary groans rumbled inside his chest.

"Damn," he whispered as he glanced at the bedside clock. It was 5:37 a.m.

Race moved off the bed and looked out the window at the glare and glitz of pre-dawn Las Vegas. Shadowy figures moved wraith-like on the walkway that extended from the hotel to the Strip. Like prowlers on the hunt for depravity. A taxi crawled slowly up the boulevard, like a shark on the hunt for prey. Even at this hour, there was activity. He considered a run on the street. It was important to stay in shape, in light of his new profession and having crossed the forty-year-old threshold. But a plastic bag that blew past the window on a violent February blast of wind persuaded him that the treadmill in the hotel's postage stamp-sized exercise room was the preferable option.

He tried to flex his shoulders as he moved to the bathroom, but the damage done to them no longer allowed the range of motion he'd once had. Not that he needed reminders of the night he lost his family, the night he was nearly beaten to death, but part of his daily ritual was to examine his body and face in the mirror. Each scar reminded him of that night, and the sight of each one rekindled the hate and anger that perpetually simmered within him. Race traced a finger along the scar that seemed to creep out of the middle of his hairline, like a snake crawling from its cover. That one was now more white than pink, to match the color of his hair that had gone from black to white almost overnight. He brought the finger down between his hazel-colored eyes, to his nose and followed the S-curve that his once-straight nose made. Another scar meandered from his left ear lobe to the top of his cheek bone. He moved his jaw from side to side and felt the tightness that had been there for over three years. Ever since the intruder broke his jaw with a tire iron, laughter, or even a full smile, was no longer easy for him. Not that he had anything to laugh about. He couldn't remember the last time he'd found anything truly humorous. He stared intently at the scars on his shoulders—zippered reminders of the work the surgeon had done to repair the broken bones and ruptured tendons.

"I guess I could be called ruggedly handsome," Race whispered to his reflection in the mirror. But he knew that was a stretch. He looked more like a punch-drunk journeyman boxer than ruggedly handsome. Good looking once; he and Mary had always been the most attractive couple wherever they went. Now his wife's beauty was a fading memory and he had become damaged goods.

After he washed his face, he dressed for a workout. He'd put in an hour on a treadmill, another hour on free weights. After his exercise routine, he'd clean up, dress, and meet Eric Matus at a diner. If things went well, he'd be on the road by tomorrow.

At 7 a.m., Eric Matus reconnoitered the exterior of the Shrine-Most Holy Redeemer Church on Reno Drive. There were only two cars in the lot behind the building. Then he went inside and sat in the last pew. He observed an elderly man and woman seated halfway toward the front, in the middle of a pew on the left side of the aisle. A very old woman sat in a wheelchair in the aisle at the front, also on the left side of the center aisle. A young woman sat in the pew next to her. Satisfied with what he saw, Matus walked the street to his Toyota Land Cruiser and dialed a number.

"Yeah, this is Salvatore Puccini."

Puccini's telephone voice was soft, but a bit shrill. That wasn't what Eric Matus had expected. He'd seen a photo of the man on the Internet. Big, beefy guy with a full head of salt-and-pepper hair and hands like catchers' mitts.

"Right on time," Puccini said. "That's good. Shows respect."

"Respect is important," Matus said.

"So, you say you're dependable."

"No one better."

"Why do you do it?"

"Do what?"

"Kill for money."

"You mean kill assholes for money."

"Yeah. But why?"

"Justice."

"Bullshit. There's got to be more to it than that."

"Do you really care?"

"Yeah, I do."

Matus hesitated for a few seconds. "Personal reasons."

"What sort of personal reasons?"

"What difference does it make?"

Puccini paused as though considering Matus's question. "I understand *personal*. This is very personal to me. But I don't want some guy working for me who likes to kill; some psychopath. I want to hire a guy who feels what I feel. Who doesn't take an assignment just for the dough. Who wants to get rid of scum."

Matus cringed at Puccini's use of the word "psychopath." What else would you call someone who murders people? He shook his head as though to rid it of the unwanted thought. He didn't like where this conversation had headed. "I assure you—"

"Just answer my question and I'll deliver the package. Why do you do it? Something happen to you? You don't answer, I walk."

Matus sat silently for a full ten seconds. He knew he would break trust with Race if he told Puccini anything personal about either of them. But Puccini's job was a threefer—three targets; sixty thousand dollars.

"I was Joe Citizen. Never even had a parking ticket." He took a deep breath and waited a long beat. "Came home one night from work and found a cop on my doorstep. He told me my wife and son had been killed in a crash with a drunk driver. The guy had thirty DUIs before he killed my family."

"What did they do to the guy?"

"His license was suspended and he got off on probation."

"What did you do about that?"

Matus's throat seemed to constrict. He swallowed, and said, "I killed him."

Puccini said, "You're the man for me. You'll have the package in fifteen minutes."

Matus watched a black Cadillac sedan pull up in front of the church fifteen minutes later. He recognized Salvatore Puccini when he exited the Cadillac. He admired the way the man carried himself as he walked into the church—erect, proud, in command. Despite the events that had occurred over the past year, Puccini seemed to have survived emotionally and physically. But, Matus thought, you can never know what goes on inside a man's brain, especially after what happened to Puccini's granddaughter. He could relate. Any memory of the smiling, beautiful faces of his own wife and son was a throat-tightening, heart-wrenching experience. All he needed to do was think for an instant about them and the face of the bastard who had murdered them that day in Salt Lake City would fill his mind's eye. Venomous hate would overwhelm him, and he would once again regret that he hadn't avenged his wife and son's deaths himself, instead of Race doing it for him.

He felt swamped with guilt about the story he'd told Puccini. At least the part about who killed the drunk who'd murdered his family. But he couldn't come up with another way to relate the tale. He didn't want anyone to know that another person was involved with him. That could only expose Race, who had as much motivation to kill scumbags as he had. Matus thought again about what had happened to Race. How he came home from work one night and came face-to-face with a guy in his kitchen. The guy beat him with a tire iron. Nearly killed him. When he came to in the hospital, he'd learned his wife and two teenage daughters had been tortured and brutally murdered. DNA and fingerprints at the scene showed there had been three men involved, but all that could be determined from the DNA was that two of the men were white and one was black. The authorities couldn't connect the DNA and fingerprints to anyone. Apparently, none of them had ever been arrested or worked for the government.

Matus's mind leaped back to the present when Puccini left the church less than a minute after he entered, returned to the sedan, and drove away.

Matus watched the church for an hour after Puccini left. Then he crossed the street and went inside. He moved to the fifth pew from the rear, on the left side of the nave, and sat down by the aisle. He knelt, reached under the pew in front of him, grasped the envelope taped there, pulled it free, and slipped it under his sport jacket. He looked at his watch as he left the church and noted that he had fifteen minutes to meet Race.

Back in his SUV, Matus removed the sixty thousand dollars in cash from Puccini's envelope and stuffed it into the glove compartment.

Parked across the street from the diner, Race watched from his blue Chevrolet Impala as Eric Matus left his Toyota SUV in the parking lot and climbed three steps to the diner door. He took a seat in a corner of the aluminum-clad building. Race continued to observe the diner and surrounding area. After ten minutes, confident no one suspicious was around, he left the Impala, walked to the front door of the building, and joined Matus in the booth.

"Everything okay?" Race asked.

Eric gave him a nervous smile. "Everything's fine." He pushed a large envelope across the table. "Big job this time."

"Why's that?" Race asked.

Eric looked around, leaned forward and, in a lowered voice, said, "Multiple bad guys."

Race waited.

"It's all in there. Client's eighteen-year-old granddaughter was raped by three college football players at a frat party. All rich kids. Parents politically connected. Claimed it was consensual. Can you believe that? Judge here in Vegas gave them all suspended sentences because the girl couldn't testify. She's been institutionalized ever since the attack."

Race felt his blood boil. He passed a throwaway phone to Eric. "As usual, it's already programmed with the number you should call next time. Make sure you destroy the phone after you call me."

"Come on, Race. How many times have we done this? I know what to do."

Race slid from the booth and went outside. He drove to his hotel and studied the file in his room. Then he walked across the street to a bank and accessed the safety deposit box he'd opened there two years earlier under one of his aliases. He'd provided the bank with a social security number and address he'd bought off the Dark Net, an overlay network that could only be accessed with specific software, configurations, or authorization, and paid for the box five years in advance. After the clerk left him alone, he removed ten thousand of the five hundred thousand dollars he'd originally placed in the box. The key to the box then went back into his wallet to accompany the keys to the safety deposit boxes he'd rented in Albuquerque, Newport Beach, El Paso, and Denver.

The wind had subsided since he'd left the hotel earlier that morning, and the temperature had climbed to a comfortable sixty-two degrees. Race drove to the neighborhoods where the three rapists lived—two in The Ridges Community, the third in Spanish Trails. The communities were gated. Access would be a problem.

He picked up the file with the boys' photos and found the name and number of the attorney who had represented the three at trial: Samuel Jacobson. He used a burner phone to call the lawyer's number.

"Samuel Jacobson's office; Maria speaking."

"Hello. My name is Walter Reidy. I've just moved to Las Vegas and want to hire an attorney who can represent me on a business deal."

"I'm sure Mr. Jacobson can assist you, Mr. Reidy. Let me check his calendar."

When Maria came back on the line, she said, "Mr. Jacobson has some time available next Monday. He could—"

"I'm interested in buying a casino hotel in Las Vegas. This is a matter of some urgency, so I need to immediately retain an attorney. I guess I'll have to call someone else. Thank you for—"

"Well, if it's urgent . . . ."

"I can meet with Mr. Jacobson this evening, say about 6:30?"

"Let me check. Please hold."

Race listened to sappy elevator music for half-a-minute, then a man said, "Mr. Reidy, this is Sam Jacobson. I understand you want to meet with me this evening. Can you give me a bit more information?"

"Of course, Mr. Jacobson. I represent an investor group that has just begun negotiations with the owner of a casino group. It is our policy to retain local counsel whenever we prospectively acquire property in a new community. I understand you are an experienced litigator. We would like to bring you on board our team in case litigation should become necessary."

"I see," Jacobson said. "I would require a retainer agreement."

"That would be no problem. If you could prepare an agreement today and meet with me tonight, I can execute the agreement and write a check then."

"That sounds acceptable, Mr. Reidy. Do you have my office address?"

"Yes. I'll see you at 6:30."

# CHAPTER 5

Jimmy Frankel was an artist. He was the best *paper hanger* in Los Angeles. So, when Frank Armbruster met with him, it was initially just another day at the office for Frankel.

"Tommy Malatesta says you're the best there is," Armbruster told Frankel.

"The diamond merchant?"

"Yeah."

"How do you know Tommy?"

"Is that really important?"

Frankel shrugged. "What can I do for you?"

"I want passports, international drivers' licenses, and credit cards that will pass muster for travel abroad. For two people."

"When do you need them?"

"Tomorrow."

"You gotta be shittin' me."

"Nope."

"That'll cost you extra. Twenty grand. Half now; half on delivery."

Armbruster handed over a stack of hundred dollar bills, passport photos of himself and of his girlfriend, and the aliases they planned to use. "Remember, I need everything by tomorrow."

Frankel nodded. "They'll be ready."

After the call, an itch started at the back of Frankel's brain. Something about Armbruster rang a bell in his memory. The man's name was unusual and Frankel thought he'd heard it before. He shook his head as though that might jar his memory, but he couldn't come up with anything.

Frankel went to work on Armbruster's documents and had completed everything but the passports by the time the sun had set. He picked up the passport photos and stared at them. The woman was a real looker. Armbruster was obviously hitting way out of his ballpark with her. Guy must have a lot of money, he thought.

Then it hit him. Money. He looked at Armbruster's passport photo again and concentrated on the warts on his cheeks and forehead. The guy had a veritable wart farm on his face. He remembered what Stan Bukowski had told him months before. Bukowski was a money launderer to whom Frankel had sold fabricated IDs for the day when Bukowski might have to jump the border to avoid American authorities. He had told Jimmy that some guy he called Wartface managed some of his money. Seven figures, he'd said.

Frankel laughed. Looks like old Stanley Bukowski is about to get screwed, he thought. His investment guy apparently planned to skip town. Then Frankel thought how grateful Bukowski might be if he gave him a heads-up about Armbruster. He picked up his cell phone and dialed Bukowski.

"Hey, Jimmy," Bukowski said.

"Hey, Stan. How they hangin'?"

"What's on your mind, Jimmy? I got no time to shoot the shit."

Frankel had a sudden urge to just tell Bukowski to go to hell. Arrogant bastard. But then he considered that he might need a favor from the man down the road.

" 'Member that guy you mentioned to me? Called him Wartface?"

"Yeah, what about him?"

"Is his name Armbruster?"

"What's this about, Jimmy?"

"Is that the guy?" Frankel asked.

"Yeah. So what?"

"I think you got a problem."

# CHAPTER 6

"Detective Lassiter, it's Martin Wulfe."

"Hey, Wulfie, you got anything for us?"

"Hmmpf," Wulfe blurted, as he always did when someone addressed him by the hated nickname. "Yeah, I got something for you. The lab report came back on O'Neil. We also received the final results of the autopsy. O'Neil died of severe hypoxia."

Barbara put her phone on speaker and waggled a finger at Susan to come over to her desk. "It's Wulfie," she whispered.

"Go ahead, Wulfie. Susan's on the line, too."

"As I was saying, Sylvester O'Neil died from severe hypoxia that brought on a myocardial infarction. He ingested a significant amount of liquid heroin, which suppressed his breathing to the point of coma and then stopped his heart. If he had survived, he would probably have had massive brain damage."

"What about the tent peg?" Susan asked.

"Inserted post-mortem. It was probably symbolic."

"So," Barbara said, "someone forced O'Neil to swallow liquid heroin."

"Probably. It's unlikely the deceased would have drunk the stuff voluntarily. It would have been possible, however. But the tent peg indicates something else entirely."

"You find any other forensic evidence?" Susan asked.

"Nothing."

Barbara drove the Crown Vic from downtown to Albuquerque's Jefferson Corridor. Victor Graves's office was on the top floor of a sprawling three-story building located in an industrial park. The marquee on the front of the building announced *New Mexico Herald-Tribune*.

"Nice digs," Susan muttered as they entered the newspaper's executive office area. The basketball court-sized space was all leather, oriental carpets, and expensive oil paintings. Even the receptionist—black dress, pearls, chignon hair style, black heels—looked expensive.

Barbara flashed her ID. "I'm Detective Barbara Lassiter. This is Detective Susan Martinez. We would like to speak with Mr. Graves."

"Do you have an appointment, Detectives?"

Barbara moved against the reception desk and glared at the woman. "No," she said in an icy voice. "Why don't you play nice and tell Mr. Graves two Bernalillo County Sheriff's Department detectives want to see him."

The receptionist broke off eye contact, picked up the telephone receiver on her desk, and punched in numbers. "Two detectives would like to see you, Mr. Graves," she said. She listened for a few seconds, put down the phone, and said to Barbara, "Please follow me." She led them to a small conference room off the reception area, pointed at the chairs at a small table, and said, "Mr. Graves will be right with you." Then she turned around and left.

"No...'would you like a cup of coffee, ladies'?" Susan said. "Maybe if you'd been more pleasant."

"That *was* me being pleasant," Barbara said.

"You're getting grumpy, partner."

"Dead bodies do that to me."

The door opened and a man entered. He was of medium height, trim, tanned, and well-dressed in a tailor-made navy-blue suit, brilliant-white dress shirt, and red power tie. Gold-framed glasses were perched on the end of his nose. He removed the glasses after he closed the conference room door and turned to look at Barbara and Susan, who stood and introduced themselves.

"Victor Graves," he said and shook their hands.

Barbara focused on Graves's eyes. Although he smiled as he took her hand, there was a deep sadness there.

Graves sat and Barbara and Susan reclaimed their chairs. He said, "I assume this is about the murder of that bastard, Sylvester O'Neil."

"That's right, sir," Barbara said.

"My reporter who wrote the story said O'Neil died of a drug overdose. Is that correct?"

Barbara nodded. "There were drugs involved in his death."

"I hope he suffered," Graves said.

"We can understand how you feel, Mr. Graves," Susan said. "But—"

"You ever lose a child, Detective?" Graves asked.

Susan shook her head.

"With all due respect then, there is no way on earth you can understand how I feel."

"Mr. Graves," Barbara interjected, "we have a murder on our hands and a job to do. O'Neil was a bad guy, but that doesn't justify vigilantism."

"Vigilantism? Why do you think that? O'Neil was a low-life. Maybe he was involved in a drug deal that went bad."

"There was evidence that the murder could have been payback for something O'Neil had done."

Graves just glared at Barbara. The sadness in his eyes had hardened to a steely aspect.

Susan said, "We hoped that you might be able to shed some light on who might have wanted to kill O'Neil."

"You mean besides me?"

Barbara coughed. "You obviously had motive."

Graves nodded, closed his eyes, and compressed his lips. After a few seconds, he opened his eyes, and said, "Let me tell you ladies something. If I didn't have a wife and two other children, I would have killed Sylvester O'Neil with my bare hands. I would have made him suffer the way he made Adam suffer." He paused, looked down at his hands, and cracked his knuckles. When he looked up, his eyes were moist. "I hope you'll never feel the way I do. I hope you'll never experience the pain, the anger, the hatred I feel." He paused again.

"I swear I didn't touch Sylvester O'Neil. I did *not* murder that sick bastard." He looked from Barbara to Susan, then back to Barbara again. "Now, if you're through here, I have work to do."

Barbara and Susan stood as Graves moved from his chair and half-opened the door. He stopped and turned back to them. "The next time you want to talk with me, call to make an appointment, so I can alert my attorney. I wouldn't want to say something, whatever it could possibly be, that would assist you in identifying the person who killed O'Neil." He added, "I consider the person who killed that monster a saint. I will be grateful to him or her for the rest of my life."

"Mr. Graves, I don't—"

He raised a finger to stop Barbara. "I've said enough. Have a good day."

Graves left the room. His "Ice Queen" receptionist then appeared in the doorway, and said, "May I show you . . . ladies out?"

Back in the Crown Vic, Susan said, "You notice that Graves said he didn't touch or murder O'Neil?"

"Yeah. He also said he wouldn't want to say anything that might help us ID O'Neil's killer. How could he possibly say anything that might help us ID the killer if he didn't hire the killer?"

Susan shrugged. "And he never said that he had *nothing* to do with O'Neil's death."

"You thinking that Graves had something to do with sending a killer after that scumbag O'Neil?"

"No doubt in my mind. But we've got two problems. First, how to prove it."

"And second?" Barbara asked.

"Do we want to?"

# CHAPTER 7

Race spent part of the afternoon working on his disguise. He touched up his hair with black dye and used theatrical makeup to make his broken nose appear straighter, to cover the perpetual dark circles under his eyes, and to conceal the scars on his cheek and forehead. He put on a pony-tail extension, blue contact lenses, and tinted wire-rimmed glasses, and wrapped a padded waistband around his torso. Race Thornton no longer looked rugged. He now presented the appearance of a sloppy, out-of-shape college professor.

Race arrived at Samuel Jacobson's office at 6:30 with a briefcase in one hand and an overnight bag in the other. He bent over slightly to conceal his six foot, two inch height.

"Mr. Reidy?" Jacobson asked when he greeted Race in the office reception area.

"Please call me Walt," Race said.

"Thanks, Walt. My name is Sam."

"Thanks for staying late to meet with me. Looks as though everyone else left for the day."

Jacobson grinned. "The employees tend to abandon ship at 5 p.m., sharp. I'm usually here later than this."

Race smiled. "That's the price of having your name on the door."

"How true. Let's go to my office."

Race followed the lawyer to a well-appointed office that was large enough to accommodate a Volkswagen-sized desk that faced two straight-backed leather chairs. There was also a large bookcase crammed with law books, a separate seating area with a three-seater leather couch, two plush leather chairs, and a glass and brass coffee table. A bar was situated in a corner of the room near a door that Race guessed led to a private bathroom.

"So, tell me which casino/hotel you're targeting."

Race pressed back in his chair and crossed his legs. "I haven't been honest with you, Sam. I'm not here to talk about casinos. It's your clients, the three college football player-rapists, who bring me here."

Jacobson leaned forward and frowned. He pointed a finger at Race. "What the hell is this?"

"It's really quite simple, Sam. You did a bad thing when you helped set three rapists free. Your clients are loathsome people, and you're just as vile for having worked with them. Now you've got the opportunity to make amends by doing the right thing."

"Get out of my—"

The pistol that Race pulled from a shoulder rig under his jacket stopped the lawyer in mid-sentence.

"Here's how this will go, Sam. You'll make phone calls to all three of your clients. You'll tell them you need to see them right away, that you have some final papers they have to sign that you must take to the courthouse first thing in the morning."

"That's bullshit. They know there are no other papers that need their signatures. I—"

Race waggled the gun at Jacobson. "Then tell them the court misplaced the original documents and you want new papers filed to prevent a problem for them down the road."

"And what if I don't do what you ask?"

"First, I'm not asking. Second, if you don't do what I want, I'll shoot you and find another way to get to your clients."

"What do you . . . plan to do . . . with the boys?"

"Boys, my ass. They're two-hundred-fifty-pound men. What I plan to do with them is kill them for what they did to Rosa Puccini. They brutalized her and left her so traumatized that she will more than likely be institutionalized for the rest of her life."

"That doesn't justify murder. You'll be breaking the law." Jacobson paused and then added, "You're making me an accessory to murder."

"Gee, Sam, you were already an accessory to rape when you helped turn your clients loose. What's a little murder?" Race stood and moved the gun to within a foot of the lawyer's forehead. "Now, pick up your phone and call your clients."

"You're working for the Puccini family, aren't you?"

"I wouldn't know the Puccinis if they walked in here right now. I don't work for anyone but myself. Ridding the world of assholes is what I do."

"You'll kill me anyway."

"Actually, Sam, I *should* kill you for helping to set those animals free, but I won't. You have my word on that."

"Your word?"

"Yeah. Believe it or not." Race took a long breath and then exhaled loudly. "Your time's up." He stretched his arm forward so that the muzzle was just inches from Jacobson's nose.

"Wait. Wait." He vented a loud breath. "I need to get the file."

Race pulled a card from his shirt pocket and tossed it in front of Jacobson. "The numbers are on there."

Jacobson picked up the receiver of his desk phone and dialed the first number.

# CHAPTER 8

Frank Armbruster used a small plastic scoop to pour his hoard of diamonds into a replica of a shaving cream canister. He bounced the can in one hand and marveled at how much wealth the stones represented. Then he placed the can into a large shaving kit.

Twelve years of work had yielded over one hundred twenty million dollars. The conversion of most of that cash into cut diamonds had cost him twenty million. And the sale of the stones in Amsterdam would reduce the proceeds by about another twenty million. By this time next week, he'd have eighty million dollars in cash to go along with the three million in bearer bonds in his briefcase. The numbers didn't come close to Bernie Madoff figures, but Madoff was in prison. A warm rush ran through him when he thought how wonderful his life would be.

"Frank, are you about ready to go?"

Armbruster shuddered at the sound of his wife's voice. He'd come to hate everything about the woman, even the cadence of her speech, the hoarseness of her voice, and absolutely everything about the way she looked. They'd been married twenty-five years. They were each forty-nine years old. But she looked sixty. Worse, she acted as though she were seventy.

He picked up his suitcase and briefcase and walked down the stairs to where Betty waited.

"All set?"

"Yep."

She looked at her wrist watch. "We'd better hurry. You know what traffic is like this late in the afternoon."

"We've got plenty of time," Armbruster said.

The ride to Burbank Airport was uneventful. His wife dropped him at the terminal.

"Call me when you arrive in Denver," she said. "Hope the trip goes well."

"I'm sure everything will go fine. Always does."

She smiled at him as she closed the car trunk and he mounted the sidewalk outside the terminal. "Love you."

He smiled back. "Bye, Betty."

Armbruster waited ten minutes until his wife merged her car into traffic and disappeared. Then he walked to the curb. Two minutes later, Astrid pulled up in the Audi A8 he'd bought her and shot him a smile that warmed him all over. He felt a stirring in his groin and wondered why he'd waited so long to dump Betty.

"Where to?" Astrid asked after he stored his bags in the trunk and dropped into the passenger seat.

"Las Vegas. We'll board the flight there for Amsterdam."

"What about my car?"

He laughed. "I'll buy you a new one when we get to Europe."

From the front passenger seat of his Lincoln Navigator, Stan Bukowski watched Frank Armbruster get into the passenger seat of a new Audi A-8.

"What do you think he's up to, boss?" his driver said.

"How the hell do I know, Richie? Just keep on his tail."

They dodged in and out of traffic as they followed along behind Armbruster.

"What do we do now?" Richie asked.

"Follow him. You lose that asshole and I'll have you dumped in the ocean as shark food." While they followed, Bukowski called a number from memory and left a message.

Eric Matus's cell phone rang. He saw it was a forwarded call from his office phone at Special Arts Agency. He listened to the message, but the man had left a number but no name. He returned the call.

"You left a message for Special Arts Agency?"

"It's Stan Bukowski from L.A."

"How the hell did you get this number?"

"Come on, Matus." The man paused and then asked, "You really want to know how I found you?"

"Yeah."

"After I dropped off the money and information at that church in Los Angeles, I had a guy watch. He saw you enter and leave the church. Then he followed you to a park where you met with some guy. You passed the stuff I left for you to that guy. After you left there, he followed you all the way to your office in Salt Lake City. Found out you hardly ever go there. It's a front. Right, Eric? Your phone there is forwarded to a cell phone."

Matus felt as though sweat leaked from every pore. His jacket sleeve came away soaked when he swiped his arm across his forehead. This wasn't supposed to happen. He remembered doing business with this guy. He shuddered as he recalled the conversation he'd had with him a year ago. The way the man had said, 'I want you to kill those fucking humps that did this to my son. Am I making myself clear? I want them scumbags dead, dead, dead.'

Matus groaned. He'd screwed up royally.

"What was that?"

"Nothing. What do you want?"

"I got a job for you."

"I might have an opening next week."

"Don't think it can wait 'til then," Bukowski said.

"We're booked up right now."

"Listen, asshole. You either do this job or I'll put the cops on you."

"What are you going to tell them, that you hired me to kill someone?"

"Nah. I'll make an anonymous call. There's no way you can tie me to the murder of my son's kidnapper."

A tremor of fear shot through Matus. "What's the job?"

"Stop an embezzler from fleeing the country. Get my money

from him. Then kill the sonofabitch."

"Embezzler? That's not my kind of job."

Bukowski's voice hardened and became louder. "This is not a negotiation."

Matus groaned again. "Where's the guy located?"

"Los Angeles at the moment, but that could change."

"I don't like this."

"What are you, finicky? Besides, I already told you, you ain't got a choice."

Matus exhaled a long stream of air. "It'll cost fifty thousand."

"Jeez, man, that's robbery. It was only twenty last time."

Matus waited.

"Aw, shit." After a long pause, he said, "I'll pay."

"How quickly can you get me the usual information?"

Bukowski said, "I've already got it with me. Where do you want it delivered?"

"I'm in Las Vegas." He gave him the address of a church. "3 p.m."

"Bullshit," Bukowski barked. "I ain't goin' through that crap again. We'll meet face-to-face. I'll call you when I know where the guy is headed. You can meet me there."

# CHAPTER 9

Susan asked, "What's with meeting at this hour?"

Barbara chuckled. "It's the FBI. They work 24/7, 365 days a year."

"Yeah, right. Or, your friend works the graveyard shift today and wanted us to accommodate her schedule."

"You're a bright and perceptive woman."

They entered the Federal Bureau of Investigation's building on the east side of Interstate 25 at 8:30 p.m. FBI Special Agent Sophia Otero-Hansen met them in the reception area.

"How many years has it been?" she said.

"At least five," Barbara answered. She turned to Susan. "This is my partner, Susan Martinez. Susan, meet Special Agent Sophia Otero-Hansen."

Susan gave Otero-Hansen an abbreviated wave and nodded. She received no response.

"What's on your mind, Barbara?" Otero-Hansen said.

"We caught a murder a couple days ago. Guy named Sylvester O'Neil."

"The pedophile. I read about it."

"Good," Barbara said. "We accessed the NSOD and discovered that O'Neil had a hell of a record. The first logical place for us to try to find a connection to his killer is among the families whose children were molested."

"Makes sense," the FBI agent said. "How many cases showed

up in the National Sex Offenders Database under O'Neil's name?"

"Enough that it could take us a while to unearth the killer. And, based on the way O'Neil was killed, we think his murderer is a pro."

"How so?"

"There was zero forensic evidence at the scene other than evidence that O'Neil died from swallowing a massive heroin overdose. We think he was forced to swallow the stuff."

"You kidding?" Otero-Hansen said. "Never heard of anyone doing that before."

"And the killer put a stake in O'Neil's heart after he died."

"A stake?" Otero-Hansen said. "Like a vampire killing?"

"Actually, it was a tent peg. What we're wondering is whether the FBI could narrow down the number of possible suspects with two filters. One, the forced ingestion of liquid heroin. Two, the tent peg. We know the NCIC database can be queried based on cause of death and other variables."

"I can check on it, but why don't you do it?"

Barbara smiled. "We figured the FBI might have access to info that we can't access."

Otero-Hansen smiled back. "You think we might have secret files, or something?"

"Heaven forbid."


"You think she'll help us?" Susan asked Barbara as they drove away from the FBI building.

"Only if it helps her as well."

"As in FBI agent solves vigilante killer murders."

"Yep. Of course, that assumes there is a vigilante killer."

"I'm not so sure," Susan said. "The tent peg in O'Neil's heart was an emotional, vindictive act. It was almost personal. Like something the father of a boy murdered by O'Neil might do.

"Another thing about the tent peg is that the Graves boy was murdered while his scout troop camped in the Jemez Mountains. The boys and their leaders all slept outside in World War II surplus pup tents. Wulfie said the tent peg found in O'Neil's chest is the type used to anchor a pup tent."

"Like the killer was sending a message," Barbara said. "That

O'Neil's death was payback for what he did to the Graves boy on the camping trip."

"Yeah. But, if that's the case, it would be pretty stupid of the killer to leave that sort of message. Leaving that tent peg was unprofessional; an emotional act. That's why I keep wondering about family members of O'Neil's victims."

Barbara put a hand on her forehead and groaned. "You're right. O'Neil's murder looks personal. As though it was committed by someone personally related to Adam Graves."

Race met the first of the three football players when he walked into Jacobson's reception area. He pointed at a conference room down a hall. "Sam will meet with you there when the others arrive."

The guy was over six feet, four inches tall and must have weighed two hundred eighty pounds. His head was shaved and he wore a goatee and mustache. Good looking kid, Race thought.

Race followed him into the conference room.

"I haven't met you before," the hulk said, as he sat on the left side of the table.

"I do odd jobs for Mr. Jacobson," Race answered as he left the conference room. The other two men arrived as Race entered the reception area. Neither one was as big as the first, but they were still enormous. They were each as tall as Race, but outweighed him by at least sixty pounds. He pointed them to the conference room and followed.

After a few seconds of fist-bumping and friendly banter, the two new arrivals sat in chairs across the table from their friend.

Race stood behind the empty chair at the head of the rectangular table and pointed at three glasses he'd placed there earlier. "How about some lemonade, fellows?"

"Sure," the big one said as he grasped one of the glasses. He downed the contents and smacked his lips.

The man directly to Race's right followed the example of his team mate, but the third man made no move for his glass.

"Not thirsty?" Race asked.

"Nah."

Race glared at the guy. "It's not polite to refuse someone's hospitality."

A confused expression came over the man's face. "Thanks, but I don't want any lemonade."

"Drink it anyway."

The man's expression changed to a hard, mean look. "I told you I don't want any damned lemonade, so take it and shove it up your ass."

"Now, that's terribly rude."

The other two men's breathing suddenly became loud and labored.

"What the hell?" the big one said as he pressed both of his hands against his chest.

Race pointed at the one without a glass in hand, and barked, "Drink up."

"Go to hell," the guy shouted as he leaped to his feet, knocked his chair against the wall, and moved toward Race. With lightning speed, Race pulled his pistol from the shoulder holster under his jacket and pointed it at the guy.

"Back to your seat."

Race took a silencer from a side pocket in his jacket and screwed it onto the barrel of his pistol. When the guy was reseated, Race said, "You pick up the glass and drink before I count to three. If you don't, I shoot you. You have any idea how painful a bullet wound can be?"

"Come on, man," the biggest one rasped. "What's this all about?" His breaths now came in gasps.

"Rosa Puccini."

The one closest to Race on his right moaned as though in severe pain. "You . . . joking," he said.

Race glared at him. "No joke, guys." Then he turned back to the one who had yet to drink the concoction waiting in the third glass. "Drink up."

The big one said, "Is it . . . money . . . you . . . want? Our folks . . . will . . . pay."

Race shook his head. The third guy had still not picked up his glass. He pointed the gun at the man's right shoulder and pulled the trigger.

The guy looked stunned for a second, and then screamed, "You shot me." He grabbed his shoulder and writhed, screaming all the while.

"You won't feel any pain after you drink what's in that glass," Race said.

The big one on Race's left whimpered, "Please . . . don't . . . do this."

Race kept his gaze on the one he'd shot. He moved the pistol toward the man's left shoulder.

"Okay, okay," the man said, and drained the glass in front of him. He made a sour face and gagged.

The other two men now perspired as though in a steam room. Their faces had turned pallid.

The one to Race's right moaned, "I'm . . . sorry."

"Too late," Race said. "Much too late. Now let me tell you what's about to happen."

Race knelt down on Samuel Jacobson's private bathroom floor and checked the ropes he'd used to bind the lawyer's feet and hands to the pedestal sink. Then he stared into the man's eyes.

"What time does the cleaning crew show up?"

"Nine o'clock."

"Good. You'll be free in a little while."

Then he gagged Jacobson with a washcloth and left the room.

Race returned to the conference room. He looked at the three men bent over the table, their heads resting on their folded arms. He put his briefcase on the table, opened it, took out three roses, and placed a rose in front of each man. Then he closed and picked up his briefcase, retrieved his overnight bag from Jacobson's office, left the suite, and went to the public men's room. He plugged up the toilet, urinal, and sinks with paper towels and left the bathroom just as water flowed onto the floor.

He carried the briefcase and overnight bag to his Impala parked behind the office building. Seven miles away, he drove behind a gas station he'd scoped out earlier—one without a security camera—and changed clothes in the rest room. He put the clothes he'd changed out of, along with his wig, tinted glasses, and rubber gloves in a black garbage bag he took from his briefcase. Back outside, he dumped the bag in a dumpster and poured a quart bottle of charcoal starter fluid over it, dropped a lit match into the container, and then drove away.

Race thought that a good night's sleep was in order, but knew it was unlikely to happen. The nightmare always seemed to be worse right after he completed an assignment. But it was worth a try. Maybe he'd get lucky. Then the throwaway cell phone in the vehicle's console rang.

"Yeah?"

"We have another job."

"Eric, I'm exhausted."

"It's a repeat customer. Says it's urgent."

"I'll consider it. Depends on where the job is."

"Where do you want to meet?"

"Same place as this morning. But in the parking lot. Stay in your car. I'll come to you."

Eric Matus had spent an hour in a mom-and-pop Italian restaurant halfway between the Las Vegas Strip and McCarran Airport. As good as the *linguini vongole* he'd ordered looked and smelled, he could barely touch it. His stomach churned like surf in a storm. He had tried to devise a way out of his predicament. Maybe he could just disconnect the telephone in Salt Lake City, abandon the office there, change his name, and set up shop in a different city. But Stan Bukowski was a connected guy. A pissed off Bukowski might, sooner or later, track him down. The result of that, Matus knew, would not be pretty. The acid level in his stomach climbed into the red zone. Race had been right all along. Money would ultimately lead to a problem. Race had been adamant about not taking money from clients. Adamant that they should always serve good people who deserved justice. That's why he was supposed to vet their clients in advance.

Matus sucked in air through his teeth. He'd violated two of Race's rules when he negotiated the deal with Bukowski. He'd charged a fee and he'd made a deal with a guy he knew right up front was connected to organized crime. The man was definitely not "good people."

He'd just have to convince Race to do the job. He had just gone out to his SUV when his cell phone rang.

"Hello?"

"It's Stan."

"Where are you?"

"Las Vegas."

Sweat popped out on Matus's brow and then leaked down his face. "What are you doing here?"

"Where should I meet you?"

"I asked you a question. Answer me. Why are you in Vegas?"

Bukowski blurted a boisterous laugh. "Because that's where the embezzler went. Right here in Sin City. I just followed the guy to the Bellagio. Bribed a bellman to give me his room number. 1713. Checked in for one night."

At least that's convenient, Matus thought. "Okay." He gave Bukowski the address of the Italian restaurant. "Meet me in fifteen minutes in the strip center lot across from the restaurant."

# CHAPTER 10

The Nguyen sisters split up as soon as they entered Samuel Jacobson's building. Lisa Nguyen always took the northern part of the building, while Lucy Nguyen cleaned the southern end, which included Jacobson's office.

Lucy vacuumed and dusted the three associates' offices, the reception area, and the hallway. Then she knocked on the conference room door because the light was still on.

"Mr. Jacobson," she quietly called out. No answer. She cracked the door several inches and peeked inside. A strong odor hit her. There were three large men seated at the table with their heads resting on their arms. They appeared to be asleep. Lucy knocked again, but the men didn't stir. She called through the cracked door, "I'm sorry to disturb you." Still no response. She pushed open the door and was immediately hit by the overpowering stench of vomit, urine, and feces. Then she spotted what appeared to be blood on one of the men's shirts.

Lucy Nguyen screamed and ran from the office, through the reception area, and into the hallway, which was now covered with running water.

The Las Vegas Police Department is one of the best and most responsive law enforcement agencies in the United States. Radio cars, homicide detectives, ambulances, and representatives from the Office of Medical Investigation were in and around Samuel Jacobson's offices within ten minutes of Lucy Nguyen's 9-1-1 call. But it wasn't until six minutes after the first patrolman entered Jacobson's building that anyone bothered to look in the lawyer's private bathroom. By the time someone released Jacobson, who lay in six inches of water, the lawyer was apoplectic with rage.

"Didn't you hear me?" he shouted.

The LVPD detectives and most of its uniformed officers knew who Samuel Jacobson was: the goddamn attorney who got scumbags off by pulling tricks and making cops look stupid in court.

The detective in charge helped Jacobson to his feet, led him to the office reception area, and told him, "Sit right there; don't move. I'll be with you in a minute."

Jacobson sputtered, but he sat down and shut up. He wanted to make certain he had his story straight about what had happened. And he wanted to remember everything about the maniac who had tied him up and murdered the three young men he'd represented. He took a pad from his receptionist's desk and snatched a pen from the set in front of the blotter. Ignoring the water which was up to his ankles, he jotted down every feature he could remember about the man: maybe forty years old; blond hair in a ponytail; smooth skin; no scars or moles; blue eyes; wire, tinted glasses; maybe six feet, one or two inches tall. He wrote down the time the man had entered his office and when he'd left.

Jacobson placed the pad back on his desk and smiled. "I got you, you sonofabitch. The cops'll pick you up before you know it."

After Matus met with Stan Bukowski, he called Race's throwaway cell phone, and said, "Thirty minutes." He then took a circuitous route to the diner to ensure that Bukowski didn't have him followed again, and waited. His heart leaped in his chest when Race opened the rear right passenger door and entered the SUV.

"Jeez," Matus said with a loud, long exhale. "I didn't see you come up on me."

"You're losing the skills they taught us at Bragg. What's the job?"

"Our client has an account with an investment advisor in L.A. The guy is apparently about to leave the country with all his clients' money. He went to the guy's office yesterday and found the place cleaned out. No files, no records, no nothing. Looks like the investment advisor skipped with his clients' money."

"That's not our type of job, Eric."

"But the investment advisor probably stole a huge amount of money, including three million from our client. I thought you'd want to do this one because the guy defrauded a bunch of retirees and charitable organizations, too. I checked the guy's website. He catered to handling money for the elderly and small charities. If we can recover some of the money he stole, we can help those people."

Race didn't respond immediately. He finally said, "Maybe that would be good. But how the hell will I find the money? It could have been transferred overseas by now. The guy can't possibly have a lot of cash with him."

"The client got a tip from a forger in L.A. who fabricated ID for the advisor. Says the guy was referred by a diamond dealer. He may have converted the money into stones and could have them with him."

After a long pause, Race said, "I'll do it. But this is different. This won't be a wet job like the others."

Matus said, "Whatever you say."

"What's the guy's name and where's he located?"

"That's the good news. He's right here in Vegas. Holed up at the Bellagio. Apparently, only for one night. He may leave the country tomorrow. He's booked at the hotel under the name Harry Whitaker."

"By himself?"

"As far as I know."

# CHAPTER 11

Barbara's cell phone ring startled her out of a sound sleep. She rubbed her eyes, glanced at her bedside clock—11:47 p.m. She cleared her throat as she reached for the phone, and answered, "Lassiter."

"Barbara, it's Sophia. Sorry about the late hour."

"It's okay. What's up, Sophia?"

"We dug up something interesting. The database gave us eight deaths where the victims ingested liquid heroin."

"Any suicides?"

"Nope. Every one of the deaths was an obvious homicide."

"How can you be so certain?"

Otero-Hansen blurted a shrill, condescending laugh that Barbara remembered from years ago. It was just as annoying now as it had been when they'd worked together.

"Easy," the agent answered. "The killer left a calling card in every instance."

"What sort of calling card?"

"Something different every time. A shell cartridge inserted in a nostril, a woman's scarf wrapped around a neck, a dollar bill stuffed in a mouth, a liquor bottle in a hand. Like the tent peg in Sylvester O'Neil's chest. Never the same thing twice."

"Huh," Barbara muttered. "Any idea about the significance of the items left behind?"

"Yeah. The victims were all people with criminal records who'd committed recent violent crimes and been released on bail or acquitted because of some police or prosecutorial error, or because of political influence. The items the vigilante killer left behind were related in some way to the criminals' victims. The cases involved murder, rape, incest, felony assault & battery, armed robbery, DUI-related auto accident, and so forth."

"You're confirming there's a vigilante killer out there who targets bad guys."

"We'll refine our database query. Search for killers who leave items behind. I wouldn't be surprised if we find more murders than the initial database query yielded."

"Can you email the eight case files to me?" Barbara asked.

"Already done."

That surprised Barbara. It wasn't like Sophia to share information that might make someone else look good. But, after all, it was Barbara who had put her onto the liquid heroin lead.

"Thanks, Sophia. I appreciate your help."

"No problem. We're on the same team, aren't we?"

Barbara was even more surprised. This was a different Sophia Otero-Hansen than she remembered.

Then the FBI agent said, "I'm telling you, Barbara, the world is a better place without the eight people—nine, including O'Neil, no longer alive."

"Of course, you know that doesn't change a thing, Sophia."

Barbara figured that if she couldn't go back to sleep, she might as well call Susan and brief her on what she'd gotten from Otero-Hansen. She dialed Susan's number and, when her partner answered, said, "Hey, Susan, you ever hear the term, *misery loves company*?"

"You are such a bitch," Susan said. "What do you have?"

After Barbara passed on Otero-Hansen's information, she said, "What do you think?"

"I think there's no way in hell I'll be able to go back to sleep. Pick me up in thirty minutes."

"Don't you have your Corvette back yet?"

"I'll need a bank loan if this goes on much longer. Mechanic

says I need a new alternator and master cylinder."
"Maybe you need a new mechanic."

# DAY 5

# CHAPTER 12

In their downtown office, Barbara and Susan stood in front of the white-board on which Sylvester O'Neil's victims' names had been written. Barbara waved a hand at the board. "You know there might be dozens more victims."

"Yeah," Susan said. "But that's not our problem at this time. It's O'Neil's killer we're after." She blew out a breath, and asked, "In how many states do we think the vigilante has been active?"

Barbara looked at the hard copy of Sophia Otero-Hansen's email and counted down: "Six."

"Coast to coast?"

Barbara looked at the email again. "No. All in the west. Arizona, California, Colorado, Nevada, New Mexico, and Texas."

"So, our boy may live somewhere between Texas and California."

"Could be," Barbara said.

Susan pointed at the white-board. "We should open a computer file similar to what you put on the board. Nine murders. Everything in chronological order. Then let's map the killer's path by location."

"Why don't you start that while I call Sophia? Hopefully, she got something from the expanded query she said she would run."

"What?"

"About killers who leave calling cards, like our guy does."

"And what if that query comes up with hundreds of murders where calling cards were left? Where there were murder methods other than liquid heroin?"

"There's a happy thought."

"Why don't *we* just query the NCIC?" Susan asked.

"Because we don't have one percent of the computing capacity the Feds have. Besides, we may need Sophia if we have to follow cases in other states."

"Follow cases? As in going to other states ourselves?"

Barbara frowned. "What have you been smoking? You really think that will happen? You think the lieutenant will approve travel for us? With the department's budget problems?"

Susan laughed. "He might if I wear my red dress. I thought his eyes would pop out the last time I wore it to work."

"Shameless. Absolutely shameless."

Race Thornton sat in one of the lounge bar's in the Bellagio Hotel & Casino, after having ordered five scotch and waters—each of which he'd dumped in a potted plant—and after making a minor scene every time the bar waitress served him. His loud and lewd remarks to the waitress had caught the attention of a uniformed guard who'd posted himself near the steps from the bar down to the casino floor. Race's last outburst had brought the guard to Race's table.

"Sir, are you staying here at the Bellagio?"

Race frowned at the guard. "Shit no," he slurred. "I can barely pay for the drinks here. No way could I afford a room."

"How 'bout I call you a cab?"

Race hiccupped and waved his hands in the air as though to say, "Whatever." The guard snagged Race's arm when he stumbled a bit as he stepped down to the casino floor.

"Thanks," Race said, as he bumped against the guard, snatched the man's passkey ID clipped to the front of his uniform shirt, and slipped it into his pocket. "Guess I had a few too many."

"It happens," the guard said.

Outside the building, the guard turned Race over to the doorman, who waved at a taxi. Race fell into the back of the cab and gave the driver the name of his motel.

Race adjusted the new gray wig and dark glasses and pressed

firmly on the false mustache and beard to assure himself they were in place. He finished off his disguise with a cane. Then he left his motel, drove his car to the Bellagio, self-parked, and walked inside to the lobby house phone.

"Please put me through to Mr. Whitaker's room," he told the hotel operator.

"My pleasure, sir. Please hold."

The phone rang ten times before the operator came back on the line. "Mr. Whitaker is not answering his phone, sir. Would you like to leave a message?"

Race declined and hung up. Then he meandered around the casino floor. He saw no one that came close to resembling the man in the photos Eric Matus had provided. Then he moved from restaurant to restaurant inside the building: Le Cirque, Picasso, Prime, Yellowtail, Michael Mina, Jasmine, OLiVES, Fix. Still no sighting of Whitaker. Once more he tried the operator, but once again no one answered in Whitaker's room.

Race wished there was a better alternative than breaking into Whitaker's room. The universal passkey he'd lifted off the security guard would give him access, but the hall and elevator cameras would record his every movement. Even with his disguise, it was risky. He doubted Whitaker was in any of the restaurants—it was already 1 a.m. The man could be anywhere, including in his room. He might have turned down the ringer on the room phone or just decided to not answer it.

Race rode the elevator to the 17th floor and leaned heavily on the cane as he shuffled down the hall to Room 1713. He brushed the passkey over the electronic lock. The mechanism clicked and the light turned green. He opened the door, slipped into the room, and quickly searched it. When he confirmed it was empty, he flipped on the lights.

He searched the room and found luggage in the closet. The luggage tag on one of the suitcases had the name Whitaker on it. The safe in the closet was locked. There were clothes on hangars, as well as in dresser drawers. Toiletries, including women's lotions and perfume, were in the bathroom. Whitaker wasn't alone. Matus's information had not been completely accurate. Race shook his head out of frustration. He turned to look around the room again just as he heard loud voices come from the hallway. Then he heard the unmistakable chime of a key card swiped over the room door lock.

He moved quickly to turn off the lights and then went into the closet.

"Frankie, that was so much fun," a woman said. "I could have danced all night. I'm so glad you decided to leave from Las Vegas instead of L.A."

"You've got to stop calling me Frankie. That could really ruin things for us. It's Harry. Harry Whitaker."

The woman giggled. "Sorry . . . Harry."

"Jeez, you have to sober up before we go to the airport in a few hours."

The woman giggled again. "Don't worry; I'll be fine . . . Harry." She broke out in full-fledged, maniacal laughter.

"Jesus, Mary, and Joseph," the man said.

"You know, you could have come up with a better name for me than Sandra Jones," the woman said in a little girl whine. "You might as well have come up with Beatrice Cumberbund, or Florence Nightingale, or—"

"This isn't funny, you hear me?"

"Oh, don't be such a bore, Frankie. I won't mess up when—"

Race stepped from the closet into the well-lit room. He pointed his weapon at the woman, and said, "It's Harry, not Frankie, Sandra."

The woman opened her mouth as though to scream. Whitaker sagged as though he was a punctured balloon.

"One sound comes out of either of your mouths and I'll shoot you both. I don't want to do that, but I will if I have to."

Whitaker nodded. The woman backed up to the bed and sat down.

"Take off your belt," Race ordered the man, "and tie your girlfriend's hands behind her back."

After the man complied, Race pointed at the bathroom. "Get a wash cloth."

Whitaker moved as though he understood the stakes and rushed back with a wash cloth.

"Stuff it in her mouth."

Again Whitaker complied.

"Put her on the floor; lie down next to her," Race ordered.

With the two of them on the carpeted floor, Race took a belt from a robe in the closet and tied Whitaker's hands. Then he pulled a case from one of the bed pillows and used strips he tore from it to bind the man's and woman's ankles. He turned Whitaker over onto his back and forced the pistol muzzle into his mouth.

"Where are the stones?" Race asked, taking a gamble that the man had converted his ill-begotten gains to diamonds.

The shocked expression that came to Whitaker's face told Race that his gamble had paid off.

"We can make a deal," Whitaker mumbled.

Race pulled the gun from the man's mouth and pressed the muzzle against his forehead. "Last chance. Where are the stones?"

The guy closed his eyes and moaned, "The wall safe."

"The only words I want to hear from you are the numbers to the safe combination. If I hear anything but those numbers, you're dead."

Race pressed the muzzle even harder against Whitaker's forehead.

"Four-seven-eight-eight," Whitaker rasped. "Four-seven-eight-eight."

Race went to the closet safe, pressed in the code. The safe hummed and popped open. He took out a shaving kit and tossed it on the bed beside the woman. The only other items in the safe were two passports.

"Where are the stones?" he demanded as he moved back toward the man.

"Maybe we can make a deal."

Race bent over the man again and pointed his pistol at his face. "I told you to shut up. You get to talk only when I ask you a question. Now, where are the stones?"

"My shaving kit."

Race went to the bed and unzipped the kit. I need some sleep, he told himself. Should have thought of that. Who the hell puts a shaving kit in a safe? He turned it upside down, dumped the contents on the bed, and picked through the items. The only things large enough to hold a cache of diamonds were the deodorant and shaving cream cans. He shook the deodorant can. Nothing. Then he lifted the shaving cream can. Even before shaking the container, its weight told him he'd found the diamonds. He turned it over and inspected it. He tried to pry off the bottom of the container. No luck. Then he tried to twist off the top. At first, nothing happened. But when he twisted with more force, the top came away from the body of the can. He peeked inside and was shocked at the hoard of brilliant stones there.

"How much is in here?" he asked Whitaker.

"Please, listen to me," Whitaker said. "We can make a deal. There's a hundred million dollars' worth of gemstones in there."

"Why would I make a deal with you when I now have all the stones?"

The logic of that statement seemed to deflate Whitaker to the point of total defeat. He moaned again.

Race noticed the woman's eyes follow his movements as he screwed the top back onto the shaving cream can. Then he went to the bathroom, retrieved a second wash cloth, and stuck it in the man's mouth. Then he had an inspiration.

# CHAPTER 13

"Yeah?" Stan Bukowski grumbled into the telephone.

Eric Matus couldn't keep the euphoria from his voice. "We recovered your money." He took a quietening breath. "The asshole converted everything to diamonds. But we got it all. I'll give you your share of the stones tomorrow."

"Tomorrow, my ass. I want them today. This morning." Then, after a beat, Bukowski said, "How the hell do you know what three million in diamonds looks like?"

"Weighed the hundred million in stones and then took out three percent of the total for you."

"What about the rest of them?"

"My partner will turn them over to the California Attorney General so restitution can be made to the other investors."

"Are you messin' with me?"

"No, why?"

"What are you, some kinda schmuck?"

After a hesitation, Matus said, "This *schmuck* just got you your three million dollars."

"Yeah, yeah. You still in Vegas?"

"Yes. I'll be—"

"Meet me at Gentleman Gil's in North Las Vegas at 9 this morning."

"Why?"

"Don't you want the rest of your fee?"

Matus made it to the meeting location with Race with barely a second to spare. He looked around the wedding chapel parking lot but didn't spot Race's Impala. Of course, that didn't surprise him. He never saw Race unless Race wanted to be seen. His heart leaped when the rear door opened and Race entered the SUV. Matus turned to look at him.

"No more jobs for a while," Race said from the backseat. "I'm running on empty. Need to get some rest."

"I understand. I plan to drive up to Salt Lake and get some rest, too."

Race passed a plastic bag to him. "That's the client's share of the diamonds."

"Did you send the rest of the diamonds to California already?"

"Why?"

"Just wondering. If you hadn't, I could have handled it." He felt his face go hot and turned away from Race.

"Thanks, but I already took them to FedEx. I sent an email message to the California Attorney General's office to be on the lookout for them." Race chuckled. "That ought to get the adrenaline flowing in Sacramento."

"Hmm."

"That's kind of an anemic reaction. I thought you wanted to see the elderly and charity investors get their money back."

"Yeah . . . of course."

"What's wrong, Eric?"

"Oh, nothing. I guess I'm just tired."

"Bullshit. I've known you too long to fall for that. Something's bothering you."

"No, no. I'm fine."

"I have a question, Eric. It's bothered me since you told me about this job."

"Yeah, Race. What is it?"

"How'd you learn about this embezzlement business? There was nothing in the news about it. I checked on the Internet. Nothing about this guy Whitaker, or whatever his real name is, embezzling from his clients."

Matus felt his face grow hot again. Sweat broke out on his forehead. "I . . . ."

"Don't lie to me, Eric. What going on?"

"Ah-h-h, jeez. I screwed up, Race. Remember that guy who kidnapped the kid in Los Angeles two years ago?"

"Of course. The Bukowski kid."

"His father was our client. I didn't tell you, but I discovered after the job was done that Bukowski was connected to organized crime. He somehow had me followed all the way to Salt Lake when I returned home afterward. He knows who I am."

"Has he seen me?"

Matus hunched his shoulders. "I don't know. But he knows I have a partner."

"How'd Bukowski contact you?"

"He called my office number in Salt Lake and left a message."

"Sonofabitch," Race cursed.

"I'm sorry, Race. I had no idea I was followed."

"That was careless, Eric, but it happened. What pisses me off is that you didn't tell me Bukowski called you. You've put both of us in jeopardy."

"I know, I should have said something, but Bukowski owes us. After all, we saved his only son. He won't do anything to hurt us."

Race thought about that for a minute. "Did you tell him that this Whitaker job isn't what we do?"

"Sure. I told—"

"What did he say to that?"

Matus covered his face with his hands. "I'm sorry, Race."

"What did he say, Eric?"

"He threatened to turn us in."

"How do you plan to give Bukowski his share of the diamonds?"

"We're supposed to meet at some club in North Las Vegas at 9 this morning."

"Then what?"

"He said he had another job for us."

"Bullshit. It's a setup. The guy wants the rest of the stones."

Matus whined, "I'm really sorry. I should never have—"

"Give me the name of the club."

"What are you going to do?"

"Just give me the name. I'll be outside when you meet him. And, for God's sake, don't tell him I already shipped the diamonds."

Matus was as frightened as he could ever remember being. He knew he had no other choice but to meet with Bukowski. If he didn't, he figured there could be one of two outcomes: the guy could call the cops, which didn't seem the most likely. Or he'd sic one of his enforcers on him. It gave him a small degree of comfort to know that Race planned to be outside the club, but it wasn't enough to prevent him from feeling as though he might void his bladder at any moment.

Matus felt his skin crawl as soon as he entered Gentleman Gil's. It took a while for his eyes to adjust to the dark interior. The place was packed with men at tables and at a bar in front of a runway on which a nearly-naked woman danced. Other half-naked women meandered around the club floor. He thought this low-life strip joint was one small notch below a whore house. Then he spotted Stan Bukowski in a corner booth and wove his way around tables.

"Hey, Eric," Bukowski shouted. "Take a seat."

"You really want to do business here?"

"Sure, why not? I got an interest in this joint. Sit down and take a load off." He laughed. "Have a drink; then we'll go back to the office."

A waitress came over. Bukowski shouted over the music at her, "Hey, honey, bring my friend here a double bourbon."

Matus waved a hand as though to decline, but Bukowski ignored him.

When the waitress walked off, Bukowski rounded on Matus. "I got a job for you here in Vegas. Another rush job."

"Yeah, but—"

"I'll pay double your usual rate."

Matus felt a chill run down his spine. This was already the most profitable week of his life. O'Neil in Albuquerque, the three rapists, and Whitaker. It's too bad, he thought, that Bukowski probably didn't have another job for them. Race was more than likely correct that the promise of another job was just Bukowski's tactic to seduce them into a compromising situation so he could steal all the diamonds. But, at that moment, he couldn't have cared less about the money. He couldn't spend money if he were dead.

"I don't think—"

"I don't give a shit what you think."

Matus's heart seemed to beat a frenetic riff. The waitress placed a drink in front of him.

"Drink up," Bukowski said, "then we'll finalize arrangements."

As soon as he walked into the office, Matus knew he'd made a terrible mistake.

"What is this?" Matus demanded. "What—?"

A large man spun Matus around and slugged him in the stomach. Matus fell to his knees and gasped for breath. He had just about caught his breath when a wave of nausea hit.

"Pull a trash can under that asshole," Bukowski shouted.

The big man slid a waste basket over just in time for Matus to vomit into it. While he retched, the big guy reached into his jacket pocket and found the plastic bag with Bukowski's three million dollars in diamonds. He tossed the bag to his boss.

"Okay, Matus, here's the deal. I know you got a partner. I figure you're the booking agent, just like in Hollywood. So, you get your guy in here, or I'll have Richie work you over." Bukowski laughed. "Then I'll have him kill you."

Matus pushed the trash can away and tried to stand. He made it to a crouch, but had to drop back to his knees as another wave of nausea struck. It took a minute before he could rise from the floor.

Matus wiped his mouth with a handkerchief he took from his pants pocket. "What do you want him for?"

"Are you fuckin' stupid? I want the diamonds. All of them."

"He might have already mailed them."

"Then you're dead."

Matus looked at the big man. He was about six feet tall, had to weigh at least two hundred fifty pounds, and had arms the size of most men's thighs. Tattooed serpents ran around his neck and down both arms. He glared back at Matus, then smiled gleefully, as though he looked forward to beating him to a pulp.

"What do you want me to do?"

"How do you make contact with your partner?"

"My guy gives me a burner phone that I'm supposed to use only once. We arrange to meet, where I hand over information about the next assignment and he gives me another phone."

"How did he give you the diamonds for me?"

"He called me on the cell. Told me to meet him."

"So you got a throwaway cell for the next contact?"

Matus patted the side pocket of his sports jacket. "Yeah."

"Good. Call him and say you'll meet him here."

"It doesn't work that way. He only meets in places he chooses."

"Smart guy," Bukowski said.

Matus nodded. "He is."

"Then call him and say you have a new job."

Matus had no doubt that Bukowski planned to kill him the second he had his hands on the diamonds, had the stones still been available. He also had no doubt that he *would* kill him when he discovered there were no diamonds. As he fumbled the throwaway cell from his jacket pocket, he told himself to think, but the adrenaline that ripped through his system made clear thinking difficult. He hit the pre-programmed number to Race Thornton's cell phone and waited.

"Yeah," Race answered.

"We have another job." Matus breathed out a loud breath. "Another assassination."

Race didn't respond for several seconds. Then he said, "Another assassination?"

"Yeah."

"Meet me in the parking lot of the big office complex on the 4200 block of Paradise. 3 p.m."

Race disconnected the call before Matus could ask any questions or try to change the meeting arrangements. In all the years he and Matus had worked together, the man had followed one of his rules to the letter: never mention the nature of an assignment over the phone. Until just now. When Matus said, 'another assassination,' Race concluded he was under duress. Bukowski had forced him to make the call.

# CHAPTER 14

At 9:15 a.m., Albuquerque time, Barbara and Susan took a break from building a victim matrix and fast-walked to the Starbucks in the Hyatt hotel lobby. The wind had come up again and a scattering of snow flurries blew wildly in their faces.

"Damn, I wish I'd worn a heavier coat," Susan yelled over the wind.

"Nah. It's not cold out. Just ask the Chamber of Commerce. They tell tourists the temperature never drops below fifty in Albuquerque."

"Aren't you cold?"

Barbara scoffed. "I'm freezing."

Barbara fought to open the hotel's front door against the wind. Susan slipped inside in front of her, and then Barbara battled another wind gust. Inside the lobby, she breathlessly exclaimed, "I'm about ready for a road trip to some place warm. You have to work on the lieutenant as soon as he gets in this morning."

"What? Without my short black skirt and red blouse."

"Bat your eyelashes at him."

"*You* bat your eyelashes at him."

"He's hot for you," Barbara said. "Not me."

Susan shrugged. "He's hot for anything in a skirt."

They each ordered a *grande* coffee and a morning bun and found a place to sit in the hotel lobby's lounge. Barbara had barely sipped her coffee when her cell phone rang. She looked at the screen and recognized Sophia Otero-Hansen's number.

"It's my good friend, Sophia."

"I thought you said she wasn't really your friend."

Barbara scrunched up her mouth. "Things change." She answered the call. "Hey, Sophia."

"The guy who killed O'Neil might be in Las Vegas. At least, we think he was there a short while ago."

"What happened?'

"Three twenty-year-old football players were found dead in their lawyer's office."

"Liquid heroin?"

"Yep. There were three nearly empty glasses on the lawyer's conference room table. Lemonade laced with heroin. And the guy left calling cards. A rose under each of the kids' hands."

"Why roses?"

"We think it's because the three guys assaulted a teenager named Rosa Puccini. She's now in a mental hospital. The killer set up an appointment with the lawyer under false pretenses. Then he threatened to kill the lawyer if he didn't call the men down to his office."

"The lawyer saw the guy?" Barbara asked. "Really?"

"No kidding. He saw him all right. We got a description, which we'll run through the computer."

"What about forensics?"

"*Nada*. Zip. Zilch. The perp even screwed up the plumbing so the place flooded. If there had been any evidence, it's washed into the Vegas sewer system by now."

"How the hell did the killer make three football players do what he wanted?"

"He shot one of them in the shoulder."

"I'll be damned. Well, thanks for keeping us informed. If we find anything, I'll be in touch."

"Don't you want to hear about the other case?"

"There's another case?"

"Our boy—at least we think it's the same guy—robbed a guy in a room at the Bellagio."

"You sure? That doesn't sound like something the vigilante

killer would do."

Otero-Hansen laughed. "On the surface, you're correct. The police learned of the crime after someone called the *Las Vegas Review-Journal* and television stations and told them a man running a Ponzi scheme out of Los Angeles was in a room at the Bellagio. Told them the man was about to skip the country with loot he'd stolen from investors. One hundred million dollars converted to diamonds. The media called the police who went to the hotel room and found a man and woman bound and gagged. The police found false ID, including passports, airline tickets to Amsterdam, and several million in bearer bonds in a briefcase."

"I still don't get the connection," Barbara said.

Otero-Hansen laughed again. "The guy left a calling card. The woman they found in the room was beside herself. She kept screaming that a thief broke into their room and forced her and her boyfriend to swallow diamonds. One each. We might not have connected the vigilante to the Bellagio room if not for the murdered football players being in the same city and the diamonds he forced the man and woman to swallow. I mean, how many crooks leave calling cards like this guy does? Three roses with the football players and diamonds with the two at the Bellagio."

"What happened to all the loot?"

"The caller to the press said he would put it in a FedEx box and send it to the California Attorney General."

"I'll be damned." Barbara chuckled. "Pretty stupid."

"Who?"

"The woman in the hotel room. She should have kept her mouth shut about the diamond she swallowed. Could have cashed in after nature took its course."

# CHAPTER 15

Race drove the ten blocks from his motel to the meeting site on Paradise Boulevard. The office complex, one of the biggest in Las Vegas, was surrounded by an expansive series of parking lots. Race reconnoitered the site until he found a spot that would serve his purpose. Then he drove to several retail stores and bought a bottle of granulated tree stump remover, table salt, a bundle of black yarn, a measuring tape, a set of measuring cups, a screwdriver, a disposable cigarette lighter, a roll of scotch tape, and four cookie sheets.

Back at his extended-stay motel room, he unpacked his purchases and lined them up on the kitchen counter. He cut off four eight-foot lengths of yarn and placed them on the bed. He put a large skillet on the stove and turned on the burner. Then he measured out seventy-two grams of the stump remover and mixed it with forty-eight grams of table salt. He vigorously shook the mixture for a full minute. When the skillet was too hot to touch, he poured 2/3 cup of water into it and then added in the stump remover/table salt mixture and stirred the concoction. When the contents of the skillet became frothy and much of the water had evaporated, he dropped the strips of yarn into the skillet. He held onto one end of each of the yarn lengths and watched as the water evaporated and the yarn became super-saturated with the chemical mixture. He then removed the yarn strips from the skillet and put one each on four cookie sheets in a serpentine pattern.

Then Race moved two of the cookie sheets to the oven that had been pre-heated to three hundred degrees. After twenty minutes, he removed the cookie sheets, placed them on top of the stove to cool, and put the other two sheets in the oven. When the second set of cookie sheets was removed from the oven and allowed to cool, Race touched the yarn and found all four lengths had dried perfectly. He then carried the cookie sheets out to his car and placed them on the backseat.

Race saw it was now 2:30 in the afternoon—thirty minutes to meet Matus. He drove back to the address on Paradise and pulled in between two parked cars near the back of the employee parking lot. The two cars had gas tank access doors on opposite sides. After Race checked to make certain no one was around, he used the screwdriver he'd purchased to pop open the fuel doors of the cars on either side of his car, unscrewed the gas caps, and inserted one end of a strip of treated yarn deep into each of the car's gas tanks. He carefully closed the gas access doors to within a half-inch of the strips of yarn. Then he taped another length of yarn to each of the first two lengths and ran them under the two vehicles to his car. He placed the two ends behind the Impala's left rear tire.

He waited behind the wheel of his car until his dashboard clock read 2:55. Then he moved to the Impala's rear end and peered through the bushes that separated the lot from the sidewalk and the street. When he spotted Matus's SUV turn onto Paradise Boulevard, he squatted by the left rear tire of his car and lit the two lengths of yarn with the disposal cigarette lighter.

Matus's SUV pulled across the front of Race's parked car and stopped just beyond it, its engine still running. Matus stepped out from behind the wheel and moved toward Race.

Matus's face was pale; he had deer-in-the-headlights eyes. He opened his mouth, but nothing came out.

Then two men piled out of Matus's vehicle. One of them was built like an NFL linebacker; the other was overweight, swarthy, had mean black eyes and was dressed in a silk suit.

"What is this?" Race said, feigning surprise.

"Shut up, asshole," the guy in the suit said.

Race estimated that the slow-burning fuses he'd fabricated

were less than a minute from hitting the gas tanks of the cars that book-ended the Impala. He said to Matus, "You set me up. This is just like the Springer job."

Matus's expression turned disconsolate. He seemed about to speak, but suddenly closed his mouth. His eyes widened even more than they were already.

"Lift your jacket and do a slow turn," the suit ordered Race.

"I'm not armed," Race told him as he turned.

"Where are the diamonds?"

Race moved slowly toward the man and dangled his car keys from his upraised left hand. He tossed them to the muscle-bound man, and announced, "They're in the trunk."

"Give me that gun," the suit told the muscle-head. "Go check the trunk." Then he said to Race and Matus, "You two come over here."

"What do you plan to do with us?" Race asked as he moved between the suit and Matus's SUV.

"Shut the fuck up," the suit said.

Race noticed that Matus was slightly bent at the waist, trying to make himself small. His mention of the "Springer job" had apparently penetrated his fear-wracked brain.

"What the hell's wrong with you?" the suit said to Matus. He laughed. "Your stomach still hurt?"

The muscle guy had just opened the Impala's trunk when Race felt the air suddenly become pressurized. Then a loud *whoosh* sounded and the rear end of the car on the right spewed flames. The stench of gasoline was immediately detectable as it poured from the car onto the blacktop, caught fire, and engulfed the muscle guy. Black smoke from the vehicle rose skyward. The bitter odor of burning plastic mixed with the smell of gas and filled the air. Race's ears felt as though they were full of cotton.

The suit screamed something unintelligible and dove to the blacktop. Race leaped on top of him and wrestled for control of the gun. As he grappled with the man, he yelled, "Eric, get in your car." The words had just escaped his lips when the pistol went off and the gas tank of the vehicle on the left ignited. He jerked the gun from the suit's hand and leaped off him. As he stood and backed away from the flames, he spotted Matus sprawled on the blacktop.

He took a step in Matus's direction, when the suit grunted as he got to his knees. Race glanced back at the man and saw him reach toward his ankle.

The suit jerked a snub-nosed pistol from an ankle holster and pointed it toward Race. He fired before Race could pull the trigger on the pistol he held. He felt a tug on his jacket sleeve and a burning sensation on the outside of his left bicep as he pulled the trigger on his weapon. The pistol roared. An instant later the suit was flat on his back; a hole punched in the center of his forehead.

Race's head ached as he turned back to where a gasping Matus lay. He rolled his friend from his side to his back. A hole the size of a quarter showed on his blood-soaked shirt. Blood drenched the pavement around him.

"Get . . . out of here . . . while you can," Matus groaned.

"No way," Race said. "I've got to get you to a hospital."

Matus coughed and sprayed blood onto Race's jacket. Then he moaned and exhaled a long, raspy breath.

He tried to find a pulse at Matus's neck. Nothing. "Dammit, Eric," he whispered. Then he searched Matus's pockets, took his cell phone, and climbed into the SUV.

# CHAPTER 16

Even with their years together in the military, Race and Matus had never been close friends. Since Race's family had been murdered and Eric had called him to express his condolences, their relationship had been more like employer/employee. Even when Matus had informed Race that his own wife and son had been killed in a car accident caused by a habitual drunk driver and he'd begged him to help avenge their deaths, their relationship never changed. That was intentional on Race's part. He couldn't afford to get too close to anyone once he'd changed his career from software entrepreneur to vigilante killer. But Matus had been an emotional and administrative support. He'd afforded Race the opportunity to maintain anonymity while he completed his missions—avenging the victims of psychopaths and sociopaths. Matus had been an integral part of the operation, but now Race was on his own, and more exposed.

He drove the SUV away. As he steered onto Paradise Road, he saw a flash of orange light in his rearview mirror. The flames from the two vehicles had apparently ignited the fuel in the Impala.

Race knew he had very little time before a manhunt ensued. He cursed himself for not taking Matus's wallet with him. But then he realized that would have only slowed the cops down, but wouldn't have prevented them from ultimately identifying Matus. His fingerprints were in the military database. They would backtrack into every crevice of his life. He needed to dump the SUV and find another vehicle. And he needed to leave Las Vegas.

Race drove to his motel and stripped off his jacket and shirt. The bullet the guy had fired had grazed his bicep. He scrubbed the arm with soap, then rinsed it and toweled it dry. He put the shirt and jacket back on and collected his suitcase and briefcase. Then he booted up his Mac and searched the local newspaper's classified section. Within fifteen minutes, he found an advertisement for a four-year-old Chevrolet Silverado LT Crew Cab pickup truck. The words Highly Motivated were in the ad. The vehicle was in Henderson, Nevada. He called the number in the ad, arranged to meet the owner at her home, and then drove the SUV to a city lot in Henderson. After he wiped down the vehicle, he backed into a corner space to conceal the pitted and scorched driver's side.

Six blocks from the garage, he took a cab from a hotel to the pickup truck owner's home. The truck was parked on the street in front of a tiny bungalow. He placed his suitcase flat in the truck's bed, then crossed a yard that was more dirt than grass to the house's front door and rang the bell.

A thirty-something brunette, who looked damned good in a pair of jeans and a sleeveless blouse, answered the doorbell and came outside. She gave Race the once over. "Mr. Crandell?"

"Yes, ma'am."

She stuck out a hand. "Christy Ledbetter." They shook. Then she pointed toward the street. "You like the truck?"

Race was in a hurry to close the deal, but he didn't want to raise suspicions by not asking questions a typical seller would anticipate.

"The ad said this is a one-owner truck. Is that right?"

"That's right." She led the way down to the street.

After he circled the truck for a minute and looked under the hood, he said, "It looks like it's been well maintained."

"That's right. Belonged to my husband. I got it and the house in the divorce settlement." She laughed. "That truck meant more to Roger than I did. That's why I fought for it in the settlement."

Race nodded.

"I'm asking fifteen thousand."

Race detected desperation in her tone. He figured he could

probably negotiate a much better deal. He could afford to pay the asking price, but didn't think a smart buyer would do so. "I'll pay you thirteen thousand five hundred cash if we can make a deal right now."

"Make it fourteen thousand and we've got a deal."

Race looked back at the truck for a long moment, then said, "That sounds fair."

The woman breathed out a long, relieved breath. "Done. Let's go inside."

Race laid his briefcase on the table in the woman's kitchen. "You have the title?"

"Of course." She stood, moved to the kitchen counter.

Race watched her move and noticed again how nice she looked in her jeans. "Sorry to hear about your divorce," he said.

She waved a hand as though to dismiss the subject of the divorce. "It's been tough financially, but I'm a whole lot happier now." She returned to the table with a manila folder and sat across from Race. She opened the folder, took out a vehicle title, and passed it to him.

He looked over the title without really reading it. He gave it back to her. "If you'll sign it on the back, we can get this done."

The woman's hand shook a bit as she picked up a pen from the table and signed the document. He wondered if she was frightened of him or just excited about closing the deal on the truck.

"What name should I write in as the buyer?" she asked.

"Crandell. Hugh Crandell."

As she wrote "Hugh Crandell" on the title, Race spun his briefcase around, opened it, and counted out fourteen thousand dollars in one hundred dollar bills.

The woman's eyes seemed to bug out as he placed the bills on the table in front of her.

"Thanks, Mr. Crandell. This sure will come in handy. Since I got laid off at Caesar's Palace . . . ."

"The economy's been hurting since 2008. The gaming industry's been hit hard."

"Tell me about it."

Race closed his case, lifted it from the table, and stood. "Nice doing business with you, Miss Ledbetter."

"Would you like a drink . . . ? You know, to celebrate the deal."

He recognized loneliness, neediness, and sadness in the woman's expression. The same things he saw every time he looked into a mirror. He was tempted, but gave her a half-smile, and touched her shoulder. "I appreciate the offer, ma'am, but I'm on a tight schedule. Maybe you'd give me a rain check for the next time I'm in the area."

The woman tried to smile back, but her expression was more sad than happy. She stood a bit straighter. "You got that rain check, Mr. Crandell. I hope you'll cash it in some day."

Race turned and walked toward the front door.

"Oh, Mr. Crandell."

He stopped and turned. "Yes?"

"You might want to get rid of that jacket. Probably the pants, too."

Race was confused. "Why's that?"

"You smell like smoke. And there's a big black mark on the back of your jacket. Musta got too close to a fire."

Race felt his face go hot. He nodded and walked out to the truck.

# DAY 6

# CHAPTER 17

"You know, Saturdays are supposed to be off-days for us," Susan said.

"Unless we're on an important case," Barbara said.

"Oh, so that's why we work every Saturday."

"And Sundays, too."

"We're so lucky to be such stars. Salas seems to feed us all the important cases. That's why they pay us the big bucks."

Barbara hummed a few bars of *Dream Along With Me*.

"How's Henry?" Susan asked.

"Why do you want to know?"

"Well, you can't have much of a love life working these hours."

"Listen, girlfriend, one night with Henry Simpson holds me over for a week. He's a real hottie."

"Aw, jeez, that's TMI."

Barbara smiled slyly. "Too much information. Really?"

"Yeah. I got this sudden picture in my head of nerdy Henry, wearing glasses and black socks, jumping into the sack with you."

"You're basically a nasty bitch," Barbara said. "I'll have you know that Henry does not wear socks or glasses in bed. And there's nothing nerdy about him."

"He sure looks nerdy in his clothes."

Barbara smiled. "So does Clark Kent. Henry's one-hundred-sixty-five pounds of twisted blue steel and sex appeal when he's naked."

Susan seemed to think about that for a few seconds. She chuckled. "Maybe you should have Henry introduce me to one of his colleagues."

"That can be arranged."

"Any hunks in the geology department that aren't igneous?"

Barbara laughed. "I'll check. Now, can we get to work?"

"Sure."

"Did you see the news about the crispy critters in Las Vegas?"

"Of course. So what?"

"There's an awful lot going on in Las Vegas, don't you think?"

Susan paused a beat and then asked, "You don't think they're connected to the Ponzi scheme guy and the murders of those three football players, do you?"

Barbara spread her hands as though to say, 'Who knows?' "There just seems to be a lot going on in Sin City."

"It's a big city. Crime happens."

"I know, but maybe we should call my new friend, Sophia."

Susan shrugged. "Can't hurt."

Barbara dialed Sophia Otero-Hansen's number and left a message.

"What's with all the IT time?" FBI Agent-in-Charge Bruce Lucas asked.

"What do you mean?" Sophia Otero-Hansen said.

"You've spent twenty hours on the NCIC database over the past three days."

"I didn't realize it was that many hours. But it's been productive."

"Productive how?"

"I began with the murder of a pedophile here in New Mexico. It's led to a mass murderer. A possible vigilante."

"And what does that have to do with the bank robbery case I assigned to you and Murdoch?"

"Uh, nothing, boss. But Murdoch's working that case and—"

"In other words, Murdoch's doing his job and you've decided that what *I* want is unimportant."

"Of course not. It's just that this vigilante has been active over the last few days. I thought we might be able to identify him."

"Active where?"

Otero-Hansen swallowed. She knew Lucas wouldn't like her answer. "Las Vegas."

Lucas's ruddy complexion turned beet-red. He leaned forward in his chair and glared up at her. "So, let me summarize what I've just heard. You've spent hours and hours sitting on your ass staring at a computer, ignoring the assignment I gave you, and are involved somehow in something that isn't even in this office's jurisdiction. Does that about cover it?"

"But . . . . The vigilante killer has murdered at least a dozen people in six states, including New Mexico. *Our jurisdiction.*"

Lucas's face went red again. "You're in enough trouble already without getting snippy." He pointed a fat finger at her. "You drop this bullshit mass murderer-vigilante and get back on the bank robbery case. And get your attitude adjusted. Or else."

Otero-Hansen gaped at Lucas like a beached fish. She was just about to ask, "Or else, what?" but controlled her anger and marched out of his office.

Back at her desk, she saw her message light blinking and checked calls. Barbara Lassiter had left a message. She immediately returned the call.

"Lassiter."

"It's Sophia."

"Hey. I called to see—"

"I just got reamed about the time I've put into our mass murderer vigilante. As of this moment, I'm off the case."

"I'm sorry, Sophia. I really think we've got something here."

Otero-Hansen groaned. "I know we do. But I'm done. My asshole boss wants me to work a series of bank robberies in New Mexico."

"Damn." Barbara thought for a few seconds. "What hours are you working today?"

"I'm off at 6."

"How'd you like to have dinner with Susan and me tonight? Just a nice, social occasion."

Otero-Hansen said, "Sounds good."

"By the way, have you followed the news about the latest event in Las Vegas?"

"Oh, yeah. What a mess."

"What happened?"

"We haven't figured that out. I just saw the IDs of the deceased come over the wire. A connected guy named Stanley Bukowski, a muscle-head who worked for Bukowski by the name of Richie Hewitt, and a guy from Salt Lake City named Eric Matus."

"Salt Lake City? What's he, some kinda Mormon Mafioso?"

"Haven't determined that yet either. All we know so far is he served in the U.S. Army and ran a talent agency."

Barbara said, "Okay, see you tonight. How about the Elephant Bar at 7?"

"I'll see you there."

# CHAPTER 18

Susan stood and stretched her back and rolled her shoulders. "Damn," she groaned, this chair is ruining my back."

"That's what happens when the county buys furniture from the lowest bidder," Barbara said."

"How 'bout leaving now. I gotta make a stop on the way to the restaurant."

"Jeez, it's only 4:30. We don't have to meet Sophia until 7."

"I have to sign some papers at the credit union. They close at 5."

Barbara stood and grabbed her purse from the floor by her desk. "Okay, let's go."

On the way down in the elevator, Barbara asked, "What's going on at the credit union?"

"I'm taking out a loan."

"That's not like you. I thought you hated owing money to anyone."

Susan shrugged and looked down at the floor. "It's the Corvette. It's going to cost more than I thought to fix it."

When Susan raised her gaze, Barbara said, "That thing's never going to be worth what you've put into it."

"You can't put a value on a classic."

"Humpf," Barbara blurted.

The drive to the credit union building took fifteen minutes. Barbara pulled the Crown Vic up to the front door of the building and told Susan she'd wait in the vehicle. After Susan walked inside, Barbara pulled around to the side of the single story structure and found a parking space there. She booted up her cell phone and accessed her email account. After she cleared out the spam emails, she put the phone away in her purse and craned her neck to catch sight of the building entrance. It was almost 5 p.m. She shook her head at the thought of driving from downtown Albuquerque to the uptown area at the height of rush hour traffic.

She decided to get out of the car to stretch her legs and to be able to spot Susan when she exited the building. Having just closed the car door, the shrill squeal of tires on concrete diverted her attention away from the building entrance. A black van came around the corner of the building and sped toward the front door. The vehicle came to a screeching stop there.

"What the hell," Barbara rasped. She moved toward the van, planning to give the driver a piece of her mind, when three young men bailed from the vehicle. All three carried shotguns and wore masks.

Barbara reached for her pistol in the holster on her hip and felt a sinking feeling when she remembered she'd clipped the holster to the strap of her purse. She always did that while driving, to avoid the discomfort of wearing the weapon on her hip while she was behind the wheel. She quickly reversed direction to return to the car, opened the door, and dropped into the driver's seat. She snatched her purse from the floor. As she pulled the pistol from the holster, she called in to the dispatcher.

Barbara identified herself and then said, "Two eleven in progress at Bernalillo County Credit Union, twelve hundred block of 4th Street Northwest. At least three armed men inside the building. One man still in a black van parked outside the entrance. I—"

The sounds of a pistol being fired stopped Barbara. Then the roar of a shotgun sounded. "Shots fired," she shouted into the mic. "Code twenty; officer needs assistance." She threw down the radio mic and exited the car. She used parked vehicles as cover while she moved toward the running black van. She was eight vehicles away from the building entrance when the front doors flew open and the three masked men stampeded onto the front pavement and circled around the van. One of the men dragged a leg as though he was injured.

Barbara cut around the back end of the pickup she was using as cover and ran toward the van. "Stop! Police!" she shouted, as she brought her pistol to bear on the vehicle. Movement to her left momentarily diverted her attention. Susan ran from the building, gun leveled toward the black vehicle. She rapid-fire shot at the van's occupants as the vehicle sped away.

"You okay?" Barbara shouted at Susan.

"Yeah. Get the car."

Barbara ran back to the Crown Vic, backed out of the parking space, and peeled out toward where Susan waited. Once Susan was in the car, Barbara asked, "Anyone hurt inside the building?"

"No, thank God. I clipped one of the guys in the leg. He fired off his shotgun into the ceiling."

Barbara shot out of the parking lot and pulled onto 4th street. She could see the top of the getaway vehicle half-a-block ahead. "Get on the radio and give them what you know," she told Susan. "I got the plate number."

After Susan got off the radio, she opened her window and placed the emergency light on the car's roof.

"You know, with this traffic, the siren and flashers probably won't help a bit," Barbara said.

"Bastards," Susan blurted. "They coulda killed someone. They were armed to the teeth. Shotguns and automatics on their hips."

Barbara saw the van turn left at the end of the next block. Traffic came to a dead stop in front of her. The oncoming lane was clogged to a standstill.

"Damnit," she yelled.

It was 8:30 p.m. before Barbara and Susan were released by the BCSD "shooting team." Barbara had called Otero-Hansen to let her know what had happened and suggested they meet some other evening, but the FBI agent had told her to call when they became available. "Those robbers could be the crew we've been investigating for months," Otero-Hansen had said.

At 8:45 p.m., Barbara and Susan sat across from one another at a table in the Elephant Bar in a shopping center in Uptown Albuquerque. They'd ordered margaritas and waited for Sophia Otero-Hansen to arrive. The first round of drinks disappeared almost immediately. Susan got the waitress's attention and ordered a second round.

"Too bad Sophia doesn't have a wonderful boss like ours," Susan said. "Sounds like he's putting her through the wringer."

"Since when did you think Salas was a wonderful boss?"

"Since I came to the conclusion that Sophia's boss makes Lieutenant Sniffles look like the boss of the year."

"Her boss does sound like an asshole. I know the Bureau takes the lead on bank heists, but you'd think the guy would have some interest in tracking down a mass murderer who's operated in multiple states."

"Maybe we can help Sophia find the bank robbers. I mean, my God, they've hit a dozen of them in the last twelve months."

Barbara scrunched her face. "There you go again, partner. Just because you think you're hot stuff, doesn't mean you can solve a case the Feds have worked since last September."

Susan pouted. "I'm devastated. My own partner doesn't think we're better than the FBI. I bet you if we were on the case, we'd quickly find the bad guys."

Barbara smiled at Susan. "If you were a better shot, that team of robbers would no longer exist."

Susan frowned. "I'll have you know, the only shot I had was the one guy I hit in the leg. The other two were screened by citizens. Any time you want to go out to the range and test my shooting prowess, just say so."

Barbara looked at her cell phone to check the time just as it rang. She saw Otero-Hansen's name on the screen.

"Hey," she answered. "Everything okay?"

"Everything's fine, except I'm running about thirty minutes late. I apologize for—"

"Don't worry about it. We'll order another round of margaritas. There'll be one waiting for you."

"Thanks. After this day, I'll need it."

Barbara put down her phone. "That was Sophia. She's running late. Sounds like she's had a bad day."

"Every day's a bad day when you work for an asshole," Susan said as the waitress delivered their drinks.

"Tell me about it," the waitress said and walked away.

Barbara smiled at Susan. "Maybe we don't have it so bad after all." Then she narrowed her eyes and said, "You never told me about that date you had the other night."

Susan frowned and shook her head. She snatched up her glass, licked salt off its rim, and downed a third of the drink. "Ah," she exhaled. "What do you want to know about my date?"

"The usual. What did he look like? Did you like the guy? Where'd you go to dinner? Any romance? You know."

Susan sipped her drink and said, "Suffice it to say that's the last time I use one of those online dating services."

"You didn't?"

"I did."

"Why would you do that? There are dozens of guys panting after you."

"Yeah, but they're all cops. I thought I'd branch out a bit. You know, maybe meet a man with interests other than murder and mayhem."

"The date didn't go so well?"

"You could say that." Susan scowled and paused, as though she considered not continuing with the story. Then she said, "You promise not to laugh?"

Barbara met Susan's gaze. "No way. It's one thing to keep your stories to myself; it's another to promise not to laugh. That's something I can't control. If you don't want to tell me, fine."

Susan took two slow sips of her drink while Barbara continued to stare at her. When Barbara thought Susan had decided not to relate her dating experience, she picked up her own drink and sipped it.

"Okay, I'll tell you."

Barbara held her drink in two hands and waited.

Susan put down her glass. "So, I signed up on this dating website. Had to put up my picture, likes and dislikes, physical description, education. You know, all that stuff. My posting's up maybe three hours and hits start coming in."

"How many hits?"

"At least fifty."

"No way."

"Yes, way. There were so many I lost track."

"How'd you decide who to contact?"

"I picked the best looking guy of the bunch. Besides he's a nuclear engineer at Sandia Labs. That's about as different from being a cop as it comes."

"How good looking?"

"Chris Pine-good looking."

"That's pretty good looking," Barbara said. "I'd say something about your superficial criteria for selecting men but I don't want to interrupt your story."

Susan scowled again. "Anyway, the guy calls me after I emailed him. We arranged to meet at Seasons Restaurant down in Old Town."

"Good start."

"Yeah, that was my reaction, too."

"I got there fashionably late. He was standing at the bar. My heart seemed to stop. I mean, this guy was drop-dead gorgeous. He's wearing a suit that's got to be Armani and it fits him perfectly. Oh my God, his eyes. They were so hazel, they were almost green. It was all I could do to not hyperventilate."

Barbara tried to keep a smile off her face, but the longer Susan's story went, the harder it became. "What happened? Did you skip dinner and go straight to his place?"

Susan squinted at Barbara. "I may be hot-blooded, but I'm not that easy."

"Sorry. Go on."

"We sat down to dinner. Nice little table in the back. Good view of the whole place. He's got his back to the room. The waitress comes over and hands him a wine list. He looks it over for maybe thirty seconds and says, 'Bring us a bottle of the Cakebread Cellars chardonnay.' "

"Henry ordered a bottle of that one time. Cost over a hundred dollars."

"It tasted like it," Susan said. "It was pure ambrosia."

"Sounds like a great date so far."

Susan sniffed. "That's what I thought. While we waited for the wine, he leans in and asks me where I grew up. I told him about being a kid in Northern New Mexico and then moving to Albuquerque when I was sixteen. While I'm telling the story, I notice he's not making eye contact. The more we talk, the more obvious it becomes. I mean, this guy's eyes are all over the place. The more his eyes wander, the more I laser in on his face with my eyes. That just seems to make him antsier. Finally, I can't take it anymore and say, 'Are you looking for someone?'

"His face goes red; then he turns pale. 'No, no,' he says. He leans in closer to me and whispers, 'It's not that I'm not listening to you; it's that I'm really tired, and when I'm really tired and look someone in the eye, that's when they take me.' "

"Who takes him?" Barbara asked.

Susan raised a hand to hold Barbara off. "I'm getting there. That's what I asked. He says, 'The little people.' I asked, 'You mean little people like aliens?' He says, 'Exactly.'

"Now, I'm thinking this guy is putting me on. But I figure I'll go along with the joke. I asked, 'How many times have the little people taken you?' He says, 'At least four times, as far as I can remember.' So, I ask, 'What do they do with you?' He tells me they experiment on him."

"What sort of experiments?" Barbara asked.

"Sexual experiments. Kinky stuff."

"This is getting interesting. Was he specific?"

Susan glared at Barbara. "If you're that interested, I could introduce you to him."

"No, that's all right. I wouldn't want to interfere with your love life."

Susan scoffed again.

"What did you do after dinner?"

"Are you out of your mind? I got out of there as fast as I could."

"You haven't seen him again?" Before Susan could respond, Barbara broke down in side-splitting laughter. When she finally got control of herself, she looked Susan in the eyes and said, "You're telling me that a guy playing with nuclear weapons out at Sandia National Laboratory believes in alien abductions?"

Susan's face reddened. "I hadn't thought about that. Nuclear weapons and psychotic behavior really don't mix very well, do they?"

"What about nukes and psychotic behavior?" Sophia Otero-Hansen asked as she sat down between Barbara and Susan.

Susan shot a warning glance at Barbara.

"Nothing," Barbara said. "Susan was telling me a joke."

"Come on, girl," Otero-Hansen said, "tell me."

Susan waved a hand as though she had nothing important to say.

"Sorry I'm late," Otero-Hansen said. "Got away from the office later than I expected. Then I had to go home to let out the dog and change."

"How's your husband doing?" Barbara asked.

"Fine. He's out of town for the week for a legal continuing education class. Poor baby had the choice between Miami and San Diego."

"Better than Albuquerque this week," Susan said. "It's supposed to rain, maybe even snow, tomorrow."

"Sorry about getting you in trouble with your boss," Barbara said.

Otero-Hansen smiled. "I'm a big girl, Barbara. You didn't force me to do anything."

"Yeah, I know. But I'm still sorry."

Otero-Hansen shrugged.

"Anything new on your end?" Susan asked.

"We discovered the black van used in the attempted robbery of the credit union was stolen a week ago. APD found it abandoned near the Indian Pueblo Cultural Center on 12th Street. The perps scrubbed it clean of evidence. The only thing we got were blood samples off the carpet in the back of the vehicle. So we'll have DNA if we ever arrest these guys. You two did good." Otero-Hansen looked at Susan and said, "I can't believe you shot one of the robbers. The lobby was packed with people."

"I had a three-inch window, so I took the shot."

Otero-Hansen looked at Barbara. The look on her face seemed to say, "She's kidding, right?"

Barbara smiled at her and asked, "Anything new from Las Vegas?"

"One of the men, Stanley Bukowski, who was killed in the Las Vegas parking lot, was shot. But the weapon that killed him wasn't found at the scene."

"Huh," Barbara said.

"Yeah. And one of the other men, Eric Matus, is a very curious guy."

"How so?" Barbara asked just as a waitress came to the table.

"Please come back in five minutes," Susan told the girl, while she continued to stare at Otero-Hansen.

"I told you earlier he was former military."

"Yeah."

"Right. Well, he ran a talent agency in Salt Lake City. We sent a field agent to his office. The landlord let him in. Bunch of glamour shots on the walls, but no receptionist. The file cabinets all empty. No computers. The place looks like a front for something."

Barbara said, "Do you find it interesting that this guy Matus was in Las Vegas around the same time that the three football players were murdered and the Bellagio incident happened? Interesting coincidence."

"Yeah. I don't believe in coincidences," Otero-Hansen said.

Barbara said, "If you checked his credit card activity, you might be able to place him on the same dates in the cities where murders occurred."

"That's a good idea," Otero-Hansen said. "But I can't do that with my boss looking over my shoulder."

Susan grimaced. "Right."

"Then we'll do it," Barbara said.


Race counted his cash before he pulled away from the Ledbetter residence. He was down to forty-three hundred dollars. He'd already decided to get far away from Las Vegas. There was plenty of cash in his Las Vegas safety deposit box, but he was too cautious to take the chance of returning to the city. He knew the police wouldn't identify him from the burned out Impala he'd left in the office building lot—he'd bought it with cash under a false name and had burned that set of ID. He'd sanitized the vehicle before he'd parked it in the lot, and the explosion and fire that had destroyed it had surely eradicated any other forensic evidence he might have left behind. But he needed cash, and his closest safety deposit box outside Las Vegas was in Albuquerque.

He followed Nevada 93 from Henderson southeast to Interstate 40 at Kingman, Arizona. From there, he went east on I-40 and finally had to stop for gas in Winslow. By that time, it was almost 11 p.m. and he was dead-tired. After he gassed up the truck, he found a motel that had seen better days. As he always did, he gave a fictitious name, paid cash, and gave the clerk a twenty dollar tip. That always seemed to discourage them from demanding ID. When he rarely stayed at first rate hotels, he presented one of several sets of false ID, but still paid cash. When they asked for a credit card, he had a standard response: "Don't believe in the damned things. Always pay cash for everything." Then he'd hand over a hundred dollar bill to cover incidentals.

Eric Matus had thought Race's ways were eccentric; thought he was unnecessarily careful. In addition to his cash-only policy, he never traveled by air; always drove cars he owned in false names. Never rented a car because the rental agencies demanded a driver's license and a credit card. He paid cash at least five years in advance for safety deposit boxes.

There was only one other car parked in the Winslow motel lot. Good, Race thought, maybe it will be quiet. I might get a good night's sleep . . . assuming the dream doesn't wake me. He turned on the television and only half-listened to a local channel while he undressed. The news anchor had just finished a report about some charity fund drive in Winslow, when he suddenly said, "We have breaking news about a home invasion in Flagstaff. A couple in the Sunrise Estates Country Club area was found murdered, along with their three grandchildren. The children's parents returned from a business trip and discovered the bodies." The anchor paused. "We warn you that the following may be disturbing for some viewers."

The words "home invasion" caused Race to stop undressing.

He sat on the bed, eyes riveted to the set.

A picture of a young female reporter, backlit by the flashing lights of a dozen emergency and police vehicles, popped onto the screen.

The female reporter said, "This is Melissa Chan. I am just thirty yards from the scene of the grisly, depraved murders of two adults and three children. The murders apparently occurred about twenty-four hours ago. The family's exterior security camera caught the suspected intruders as they entered the residence and then fled two hours later. If anyone has any information about these men, please call the telephone number at the bottom of the screen."

A grainy video played. The time clock at the bottom left side of the picture read 1:13 a.m. The camera must have been mounted directly above the residence's side door. It caught what appeared to be a dark-colored Ford Explorer approach the house. Three men quickly bailed from the Ford and ran to the side door. Each of their faces were tinged green from the infra-red video. The first man kicked in the door; then all three charged inside. Then the video went dead until the men exited the house carrying boxes, and they casually walked back to their vehicle. They all seemed to be laughing. The time clock at the bottom of the video now showed it was 3:22 a.m., a little more than two hours after the men had busted down the door.

Race suddenly gasped. He hadn't realized he'd held his breath. It was the third man in line at the back door who he recognized. The beak-of-a-nose, the tattoo of a knife on his neck, the scar that bisected his left cheek and lips were all unmistakable. Even as grainy as the video was, he was absolutely certain it was the same man who had beaten him with a tire iron over three years ago. The same man who, along with two other men, had tortured and murdered his wife and daughters. Perhaps all three of the men in this video were the ones who'd invaded his home.

His nerve endings tingled as though electrified. The emotional pain that had engorged his mind after the deaths of his family, and which, at times, had simmered under the surface, and, at others, had boiled to the point of uncontrolled rage, now exploded inside him. His mind reeled with thoughts of the home invasions and murders that he'd researched. More than a dozen of them over five years. In multiple states, from one side of the United States to the other. But there'd never been enough evidence to identify the perpetrators . . . until now.

# DAY 7

# CHAPTER 19

It took an order from a District Court judge to get the credit card company to release Eric Matus's records. Once the court order was presented, the credit card company emailed the records to the Second Judicial District Attorney of Bernalillo County, who forwarded them to Barbara Lassiter at the BCSD.

"Sonofabitch," Susan exclaimed. "It's him. It's really him."

"I'll be damned," Barbara said. "Matus was in every one of the places on the exact dates when a vigilante murder took place." She tapped the copy of the credit card bill with a finger. "Look at these entries. Fastway Gas and Frontier Restaurant in Albuquerque the day before the O'Neil murder; Motel 6, Thrifty Gas, and Sunshine Café in Las Vegas the day before and the day of the crimes at the law office and at the Bellagio; Residence Inn—"

"Don't forget the car fires and the three bodies in Vegas at that same time," Susan interjected.

"There's that, too. There's been what appears to be a vigilante killing in every city when Matus was in that city."

"It's interesting that there are no charges for flights or rental cars. You think he drove to all the locations?"

Barbara shrugged. "Coulda taken a bus, for all we know. But, if I had to bet, I'd say he drove. Should have paid cash instead of using credit cards."

"Huh. I feel kinda let down. Didn't expect to find the guy this easily."

"Neither did I. He's been ultra-careful all along. The incident in the office building parking lot in Las Vegas seems out of pattern. That's why it's been difficult for me to accept that the same guy was responsible for those deaths."

"Maybe you ought to call Sophia. I'm sure she'll want to hear the news."

Barbara nodded, picked up her cell phone, dialed Sophia Otero-Hansen's number, and punched the speaker button.

"I was just about to call you," Otero-Hansen said.

"Oh, yeah?"

"You first. You called me."

"We placed Eric Matus in the vicinity on the same day of every one of the killings you identified."

"I hate to ruin your happy moment, but before you put out any press releases you might want to try to answer a question: how did Matus's SUV wind up in a parking garage in Henderson, Nevada?"

"He could have left it there before going to the meeting in the parking lot," Susan offered.

"Nope," Otero-Hansen said. "First, there was no vehicle in the parking lot that could be tied to any of the three men who were killed there. So, how'd they get there? We checked with cab companies, and none of them dropped off the men at that site or in the immediate area at the time of the incident. We think they got there in Matus's vehicle."

Susan responded, "They could have been dropped off by someone."

"Yes, that's a remote possibility."

"You said *first*; is there a *second*?" Barbara asked.

"The driver side of the vehicle found in the Henderson parking garage is fire-damaged. It had been wiped down. No prints."

After a moment, Barbara said, "You mean Matus had a partner?"

"Yep."

The three women went quiet for a few seconds. Then Susan said, "You know, I've wondered how people get hold of the killer. I mean, it's not like you go to Google or the Yellow Pages and look up Assassin or Vigilante."

"Hmm," Otero-Hansen said. "Maybe there's a killer-for-hire network out there."

"Think about it for a minute," Susan said. "Maybe after you've knocked off a dozen or so scumbags, you develop a reputation and then word of mouth kicks in. But there's a problem with that."

"Yeah," Otero-Hansen said. "Word of mouth can sink you. Word gets to the wrong people, like the police, and you're screwed."

Barbara interjected, "Also, how do you get your assignments before you develop a reputation? How do you get your first assignment?"

More silence.

Susan said, "You could get your assignments by meeting with a family member of a victim and offering to take revenge. You screen the families before you make a call to determine whether they have the wherewithal to pay your fee. Then you make the deal."

"But what if you call someone and they tell you to go to hell and then call the cops?" Otero-Hansen asked.

"Good point," Susan said. "Maybe it's all done electronically. No one sees your face or knows your name."

Otero-Hansen countered, "The lawyer in Las Vegas and the man and woman in the hotel room at the Bellagio saw his face."

"But their descriptions of the guy were very different," Barbara said. "Maybe he's a master of disguise."

"Or, there's more than one guy out there. There could be a whole crew of these guys. Dark angels wreaking murder and mayhem against bad people. We need to consider something else, ladies," Otero-Hansen said. "If Matus had a partner or partners, maybe it was that partner or partners who committed the murders."

Race barely slept after he watched the previous night's news report about the home invasion and five deaths in Flagstaff. At 8 a.m., he booted up his laptop and tried to find updated information about the crime. There was nothing new available other than an announcement that the chief of police would hold a news conference at 11 that morning. Race could barely sit down during the three hours until the news conference.

"Will you guys shut the hell up?" Reese McCall shouted as he drove onto Interstate 40 and sped east toward the New Mexico state line. He stroked the knife tattoo on his neck, as he always did when he was aggravated.

"Whatsamatter?" Kiley Lewis said from the front passenger seat.

Gerome Bryant, in the backseat, said, "He's pissed off about his cut from the jobs we've done." Bryant laughed.

"Is that right, Kiley?" McCall asked. "You unhappy about our arrangement? You and Gerry been talking about things?"

"Hey, wait a minute," Bryant blurted.

"I told you to shut up." McCall flipped on the radio and tuned it to a Country & Western station. No more than five seconds of music had passed before the only sound in the Explorer was the voice of a radio station DJ.

"We have news about the mass murder in Flagstaff last night. As we reported earlier, the scene of the murders is gruesome, savage. Five people were killed, including three children aged seven to thirteen. The Flagstaff Police Department—"

"Holy shit," Gerome Bryant said. "They found them already. How the hell—"

"Quiet," McCall shouted.

"The children's parents returned from a trip and went to pick them up at their grandparents' home. They found the bodies and called the police."

"That musta been a shock for Mommy and Daddy," Kiley Lewis said. He chuckled.

The radio DJ continued: "The Brownell home was equipped with a motion detection, infra-red security camera. A source with the Flagstaff Police Department told us the camera captured the perpetrators and their vehicle. They've broadcast that information to all law enforcement agencies in the region, as well as to the FBI."

"Oh, shit," McCall groaned.

At one minute before 11 a.m., Race moved a chair so that he was perched on it less than three feet from the television screen. He watched a gray-haired, uniformed man climb three steps to a stage and stop behind a podium.

The man announced, "I am Wilbur Hamilton, Chief of Police of Flagstaff, Arizona. I'll make a statement and then take a few questions." He waited for the reporters in the audience to settle down. "At 1:13 the night before last, three men—two white and one black—broke down the back door of William and Yvette Brownell's home in the Sunrise Estate's Country Club community. They brutally murdered the Brownells and their three grandchildren, aged thirteen, eleven, and seven. They were in the Brownell home for approximately two hours. It appears the men robbed the Brownells after they murdered them."

Race was so fixated on the screen that it took a minute before William Brownell's name jogged something in his memory bank, but he couldn't immediately drag it up.

"We are communicating with the Federal Bureau of Investigation and all law enforcement agencies in Arizona, as well as in surrounding states," the police chief continued. "The suspects in these crimes are believed to be in a three-year-old, dark-red Ford Explorer."

The chief looked around the room and then stared into the camera. "The men who committed these crimes are suspects in similar crimes that occurred in multiple states over the past five years. I encourage the media to broadcast the video from the Brownell home security system every day, multiple times a day, until we catch these sadistic killers. This is the first time we have had pictures of these men. We must find them before they strike again."

The police chief's eyes half-closed as he visibly swallowed. He took a deep breath and said, "Finally, I want to warn everyone these men are probably armed and extremely dangerous. Anyone with information about them should call their local police or the FBI." He cleared his throat. "I will now take questions."

The media reps immediately went into hyperactive mode and shouted en-masse at the chief, who raised his hands until quiet had been restored.

"Another outburst like that and I'll walk away. Raise your hands if you have questions. I'll point at whoever I want to hear from."

A communal groan came from the press reps, but they followed the chief's instructions. The first reporter asked, "Can you tell us anything about how the victims were killed. Were they sexually assaulted, or—"

The police chief glared at the reporter. "No comment." He looked at another part of the room and pointed at another reporter.

"Would you go through events from the time the children's parents discovered the bodies to the present time?"

The police chief briefed the reporters on the general activities associated with the investigation, from the time the 9-1-1 call came in.

Another reporter asked, "Have you been able to determine why the Brownells were targeted?"

The police chief shook his head. "At this point, we assume the murderers picked the Brownell home at random."

Race turned down the volume and thought about what he knew. There was no question the killers were psychopaths. What they did to their victims was inhuman. They enjoyed inflicting pain as well as committing murder. But, despite their heinous crimes, they were clever enough to not have been identified or caught. They'd been on a rampage for years. They'd left DNA and fingerprint evidence behind when they'd murdered Race's wife and children—and had done so at other crime scenes—yet the police hadn't been able to identify them. The men had probably never been fingerprinted.

"What would I do now if I were them?" Race said aloud. He had a momentary sinking feeling as the thought hit him that he, too, was probably considered a psychopath because of the murders he'd committed. He shook his head as though to clear it of that errant thought and then took a pen and piece of paper from his briefcase. His mind worked in an organized, logical fashion, as though it was fabricated out of computer code. He considered the actions he would take if he was a member of the gang. He'd dump the Ford Explorer; get another vehicle. Then he'd get as far away from Flagstaff as possible and lie low somewhere. He also figured they would need to offload the loot they'd stolen.

He tried to come up with other answers, but nothing came to him. "Come on, come on," he rasped as he paced the motel room. "What else?"

Then it hit him. They had a problem. Their faces had been

caught on the security camera. The infra-red images had not been the best, but they were clear enough to show features and had picked up the scars and tattoo on one of them. Every person watching television or accessing the Internet would now know what they looked like. And they would know that the threesome included two white men and one black man.

Race added to his mental list: the men would need to change their appearances and split up. Two white men and one black man traveling together would attract attention now that their descriptions had become public.

Race prioritized what he thought the men would do. Number one on his list was stealing another vehicle. If and when that happened, he suspected the police would broadcast the news. But that wasn't a certainty. Maybe only law enforcement agencies would be notified. Wherever they got rid of the Explorer and replaced the vehicle with another one . . . or two, or three vehicles, if they split up, would broaden the search zone. He snatched a burner phone from his briefcase and dialed a number in Amarillo, Texas.

"Forrester."

"Detective Forrester, it's Race Thornton."

There was a slight pause before Forrester said, "Hello, Mr. Thornton. How've you been?"

"Fine. How about you?"

"Same here. I assume you heard about Flagstaff."

Race took in a quiet breath, let it out. "Of course. That's why I'm calling."

"You think they're the same guys who killed Mary and the girls?" Forrester said.

"I can tell you one thing with a certainty, Dennis. One of the men in the video from Flagstaff is the one who tried to kill me with the tire iron. Same nose, same tattoo, same scars down his cheek and across his lips."

"You absolutely certain?"

"Without a doubt."

"Sonofabitch. I thought so. When I saw the video on television this morning, your description of your attacker immediately came to mind. Maybe the same three men. Hopefully, we can compare

DNA and fingerprint evidence. That still won't identify them, but it will tell us if it's the same crew."

"Anything new on them?"

"You know I'm not supposed to put out that information."

"What harm will you do telling me anything?"

Race waited for an answer, but none came.

"You *can* do some good, Detective. Keeping me apprised of progress in finding these guys will give me some relief from the pain I've suffered for all these years."

Again, Forrester didn't respond, but, this time, Race waited him out.

Finally, the detective said, "They abandoned their vehicle in an arroyo in Gallup, New Mexico."

"Any reported stolen vehicles in the Gallup area?"

"Yeah, but that's a regular occurrence there. The New Mexico State Police put out BOLOs on all stolen vehicles, but nothing's come up yet."

"I hope someone gets these guys before they murder more people."

"Me, too, Mr. Thornton."

Race was about to thank Forrester, when he remembered why the name William Brownell had tickled his memory. He sucked in a huge breath and his heart seemed to stop for a second.

After a long pause, Forrester asked, "Are you still there?"

"Oh, sorry, Detective. I just had a thought."

"Yeah?"

Race cleared his throat. "I'm not sure."

"Come on, Mr. Thornton; tell me what's on your mind."

"Can you check something for me?"

"Depends," Forrester said.

"I understand." Race took in another long breath. "I knew a man named William Brownell . . . by reputation only. Was a big-time coin collector. The man murdered in Flagstaff might not be the same guy."

Forrester paused. "Coin collector, huh?"

"Yeah. I was just wondering. I read an article by a William Brownell several years ago about pre-Civil War U.S. coins. I'm not certain, but I seem to recall he lived somewhere in Arizona."

"Okay, I'll check. There was nothing on the wire or in the NCIC system about a coin collection. What are you . . . hey, I remember you had a big coin collection."

"I did. But there are a lot of people with coin collections. This is probably just a coincidence." Race spread his arms. "But if it's the same Brownell, and they stole his coin collection, that stuff won't do them any good unless they can find a buyer with a lot of cash. The coins stolen from my house never turned up on the market."

"Makes sense. But with their faces plastered all over television and the Internet, what legitimate coin dealer will do business with them?"

"The operative word is *legitimate*. What if you were to query the NCIC for people who had charges against them or who had served time for dealing in stolen goods? Especially rare coins."

"Interesting theory. But do you have any idea how many people you're talking about across the United States?"

"I understand. But what if you concentrated on Gallup and other towns east of there? Grants, Albuquerque, Santa Rosa. Maybe south on Interstate 25. Towns like Los Lunas, Belen, Socorro."

"What about north? Or they could have backtracked and headed toward California. It's a needle in a hay stack."

"I know, I know."

"Tell you what I'll do. I'll try to find out if William Brownell had a coin collection. If he did, I'll check NCIC for fences who specialize in coins. Maybe I'll get lucky."

"Thanks, Detective."

"Where will you be?"

"I'm in Philadelphia on business," he lied. "Would you mind if I called you for updates?"

"Any time, Mr. Thornton."

Detective Dennis Forrester processed the information Race Thornton had given him about the man caught on the security camera during the home invasion in Flagstaff. Then he went over every detail in the Thornton case file. There was nothing in it that stimulated new thinking. But Thornton's identification was a lead that no law enforcement agency had before. Then Forrester opened the NCIC database and referenced the Thornton case from almost forty months ago. He went through the file and thought, at first, he'd glossed over something. He went back through the file, but he found information missing that he had put into the case file. That information might have been unimportant at the time the file was loaded in NCIC, but, unimportant or not, it should be in the database. He might have missed it altogether if Thornton hadn't asked the question about William Brownell's coin collection.

Forrester knocked on his captain's open door. "Got a minute?"

"That's about all I've got. The mayor wants me in his office."

"I'll make this quick. Got a call from Race Thornton."

"Ah, jeez. Is that poor man still obsessing over what happened to his family?"

Forrester frowned. "No disrespect, Captain, but what would *you* do if your wife and kids had been brutally assaulted and murdered?"

The captain nodded and waved at Forrester as though to tell him to finish up.

"Thornton saw the video captured at the Flagstaff break-in. Claims one of the men in the video was the one who attacked him and murdered his family."

"After all these years, he claims it's the same guy?"

"He's absolutely certain."

The captain swiveled around in his chair and looked out the window. When he swiveled back to look at Forrester, he said, "If I recall correctly, this gang left DNA and fingerprint evidence behind on multiple occasions. In a dozen cases in many states."

"That's right."

"But this is the first time photographic evidence is available."

Forrester nodded.

"Then the Feds must be on these guys."

"I have no idea. I mean, we uploaded information into the NCIC database about the Thornton case, but we've never been contacted by anyone from the FBI about it."

"I think it's time you called the FEEBs and asked them if they inputted the video into their facial recognition system."

"You know, Captain, Thornton asked me something that now

has me confused. He said he knew a guy named William Brownell who had a coin collection. He wondered if the man murdered in Flagstaff was the same guy."

"So?"

"Race Thornton had a very valuable coin collection that was stolen the night he was beaten and his family killed. I checked the NCIC database and there is no reference to that collection in the Thornton file."

"Stuff happens."

"Yeah, but many of Thornton's coins were so rare that it was important to put their descriptions in the NCIC system. If one of those coins turned up, it could lead to the killers."

"What's your point?"

Forrester shrugged. "Just curious. What if the man in Flagstaff was also a coin collector?"

"So what? There must be millions of coin collectors in the United States."

# CHAPTER 20

Barbara followed Susan into Rudy Salas's office. This was Susan's show.

"What can I do for you, Detectives?" Salas asked.

Susan moved to within an inch of the front of Salas's desk. "You read the report we put on your desk this morning?"

"Of course," Salas said.

"Listen, Lieutenant, we think there's a serial killer out there murdering people for money, and—"

Salas interrupted, said, "He's not just murdering *people.* He's murdering *really bad people* who have slipped through the cracks in the criminal justice system."

Susan nodded. "That's right. But he's still a murderer who needs to be taken off the streets."

"No shit," Salas said. "So you and your partner are about to ask my permission to take a road trip to someplace to try to track this guy down."

"Well . . . that's right."

"Getting tired of the bad weather we've had around here lately?"

"I don't understand, Lieutenant."

Salas stared at Susan for a good five seconds. Finally he said, "You have three work days and a budget of three thousand dollars. Make sure your other cases are covered while you're out gallivanting around the country."

Barbara had made hard copies of Sophia Otero-Hansen's original case files of the vigilante's victims, including recent murders in Las Vegas. All the incidents had occurred over the past thirty-six months. She culled the files on cases in Phoenix and Las Vegas.

"How do you want to do this?" Susan asked.

"First, let's go see Victor Graves. Show him the photos of Eric Matus."

"If our theory's correct, Graves may never have met Eric Matus. Matus, or his partner, may have contacted clients anonymously."

"That's right. But maybe the shot of Matus in a pool of blood with a chunk of metal in his chest will shake up Graves enough to get him to talk."

"Then what?"

"We fly to Las Vegas. There are two families there whose loved ones were crime victims. The men who victimized their family members were all killed."

"The Smiths and the Puccinis, right?" Susan asked.

"Right. Then we'll fly to Phoenix."

Victor Graves's receptionist was no friendlier this time than she had been the first time Barbara and Susan dropped by his offices. But, this time, they'd called ahead. Graves came out to the small conference room with another man in tow.

When they were all seated, Graves said, "Detectives, this is my lawyer, Jefferson Hartley."

Hartley skidded business cards across the granite table-top. "Mr. Graves obviously wants to cooperate with your investigation. But I may have to object if you ask any inappropriate questions."

"Inappropriate questions, Mr. Hartley?" Barbara said. "We're trying to identify a serial killer who has murdered at least twelve people, including three in Las Vegas in the past two days alone." She smiled, laughed, then added, "Unless Mr. Graves has been roaming the country wiping out people, what could I ask that would be inappropriate?"

"My client is a busy man. If you have serious questions to ask, let's get to it."

Susan opened a folio she'd carried into the room and pulled out half-a-dozen photographs Sophia Otero-Hansen had provided. She turned the first one over to Graves. "You ever see the man in that photograph?"

Graves's complexion paled after he turned the photo around. "Holy . . . ." He pushed the photo to his attorney and looked up at Susan, who slid another five photographs to him in rapid succession. He looked at one more and then pushed them all back at Susan.

"Why would I have seen that man?"

Barbara said, "I mentioned that a killer has murdered at least twelve people. Every—"

"I fail to see what my client would have to do with a murderer," Hartley said, his voice full of indignation.

"Why don't I explain it to you, Mr. Hartley?" Barbara said. "Every one of the people murdered by this serial killer had committed a serious crime against an innocent victim. One of the serial killer's victims was Sylvester O'Neil, the man who murdered your client's son, Adam."

Barbara paused and looked at Victor Graves. The man sat rigidly in his chair; his eyes bored into hers as though they were heat-seeking missiles. She turned to look at Hartley. "As an officer of the court, Mr. Hartley, you should know better than most people that we can't allow vigilantes to commit murder, regardless of how hideous their victims are."

"I say again," Hartley said, "I fail to see what my client would have to do with a murderer."

Susan had been rocking in her chair. She suddenly stopped and shifted forward in her seat. "As Detective Lassiter said, every one of the people murdered by this vigilante killer had committed a heinous crime. What's interesting about the murdered men's victims is that they all came from well-to-do families who presumably could afford to pay the vigilante a fee." She looked from Hartley to Graves. "But sooner or later the killer will get it wrong. One of these days, he'll kill an innocent man or woman. That person's death will be on the heads of all the people who paid this vigilante to exact retribution."

Hartley pushed back from the table and stood. "You've obviously run out of questions and are now preaching. This meeting is over."

# CHAPTER 21

His lack of access to current information about the home invasion team frustrated Race. Even if Detective Dennis Forrester in Amarillo helped him, there was just so much that the detective would give him. So, Race was dependent upon whatever news hit media outlets. But by the time he read or heard news reports, the information in them was untimely. He needed unfettered access to law enforcement. The only people with that sort of access were cops themselves, prosecutors, and the media. He considered hacking into the servers of a media outlet, or the FBI, but that would take time that he didn't have.

Based on the information about the Ford Explorer abandoned in Gallup, the three Flagstaff murderers had obviously moved eastward from Flagstaff, so Race decided to try to get as close to them as possible. He left the Winslow motel and pushed the pickup truck eighty-five miles an hour toward Gallup. He estimated he would reach the city by 5 p.m.

It was on the leg between Flagstaff and Gallup that an idea occurred to him.

"*Herald-Tribune*," a woman said.

"Victor Graves, please."

"Hold, please."

A long half-minute went by before another woman came on

the line. "Mr. Graves's office. May I help you?"

"Mr. Graves, please."

"Mr. Graves has already left his office. He won't be back again until tomorrow morning. May I ask who's calling?"

"I assume you can reach Mr. Graves on his cell phone."

"Who's calling, please?"

"Tell Mr. Graves I'm the man who helped him to finally sleep at night. Tell him to call this number in fifteen minutes." Race recited a phone number.

"Sir, is this some kind of joke?"

"I assure you it is not."

"What if I can't get hold of Mr. Graves?"

"That would be very problematical for your boss."

Ten minutes later, Race's cell phone rang. Victor Graves's name showed on the screen.

"Thanks for calling back," Race said.

"Did I have a choice?"

"Not really."

"What is this, some sort of extortion game? You want more money?"

"What are you talking about?"

"I paid . . . ."

Graves stopped in mid-sentence. Race thought it was because the man worried that he might be recording the call. That didn't surprise him. What did surprise him was that Graves had apparently paid money to Eric Matus. Race felt violated. Eric had lied to him.

"I assure you, Mr. Graves, this isn't about money. I need your help."

"What sort of help?"

"You must have heard about the murders in Flagstaff."

"Of course. Horrible."

"You also heard that the men who murdered the family there are suspected in other home invasions and murders?"

"Yes."

Race didn't want to give Graves information that might compromise his own identity, so he improvised a story: "I've been hired by a distraught family member whose wife and children were tortured and murdered by these same men. I am on their trail, but the only information I can get is so dated it's almost useless. By the time a story is published in your paper, it's old news. If the murderers steal a vehicle in Albuquerque, for instance, they could be in Amarillo, Denver, or anywhere, by the time I hear about it. I know you have access to the authorities, to people willing to share current information with them. I need you to share that information with me as soon as it is available."

"That would be—"

"What, Mr. Graves? Were you about to say that would be unethical or illegal?"

Graves didn't respond.

Race continued, "So is hiring someone to murder the man who killed a boy."

After several seconds, Graves said, "That's all you want? Information?"

"That, and press credentials in the name of Phillip Taylor."

Graves asked, "How do we communicate?"

"I'll call you."

"What about the press credentials?"

"If I recall correctly, there's a sandwich place in the little shopping center across from your building. Leave the credentials taped under the table closest to the men's room at 11 a.m. tomorrow."

"A press pass needs a photograph."

"Don't laminate the pass. I'll deal with the photograph myself."

# CHAPTER 22

Reese McCall drove the Dodge van he'd stolen in Gallup off Interstate 40 at the Milan, New Mexico exit, pulled behind what appeared to be an empty warehouse, and turned off the ignition. "Sooner or later, we need to dump this van and split up," he said. "The cops will be looking for three men together."

"Two pale faces and one brother, to be precise," Gerald Bryant said. He scoffed. "I'm feeling a lot exposed hanging with you two."

Kiley Lewis, in the van's backseat, yelled, "This ain't funny, Gerry. You were supposed to check the place in Flagstaff for cameras. How the hell did you miss it? Look at the shit we're in because you didn't do your job."

"Screw you, Kiley. There was no fuckin' camera on the side of that house."

"Apparently there was," Lewis said. "How else did the cops get our pictures?"

"Let's take it outside," Bryant growled.

"Fine with me," Lewis shouted and opened the sliding door.

"Shut the damned door," McCall ordered Lewis, "before some cop sees the light. And both of you shut the hell up. We won't accomplish a thing turning on one another."

"Screw you, Gerry," Lewis mumbled.

"And the horse you rode in on, Kiley," Bryant retorted.

"I said that's enough," McCall said. "You guys are like little kids."

The three men sat in silence, until McCall said, "We need to get out of the country for a while. We've already got enough cash on us to last a while in Mexico. Once we turn over the loot from the Flagstaff job, we should be fixed for two years, at least."

"How the hell are we gonna make it to Mexico?" Bryant said. "First, I agree with you; we need to split up. That means we'll need at least one more vehicle, assuming I take off on my own. And, if I were you, I wouldn't be too confident about staying in this damned van much longer. It's probably been reported stolen from that used car lot in Gallup by now."

McCall nodded. "You're probably right on all counts." He looked at his cell phone. "It's 9:15 and we haven't eaten since noon. I noticed a Mickey D's three blocks back, on the main street. Kiley, why don't you walk back there and get us something to eat. Then we'll wait until midnight and dump this piece-of-shit. We'll take two vehicles off another used car lot and take off for Mexico."

"We going through Albuquerque, then heading south on I-25?" Lewis asked.

"Not a good idea," McCall answered. "Too many cops in a city that size. I checked on my cell. There's a State Road 6 off I-40 that runs to I-25, south of Albuquerque. About an hour-and-a-half drive. Then we can head south to El Paso. Another three hours, or so. All goes well; we should be at the Juarez border crossing by around 5 a.m."

"Yeah, if some cop doesn't spot one of our stolen vehicles," Bryant whined. "Or the cars don't break down. Or—"

"Waa, waa-waa, waa-waa," Lewis said. "You sound like a little bitch."

Bryant jumped out of the front passenger seat to the ground and opened the side sliding door.

"Shit," McCall muttered as he got out from behind the wheel. He rushed around the front of the van and ran at Bryant, who landed a hard right to Lewis's face, bloodying the man's nose.

McCall threw Bryant on the pavement and kicked him in the stomach. Then he dragged Lewis from the van, cuffed the side of his head, and knocked him down next to Bryant.

"You dumb shits. I've got half-a-mind to dump you both right here and take off without you."

"You can't do that, Reese," Bryant said as he sat up and tried to breathe. "You dump us and we call the cops and put 'em on your trail."

"Good point. That would be pretty stupid of me, leaving you behind to rat on me."

Lewis groaned as he wiped his nose with his hand. "That's right," he blurted. "It's all for one and one for all."

McCall turned back toward the front of the van, reached into his jacket pocket, and slipped out a .22 caliber pistol. He wheeled on Bryant, pointed the pistol muzzle at the man's forehead, and pulled the trigger. The little pistol's report wasn't completely silent, but it was relatively subdued compared to the noise the old Colt .45 automatic in the glove compartment would have made. Bryant flopped backward onto the pavement and convulsed.

"Oh shit, oh shit," Lewis moaned when McCall turned the pistol on him. He showed his palms to McCall. "Don't do it, Reese. I—"

McCall shot once into Lewis's face. The bullet pierced the man's left eye. Lewis covered the eye with a hand and screamed loudly and shrilly.

McCall shot him again; this time in the temple, which shut Lewis up for good.

McCall dragged the bodies into the back of the van, remounted the driver's seat, turned on the ignition, and drove away from the alley. He parked the vehicle at the far end of a truck stop parking lot, dumped the contents of his backpack on the van floor, sorted through the loot they'd taken from the Brownell home, and loaded the cash, coins, and jewelry into the backpack. Then he picked up a turtle-neck shirt, underwear, a clean pair of jeans, and a red baseball cap from the floor. He put on the shirt and pulled up the collar to cover his tattoo. But the collar slipped down enough to expose the knife tattoo's top two inches. He shook out the contents of Bryant and Lewis's packs and found a blue bandanna. He tied it around his neck above his collar. Then he donned the ball cap, walked with the bag over to the truck stop's restaurant, and took a seat at the counter.

"What can I get ya, honey?" a waitress asked.

133

"Burger, fries, a slice of blueberry pie, and coffee."

The waitress wrote down his order on a small pad and walked away. She returned a moment later with a cup and a pot of coffee. "Your food will be up in a minute."

"Thanks. You wouldn't happen to know if one of the truckers here might be willing to give me a lift, would you?"

"Honey, these boys are always looking for company. Driving's a boring business. But you'll have to find an independent. The big companies don't let their drivers pick up hitchhikers. Too much liability."

McCall pulled a twenty dollar bill from his jeans. "That's for you if you can get me a ride."

The woman snatched the bill from his hand with rattlesnake quickness. "I'll be right back, honey."

# DAY 8

# CHAPTER 23

Reese McCall caught a ride with a long-haul trucker by the name of Terry Driscoll who told him he was on his way to Las Cruces. He told Driscoll his name was Gene.

"Where ya headed?" Driscoll asked in a rich Texas twang as he pulled the truck onto Interstate 40.

"Dallas. I got a sister there who's been nagging me to come visit."

"You should be able to catch a ride out of Cruces for Dallas. Lot of rigs cover that route."

"Sounds good."

"You got any other family?"

"Nope." Nosy bastard, McCall thought. He hoped curt responses would discourage conversation, but he quickly learned that nothing discouraged Driscoll.

"I got three kids and seven grand kids. My youngest, Bernadette, just had a little girl. Beautiful baby. Roni's her name. They got a little boy, too. Turned three last week. Can't wait to see him." He laughed. "Kid's a holy terror. Like a force of nature. Can't slow him down. Runs around like a loose bowling bowl. Bernadette and her husband live in Deming. He works for the Border Patrol. You can't believe the shit he tells me about what they have to deal with down there, what with all the illegals sneaking across the border."

After fifteen minutes of non-stop monologue from Driscoll, McCall had seriously considered slitting the truck driver's throat and stealing his truck. He faked sleep before they were twenty miles east of Milan. Somewhere after that he dozed off for real. Sleep easily came to him because he was exhausted and it seemed like a better alternative than listening to Driscoll's inane banter about his seven grandchildren.

He was in the middle of a very satisfying dream about sex with a tall, buxom woman when he was startled awake and thrown forward against his seat belt. Brakes hissed and squealed; and Driscoll, cursed, "Damn Albuquerque drivers."

McCall looked through the windshield and saw the rear end of a compact car not more than two feet from the truck's front bumper. A flatbed carrying a large mobile home had stopped in front of the little car.

"Phew, that was close," Driscoll said.

When traffic moved again, McCall noticed they now approached what New Mexicans called the Big I, the intersection of Interstate 40 and Interstate 25.

"Terry, let me know if you want me to spell you at the wheel," McCall said.

"Will do, Gene." Driscoll laughed. "You were snoring like a bull moose in rut a minute ago. I was thinking you were turning out to be poor company."

"Sorry about that."

"Aw, don't apologize. You look like you've had a bad day."

"Thanks, Terry. You can't imagine." McCall looked at his watch. "It's a little after midnight. Tell you what. You let me sleep until we get to Socorro and I'll drive the rest of the way to Las Cruces. I used to drive a big rig years ago."

"Sounds like a plan, partner."

As McCall shifted to get more comfortable, Driscoll asked, "How long you been on the road?"

"Little over five years."

"Holy shit. Just bouncing around the country? If you don't mind my asking, how the hell do you support yourself?"

"I get odd jobs here and there. Pick up a few bucks and then move on to the next place."

"Tough way to live."

"It's not so bad. I've had some really amazing experiences."

"Don't you get lonely?"

"Heck no. I meet all sorts of people. Probably get laid more than most, too."

"Now, I've got to hear some about that," Driscoll said.

"Maybe when we stop for something to eat."

Driscoll laughed. "I always stop in Socorro on this run. Good place to gas up and grab a bite."

# CHAPTER 24

Barbara and Susan's red eye flight put them in Las Vegas at 2 a.m. They picked up a rental car and drove to a diner off the Las Vegas Strip. Despite the hour, the place was crowded.

Susan carefully reconnoitered the diner. "How many people in here you think won money tonight?"

Barbara glanced around, then said, "Not a one."

"What makes you say that?"

"Not a smile in the joint."

Susan nodded. "Probably right."

"To follow up on our conversation on the plane, do you have any more thoughts about that home invasion in Flagstaff?"

"Wouldn't it be great if our dark angel could find the guys who murdered that family?"

"You sound as though you admire what the guy's done."

Susan spread her arms and compressed her lips. "Sometimes I hate my job. Psychopaths like these should be wiped off the earth. The criminal justice system is not always the most efficient or effective mechanism for doing that."

"You know there's a chance the murderers went east from Flagstaff. They could be in the Land of Enchantment right now."

"I don't think so."

Barbara squinted at Susan. "Why not?"

Susan smiled. "Because that's *our* territory. There's no way they'd risk coming up against Bernalillo County's best detectives."

"Better be careful, partner. You might start to believe your own fairy tales. Besides, we're not in New Mexico at the moment." She smiled back at Susan. "Let's call Sophia. See if she has any new information."

Susan looked at her watch. "It's two in the morning. You can't call her now."

Barbara shot Susan a toothy grin. "Wanna bet?"

Barbara dialed Sophia Otero-Hansen's cell number and put her phone on speaker.

"Agent Otero-Hansen."

"Why are you whispering?" Barbara asked.

"Because I recognized your number and I'm not supposed to talk to you. My boss has hovered over me like he wants to catch me doing something wrong."

"You're in the office?"

"Yeah. Why?"

"Oh, nothing. I was just hoping I woke you up at home."

Otero-Hansen laughed. "What do you need?"

"You didn't happen to check your great big FBI computer in the sky to see if there have been any more killings?"

"Nope. No time. Nearly every agent here in our office, and in every Bureau office in Arizona, California, Nevada, New Mexico, and Texas has been assigned to the *Three Ghouls* case."

"The *what*?"

"The three men who killed the family in Flagstaff."

"Susan and I were just talking about that."

"There's been a task force assigned to these home invasions for years, with no success identifying the perps. Those three have ruined several careers here at the Bureau. We've got DNA and fingerprint evidence out the kazoo and still haven't been able to ID the killers. The video from the Flagstaff break-in generated all kinds of excitement around here. The faces from the video were run through our facial recognition system, but we got nothing. Absolutely nothing. But at least we have pictures for the first time."

"Well, we're still on our vigilante killer," Susan said. "Must be the year for mass murderers. Any common element apparent at the crime scenes of the Three Ghouls?"

"You mean, like with your vigilante?"

"Yeah. Do they use the same weapon, or murder people in identical ways, or leave calling cards?"

"All of their invasions are gruesome in the extreme. They don't just murder their victims; they make them suffer." She muttered something unintelligible.

"Say again," Susan said.

"They're sick bastards. They murder their victims, regardless of their age or sex. It's obvious they're in it for the money; they have a pretty good eye for valuables. But they seem to enjoy committing mayhem, too."

"Any calling cards, like with our killer?"

"Nope, nothing like that." She paused. "The only commonalty of all the crimes . . . . Nevermind."

"What?" Barbara asked.

"It's nothing. Anything else?"

"How many jobs have these guys done?" Susan asked.

Otero-Hansen said, "We have forensic evidence from thirteen home invasions that tie these same guys to each of them. There are other crimes we think they did, but can't tie them to those because of a lack of forensic evidence."

"Okay, Sophia," Barbara said. "We'll call if we come up with anything."

After Barbara terminated the call, Susan rasped, "You have to be friggin' kidding me."

"What?"

"Sophia was about to say something, but she clammed up."

"So much for sharing."

# CHAPTER 25

Terry Driscoll pulled into a truck stop on the south side of Socorro, New Mexico at 9:10 a.m. He parked his rig and touched Reese McCall's shoulder.

"Hey, man, you want to grab something to eat?"

McCall felt out of sorts as he came out of the fog of sleep. "What d'ya say?"

Driscoll chuckled. "Man, I wish I could sleep as soundly as you do."

McCall rubbed his face. "Where are we?"

"Socorro."

"Shit. Already?"

"Yep. Your turn to drive. But let's get something to eat in the truck stop first."

"Sounds good."

McCall lifted his backpack by one of the straps and opened the passenger side door.

"You know, you can leave that here. I'll lock up."

"Nah. I think I'll change into some clean clothes."

Driscoll shrugged.

McCall slung his backpack onto his shoulders. As they walked to the truck stop restaurant, he felt his cell phone vibrate in his jeans pocket. He jerked it out and looked at the screen. "I have to take this," he told Driscoll. "I'll be right with you."

Driscoll waved and continued to the restaurant.

"Yeah?" McCall said.

"Hey, bro, did you get the merchandise?"

"Of course."

"Excellent. When can I expect delivery?"

"I'll FedEx the stuff tomorrow."

"What about today?"

"I had a bit of a problem. Need to straighten some things out."

The man on the phone hesitated, then said, "You talking about New Mexico?"

"What?"

"I assume that's the problem you referred to. It's on the news. The police found two bodies in a van in Milan, New Mexico, wherever the hell that is."

McCall's stomach erupted as though an acid tap had been turned on. "Why would you tie that to me?"

"The media's all over it. The cops matched the two dead men to the Flagstaff job."

"How?"

"The security video at the Brownell house. They recognized their faces from the video. And fingerprints."

McCall groaned. He'd hoped he would have a bigger window of time to get out of New Mexico before the cops discovered and ID'ed the bodies. "I need to lie low for a while."

Another pause and then the man said, "I've got a proposition for you, bro. You fulfill this new assignment and you'll be able to retire someplace with lots of sand, sun, and nubile women."

"You'd have to pay a lot for me to do another job, what with all the heat on right now. Besides, I've already got a backpack and a bank account full of dough."

"Would a million dollars change your mind? And, with your partners out of the picture, you won't have to share it."

McCall smiled to himself. His former partners never had a clue about his share of the money they made: ninety percent for him; ten percent for them. "Yeah. That would work."

"I'll have your fee for the Brownell job wired to your Caymans account as soon as the coins get here."

"Where's the new job?"

"Farmington, New Mexico."

"You shittin' me. The only things in Farmington are oil, gas, saloons, and Indians."

"Oil and gas money can buy a lot of gold and silver."

"I assume you have a specific laundry list."

"Just like always."

"Email it to me."

McCall terminated the call and quickly calculated the balance that would be in his bank account after the Farmington job: a little over two million dollars. And that didn't include the two hundred grand in his backpack. Not bad, he thought, for a guy without a high school diploma. "Wonder what my asshole-old man would think of me now," he whispered. He turned back toward the gasoline pumps and spotted a thirty-something woman gassing up a dark-gray Infiniti QX-80 SUV. She appeared to be alone.

From a corner of the truck stop building, Reese McCall watched the blonde. He could see through the passenger side windows that she'd closed the driver's door while the gas pump operated automatically. Too cold to wait outside, he guessed. She had her visor down and seemed to be fussing with her makeup. *Dumb shit*, he thought. When will women learn? Instead of paying attention to who and what was around her, they often primped or read email. He waited until the automatic shut-off on the pump handle clicked and the woman opened her door and dropped off her seat to the pavement. Then he moved quickly and circled the rear of her vehicle. She'd just replaced the gas cap when he made his move.

McCall looked at the woman's eyes while he slapped the gas tank access door closed. A confused expression came to her face. It lasted a second or two, but was then replaced with wide-eyed terror. Her hands froze in mid-air and her mouth opened in a silent scream. She turned as though to run away, but ran into her open car door. McCall took two quick steps, shoved the barrel of his pistol into her side, and said, "You scream, you die."

The woman sagged. McCall gripped her left arm and growled, "Get into your car right now; climb over to the passenger side. You do what I say, you live."

The woman whimpered, "Please, don't hurt me; I won't scream."

"Good girl," McCall said as he watched her climb aboard. He opened the door to the backseat and tossed in his pack. Then he quickly shut that door and followed the woman inside the SUV's front row.

Terry Driscoll stepped from the truck stop building and saw his hitchhiker climb behind the wheel of a late model SUV. There was a damn fine-looking woman in the passenger seat. He was pissed off for a second, but then chuckled and muttered, "I guess the bastard got a better offer."

# CHAPTER 26

Race drove well over the speed limit all the way to Albuquerque. He'd estimated he would arrive in the city by 10:30 a.m. He was early by ten minutes. It took twenty minutes to drive from Tijeras Canyon to the I-25 Jefferson Exit on the north side of the city, to a small retail center across from the newspaper's headquarters. He parked next to a bank. Then he walked fifty yards across the parking lot to a Starbucks and camped inside with a *grande* coffee and a morning bun. He thought about the risks of picking up the press pass that Graves was supposed to leave for him. Graves was a rich, powerful man, who might hire muscle to eliminate him. The man had already paid to have O'Neil murdered. He might even alert the police. He could do so without implicating himself. Race had no proof that he'd murdered Elmo O'Neil for Graves. Who's to say Graves wouldn't pay to have him killed because of the potential risk he posed for the man? He still considered his options when, at 11:05, a teenage boy pulled up on a bicycle outside the coffee shop. Race watched the kid dump his bike on the patio, enter the shop, and go directly to the counter. When he was served a drink with what appeared to be two inches of whipped cream on top, the kid sat down at an inside table.

Race walked outside, picked up the bike, and pushed it toward the parking lot.

The kid burst outside, whipped cream on his upper lip.

"Hey, dude, where you going with my wheels?"

Race chuckled. "Thought that would bring you outside."

"Huh."

"How'd you like to make a hundred dollars?" Race asked and pushed the bike at the boy.

The kid's eyes widened as he caught his bike. "What are you, some kind of pervert?"

This time, Race laughed. "It's simple. You run an errand for me, bring me back a package, and you get a "C" note."

"A what?"

"Aw, jeez," Race muttered. "One hundred dollars."

"I only got the bike. I can't go very far."

"No problem." Race wagged a finger at the kid and moved off the patio to the curb. "See that sandwich shop?"

"Yeah."

"You go to the table closest to the men's room, find an envelope taped to the underside of the table, and bring it here to me."

The kid seemed to think about that for a while. "It ain't drugs, is it?"

Race gave the kid a big smile. "No, it *ain't*."

"How come you don't get it yourself?"

Good question, Race thought. "Because my ex-wife is in there and I don't want to get into a hassle with her."

"I don't know," the kid said.

"Forget it. I'll find someone who needs the money."

"Wait. I'll do it."

The kid was back on the Starbucks patio in less than a minute. He waited for Race to hand over the money before he reached out to hand him the envelope. When the exchange was done, Race told the kid, "Thanks."

"Your wife have red hair?"

Race didn't know where the kid was going with his question, but he played along and said, "Yes."

The kid shook his head. "She was the only woman in the place. I can understand why you didn't want to meet up with her. What were you thinking?"

"What do you mean?"

"When you married her. What were you thinking?"

Race blurted a laugh. "I guess I wasn't thinking."

"Thanks, Mister," the kid said and rode away.

Race took a "selfie" with his cell phone, then found a Kinko's, where he made copies of the photo. He bought a tube of glue, affixed one of the photos to the press pass Victor Graves had left for him, and had a clerk laminate his Phillip Taylor press pass. He flicked a finger against the edge of the pass and mumbled, "This ought to do it."

Race selected one of the burner phones from his briefcase and dialed the *New Mexico Herald-Tribune*. He asked the operator for the name of the crime beat reporter. The woman told him he needed to speak with Betsy Jaramillo. Race disconnected the call and dialed the Albuquerque Police Department. When an operator answered, he asked to be connected to the Public Affairs Officer.

"Lieutenant Carter."

"Lieutenant, my name is Phillip Taylor. I just signed on as a freelance writer with the *Herald-Tribune*, on the crime desk. Betsy Jaramillo suggested I call you to introduce myself."

"Welcome, Mr. Taylor. You new to Albuquerque?"

"Thanks. Yes. I worked in Sacramento before here."

"What happened to Betsy?"

"She's still here. Like I said, I'm a freelancer."

"Well, thanks for the call. I'm sure we'll run into one another at some point."

"I did have a question, if you have a minute."

"Make it quick. I've got a presser in fifteen minutes."

It took Race a long beat to guess that a "presser" was a press conference. "Just one question. Has the APD developed any contingency plans in case the men who murdered the Brownell family in Flagstaff come this way?"

"You doing a story about those guys?"

"I am. The video from Flagstaff kinda changed things. We understand that crew has operated for years and has savaged a lot of people. We'd like to get some information about their crimes."

"First of all, Mr. Taylor, we have a plan in place, but I'm not at liberty to disclose the details just yet. As far as their crimes are concerned, descriptions of most of them are on various Internet sites and blogs."

"Most of them?"

"Well, we can't be certain that all the crimes committed by this gang have been tied to them."

"That's why I called you. I was hoping to get accurate information."

"I don't know that I can—"

"Lieutenant Carter, when these guys go down, the press coverage will be huge. I want to get the jump on all those big city rags that will have an inside track to the Feds. I'll write most of my piece before these criminals are captured, so the story can run when they are." He paused a moment and then added, "I can make you and APD look damned good, or I can just plain leave you out of the story."

"For someone new to town, you sure play hardball."

"Let's help one another out."

Carter didn't respond immediately. Finally, she said, "I'll meet you for coffee at the Gold Street Cafe at 3."

# CHAPTER 27

Rudy and Louise Smith lived in a gated Las Vegas community, in a house the size of a Ramada Inn. Barbara knew, from the case file, they were in their forties, but they each looked to be well over fifty. *Personal tragedy will do that to people*, she thought.

"Thanks for meeting with us," Barbara said.

"Sure," Rudy Smith said. "Please come in."

They sat on a patio that backed onto a golf course. Glasses and pitchers of iced tea and lemonade were set on a serving cart. A uniformed maid poured drinks for Barbara and Susan and then returned to the house.

Barbara noticed that Louise Smith had a hi-ball glass in front of her that was half-full of a clear liquid. She didn't think the woman was drinking water based on the bloodshot appearance of her eyes and her less-than-attentive expression.

"We are very curious about the reason for your visit, Detectives," Rudy Smith said. "It's been two years . . . and you being from Albuquerque, and all."

"Would you be willing to look at a few photos?" Susan asked.

The husband shrugged. "Photos of what?"

"We wondered if you might recognize the man in the photographs."

Susan pulled three headshots of Eric Matus from a folder, turned them right side up, and passed them to the man.

The man took his time with the photos and finally, said, "Never saw the guy before." He swallowed and added, "He looks dead."

"He is," Barbara said. "You never saw him before?"

"That's what I said."

"What about the name, Eric Matus?"

Rudy Smith shook his head.

Susan said, "After your two sons were killed, were you ever approached by anyone about Ray Gorchek?"

A small whimper came from Louise Smith. Barbara looked at her and saw tears dribble down her cheeks. Barbara looked back at the husband and saw that whatever affability had shown on his face was now gone.

"What the hell are you babbling about?" he growled.

"Ray Gorchek had twelve DUI arrests before he ran into your sons' car. He'd only spent a total of fifty-three days behind bars. In fact, he was out on bail for a DUI charge when he killed your sons. The breathalyzer he was given that night showed he blew almost three times the legal limit. He wasn't just drunk; he was nearly comatose."

Louise Smith clutched her glass in two hands as though she was afraid it might take off at any moment.

Rudy Smith blurted, "If your purpose here today is to upset my wife, then you've accomplished that." He stood. "It's time you left."

Barbara and Susan stood. Barbara said, "Just two more questions, please. What can you tell us about Ray Gorchek's murder six months after he ran into your boys? Someone forced him to swallow liquid heroin, soaked his clothes with tequila, and set him on fire."

Barbara noticed the man's jaw clench. Louise Smith's eyes bounced around like plastic balls in a bingo parlor.

He said, "I understand Gorchek was already dead when he was lit up. Our boys didn't have that luxury. They . . . ." his voice broke and he stopped for a moment. He grimaced. Then he smiled. "I can tell you that whoever murdered that sleazebag is a saint and will have my undying gratitude."

"What did—?"

"We're done here," he said.

Back in their rental car, Susan said, "That really went well."

"Did you expect anything else?"

"Nah. None of these people will ever admit they hired a killer."

"Any doubt that the Smiths hired a vigilante killer?" Susan asked.

"Not a doubt in the world."

# CHAPTER 28

Out of a sense of caution and his usual paranoia, Race waited in his vehicle down and across the street from the Gold Street Cafe. He saw an APD cruiser turn onto Gold Street from 3rd Street and take a parking spot across from him. He watched a woman exit the vehicle and slip on a uniform cap. She was maybe five feet, four inches tall, with short blonde hair, and a runner's figure. She looked good in her uniform. She carried a folio. He waited until she entered the café, then left the truck and followed her. She had taken a seat at a small table at the back.

"Lieutenant Carter?"

"Mr. Taylor?"

Race nodded, shook her hand, and sat across from her. "Thanks for meeting me."

"Well, like you said, 'Let's help one another out.' "

"I appreciate you assisting the new guy in town. I think this story has legs."

She opened her arms as though to say, "We'll see."

A waitress came over and took their orders of coffee.

"How long have you been in Albuquerque?" Race asked.

"Two years. I was in Cleveland for ten years before."

"So, you're new in town, too?"

"You could say that." Carter looked at her watch. "I've got a four o'clock. Let's get down to business."

Carter waited for the waitress to place their coffees on the table and to walk away. Then she took her folio from a side chair, unzipped it, and extracted a manila folder.

"That's a list of home invasions the APD pulled off the NCIC database that have similarities. Lots of violence leading to murder. The names and ages of the victims are there, along with the dates of the incidents."

"Thanks. I really appreciate your help. Anything new on the gang?"

"Yeah."

Race felt his heart leap. "Don't tell me they struck again."

"No, nothing like that. Two bodies were found in an abandoned van in Milan. The two men have been identified as two of the men seen on the security video taken at the Brownell residence in Flagstaff. Their fingerprints match those found in at least a dozen homes where the residents were murdered." She opened the folder, removed two photographs, and passed them to Race. "These are the two whose bodies were found."

Race stared hard at the faces in the photos. Neither was the man with the facial scars and tattoos who'd clubbed him with a tire iron.

"DNA samples from the two are being examined as we speak," Carter said. "But DNA is probably not needed, now that they have fingerprints and the video." She took a long breath. "I guess the Feds will have to change their name for the bastards."

"What do you mean?"

Carter laughed, but there wasn't much humor in it. "They had just labeled the crew as the Three Ghouls. But if two of them are dead, there's only one ghoul left."

Race shook his head. "Any information on the vehicle?"

"Yeah. It was stolen in Gallup. Where the crew dumped the Ford Explorer they had when they invaded the Brownell home."

"Sounds like the gang had a falling out."

"Does, doesn't it?"

"Hmm." Race rested his chin in a hand. "Any reported stolen vehicles in Milan?"

"Good question," Carter said. "Nope."

"Which means, the third member of the gang found another

way to get out of town."

"Or is holed up in New Mexico somewhere."

Race thought about that. "That wouldn't be the smart thing to do."

"I agree."

"So what's your guess?"

"He probably hitched a ride."

# CHAPTER 29

After Barbara and Susan cleared the gate guard and parked in the circular driveway that fronted the Puccini estate, Susan looked up at the palatial residence and slowly took in the grounds. "Wow. So this is what you get from owning a casino."

"And Puccini's casino is just a little one."

They walked up to the front door and were greeted by a tall, elderly man with a full head of salt and pepper hair and hands that appeared to be too large even for his large body.

"Detectives, I am Salvatore Puccini."

"Hello, Mr. Puccini." Barbara flashed her cred pack. "I'm Detective Barbara Lassiter. This is my partner, Susan Martinez."

"Detective, people who want to suck up to me call me Mr. Puccini. I prefer Salvatore, especially when I am addressed by beautiful young women."

Susan smiled at Puccini. "You married, Salvatore?"

"Widower," he said. "Why?"

Still smiling, Susan said, "Because I want to keep all my options open."

Puccini chuckled. "I think you're sucking up to me, Detective."

Barbara interjected, "We're supposed to meet with Rose Puccini's parents. Our information is that they are in their late thirties. You—"

"I'm Rosa's grandfather. My son and daughter-in-law are inside.

156

Please follow me."

The interior of the house was even more splendid than the exterior. It looked a lot like an only-slightly understated Venetian *palazzo*, with statuary, large oil paintings, columns, and marble floors. The Puccinis were in a tennis court-sized room, with Persian carpets that covered almost every inch of the marble floor, Italianate furniture, and floor-to-ceiling bookcases on one of the long sides of the room. Opposite the bookcases were three sets of French doors that rose to within two feet of the fourteen-foot ceiling. The room was bracketed by a magnificent stone fireplace on one end and a grand piano on the other. Giuseppe Puccini stood next to the piano, as though posed for a shot in *GQ Magazine*. Francesca Puccini sat demurely on a brocade sofa; her shapely legs crossed; a book in her lap.

"Giuseppe, these are the detectives from New Mexico," Salvatore announced.

Giuseppe walked over and shook Barbara's, then Susan's hand. "I hope your visit to Las Vegas has been fruitful."

"Police work requires a great deal of digging and plenty of patience," Barbara said.

"Please, let's sit down." He pointed them toward two chairs across from where his wife sat.

The woman placed her book on the lamp table to her left and nodded at Barbara and Susan.

Mr. Puccini sat on the couch next to his wife. The old man took a chair between the Puccinis on the couch and Susan's chair.

"Can I offer you something to drink?" Mr. Puccini asked.

"Thank you, sir, but we just had lunch," Barbara said.

Susan nodded her agreement.

"Well, then we should talk about why you're here?"

"As I mentioned on the phone, Mr. Puccini, we wanted to talk with you about the deaths of the three young men who assaulted Rosa."

"Yes. And what do two detectives from New Mexico have to do with that?"

"Whoever killed those three young men, we believe, has murdered at least a dozen other people in the southwest and

Rocky Mountain areas. At least one of those murders occurred in Albuquerque."

"I see. But how in God's name can we assist you?"

"Were you ever approached by anyone who offered to avenge the attack on your daughter?"

Giuseppe's mouth dropped open for an instant. "Is that a joke?"

"I assure you, Mr. Puccini," Susan said, "twelve murders is no joke."

"Of course, of course." He hesitated a few seconds. "First, I unequivocally state that no one ever contacted us about seeking revenge for Rosa. Second, if they had, and we had accepted such an offer, do you think I would admit to it?"

Barbara glanced at Francesca Puccini and saw a slight smile crease her perfect, full lips. The smile disappeared as soon as she met Barbara's gaze. The woman's eyes diverted toward her father-in-law, whose face was expressionless.

"We have a job to do, Mr. Puccini," Susan said. "We can't have a mass murderer play judge, jury, and executioner, regardless of how vile the crimes perpetrated by his victims."

"I can understand that, Detective. Murder under any circumstances is wrong. But I have no idea what you're talking about."

Barbara looked back at Mrs. Puccini. "Do you feel the same way, ma'am?"

"My husband and I agree about everything, Detective."

Salvatore Puccini suddenly stood. "Perhaps you would like to take a tour of the grounds."

Barbara was surprised at the suggestion, but she accepted.

The old man led them toward the back of the house and exited through a French door onto a flagstone patio. He moved to a stone path that weaved away from the patio, through trees and shrubs that punctuated a large expanse of lawn. The path was broad enough for the three of them to walk abreast.

They had walked out of sight of the patio before the man spoke. "Why are you wasting your time here?"

"You think we are?"

"Of course. As my son said, if we had hired someone to avenge our Rosa, why would we ever admit it?"

"Guilty conscience," Susan said.

The man laughed. "Don't be naïve, Detective."

"You think vigilantism should be condoned?" Barbara asked.

"How else do the innocent find justice?"

"That's the purpose of our legal system."

The man laughed again, but there was a knife-sharp edge to it this time. "Now you truly are being naïve. The legal system did nothing to bring justice to our sweet Rosa. Nothing!" He sighed deeply. He seemed embarrassed that he'd raised his voice. "Go home, ladies. Stop wasting your time and ours."

Barbara was lost in her own thoughts on the way to McCarran International Airport for their 5 p.m. flight to Phoenix, when Susan said, "You know, we *are* wasting our time."

"Uh-huh."

After a short silence, Susan said, "You wanna hear my interpretation of our meeting with the Puccinis?"

"Sure."

"Giuseppe Puccini was telling the truth. He didn't know a thing about hiring a hit man to take out the three guys who assaulted his daughter."

"I agree."

"But Mama Francesca was involved up to her French twist die job."

"Yep. And what about Grandpa Salvatore?"

"He made it happen. With Mama Francesca's encouragement."

"That's why we're so good together. We both know when we're being lied to."

Susan laughed. "As I already mentioned, we're wasting our time. So, why don't we just catch a flight home?"

"Probably not a bad idea."

"But we're still flying to Phoenix."

"Yep."

"Because Barbara Lassiter's stubborn?"

"I'd prefer to think of myself as diligent, professional, and disciplined. But I'll accept stubborn if that's all you're willing to concede."

Susan said something under her breath.

"What was that?"

"I said you're a pain in the ass."

"I'll accept that as well."

# CHAPTER 30

Race hadn't had much to eat all day, but it never crossed his mind to stop for a meal. He'd been holed up in a run-down motel on Central Avenue near San Pedro Boulevard. He suspected the motel had been built when Route 66 was the way through the city. He also suspected, other than a paint job and new carpeting maybe ten years ago, nothing had been done to improve the place since the early 1950s.

But Race couldn't have cared less about his surroundings. The information that Lieutenant Maggie Carter had given him had appeared fairly innocuous at first. But, as he went down the list of victims, he thought he recognized another name. That sent chills up his spine. The odds that he would know two of the Three Ghouls' victims—William Brownell in Flagstaff, and now Susan Grabowski in Cincinnati, Ohio—were staggering. Race's heart throbbed and he felt short of breath.

He didn't actually remember Susan Grabowski's name. What clicked with him was that Carter's information showed that Susan Grabowski's maiden name was Kellerman. She'd married Ronald Grabowski five years ago. When Race met her eight years ago, she was single: Susan Kellerman.

The fact that he'd known two of the Three Ghouls' victims was difficult to reconcile. But what was even more astonishing was that the victims were serious coin collectors.

Race set the folder aside and thought about his telephone conversation with Amarillo Police Department Detective Dennis Forrester. He'd asked him if William Brownell was the same person he knew from his coin collecting days. Forrester had told him there was nothing on the wire or in the NCIC system that indicated Brownell had owned a coin collection. He stood and paced. A thought had hit his brain as though a bell had rung inside his skull when he'd remembered that he'd read an article written by a coin collector named Brownell. That bell had rung louder when he read the Grabowski/Kellerman name. Three numismatist-victims of the robbers were too strange to ignore: Brownell, Kellerman . . . and himself.

He rushed back to the table and sat down. On the back of one of the sheets of paper in Carter's folder, he wrote down a list of things he needed to do. When he'd finished, he felt a rush of frustration. It was already 10 p.m.; too late to follow up on most of the things on his 'to-do' list. But then he thought there was one thing he could do now, right here in Albuquerque.

Race found James Dunhill's home telephone number on the Internet.

"Jeez, do you know what time it is? Who the hell is this?"

"Hey, Jim. Sorry to call so late. It's Race Thornton."

Dunhill didn't immediately respond. A full five seconds passed before he said, "My God, Race. Is it really you?"

"Yeah, Jim. I know it's been a while. But—"

"Shit, Race, it's been about three years. I tried to contact you after . . . you know; what happened at your home. But your number was no longer good. No one knew what had happened to you." Another pause, then: "How are you doing?"

"I'm okay, Jim. Listen, is there any chance we could get together?"

"Sure. Are you in Albuquerque?"

"Yes."

"Why don't you come by the shop tomorrow?"

"Uh. I was hoping we could meet tonight."

Dunhill hesitated for no more than a second this time. "You sound like it's important."

"Yeah. Really important. Life and death important."

"Why don't you come by the house in the morning? I'm still in the same place. In the Tanoan Country Club area. You remember how to find it?"

"You have old Worldwide Coin Collectors' directories at your home?"

"No. They're in the shop."

"Would you be able to meet me there tonight?"

"I'm already in bed, Race. This can't wait until tomorrow?"

"I guess it could. But another coin collector could be murdered by then."

"What are you talking about?"

"I think someone's been targeting collectors all over the country."

"I'll meet you in thirty minutes."

Dunhill's shop was a tiny place squeezed into the base of a horse-shoe-shaped neighborhood shopping center on Eubank Boulevard in Albuquerque's Northeast Heights. Race beat Dunhill to the shop and waited in his truck until his old friend and coin dealer arrived. They shook hands in front of the shop, then Dunhill unlocked the front door, flipped on the lights, and shut off the alarm.

"Looks the same," Race said.

Dunhill chuckled. "The only thing that changes from one day to the next is the inventory." He went to the back of the store and slipped behind the glass display cases. "You mentioned the Worldwide Coin Collectors' directories."

Race bellied up to one of the cases and placed Carter's folder on the glass top.

"What's that?" Dunhill asked.

"Bear with me for a bit. I'll explain as soon as we check the directories."

"Which directory do you want?"

Race checked Carter's list and looked at the name Sam Jones. Jones and his wife were murdered on July 31, two years ago.

"Let's look at the directory from three years ago."

Dunhill went to a bookshelf behind him and fingered through a row of directories. He pulled one from the middle of them, turned, and placed it on the counter.

"What do you want to know?"

"Check for the name Sam Jones."

Dunhill flipped through the alphabetical listing of member names and stopped at the Sam Jones listing.

"Here it is," he said. "Providence, Rhode Island."

"Does the directory still list the WCCA conferences members attended?"

"Yes."

"Did Jones attend any conferences?"

"Nope."

"That's interesting."

"What?" Dunhill's eyebrows arched and his eyes widened.

"Let's check the other names."

Race consulted Carter's list and threw out a name to Dunhill. This time, the man was from Arkansas. He'd been a member of the WCCA for eighteen years. His membership terminated four years ago, the year after he'd been murdered in his home. He, too, had never attended a conference.

He and Dunhill went through the list of names and their listings in the WCCA directories for over an hour.

After they'd finished, Dunhill said, "Out of the names you gave me, eleven were members of WCCA. Only one—Kellerman—ever attended a conference. Why's that important?"

"First, let me tell you that every person you looked up in the directories has been murdered."

"Murdered?"

"Yeah, murdered. By a vicious home invasion gang that's operated all over the country for about five years."

"Holy Mother of God. So, why did you want to know if they'd attended conferences?"

"Because, one of the thoughts I had was that the collectors might have been targeted after they'd attended a conference. Maybe there's a thief who attends conferences, identifies big collectors, and then goes after them later. But that theory is now shot to hell."

"How's it possible that coin collectors have been murdered in these kinds of numbers without the FBI and the press making a big deal out of it? I mean, wouldn't it be all over television and in newspapers about coin collectors being targeted?"

"Good questions. Maybe the Feds have intentionally held back that information. Maybe they hope to use it at some point as confirmation when they finally arrest someone."

"We have to put out a warning through the association. They could be about to kill someone right now."

"Yeah, they might very well be. But there's something that really bothers me. How do these guys know where to strike?"

"Maybe they have access to the WCCA directory."

"Maybe. But that wouldn't tell them who to target. There are members of the association who are vendors who sell stuff to collectors and people who are interested in coins but don't have the money to collect coins. Is there a way to tell whether the people who were murdered had serious coin collections? I think Brownell and Kellerman fit that description, but I have no idea if the others did."

"You had a world-class collection," Dunhill said. "I know what I sold you. Those coins alone were worth a lot of money."

"How can we determine if the other victims were in the same class of collector?"

Dunhill's hands shook as he stared at Race. He looked frightened to death. "Hell, I don't know." He remained silent for a while. "Other than you and Kellerman, the others on your list never attended a conference, according to the directories, which tells me they were very private about their collections. Perhaps we could check with dealers in the cities where the collectors lived."

"That's a good idea. Could you do that tomorrow?"

"Sure. What will you do?"

"I'll try to find some common element that ties all the victims together."

"What about warning other collectors? Shouldn't we also share this with the police?" Dunhill waited for Race to respond. When he didn't, he added, "How could the police not have made this connection?"

"I could see how police departments might not relate one murder to another. Law enforcement is very fragmented; they might not see the whole picture. It's the FBI that I wonder about. They should have made the coin collector connection and loaded it on the NCIC system. That would have alerted local police departments. That would have spread the word through the media."

"We have to put out a warning," Dunhill said again.

Race knew Dunhill was right. Hell, he could call Victor Graves at the *New Mexico Herald-Tribune*. There's a story the guy would love to break. But he wanted a chance to find the last of the three men who'd murdered his family. Besides, Graves would expect him to identify himself and would want his personal story. He couldn't survive that sort of exposure. Having met with Lieutenant Maggie Carter had been risky enough.

"You know, any story we tell the media or the authorities will carry a great deal more weight if we verify that all the victims were major collectors. And, it would be nice if we could come up with a theory about how the killers identified their victims."

"You were the one who told me on the phone that someone else could die if we waited to meet in the morning."

Race nodded. "You're right, Jim. So, let's do this. Do you have access to a broadcast email list of the WCCA members?"

"Yes."

"Good. Then why don't you send them all a message that you heard a rumor that valuable coin collections are being targeted by a gang of thieves. Warn them to turn on their alarms and to notify their local police if they see anyone suspicious hanging around. Whether we come up with more information tomorrow, or we don't, we'll call the media and the Albuquerque police by the end of the day."

"Why not notify the police at the same time?"

"Which police? Every department in New Mexico? In the country?"

"Then what about the FBI?"

"That makes sense except for one thing. You already wondered why the FBI isn't all over these guys. Maybe it's because they couldn't identify any of the gang . . . until the Brownell murders. Maybe the Bureau didn't want to release anything as long as they didn't know who the Three Ghouls were. It could make them look ridiculous. Or, as I said before, they're intentionally holding back information for later confirmation purposes."

Dunhill looked skeptical, but nodded.

"Do you have a place to stay?" he asked. "You can spend the night at my place."

"Thanks, but I already have a motel room. If it's all right with you, I'll meet you back here in the morning."

"I open at 10, so I'll make calls to dealers before that. Why don't you drop by here at noon? I'll close the shop then."

"Sounds good."

Race thanked Dunhill and shook his hand. As he turned to leave, Dunhill asked, "What have you been doing all these years? You used to have a software company, if I remember correctly."

"Consulting, Jim."

It took almost two hours to drive north from Socorro to Bernalillo, New Mexico in the Infiniti QX-80. The woman had just about driven McCall crazy during the drive. She'd lectured him about the legal consequences of his actions. She'd promised to never tell a soul about the kidnapping if he let her go. Then she'd whimpered and begged. On the far side of Bernalillo, he'd finally had enough and slugged her on the side of the head. She'd gone out like a light and slumped down in her seat. When she came to fifteen minutes later, she didn't say a word. Seventy minutes later, he drove through Cuba, New Mexico and turned right on the road to Regina. Three miles up that road, he found a steep, snow-packed driveway that meandered up the side of a hill for a hundred yards and leveled out on a flat, wooded parcel of land. The driveway continued on for about a quarter-of-a-mile toward a cabin that appeared to be under construction. Concrete footings had been laid, but it appeared that work had ceased, perhaps with the advent of bad weather.

"Perfect," McCall muttered.

# DAY 9

# CHAPTER 31

Race didn't even attempt to sleep after he returned to his motel room. Something had niggled at the edges of his memory banks since he'd recognized two of the names on Lieutenant Maggie Carter's list of home invasion victims. That niggling had only accentuated as he'd met with Jim Dunhill and they'd discovered more coin collectors among the list of victims.

He focused on his own stolen coin collection, the conferences and conventions he'd attended, the communications he'd had with dealers and other collectors in an attempt to determine how he himself had become a victim. He racked his brain to find some action he might have taken that would have made him a victim. All the while, his thoughts were overlaid with onerous, painful guilt. What if he'd done something to make them vulnerable, and thereby been responsible for the deaths of his wife and daughters? Race had suffered from survivor's guilt for over three years. Now that guilt had ratcheted to an entirely new level. Perspiration poured off his forehead and his head ached.

He'd invested millions in his coin collection. The worth of the collection was certainly sufficient justification for thieves to target him. Eight years ago, his coins appraised for insurance purposes at seven million, two hundred thousand dollars. He suspected that value would have risen dramatically since then. Hell, he thought, the 1742 Brasher Doubloon and the 1927-D twenty dollar gold piece would bring about two million, seven hundred thousand dollars alone.

But how had they learned about his collection? Sure, he'd attended conventions and auctions, but it wasn't as though he bragged about what he'd purchased or about the total value of his holdings. In fact, he couldn't think of one person with whom he'd ever talked about the specifics of the coins he owned.

Although he'd initially considered attendance at conferences to be a way that collectors had been targeted, his and Jim Dunhill's research had shown that most of the victims had never attended a WCCA conference. Of course, they could have attended other conferences, but Race no longer believed that was how the thieves had identified large collections.

There was another thought that consistently burrowed into his brain: What's the connection between the psychopaths who commit the home invasions and someone who provides a market for the coins they steal?

There was either someone out there who could fence the stolen items or there was a collector who bought the coins directly from the robbers. Although he had no proof as to whether or not the gang stole coin collections for someone else, he couldn't fathom that they stole for their own account. If they sold stolen coins to someone else, who could that person be?

Now, something else pricked at the corners of Race's memory. Something he'd just remembered had generated a seed of a thought. But his brain and body were so exhausted from non-stop activity, inadequate sleep, and irregular meals, he couldn't dredge up anything of value.

# CHAPTER 32

"You think Rubinstein gets in this early every day?" Susan said. "I mean, 7 a.m. is downright uncivilized."

Barbara stood beside Susan in the Rubinstein Real Estate Development reception area as they waited for Jerome Rubinstein to grant them entry to his inner sanctum. She swept a hand around the space. "You don't get this by working 9 to 5. Nice place, huh?"

"Reminds me of our offices," Susan said.

"What offices?"

"Okay, our cubicles."

Barbara rolled her eyes and shook her head.

A tall, sinuous blonde in a sleeveless dress stepped through a door into the reception area. Her five-inch spiked heels beat loudly on the marble floor as she approached them. Barbara thought the woman would have looked more at home on an episode of *The Housewives of Beverly Hills* than here in a business office in Phoenix.

"I'm Janette Willis, Mr. Rubinstein's assistant. He can see you now."

She did an about face and marched back across the lobby.

They were shown into an office that was big enough to hold a meeting of forty people.

"Mr. Rubinstein, your visitors are here," Willis announced.

Rubinstein stood and came around his desk. He walked to Susan and offered her his hand. Then he greeted Barbara. "Please sit down over here, Detectives."

They followed him to a seating arrangement that included two facing couches, four chairs, and a coffee table, and sat on one of the couches. Rubinstein sat on the other couch.

"When you called, you said you wanted to discuss the man who murdered my son."

"That's right," Barbara said.

Rubinstein met her gaze. "What could I possibly tell you about that sick bastard that you don't already know?"

"Of course you know someone murdered Virgil Patterson?"

Rubinstein nodded.

"Whoever killed your son's murderer placed a .45 caliber bullet in Patterson's mouth after he was dead."

"I heard that from the Phoenix detective who handled the case."

"Why do you think that was?" Barbara asked.

Rubinstein shrugged.

"Do you think it might have had something to do with your son, Lee, being shot with a .45 caliber pistol?"

"What's your point?"

"Look, Mr. Rubinstein, we're attempting to identify a mass murderer. We think the person who killed Virgil Patterson assassinated many other people."

Rubinstein rubbed his face and then dropped his hands to his lap. "Were the other people killed by this . . . *assassin* . . . also released on bail after murdering an innocent kid?"

"How is that relevant?" Susan asked. "Murder is murder."

"I'm just interested, Detective. You see, we have a fundamental difference of opinion if you equate the murder of my fifteen-year-old son with the murder of a career criminal who had spent eighteen years in prison for a previous murder, and who shot and killed my son for his bicycle and pocket change."

"As I said, murder is—"

"Bullshit!"

Barbara didn't like the way the conversation was headed. "Mr. Rubinstein, did anyone contact you after Lee was killed and Patterson was released on bail?"

"Sure, hundreds of people called me to express their condolences."

"I mean, did anyone call you to ask if you would be interested in seeking revenge for Lee's murder?"

"You actually expect me to answer that question?"

At 9 a.m., Barbara drove to their next—and last—appointment in Phoenix. Unfortunately, the result was almost identical to the results of their two meetings in Las Vegas and the meeting with Rubinstein.

"There's a noon flight to Albuquerque," Barbara said. "Let's grab a late breakfast and then head out to the airport."

"Sounds good to me. Wonder what Lieutenant Salas's reaction will be when we tell him we spent money and accomplished nothing?"

"Well, we did accomplish something."

"Yeah, we escaped cold weather in Albuquerque for a little while."

Barbara laughed. "We also learned that the families of victims hired an assassin to take revenge for attacks on their loved ones."

"Yeah, but prove it."

"You know I can't. But, based on your observations during the four interviews, do you have any doubt about it?"

"Nope. But where's that get us?"

"Hell, I don't know." Barbara drummed the steering wheel for a few seconds. "I'll tell you one thing I'd bet a month's pay on."

"What's that?"

"Whoever committed the murders probably contacted the families. Not the other way around."

"That makes sense. Some guy reads about the rape of Rosa Puccini and waits to see how the justice system deals with the perpetrators. When, as with the case of the three Las Vegas college football players, they get off without even a slap on the wrist, our vigilante calls the family and says, 'Let's make a deal.' "

"You know, we both had some sympathy for this vigilante asshole, because he targets low-life scumbags. But I'm beginning to have another take on this guy. You notice something about all the people we've talked with. From Victor Graves, to the Puccinis, to Rubinstein, to—"

"Yeah, they're all richer than Croesus."

"Our vigilante killer is doing this for the money, not because he's got some desire to right wrongs. If he was in it to do good for goods' sake, why didn't he take revenge against criminals who had victimized poor people?"

"Good observation," Barbara said.

As Barbara took a right turn into a Denny's lot, Susan said, "It would be great if we could get a copy of the phone records of the families. Maybe we'd find that they all received calls from a common telephone number."

Susan scoffed. "Don't hold your breath on that one. First of all, we'd never get a court order allowing that. Second, the vigilante is way too smart to use the same phone. This guy's operated for years without leaving behind any evidence. He's like a ghost."

"More like a dark angel," Barbara said. "At least that's the way the families see him."

Inside the restaurant, the hostess pointed them to the only empty booth, big enough for six people.

"I'm in the mood for some comfort food," Susan said as she opened a menu.

"Might be the only comfort you get," Barbara said.

"There's pessimism if I ever heard it."

A young woman with strawberry-colored hair and a large hickey on the left side of her neck took their order.

Barbara watched the young woman slump away, as though she was worn out. "Looks like our waitress had some comfort recently," she said.

Susan laughed and looked toward the restaurant's glass-doored entrance as three very large men entered. The hostess raised a hand to them, as though to say hello, but the men ignored her and moved quickly toward Barbara and her.

"Uh-oh," Susan muttered.

Barbara followed the direction of Susan's gaze, then slid toward the edge of the booth. Susan did the same on the other side. But before they could stand, two of the men arrived at the booth and blocked the sides. The third guy—a square-headed, long-jawed man who was well over six feet tall and weighed at least twenty pounds over two hundred—placed his hands on the table, leaned over, and smiled.

"Hello, ladies. Enjoying your visit to Phoenix?"

Susan smiled back. "Who the fuck are you, the Welcome Wagon?"

The man chuckled. "Feisty, huh. I like my women that way. Unfortunately, I don't have time to discuss my personal likes and dislikes at this moment."

"You mean that this isn't a social call?" Susan asked.

The guy chuckled again. He looked at Susan and then at Barbara. Then he looked back at Susan and, humor in his tone, said, "I'm damned glad that you had to leave your pistols back in Albuquerque. From the looks in your eyes, I suspect you would have drawn down on us by now."

While Susan glared at the man, she said, "What do you think, Babs, do we need weapons to deal with riffraff like these guys?"

Barbara said, "Why don't we listen to what these gentlemen have to say before we start a brawl. If we don't like what they say, then I'll stick this fork into this guy's balls."

The man pressed up against Barbara looked down and grimaced. "Aw, shit," he murmured.

"Don't move an inch, sweetheart," Barbara said. "I might think you're going to do something bad and I'll have to stick this little old fork into your little old nuts."

The guy who leaned on the table moved in closer and, in a lower voice, said, "Just some friendly advice. You're poking your noses in the wrong place. You've made some friends of ours very angry. I think it's time to go back to New Mexico and focus on cattle rustling and drug smuggling, or whatever you usually do back there."

"You wanta tell us which friends of yours that we've made angry," Susan said.

The man laughed and straightened up. "You're as cute as a button, honey. Maybe someday we can get together under different circumstances."

Susan lifted her purse off the booth seat and placed it on the table. She reached in and took out her badge case and took a calling card from one of the small pockets. She slid it across the table to the man and said, "Look me up the next time you're in Albuquerque. I'd love to get you on my home turf."

The guy ignored the card. "Thanks, honey, but I know how to find you." He backed up a step and said, "Let's go boys."

Susan watched the three men walk outside and followed their progress across the parking lot to a Cadillac Escalade. After they drove off, she looked at Barbara. "Now, wasn't that interesting?"

"I suspect one of the families we talked with in Las Vegas or here in Phoenix sent them."

"Maybe," Susan said. "Or maybe it was our dark angel."

# CHAPTER 33

Farmington, New Mexico was exactly as Reese McCall remembered it from five years ago when he and his crew drove through the town on the way to Colorado. Lots of pickup trucks, retail stores, bars, and businesses that serviced the oil and gas industry. A good number of Native Americans, too. He pulled into a motel lot near the juncture of the Animas and San Juan Rivers and booked a room. He'd swapped the Infiniti QX-80 for a black Ford F-150 pickup with a Navajo man in Aztec, New Mexico who'd thought he'd died and gone to heaven. An eighty thousand dollar SUV for a thirty thousand dollar pickup truck. No paperwork exchanged. McCall suspected the pickup was hocked to the gills or stolen, and the Indian was happy to dump it. He also guessed the Indian would take the SUV to the reservation where the lender or the cops might never find it.

In his motel room, he looked at a map of Farmington and found the target's street. It was nearly 10:15. He would FedEx the package of coins he'd taken from the Brownell home in Flagstaff. After that, he'd scope out the Farmington target's place while it was still light. Then he'd wait for dark.

Race jerked awake, startled. The nightmare again. He was bathed in sweat and his head rang with the echoes of terrible screams. The dream images had seemed to be awash in blood. He pressed his hands against the sides of his head, then groaned when he saw the time on the clock next to the bed: 10:15.

"Damn it." Although he hadn't fallen asleep until 6 a.m., he hadn't intended to sleep so late. He scrambled out of bed and quickly showered and shaved. Within twenty minutes, he was seated in front of his computer. He went through the notes he'd made earlier that morning before he collapsed on the bed. The niggling feeling returned as he read through them. He read from the beginning again and, this time, read his notes more slowly. His stomach seemed to flip when he stopped at the words *Four years ago, had coins appraised for insurance purposes.* What if there was a connection between the appraisal and the Three Ghouls? His appraisal was done about eight months prior to the invasion of his Amarillo home. Could that just have been coincidental?

Then another question came to mind: what if the appraiser was somehow involved with the robbery? Then he said aloud, "What if the other victims used the same appraiser?"

Race looked at his watch and saw he had about an hour until he would need to leave to meet Jim Dunhill at his shop. He recalled the name of the appraisal firm he'd hired: Holmsby Rare Coin Valuations. The company had emailed and snail-mailed a copy of his appraisal to him. He inputted the company's name in Google and found its email address on its website. Then he opened his "brute-force" password cracking software, which used eight million combinations of letters and words per second to crack a password, and queried Holmsby Rare Coin Valuations/Invoices. The software put in motion a "dictionary attack" that would hopefully grant him access to the appraisal firm's list of clients by digging up the password. The dictionary attack was a method to defeat a cipher or authentication mechanism by trying to determine its decryption key or password by trying millions of possibilities. Anyone for whom it had conducted an appraisal would have received an invoice. If that client invoice file included the names of the other victims of the gang, then Race knew he would have taken a huge step forward in identifying how the home invaders chose their targets.

He paced while he stared at his computer and listened to the hard drive hum as the cracking software seemed to agonize over its mission. It had still not discovered the password into the appraiser's accounting system when it came time for Race to leave for his meeting with Dunhill.

"I talked with eleven dealers in eleven cities where the home invasions occurred," Jim Dunhill said when Race entered his shop. "Every single one of those guys acted like I was some weirdo, calling about dead people." He paused a beat, then said, "Not just dead people, but people who were viciously murdered."

"I can imagine," Race said.

"And I didn't get a thing. Each dealer was intimately familiar with the victim in his city. Hell, he'd sold coins to the guy. All the victims had impressive collections. I asked each dealer if anyone had ever contacted them about any of the collectors. You know, like someone might have wanted to know about their collections, or might have wanted the dealer to contact a collector about selling a coin. But they all said that had never happened." Dunhill blew out a long sigh. "I'm sorry, Race. I got zilch."

Race patted Dunhill's arm. "No sweat, Jim. Let me ask you something. Is there an appraisal firm that's recognized as the best in valuing rare coins?"

"Sure. Even the WCCA recommends Holmsby. I recommend them to my clients. They're the best around."

Race nodded. "That's the firm I used for my coin collection."

"You don't think Holmsby had anything to do with these robberies and murders, do you?"

"It's just a thought at this point."

"Holy shit."

Nelson Begay drained the last of a Coors six-pack. He crushed the can and tossed it out the window. He smoothed his right hand on the SUV's leather upholstery and giggled like a kid. "One righteous ride," he muttered as he drove through Bloomfield on his way to Nageezi. He laughed as he thought again about that stupid paleface. He'd traded the dumbass a stolen Ford pickup for this beautiful Infiniti.

He wondered how fast the SUV would run. It sounded as

though it had a pretty powerful engine. When he crested the hill on Highway 550, south of Bloomfield, a little distance past the refinery, he goosed the motor. The vehicle took off. Begay smiled. He'd never driven anything this powerful, or this fast. He had it up to one-hundred-ten miles per hour and wondered what this monster would top out at, when the sickening sound of a siren penetrated his alcohol-induced buzz.

"Aw, shit," Begay said. He saw flashing lights in the rearview mirror. For a moment, he considered stopping, and tapped the brake pedal. But then he thought the cop behind him was from Bloomfield, and not from the Rez. He wouldn't screw with a Navajo Tribal policeman on the reservation. But the Bloomfield cops wouldn't be able to follow him onto Navajo land. He decided to try to outrun the guy to the first cut-off onto the Rez.

Begay pushed the accelerator to the floor and saw the speedometer hover at one-hundred-twenty miles per hour. His hands felt as though perspiration leaked from every pore. He wiped one hand and then the other on his jeans and gripped the steering wheel with force. The turnoff was about one mile ahead. He came over another hill and eased off the accelerator a bit. The dirt road on the right side of the highway approached at seemingly blinding speed. He stepped on the brakes and tried to control the huge SUV as he turned the steering wheel. He knew he was going too fast as the front wheels of the vehicle hit the surface of the muddy dirt road and the rear end fishtailed. Then everything seemed to happen in slow motion. The back of the SUV broke loose from the road and Begay felt as though he had been launched into the air. Then the vehicle crashed into a ditch beside the road, rolled three times, and came to rest on its roof.

Bloomfield Police Officer Clarence True watched as the Infiniti he'd chased went airborne, rolled, and then, finally, came to rest upside down. He tried to keep his voice steady as he called in the accident to Dispatch: "Unit 12 to Base. I am on the scene of a 10-45, on Highway 550, three miles south of Bloomfield."

True parked beside the ditch and ran through a foot of snow to the SUV. He was prepared to see blood and gore inside the vehicle.

The windows had all been blown out, side panels had been dented, and the roof had collapsed about six inches. None of that surprised True. He also wasn't surprised to find Nelson Begay behind the wheel. True had arrested Begay multiple times on DUI, Drunk & Disorderly, Aggravated Assault, and Breaking & Entering charges. What did surprise him was that Begay was driving an expensive vehicle and, despite blood that had sprayed the front seat and dashboard, Begay was still alive. He groaned when True checked his neck for a pulse.

"You've got a guardian angel, Begay," True said.

The radio in True's cruiser squawked and a message came over his shoulder mic. "Base to Unit 12, that vehicle you called in was reported in connection with a 10-28 and a 10-75. A Richard Katz reported his wife missing when she didn't return to her Albuquerque home after a business trip to Las Cruces. She last called him from Socorro where she stopped for gas yesterday morning. Is the woman in the vehicle?"

"No sign of her."

# CHAPTER 34

The Southwest Airlines flight from Phoenix landed at the Albuquerque Sunport just after 3 p.m. Barbara and Susan retrieved their Crown Victoria from long-term parking and drove to their downtown office. On the elevator up to their floor, Susan said, "If we're lucky, Lieutenant Salas won't be in today."

"Uh huh," Barbara said. "Don't count on it."

As the elevator door opened, they came face-to-face with Salas.

"Well, well, look who's back." He waggled a finger at them. "I was on my way to drop something off for the sheriff, but I can't wait to hear what you have to report from your gallivanting in Nevada and Arizona."

Salas turned around and marched toward his office.

Susan shot Barbara a tight-lipped, wide-eyed look.

Barbara nodded.

Salas sat behind his desk but didn't invite Barbara and Susan to sit. He looked over his reading glasses at each of them, in turn. "So-o-o?"

"You want the good news or the bad news?" Susan said.

Salas removed his glasses, lowered his head, and ran his hands through what was left of his hair. When he looked back up, Barbara thought he looked grim.

"It's that smart-ass attitude of yours, Martinez, which will prevent you from ever getting promoted again." He turned to

Barbara. "You got ten seconds to tell me if anything productive came from your trip."

"No, Lieutenant, nothing productive that we can take to court. We're convinced that the people we met with paid a vigilante to take revenge for violent crimes committed against family members. But we can't prove it."

"So, you wasted time and money?"

Barbara shrugged. She could sense heat emanate from Susan and sent a silent prayer that her partner would control her emotions and her mouth until they were out of Salas's office.

"You got anything to add, Martinez?"

"Not a damned thing . . . Lieutenant."

"I want a written report on my desk before you leave tonight. Now get out of here."

Barbara spun around and took a step toward the door. But Susan didn't move. Barbara grabbed the sleeve of Susan's jacket and jerked her out of the office. They had barely cleared the door when Salas shouted, "Get back in here."

"What now?" Barbara said under her breath.

When they were back in front of Salas's desk, the lieutenant held out a file. "This came in a few minutes ago. I planned to assign it to another team, but since you've been vacationing for the last two days, you might as well do some work. Missing person. Heather Katz. Wife of Richard Katz."

"The symphony conductor?" Barbara asked.

"That's the one. Her car was involved in an accident up in San Juan County, just outside Bloomfield."

"Is she okay?" Barbara asked.

"She wasn't in the vehicle. The last her husband heard from her she was getting gas in Socorro, on her way back to Albuquerque from Las Cruces."

"And the car was found in San Juan County? That can't be good."

"Nope."

"You want us to do the report on our trip first?" Susan asked, a hint of sarcasm in her tone.

Salas smiled at her. "Oh, no, Detective Martinez. I want you to look into Mrs. Katz's disappearance. Then you can do the report."

Susan looked at her watch.

"Yeah, it'll be a damn late night for both of you." He smiled again. "Have fun, ladies."

The Katzs lived in the Four Hills neighborhood, nestled against the foothills of the mountains on Albuquerque's southeast boundary. The area had once been one of the premier residential areas in the city, but had become a bit tired over the years. It was now experiencing revitalization. The Katz home sat in the middle of a block, atop a rise that offered a view all the way to the west side of the city.

Richard Katz answered the door to Barbara's knock. She was immediately struck by his haggard look—his face seemed to droop.

"Thanks for seeing us," she said after she and Susan introduced themselves.

"Of course; please come in. Let's go into the studio."

Katz led them through a living room and dining room and stopped in the kitchen. He introduced Barbara and Susan to his twin sons, who were doing homework. Then they all passed through the kitchen to a room that appeared to be a recent add-on to the back of the house. One wall was all windows. A grand piano took up a good part of the space.

Katz closed the door between the studio and the kitchen and pointed at four chairs around a small table.

"How old are your boys?" Barbara asked.

"Eight. Next week."

"Do they know about their mother?"

"No. I'm hoping for the best. No point in upsetting them over maybe nothing. I kept them out of school today." He shrugged and looked from Barbara to Susan. "You know how kids talk." He swallowed and added, "Have you heard anything?"

"That's why we came out, Mr. Katz. Your wife's SUV was found near Bloomfield."

"Bloomfield? That's way up by Farmington. How's that possible?"

"It was involved in an accident."

"Was Heather—?"

"Your wife wasn't in the vehicle. The driver was badly injured and is still unconscious. We hope he regains consciousness and can tell us something."

Katz's features seemed to sag even more. He closed his eyes, rubbed his forehead, and breathed a long sigh that seemed to carry with it the worries of the world. "I don't understand. She attended a legal conference in Las Cruces and called me yesterday morning from Socorro when she stopped for gas. How could—?"

He apparently came up with an answer to his own question. "She could have been carjacked there, or somewhere else between Socorro and Albuquerque."

Barbara asked, "Did she plan to stop anywhere else?"

"No. She told me she would drive all the way through after she gassed up."

Barbara glanced at Susan and received a sympathetic look back. There were tough questions that had to be asked.

"Mr. Katz, I apologize in advance, but we need to exclude things in order to focus our investigation."

Katz nodded.

"How's your relationship with your wife?"

A slip of a smile played on his lips, but quickly disappeared. "This will sound trite, but we're as much in love today as the day we married."

"No other . . . relationships?"

Katz's face showed confusion for an instant, then his mouth made an "O." He shook his head. "You're asking if Heather or I have had affairs with other people. Absolutely not."

"Can you think of any enemies that you or your wife might have?" Susan asked.

"Heather is a defense attorney. She has probably angered half the cops in New Mexico over the last eight years, since we moved here."

"Are you suggesting—?"

"No, no. I have too much respect for the police to think they could be responsible for my wife's disappearance."

"Anybody else?"

"No. I just can't imagine anyone would want to harm Heather. She's the kindest person you would ever . . . want to . . . meet." His voice broke and tears flooded his eyes.

"One more question, sir," Barbara said. "Would your wife have used a credit card to buy gas? If so, which one?"

"She always uses her American Express card for business travel."

"If you have access to the card number and are a signatory on her account, there's something you could do."

"Anything," he said as he wiped his eyes with a handkerchief.

"Go online and check the latest charges put on the card. Or call American Express."

Katz leaped from his chair. He looked energized to have something to do that might help. "Wait here, please," he said, and fast-walked to the door. He disappeared for a few minutes, then returned with several sheets of paper.

"This is her most recent statement. I can call the customer service number. I'm on her account."

"Please," Susan said.

Katz settled back into the chair and picked up a cordless receiver from a telephone console. He dialed a number, then hit the speaker button, and placed the receiver on the table between him and Barbara and Susan. Within two minutes, he had discovered the date and time of the last charge on Heather Katz's card, and the name, address, and telephone number of the gas station in Socorro. Susan wrote down the information in her notebook as Katz recited it.

# CHAPTER 35

In the Crown Victoria, on the way back to their office, Susan called the number in Socorro and asked to speak with the gas station manager.

"Herb's not available right now. Can I take a message?"

"When will Herb be available?"

"After he finishes his dinner. He's on break."

Susan opened her mouth and took in a long, slow breath. She saw Barbara's questioning look and held up a finger to hold her off. She said to the woman on the other end of the line, "My name is Susan Martinez. I am a detective with the Bernalillo County Sheriff's Office. I need to speak with Herb right now."

"I'm not supposed to bother Herb when he's on break."

"What's your name, honey?"

"Mary Beth."

"Okay, Mary Beth, let's do it this way. If you don't put Herb on the phone in exactly five seconds, I'm going to call my cousin with the Socorro Police Department and ask him to arrest you for interfering with an investigation, obstruction of justice, and aiding and abetting a violent crime."

Barbara's eyebrows rose. She whispered, "Laying it on a bit thick, aren't you?"

Susan smiled back at her when a man came on the line. "This is Herb Watson. How may I help you?"

"Mr. Watson, this is Detective Susan Martinez with the Bernalillo County Sheriff's Office. We are conducting a missing person's investigation. We have information that a missing woman fueled up yesterday morning at your station." Susan crossed her fingers and closed her eyes as she then asked, "Do you have a video camera at your location?"

"Yes, we do. Both inside and outside our building."

"If I gave you the time that the missing woman used her charge card at your station, would you be able to provide me with a copy of the video from your cameras for, say, fifteen minutes on either side of that time?"

"Absolutely. I would be happy to help."

"Bless you, Mr. Watson. Please do me a favor and do not erase or tape over the contents of that tape. We may need it as evidence down the road."

Susan gave Watson her email address and thanked him.

"One question, Detective. What did you say to Mary Beth? She looks scared to death."

"Gee, I can't imagine, Mr. Watson."


Back at BCSD headquarters, Barbara and Susan pulled up the video from Socorro on Barbara's computer and cycled through it.

"Stop," Susan said, ten minutes into their viewing. "I think I saw something."

Barbara paused the video and backed it up to the point where an Infiniti SUV pulled up to a pump and stopped. The camera's orientation was from an elevated position that may have been on a pole. The near-left side of the picture showed the corner of a building.

"Must be the convenience store or restaurant at the station," Barbara suggested. She ran a finger across the screen. "There are two gas pump islands on the far side of the property, and two between there and the building. What looks like the Katz vehicle is at the near-right pump."

Barbara played the video again, but this time in slow motion. A woman slid down to the ground from the SUV's driver's side and turned her back to the camera.

"Probably putting her credit card in the machine," Susan said.

"Yep. Look at the time on the bottom of the video. It's nearly identical to the time the card was used, according to the card company."

They watched Heather Katz turn and put the fuel nozzle into the gas port and then climb back into her vehicle. She leaned forward in her seat and appeared to be touching up her make-up.

"What was the time of her call to her husband?" Barbara asked.

Susan consulted her notebook and said, "9:10, according to Richard Katz's cell phone. He said she called him as she exited the interstate."

Barbara tapped the screen. "That's about right."

Almost four minutes passed before Heather Katz again slid down off the driver's seat to replace the gas hose.

"Sonofa—" Susan blurted as a man suddenly showed on the video, circled the back of the SUV, and moved up against Katz. The SUV blocked most of the view of the woman and the man, but there was just enough of a shot through the vehicle's windows to see that the woman seemed unsettled.

They continued to watch as she climbed back into the Infiniti and crawled over the center console into the passenger seat. The man shrugged out of a backpack, opened the left side back door, and tossed the pack onto the seat. For a flash of an instant, Barbara thought she saw something in the man's hand before he stepped up behind the wheel and drove out of camera coverage.

"Play it again," Susan said.

After the fourth time through the video, Barbara was as frustrated as she'd ever been. "Nothing," she said. "Other than the man's back, we got nothing."

# CHAPTER 36

Alberto Baca was going stir crazy. Since the last snow storm that had hit Cuba, New Mexico, the temperature had stayed around twenty-eight degrees. The snow hadn't melted; there was still about a foot of accumulation packed on top of ice. He'd hoped to have framed in the cabin he was constructing on the north side of Cuba, but all he'd accomplished so far was to put in the footings.

"You're drivin' me crazy, *hijo*," Consuela Baca said. "What with all your marchin' around *mi casa* like an *hombre loco*."

"Mama, *es la nieve*. The damned snow won't let me get to work on Juan Padilla's new cabin. If I don't get it done soon, he'll fire *mi culo*."

Mrs. Baca shook a wooden spoon at her son. "You watch your language, boy. You're not too big for me to knock you on your *cabeza*."

"*Lo siento, Mama*."

She moved to her son and wrapped her arms around his neck. "Why don't you go up to the job site and check things out? That will give you something to do."

Although he didn't see much point in going up to Juan Padilla's cabin site, what with the weather and all, Alberto Baca figured he'd give his mother a break. He piled into his pickup truck and drove down out of the foothills on the east side of Cuba to the road that ran through town. He turned right and drove north toward the edge of town. Halfway through town, he saw his old high school classmate, Tomas Bustamante, parked in a vacant lot in his Cuba Police Department cruiser on the lookout for speeders. Travelers through Cuba who were headed for Albuquerque or the Four Corners area and who ignored the town's speed limit were a major income source for Cuba. He honked and waved at Bustamante, who gave him a thumbs up.

The ride to the job site took less than ten minutes. As he turned off Regina Road onto the driveway he'd plowed onto the site, he noticed fresh vehicle tracks in the snow.

"Sonofabitch," he cursed. "Some *pendejo's* been screwing around up here." The good news, he told himself, was that there were no tools or construction materials anyone could steal.

On flat ground, at the top of the driveway, he marveled, not for the first time, at the splendor of the site that Juan Padilla had picked. It was heavily wooded on the back end and two sides of the land. The cabin site was up against the rear tree line. He drove forward and then smashed his foot down on the brake pedal. The rear end of the truck slewed to the right as he cranked the steering wheel to the left.

Despite the freezing temperatures, the sun was bright and the glare intensive. Baca wasn't certain what he'd seen. Maybe a deer. He grabbed a .38 caliber revolver from the glove compartment and jumped out of the truck. He cautiously rounded the front of the vehicle and stopped by the right end of the front bumper. He gulped and knocked himself in the mouth with the pistol when he crossed himself with his right hand.

"*Madre de Dios*," he muttered. "*Madre de Dios*."

# CHAPTER 37

When Race returned to his motel room, he checked his computer. The Mac Book Pro still ran its password cracking software. The dictionary attack against the Holmsby Rare Coin Valuations accounting system had continued during his meeting with Jim Dunhill. But it had yet to come up with a system password. He thought he might be able to facilitate the process by performing tasks he hadn't had time to do before he left to meet Dunhill. He accessed the appraisal company's website and clicked on the "PERSONNEL" link. There he found the name of the company's accounting manager: Clyde Zimmerman. He Googled Zimmerman and found a wealth of information about the man, including a bio on his high school alumni site. There he learned that Zimmerman was married to Anne Zimmerman, had two grown daughters—Louise and Eleanor—a college-bound son Alexander, and a dog named Scamp. Race then went to Facebook and found that Zimmerman, his wife, and their three children each had their own Facebook pages. He wrote down the birthdates that he found there.

Race paused the cracking software. On the assumption that Zimmerman would have authored the appraisal firm's accounting system's password, Race included a series of teasers into the software's instructions, including several dozen combinations of birthdates, family first names, and Scamp. Within two minutes of making these changes, the software hit the pot of gold with *Louise9141962scamp*.

The password included Zimmerman's oldest daughter's name, his youngest daughter's birth date, and his dog's name.

Within another two minutes, Race accessed the appraisal company's entire accounting records, including its customer list, its accounts receivable ledger for the years 1999 to the present date, and every appraisal it had prepared since 1953.

A review of the accounts receivable ledger showed that every coin collector murdered by the home invasion gang had been a customer of Holmsby Rare Coin Valuations, Inc. Race jotted down the dates of the appraisals the firm had done for those collectors and then compared those dates to the dates of the home invasions. By the time he'd compared the first three appraisal dates against the incident dates, he knew he had discovered the link between the firm and the crimes. He had to concentrate on breathing; he was so stunned that his heart seemed to have stopped and his lungs felt paralyzed. When he'd finished his analysis, he'd discovered that the average period of time between the completion of an appraisal and the murder of the collector for whom the appraisal had been done was sixty-three days. The longest period of time differential was ninety-one days; the shortest was twenty-three.

Then Race had a thought. He went to the appraisals themselves and looked for the names of the company employees who had done the appraisal work. In every instance, the appraiser was shown as: Sylvan Tauber. Race stared at the man's name on his computer screen and collapsed back into his chair. He remembered Tauber. The man had appraised his collection, too. He was renowned as one of the premier rare coin appraisers in the world. Even four years ago, when he'd appraised Race's collection, Tauber had been elderly: his hair snowy-white; slightly stooped; gnarled fingers. His blue eyes had an almost milky hue to them, and his right eye had a permanent squint that he'd laughingly told Race was from using a magnifier loupe to examine coins.

Race felt heat rise from inside himself. Tauber had been a genteel man who'd interacted well with Mary, Sara, and Elizabeth. He'd joined them all for dinner the evening he'd finished appraising Race's collection. If he'd been forced to come up with the name of someone responsible for the deaths of his wife and daughters,

Sylvan Tauber would not have come to mind.

Another search of the appraisal firm's website showed that Tauber was still employed there, but was no longer in the home office in Stamford, Connecticut. He now worked out of the company's Hermosa Beach, California, satellite location.

Race had never believed in coincidences. Two murder victims who had used Holmsby's services might have been a coincidence. Thirteen were staggering.

His computer screen showed it was now 8:27 p.m. He hadn't eaten all day and suddenly felt weak. He found a list of local restaurants on the dresser in his motel room and called a pizza place that offered delivery. After he'd placed an order, Race went back to his computer, but, after twenty minutes, couldn't concentrate. He turned on the television. A local station broadcast some inane reality show. He was about to change the channel when a "Breaking News" streamer scrolled across the bottom of the screen. After a few seconds, the show segued to a live reporter seated behind a desk in a news room.

"This just in," the reporter said. "The body of Heather Katz, the wife of the Albuquerque Symphony Orchestra conductor, was discovered near Cuba, New Mexico. Initial reports are that she had been shot at least once. Mrs. Katz's vehicle was involved in an accident near Bloomfield earlier today, and Channel 9 has just received video captured by a service station security camera in Socorro. We will show that video momentarily. The New Mexico State Police ask that if anyone recognizes the man in the video, please contact your local law enforcement or the state police immediately."

As depressed and angry as Race felt, the fact that someone had murdered a woman ratcheted his emotions to another level. He watched the screen as the security video came up. His heart ached when he saw the woman seated in her SUV, fixing her make-up. She didn't seem to be alert to her surroundings. Always a mistake, he thought.

Then Race became even angrier. His pulse beat like a metronome on steroids. A man suddenly appeared on the video and quick-walked—predator-like—around the SUV. He wore a baseball cap, jeans, and a dark-colored insulated jacket.

Race wanted to scream out to the woman, to warn her.

The man looked somehow familiar. The way he was dressed. The way he moved on the balls of his feet. Race moved closer to the TV screen and watched as the station replayed the video. Then the station returned to its regular programming.

Where had he seen this guy before? He tried to dredge up the memory, but it just wouldn't come. He was too tired to think clearly. Then there was a knock on his door. He parted the curtains and looked out on the pathway in front of the room. A kid stood there with a pizza box in hand. Race opened the door, paid for the delivery, and tipped the kid. He closed the door and dropped the box on the dresser. The smell of the pizza seemed to push everything from his mind. He took a slice, sat at the table, took a large bite, and sighed. About to take another bite, a sudden thought struck. He pulled up the television station's website and looked for the video they had just shown. Once he brought it up, he focused on the man in the video. He hoped something there would jangle his synapses enough to remember what it was about the man that seemed familiar.

Race accessed the Brownell video on YouTube and compared it against the service station video. He put the two videos up on split-screen and watched the man in each one. There was no question the two men walked similarly, and they dressed alike. But baseball caps, jeans, and short, insulated jackets were ubiquitous in New Mexico. There was something else that Race felt he had missed, but whatever that something else was just didn't come to mind. Even after looking at the screen dozens of times, there just wasn't enough there for him to conclude the men in the two videos were one and the same.

# CHAPTER 38

"Clarence, I want you to stay at the San Juan Regional Medical Center in Farmington and keep me informed about Begay."

"Really, Chief?"

Bloomfield Police Chief Randall Cummings said, "Yeah. This is no longer a traffic accident, or even grand theft auto. That wrecked SUV was carjacked in Socorro by a man who apparently murdered the vehicle's owner and dumped her body near Cuba. We need to question Begay about that."

"Begay's a loser, Chief. But he's smalltime. No way he'd carjack a woman and then kill her. While I'm sitting on my ass at the hospital, the real killer could be putting a lot of distance between us."

"That might be so, but I want you there if he regains consciousness. You understand?"

"Sonofabitch," Reese McCall screamed at the television in his motel room. "That damned Indian." He imagined the heat the cops would bring down in the Farmington area if they learned from Begay that he'd swapped vehicles with him. They'd have his description and a description of the pickup he'd gotten in the trade. The only good news at this point, McCall thought, was that Begay was unconscious in a hospital according to the news.

It was 10:15 p.m. He'd planned to break into the target's house after midnight, but now wondered if he ought to go in earlier, and then get the hell out of Farmington. Maybe cross into Colorado and haul ass north. But he knew the earlier he went in, the more likely it would be that he might be seen by a neighbor or that the target would be awake.

"Haven't you seen enough of that video?" Barbara asked.

Susan took her eyes off her computer screen and stretched her neck and shoulders. "There's something there, Babs, that's setting off sirens inside my head."

Barbara stood and walked around her desk to Susan's. "Like what?"

Susan turned back to the screen and pointed. "Like the guy there seems familiar."

Barbara looked over Susan's shoulder. "Looks like half the men in New Mexico. Boots, jeans, ski jacket, and ball cap."

"Something else."

"You think you've seen him before?"

"Yeah."

"You mean, in person."

"Maybe."

"How many men do we see on any given day, let alone a week or a month?" Barbara huffed, then added, "Maybe you saw him in a photo."

"Nah. The guy's face doesn't show in the video. It's the way he moves, or his clothes." She shrugged. "There's something familiar about the guy."

"What about videos?"

Susan shrugged. "Could be."

"What videos have you looked at recently?"

"I'll be damned. Maybe that's it. Besides this video, the only other one I've seen lately was the security video from the home invasion in Flagstaff."

"Pull it up and watch it again."

Susan shook her head. "That can't be it. I mean, what are the odds that a guy caught by a camera in Flagstaff would be filmed in Socorro a short time later. It's probably just my imagination. Are you finished with the report for Salas?"

"Yeah. I'll email it to you."

"Sounds like a plan."

Barbara went back to her desk, but before she returned to the report for Salas, she said, "Susan, do yourself a favor and watch that Flagstaff video one more time. Otherwise, you'll wake up in the middle of the night thinking about it."

Susan waved her arms in exasperation. "You are such a nag."

She pulled up the Flagstaff video of the Three Ghouls. The camera had captured the three men as they entered the Brownell home. The first man in line obscured the camera's view of the two other men behind him. There was nothing about that first man that reminded her of the guy in the Socorro video. Besides, that guy was dead.

The camera had stopped after the men entered the Brownell home. Then, about two hours later, when the three men exited the home, it went into action again. The first man out appeared to be the one who had entered the home last. Susan concentrated on him as he walked down the steps to the driveway. She gasped and said, "I'll be damned."

Barbara stood and came around behind Susan again. "What is it?"

Susan tapped the computer screen. "Watch the way this guy moves." Susan booted up the Socorro video. "Now watch the man here."

"I think you're right," Barbara said. "Play them again."

After they'd looked at both videos again, Barbara said, "There's something else. Look at his boots. The chains."

"I'll be damned," Susan said. "I'll be damned to hell."

Barbara used her cell phone to call Sophia Otero-Hansen's cell.

"Federal Bureau of Investigation, Agent Otero-Hansen's phone," a man answered.

"Please put Agent Otero-Hansen on," Barbara said.

"She's away from her desk. I heard her cell ring as I passed her office."

"Who am I speaking with?" Barbara asked, wondering if it was FBI custom to answer one another's cell phones.

"Special Agent Bruce Lucas; who's calling?"

The man's voice irritated Barbara. It was shrill and officious at the same time.

"When will Agent Otero-Hansen return?"

"I asked you a question, ma'am. Who's calling?"

Barbara was about to tell the man she'd call back, when Lucas must have seen her name on Otero-Hansen's cell phone screen.

"Oh, it's you, Detective Lassiter. In what wild goose chase do you now want to involve Agent Otero-Hansen?"

Barbara hesitated a moment to decide how she wanted to handle Lucas. She didn't want to do anything that would cause him to retaliate against Sophia. Finally, she said, "I have some information that I am certain Agent Otero-Hansen would like to have."

"Is that so?"

Barbara felt her self-control about to break loose. "She has my number; please have her call me."

"It'll be a cold day in hell—"

So much for self-control, Barbara thought. "Listen, asshole, I have information about the surviving Three Ghouls killer. If you aren't interested, I'll just call a friend in the Denver office. I'm certain she'll be thrilled to take credit." She terminated the call.

"What in God's name did you say to my boss?" Sophia Otero-Hansen asked, sixty seconds later.

"Well, I called him an asshole."

"Ha. Good for you. What's this about the Three Ghouls?"

Barbara put her phone on speaker and moved to Susan's desk. "We're working the Heather Katz homicide. Susan may have tied the remaining Three Ghouls killer to the murder of Mrs. Katz." Barbara waved at Susan to continue the story. When she had done so, Otero-Hansen was silent for a long few seconds.

"You still there?" Barbara asked.

"Yeah. Sorry. So what you noticed was the way the guy walked and his clothes?"

"At first," Susan said. "But then I noticed the chains on the back of the guy's boots. Same walk, same clothes, and same chains in both videos."

"Let me look at the two videos and I'll get back to you."

# CHAPTER 39

Police Officer Clarence True called his chief and tried to maintain professional calm while he waited to be put through. When Cummings came on the line, True's voice broke. He swallowed, took a deep breath, and started again. "Begay's conscious. He told me how he got the Infiniti SUV."

"Are you going to share it with me or do I have to ask?"

"Oh, sorry, Chief. He swapped a stolen pickup for the SUV with a guy in Aztec. He gave me a description of the truck and of the guy he gave it to. I just emailed the descriptions to you."

"Good job, True. Damned good job."

Lieutenant Maggie Carter had called an emergency presser at APD headquarters for 10:30 p.m. Such a late press conference was highly unusual, but so was the murder of a prominent Albuquerque citizen that now involved law enforcement in four different counties: Bernalillo, Sandoval, Socorro, and San Juan; and the FBI. At 10 p.m., she took the elevator down to the press room and checked to make certain the lights and the audio/visual system were in working order. She found Betsy Jaramillo, the *New Mexico Herald-Tribune's* Crime Desk reporter, seated in the first row, while her cameraman set up his equipment on the floor below the dais.

"Hey, Betsy. What's up?"

"You tell me, Maggie. They dragged me out of bed and told me

201

it sounded like something important was about to go down."

"Be patient, Betsy. All things in their right time. By the way, I met Phillip Taylor recently, your new freelance guy. Seems like a nice fellow. But maybe a little overanxious."

"Who?"

"Phillip Taylor. Said he works for you guys on the crime desk."

"News to me, Maggie. Never heard of him."

Carter was confused. She thought about Phillip Taylor as she went back up to her office, but quickly put him out of mind when her boss, the chief of police, came in and asked, "Is everything set?"

Race had a tingling sensation at the top of his spine as he watched the televised late night press conference. He recognized Lieutenant Maggie Carter behind the podium. Next to her was a guy with silver-colored hair, dressed in a bemedaled blue uniform. She introduced the man as the Albuquerque Chief of Police, then stepped aside as the chief spun a story that electrified Race's nerve endings.

The presentation included video clips of the Brownell home invasion and the carjacking in Socorro. When the chief talked about the murder of Heather Katz and the discovery of her vehicle in San Juan County, in the Four Corners area, Race stood and paced in front of the television set and tried to identify an anomaly that seemed to be present in the presentation.

"We believe the man in this video recently invaded a home in Flagstaff with two other men and murdered the occupants," the chief continued. "Those two other men were recently found shot to death in Milan. We assume the man in the video killed his associates and hitched a ride from Milan to Socorro, carjacked Mrs. Katz at a service station there, and drove to Cuba, where he murdered her. We know he then drove to Aztec where he traded the SUV for a pickup truck. Our assumption is that he is either still in San Juan County, or has left the state and gone into Utah, Colorado, or Arizona. Police checkpoints are being established on all roads that lead into those states from New Mexico."

Something didn't seem right to Race. Something was out of place. He was exasperated when he finally determined what it was, because it was so simple, so obvious. Why would the man in the video have gone from Flagstaff to Socorro, hijack Heather Katz, and drive all the way to San Juan County? He's gone east, then south, then north, and finally northeast. For a moment, Race considered that the man had backtracked to throw off the authorities. But that didn't seem right. If he wanted to get out of New Mexico, the smart thing for him to have done would have been to continue south from Socorro to Mexico.

Race could come up with only one logical conclusion: the guy had had a change of plans caused by something or someone. "What does the guy do?" Race asked out loud. He answered his own question: "He murders and steals valuable coin collections." Then he asked, "What does he do with the collections?" Race suspected the coin robberies were performed by the home invader on behalf of someone else. "What if that someone else had called the killer and given him a new assignment? A new target?"

Race pulled up a map of the Farmington area on his laptop and located all the communities in the general area. In addition to Bloomfield, Aztec, and Farmington in New Mexico, he identified other towns like Chinle, Arizona; Silverton, Telluride, Cortez, and Pagosa Springs, Colorado; and Monticello, Utah. He shook his head out of frustration. The territory was huge.

Race groaned and wondered how he might be able to narrow the hunt. He looked at his computer. He had been an IT professional most of his life. Before that he'd been a combat soldier. The Army had trained him to improvise. That's what he needed to do. And, in that instant, something seemed to go off like a grenade in his head. It was as though scar tissue had blocked an idea from surfacing, but had suddenly been excised. He went back to his hack of the Holmsby Rare Coin Valuations, Inc.'s accounting system and searched the appraisal file in chronological order. He keyed on appraisal firm clients who lived in the Four Corners area and who had appraisals conducted within the last ninety days. There were two. One in Farmington, New Mexico. Another in Monticello, Utah. He wrote down the clients' names, addresses, and phone numbers. Then he accessed the appraisals prepared for the two clients. He was shocked at the extent of both collections. A collector in Utah had a massive number of rare coins. The total appraised value of the collection was a few dollars short of twenty million dollars. The Farmington, New Mexico collector had an incredible collection of Colonial and Post-Colonial coins. In fact, Race hadn't known that such a collection even existed. The total appraised value of that collection had been set at thirty-two million dollars.

Race gathered up his possessions and loaded them into his pickup truck.

"You want to go on a road trip?" Sophia Otero-Hansen asked.

Barbara cleared her throat and tried to shake the foggy feeling from her head. She looked at her bedside clock and groaned. "It's 11. And we're already in trouble because of the last road trip we took."

"I'm flying to Farmington on our jet. I got my boss to agree to let you and Susan come along if you can be at the airport by midnight. We're trying to locate the Three Ghouls guy."

"Your boss wants us along?"

"Well, I may have misspoke. Lucas did everything he could to dissuade a guy here from D.C. who suggested you and Susan be invited along. But he wasn't successful. The D.C. guy thinks you might be valuable resources considering that you noticed the similarities in the Brownell security video and the one at the Socorro gas station."

"I'd have to clear it with my boss."

"Remember my motto, Barbara. It's better to ask for forgiveness than to ask for permission."

"How's that worked for *you* so far?"

"Not very well."

Barbara laughed. "I'll call Susan. See you soon."

Race drove his truck with complete abandon. He'd used one of his burner phones to call the Farmington collector, Nicholas Franchini, who he'd identified from the Holmsby server, but there'd been no answer at the number he'd found in his hack of the appraisal firm's computer. He left a message on the answering machine. He then called Winston Abbott in Monticello, Utah.

A woman answered.

"Winston Abbott, please. Tell him Robert Thornton is calling."

"What is this? Do you know what time it is?"

"Is this Mrs. Abbott?"

"Yes. Who is this?"

"May I speak to your husband?"

"My husband passed away last year. Who are you?"

"Listen, Mrs. Abbott—"

"If you don't stop bothering me, I'll call the police."

"That's exactly what I want you to do. Call the police. Tell them there's a man who may be on the way to your home. That same man broke into my home several years ago, murdered my wife and daughters, and stole my coin collection. He may be targeting your coin collection. I don't have a lot of time to explain and you don't have a lot of time to get to someplace safe."

"What did you say your name was?"

"Robert Thornton."

"Oh, my God. I remember your name. When your family was murdered, my husband told me he'd met you at an International Coin Show in Tucson a while back."

"I want you to call the police, Mrs. Abbott. If they can't immediately send an officer to your place, you should drive somewhere safe. Can you do that?"

"Of course. But do you think that is absolutely necessary?"

"Mrs. Abbott, I have no way of knowing whether your husband's coin collection is the target of the maniac who murdered my family, but I think there's a fifty-fifty chance that it is."

"Oh my Lord," she said. "I'll call the police right away, and I'll drive to my daughter's place. She's close by."

"Good," Race said. "I hope it will prove to have been unnecessary, but it's better to be safe."

"Thank you."

Race hung up and again tried the Farmington number. Still, no answer. He left another message. Then he called Jim Dunhill.

"Do you ever sleep?" Dunhill asked.

Race apologized for calling so late again and then briefed Dunhill on what he'd discovered in his hack of the Holmsby computer system. "There are two big collections in the Four Corners area. Winston Abbott and Nicholas Franchini."

"You think the killer might be targeting Abbott or Franchini?"

"Jim, it's the best theory I can come up with."

"God help us if he's going further north," Dunhill said. "Denver, for instance. It'll be nearly impossible to pinpoint a target there. There are dozens and dozens of big-time collectors in a city that size. I sell to at least two dozen up there myself. And many of them may have used Holmsby to appraise their collections."

"You can help me with one thing, Jim. I talked with Mrs. Abbott in Monticello, Utah and warned her. She should be okay. It's Franchini in Farmington I'm worried about. I've called several times. No one answers. I left several messages on the answering machine. Could you try to reach him?"

"Sure."

"That would be great. I suspect telephone coverage between here and Farmington might become a little sketchy."

"I've sold coins to Franchini over the years. He made a ton of money in oil and gas. Now he owns a fast food franchise. I'll try to reach him."

After he hung up with Dunhill, Race considered calling the Farmington Police. He burned with the need to take revenge against the man who'd murdered his family, but he knew he wouldn't be able to live with himself if another innocent person died because he hadn't done the right thing. He pulled up the Farmington Police Department number and called it.

"Farmington P.D. How may I help you?"

"I need to talk to a detective."

"Can I have your name, sir?"

"Ma'am, here's the deal. I will not give you my name. I have information about the man who murdered Heather Katz down in Cuba. I think he's in Farmington and plans to steal a valuable coin collection at 127 Chaco Loop. This man has murdered dozens of people in home invasion robberies."

"Is this some kind of joke?"

"Listen, lady, do you hear me laughing?"

"We don't have any detectives on duty right now. I'll contact the one on call."

"Great. Thank you."

# CHAPTER 40

Barbara and Susan arrived at the Albuquerque Sunport's private terminal at ten minutes to midnight. Bruce Lucas didn't even make an effort to hide his disdain for them as they marched into the terminal in jeans, above-the-ankle insulated boots, sweaters under ski jackets, and ski caps. The FBI representatives were all dressed for a business meeting. But at least they had the sense to bring parkas along, which they each carried under an arm.

"That was quite a nasty look Brucie gave Barbara and me," Susan said to Sophia Otero-Hansen. "Don't I look good in these jeans?"

Otero-Hansen chuckled. "Bruce Lucas isn't happy about you and Barbara coming along. Of course, he's probably also unhappy that you're not dressed as professionally as we are."

"Ouch," Barbara said.

# DAY 10

# CHAPTER 41

Reese McCall had abandoned the F-150 pickup in a Wal-Mart parking lot shortly after he saw the news report about Nelson Begay being taken into custody. He hiked the mile back to his motel and hid out in his room until 12:15 a.m. Then he walked six blocks to a bar with a flashing neon sign of a cowgirl above the front door. The booming sounds of Country & Western music had drawn him to the place from two blocks away. By the time he opened the front door, he was hunched over from the cold. A thermometer outside the bar entrance showed twenty degrees.

He exhaled a satisfied sigh as he stepped inside and looked around the place. The warmth of the bar felt damned good, and the people there were his kind of people. Most of the men either wore ball caps or cowboy hats. Jeans appeared to be required dress for men and women.

McCall moved to a stool farthest from the door. Seated on the next stool over was a lean, forty-something woman who looked as though she'd been rode hard and put away wet. Her hair looked wind-blown and her western blouse and leather coat were wrinkled and worn. When the woman turned toward him, McCall eyeballed her and thought she'd been a looker maybe ten years ago. She now had the appearance of a woman who'd experienced a life full of disappointment. And she had the red, glassy-eyed look of a drunk. He smiled and thought, *Perfect prey.*

"Buy you a drink, Miss?" McCall asked.

She wore a surprised expression when she swiveled around to face him. "Were you talking to me?"

McCall laughed. "I sure was. How about that drink?"

Surprise still showed on her face, but she now smiled and her eyes sparkled a bit. "Why, that would be very nice."

McCall raised a hand and caught the bartender's attention. He pointed at the woman's glass and raised two fingers. Based on the red in her eyes and the slur in her speech, he guessed she'd had at least several drinks before he'd arrived.

"My name's Reese; what's yours?"

"Kathy."

"Nice to meet you, Kathy. Looks like you're drinking tequila."

"My favorite," she said. "Used to drink margaritas; that's how I got a taste for tequila."

"Margaritas are for girls and girly-men. Tequila straight up is what real women drink."

She seemed to like being included in the "real women" class. She patted his hand and said, "You're a real charmer, aren't you?"

While McCall nursed his first drink, his new friend Kathy downed three. When the bartender told them it was last call, McCall ordered his new friend another drink.

Kathy had long since devolved into giggles and swishy speech. The more she drank, the more she seemed to appreciate McCall's sense of humor . . . even when he wasn't trying to be funny. The more she drank, the more she touched, patted, and rubbed his body.

"How'd you get those scars on your face?" she asked as the bartender went to retrieve her drink.

McCall had always been super-sensitive about the scars. He'd gone through a windshield when he was a senior in high school. The kid who was driving had been killed. He knew he wasn't handsome. The scars only made him less attractive. But Kathy seemed to not be put off by them.

"I don't like to talk about them."

"Aw, come on, sweetie. I think the scars and that tattoo on your neck make you look like a pirate." She lazily waved a hand around as though she brandished a sword. "Ho, ho, ho," she said, and giggled. "If you had a wooden leg, you'd look like Long John Silver." More giggles.

"How do you know I don't have a wooden leg?"

She licked her lips and seemed to sober up for a moment. "Do you?"

"You'd have to take off my boots and pants to find out."

The bartender placed a drink in front of Kathy. She turned to the bar, downed the drink, and then turned back to McCall. "Well, sugar, I think we should go see if you have a wooden leg."

"Your place or mine?"

She winked at him, took his arm, and slid off her stool. "Why, my place, of course."

McCall supported her as they walked outside. The wind blasted him and the temperature felt as though it had dropped ten degrees in the last hour.

"Maybe you'd better give me your car keys."

"You are such a gentleman." She fumbled in her jeans and came up with a key ring. She giggled as she handed it to McCall. "Now I have to remember where I left my car."

He pressed the unlock button on the remote on the key ring. The headlights flashed on an Audi sedan parked across the street. He helped her to the vehicle and into the front passenger seat. Then he got behind the wheel, cranked the motor, and drove off.

"Where do you live?" he asked. When she didn't answer, he looked over and saw she'd fallen asleep. "Well, ain't that the shits?" he mumbled.

Reese had never been particular about who he had sex with. Sex for him was all about release of tension. Kathy would have served that purpose. But he liked to inflict pain. Screwing a comatose drunk would have been less than satisfying. But what he was really after was a vehicle. That much he'd accomplished. He drove back to his motel, dragged Kathy into the room, and struggled to put her on the bed. He carried his backpack to the Audi and drove toward the south side of Farmington, toward 1456 Burro Drive, the address his brother had given him.

# CHAPTER 42

The FBI plane took off just after midnight. The Beechcraft Premier IA jet landed at the Farmington Airport thirty-five minutes later.

From across the aisle, Barbara smiled at Otero-Hansen as they taxied to the terminal. "Nice wheels. Turns a three-hour drive into a thirty minute magic carpet ride."

Otero-Hansen leaned toward Barbara. "The guy I introduced to you in the terminal, Sanjay Darzi, is a big guy in the Criminal Investigative Division out of D.C. He flew out here on this wet-dream-of-an-airplane to find out how my boss is handling the Three Ghouls investigation. He asked me how I linked the man in the Brownell video to the Socorro video. I told him you and Susan had discovered that connection and passed the information to me because of"—she smiled—"our longtime, solid relationship. Part of our successful outreach program with local law enforcement. He suggested to Lucas that he invite the two of you along on this little trip. Thought you might like to be in on the action."

"You said that Lucas wasn't happy about Darzi's suggestion."

"Actually, I thought he would have a heart attack. You should have seen his face. You realize you coming along is a slap in his face."

"Like he couldn't perform this little mission to Farmington without the help of two detectives from the BCSD?"

"Exactly."

"Maybe he's also pissed because I called him an asshole."

"Nah. I can't imagine he would hold a grudge over something like that."

Barbara chuckled.

Susan, who sat in front of Barbara, turned and looked at Otero-Hansen. "Is there going to be a briefing?"

"In the terminal here."

"Good. If I'm going to shoot someone, I'd like to know who, when, where, and why."

"By the way, Susan, nice jeans."

"Why thank you, Sophia. What a nice thing to say. I wish Brucie-boy felt the same. I think he's kinda cute, in a weird, FBI-sort-of way."

Barbara and Susan followed the FBI contingent—Darzi, Lucas, Otero-Hansen, and another Albuquerque agent, Allen Vincent—across the tarmac to a room the FBI had reserved in the Farmington Airport terminal. There were a man and woman who greeted Lucas and Darzi. FBI, Barbara thought, because of their dress and their obsequious attention to Darzi. The woman introduced Lucas and Darzi to a middle-aged guy in a blue police uniform and a thirty-something man in tactical gear. Then SAC Bruce Lucas moved to the front of the room and asked everyone to take seats. There were two easels at the front of the room, to Lucas's right, with blown-up satellite photographs mounted on poster board.

Lucas asked everyone in the room to introduce themselves. Then he said, "Here's the situation." He pointed at the uniformed man. "Farmington Police Chief Ben Summers called to let us know an anonymous tip had come in. A caller advised that Heather Katz's murderer may be on his way to an address here in Farmington. We have reason to believe that Katz's killer is a member of the gang the Bureau has coined the Three Ghouls. The bureau has had a task force working on the Three Ghouls for years." Lucas paused and looked around the room. When he continued, he said, "Two of the gang's members were shot and killed in Milan, New Mexico two days ago. Based on the gang's MO, and the tip the Farmington Police received, we feel there is a high probability the killer might be targeting 127 Chaco Loop, the address the caller gave us." He rapped the photograph on the right with a pointer. "A couple named Nicholas and Karla Franchini live at that address.

"Thanks to the people in our Farmington office for providing these photographs." He nodded in the direction of the man and woman now seated in the second row of five rows of metal chairs. "The Sat image on the left shows a two-and-a-half square mile quadrant that includes the target location."

There was a red "X" painted near the center of the photo. Lucas rapped the "X" with a pointer.

"We'll drive in from the north and park at the two ends of the loop. As you can see, there are plenty of vehicles parked on the street, so we'll be able to position our vehicles without raising suspicion.

"We'll be in a support role. Farmington P.D. SWAT will take the lead, under the command of Lieutenant Whaley. They have a four wheel drive armored vehicle parked behind an office building around the corner from Chaco Loop."

Susan, seated in the back row next to Barbara, caught Barbara's eye, hunched her shoulders, and whispered, "What the hell is this, World War III?"

Barbara arched her eyebrows and put a finger to her lips.

Lucas stepped to the second easel. "This photo shows the target property and homes on either side and across the street. 127 Chaco is a two-story house on one acre. You can't miss it. It's the only house on the block with a metal sign in the front yard. I'll turn this over to Lieutenant Whaley for now."

Scott Whaley, the guy in tactical clothes, stood. "We have two pickup trucks here"—he tapped the photo on the right—"and here." He tapped the photo again. "There are two SWAT officers in each of those vehicles. The rest of my team will be in our tactical vehicle. Anyone who approaches the target will immediately be challenged." He looked out at the audience and asked, "Are there any questions?"

Barbara looked around, expecting someone to have a question. She had several she wanted to ask, but didn't think it was her place. Her stomach flip-flopped when Susan raised her hand.

"Yes?"

"Do you have any officers stationed inside the target property?"

"No. In fact, there doesn't seem to be anybody in the house. We've used "through-the-wall" infrared radar and fiber optics and haven't picked up any indications of body heat. We've called the home number several times without a response. The Franchini's appear to be out. We sent an officer in street clothes to the residence. He knocked a number of times and walked around the property. All the doors and windows were locked tight and covered with drapes or shutters. Couldn't see into any of the rooms. No lights on."

"Or, already dead," Susan whispered.

Whaley turned to see if there were any other questions, but Susan stopped him. "I have a question for Mr. Lucas."

Whaley stepped aside and Lucas came forward. He glared at Susan as though she was the Anti-Christ and grumbled, "Yes, Detective?"

"You said something about a metal sign in the front yard."

"Yes."

"Is it a For Sale sign?"

"No. It's from a construction company." He pointed at one of the photographs. "You can see heavy tracks from construction vehicles that must have crossed the lawn at some point." Lucas squinted and sarcastically asked, "Anything else, De-tec-tive?"

"You mentioned something about the Three Ghouls' MO. Can you clarify what you meant?"

"No, that's classified." He looked around the room. "Well, if there are no other questions—"

Susan came out of her chair and raised her hand. "Mr. Lucas, I have more questions."

Barbara watched Lucas's face redden. She held her breath. Conflicting emotions ran through her. She was nervous anticipating what her partner might ask, but, at the same time, was very interested in what Susan might say. She knew how sharp a mind Susan had and knew whatever she would ask would be important.

"Were the neighbors asked about the whereabouts of the Franchinis?"

Lucas blew out a loud stream of air. Barbara thought he looked exasperated. His face had turned almost crimson. He looked at Whaley and asked, "You want to answer that?"

"We cleared out the neighbors from the houses close to the Franchini place." He suddenly looked embarrassed. Red-faced, he said, "We never got around to asking any of them if they knew where the Franchinis might be." Besides, it's unimportant where the Franchini's might be. In fact, it's an advantage that they're away from their home. If the killer shows up, we'll be able to act without endangering the Franchini family."

"So the Franchinis could already be dead."

Lucas ignored Susan and looked around the room.

Barbara caught Darzi's surprised expression. He seemed about to interject as he half came out of his chair, but appeared to have second thoughts and sat back down.

"If there's nothing else . . ." Lucas said.

Susan, still standing, said, "Can you at least tell us what's in this house that's so important to attract a man who tortured and murdered a family in Flagstaff, who apparently executed his two partners in Milan, who carjacked a vehicle in Socorro, who may have murdered a woman in Cuba, who swapped vehicles in Aztec, and who is now possibly in Farmington?"

"I already explained. The information is classified."

After the briefing ended, Barbara and Susan waited for the rest of the people in the room to exit. They then moved down their aisle to follow them, when Bruce Lucas came back into the room and blocked their departure.

"I'm going to make something very clear so there's no chance you two will misunderstand." He paused a second and then continued, "You are here as observers only. You are to take no part in the operation. I don't want you to open your mouths. You are not to draw your weapons. You got it?"

Susan half-raised a hand. "Would it be all right to ask a question?"

Lucas frowned at Susan. "What is it?"

"Let's say the killer is at the Chaco address and he has a weapon pointed at you. Would it be all right with you if I pulled my weapon and shot the bastard?"

Lucas growled, turned, and fast-walked from the room.

"Oh, Bruce—"

Barbara grabbed Susan's arm and said, "Shut up."

Race sped into Farmington. Despite being fatigued, he'd been able to stay awake, fueled by pure adrenaline and continuous thoughts about the killer he hoped he would find in Farmington. He was so stressed by the time he reached the city that he felt as though every nerve ending in his body had been stripped.

He'd accessed Google Maps on his phone to find the address on Chaco Loop. He approached the street from the west, turned slowly onto it, and passed the address. He circled the block and was angry that there were no police vehicles in sight. His call to the Farmington P.D. had apparently been blown off as a crank call. On his second circuit of the Franchini's street, he spotted a parking place three doors down from 127, and tried again to reach Franchini. Still no answer. "Aw, hell," he whispered. He opened his door and stepped down to the street. As he closed the door, someone grabbed him from behind and slammed him to the ground. The air went out of his lungs as emergency lights flashed and what sounded like a hundred voices shouted.

# CHAPTER 43

"A reporter?"

"Yeah, Chief," SWAT Commander Scott Whaley said. "He's carrying *Herald-Tribune* credentials. Phillip Taylor's his name."

"Sonofa—how the hell did he learn about this?"

"He won't disclose his source. What should I do with him?"

Chief of Police Summers turned to the FBI contingent and shot Lucas a questioning look. Barbara and Susan hung back a few feet and watched.

"Tell him to get out of here," Lucas said. "If he doesn't cooperate, throw him in a cell."

Whaley smiled. "I hope he doesn't cooperate."

"Don't you think we should—?"

Lucas interrupted Barbara. "When I want your opinion, Detective, I'll ask for it."

Barbara noticed a sour look on Sanjay Darzi's face, but the man didn't say anything.

Barbara stepped forward and tried again. "You said the guy's name is Phillip Taylor."

Chief Summers said, "Yep. That's the name on his press pass."

"Never heard of him," Barbara said.

Lucas scoffed. "You know every damn reporter in the state?"

"No, but I do know the people at the *Herald-Tribune*."

Lucas shook his head and snarled at Barbara, "If you want to waste your time, why don't you call the paper and check on the guy? Go ahead, make a fool of yourself." Lucas turned to Whaley. "Get that damned reporter out of here."

Barbara turned away, took her cell out of her coat pocket, and called Betsy Jaramillo's cell number. She heard Lucas snort and say, as he walked away, "Women cops. What a waste."

Reporter Betsy Jaramillo answered as though she was in a sleep-drugged haze. "Hell-o-o."

"Betsy, it's Barbara Lassiter. Sorry to call so late."

"Jeez, Barbara. Calling me at this ungodly hour, I hope you've got a good story for me."

"I might. But I first need to check on a guy who claims to work for your paper."

"Don't tell me. Phillip Taylor, right?"

"How'd you know?"

"Maggie Carter asked me about Taylor at a press conference last night."

"Does he work for the *Herald-Tribune*?"

"I told Maggie I'd never heard of the guy. But when I went back to the office, I checked to make sure. I don't know how he got his hands on press credentials, but I assure you Phillip Taylor does not work for us."

"Thanks, Betsy. I'll be in touch."

Barbara moved to where Susan and Otero-Hansen now stood.

"Sophia, where's numb nuts?"

"You mean my boss?"

"One and the same."

"He's in the SWAT vehicle in that office parking lot down the block, pretending to be one of the boys."

"Let's go see him."

"What's up?"

"You'll find out in a few minutes."

They walked down the street and turned the corner. Half-a-block down, they circled around behind an office building. Sophia Otero-Hansen banged on the side of the SWAT vehicle parked behind the building. When Lieutenant Whaley came out, Barbara said, "Is Bruce Lucas in there?"

Whaley sneered as though he'd had more than enough of Lucas. "Yeah."

"Would you kindly ask him to join us?"

Whaley opened the vehicle passenger door and called out, "Hey, Agent Lucas. Someone out here wants to talk with you."

Lucas joined them on the street. When he saw Barbara, Susan, and Otero-Hansen standing together, he asked, "What's this? A tea party?"

Lucas's comment was so blatantly sexist and insulting that Barbara was barely able to keep her feelings under control. She put her arm out and blocked Susan when her partner moved toward Lucas.

"I believe you said something about female cops being a waste. Well, I checked on the reporter you just released. He doesn't work for the *Herald-Tribune*, which means he's carrying forged press credentials." She let that settle in. "Which could mean you just released the killer." She paused again, then said, just as Sanjay Darzi walked up, "If women cops are a waste, then what are incompetent, misogynistic FBI agents?"

Lucas babbled for a few seconds and appeared to be about to respond, when Darzi said, "Come over here," and led Lucas away.

# CHAPTER 44

It took several minutes for Race's breathing to slow down to normal. It was bad enough he'd been surprised by the police on Chaco Loop. The fact that he could have been taken in and questioned had made it difficult to take even a shallow breath. He'd blown it. He'd almost irreparably blown it. Thank God he'd taken the time to disguise his appearance. He scratched at the phony beard, which had become hot and itchy.

He drove away from Chaco Loop and, by the time he'd parked on a residential street a few blocks away, had come to the conclusion that the police had things under control. If the Three Ghouls murderer aimed to rob the Franchini home, the cops would surely grab him. The same thing would probably transpire if he was after the Abbott collection in Monticello, Utah. Of course, the man could be after some other collector altogether, but how he could determine who that might be, Race had no clue.

The only option he seemed to have was to leave things in the hands of the police and return to Albuquerque. He'd never had the chance to go to the bank there where he had a safety deposit box. He would need to do that pretty quickly as he was low on cash. Maybe he'd stop for something to eat, drink a couple caffeinated colas, and hit the road. As he pulled away from the curb, he wondered if Jim Dunhill had ever contacted Nicholas Franchini. He called Dunhill's number.

"Jeez, Race, I've racked my brain for over an hour trying to figure out how to get hold of you."

Race realized he hadn't given Dunhill a number to call. He was so used to calling with burner phones and never giving out his numbers to anyone but Eric Matus that he'd stuck with normal procedure.

"Sorry, Jim. What's going on?"

"Nicholas Franchini moved to another address in Farmington about six weeks ago."

"Are you certain?"

"Yeah. When I didn't hear back from Franchini after ten calls, I accessed the Worldwide Coin Collectors website. They always post new members and change of contact information for old members on the site until the next annual membership directory is published. I checked to see if Franchini had moved. There was a cell phone number on the website that wasn't in the directory. I checked Franchini's Facebook page and learned from a post he'd placed weeks ago that they had a major water leak in their home and are renting a place across town until the reclamation work on their home is finished. After I couldn't get in touch with you, I tried to contact Franchini. Called the cell number ten minutes ago. No one answered."

Race's pulse pounded in his temples. "What's his new address?"

Dunhill recited the address and cell number. "Where are you now?"

"A few blocks away from the Franchini home on Chaco Loop."

"You're about a mile-and-a-half from the Franchini's new address."

"Hold on. I'm pulling it up on Google Maps."

While his cell phone uploaded the new address, Race muttered. "I noticed a sign in the front yard of the Chaco Loop place. Paul Shepherd Reclamations, or something like that."

"That's a national franchise operation," Dunhill said. "They come in when there's been storm damage or a water leak. Mold. That kind of stuff."

"That's why Franchini didn't shut off the phone at the Chaco place. Where he's staying now is just temporary."

"That makes sense. But I guarantee you he moved his coin safe with him. A serious collector would never leave his collection behind, even if he had a safe as solid as a bank vault."

Race shouted, "I got the directions to the new address. I'll call after I get there." He disconnected the call to Dunhill and dialed the Franchini cell number. It rang, but no one answered. He bounced his left foot on the floor board as he steered the truck away from the curb.

The route to the Franchini place on Burro Drive took him down to Main Street and onto the small bridge over the San Juan River. The thought crossed his mind that he should call the police, but this time he held off doing so. He could reach the Franchini home before the police could. He might be able to get the revenge he'd wanted for three years. But, if everything was okay at the Burro Drive location, he'd let Franchini call the police while he got out of town.

The pickup went airborne when Race hit a rise on the far side of the river bridge. The vehicle slewed left and Race almost lost control. He dropped his cell phone on the seat next to him as he grabbed the steering wheel with both hands to get control of the vehicle.

He picked up the cell phone as he raced toward Burro Drive and redialed the Franchini number. No answer again. He felt in his gut something was wrong.

He found the turnoff that would take him to Burro Drive and took the turn at speed. The vehicle slid sideways into the straightaway after he made the turn. His head slammed into the driver's side window as he tried to control the truck. Race cursed himself but didn't slow down. He turned right onto Burro Drive and looked for 1456.

The neighborhood was a collection of high-end residences on large lots. The only car Race saw parked on the street was a late model Audi across from 1456. He passed the sedan, executed a U-turn up the block, turned off his motor and headlights, and coasted back down the street. He stopped in front of the house one up from the Franchini residence, took his pistol from his briefcase, and left the pickup. He quietly closed the truck door and crouched as he approached the front of the house. He tested the door handle. Locked.

Race bent over as he moved toward the rear of the house. There were no lights on in rooms along the side of the place. But there appeared to be lights on at the back. When he reached the back corner, he saw that motion detector security lights were on along the rear of the residence. What he knew about this type of security light told him that movement would illuminate them and they would stay on for maybe a few minutes—depending on the setting. This told him that someone or something had recently tripped the motion detectors. He hoped he had arrived in time.

The rear of the house seemed to be relatively straight, except for a recessed area near the far end. A brick path led to a patio and the recessed area. Race moved to the patio and noticed that something flapped in the light breeze. As he came closer, he saw it was a curtain or drape caught in the patio door. He rushed to the door, tested the handle, and pushed inward.

He stepped into a large den, quietly closed the door behind him, and crept across the room to a corridor that appeared to parallel the back of the house. He stopped and listened for sound, but heard nothing. He saw the kitchen and dining room at the end of the corridor, to the right. He moved left, toward where he presumed the bedrooms were located.

The hall floor was Saltillo tile, covered intermittently with Navajo throw rugs. Race padded past the front entrance alcove to the first room on the left. He cracked the room door and saw in the slight bit of glow that leaked through a window a desk, two chairs, book shelves, and a six foot tall safe. The safe appeared to be closed.

The Amarillo police had guessed that the robbery at his house happened after the men beat Mary and threatened to hurt their daughters. Probably to coerce her into giving up the combination to Race's coin safe. If this invasion followed that MO, the intruder would threaten Nicholas Franchini or the man's wife, if he was married, get access to his coin collection, and then murder the couple.

He could wait in the hall outside the room with the safe. Sooner or later the intruder would force Franchini to open it.

Then a woman's scream reverberated through the house.

# CHAPTER 45

The fact that repeated phone calls to the Franchini phone at the Chaco Loop location were unanswered and had gone to voicemail had bothered Sophia Otero-Hansen for the last hour. Great, if Franchini was out of town. But what if he wasn't? What if the killer had already been here and gone? She moved to where Barbara was in conversation with Susan and shared her concern.

Barbara responded, "I've been thinking the same thing. Why don't you talk to Lucas about it? I have a very bad feeling we're wasting our time here."

Otero-Hansen did as Barbara suggested, but Lucas blew off her concern with, "They're probably just out of town."

"Then maybe we should pop the front door just to make certain they're not in there. The killer might have beaten us here."

Lucas poked her in the shoulder and growled, "Get out of my face."

Sanjay Darzi walked up at that moment and cleared his throat. "Perhaps you'd give Agent Lucas and me a moment," he told Otero-Hansen.

Obviously exasperated, she nodded and went over to where Barbara and Susan now stood by a sedan parked on the street.

"Didn't go well, did it?" Barbara asked.

Otero-Hansen told them what Lucas had said.

Barbara glanced at Darzi and Lucas. It seemed that the man

from Washington was giving Lucas an earful. She looked back at Susan and Otero-Hansen and said, "Lucas is such a dumbass; whatever he thinks has to be wrong." She pulled her cell phone from her jacket pocket and looked at the 800 number on the contractor sign in the front yard of the Franchini home.

Susan asked, "What are you doing?"

"Calling the contractor to see if he knows if the Franchinis are out of town."

Susan squinted. "Someone with the Farmington Police or the FBI must have already done that."

"Too obvious to have been skipped over, right?"

"Exactly. We couldn't be the only ones who thought about that."

Barbara said, "Wanna bet?" She stared at Otero-Hansen. "You aware of anyone checking with the Franchini's contractor?"

"For what reason?"

"Maybe the Franchinis moved . . . I don't know."

Red-faced, Otero-Hansen shook her head. "We got this address from the Farmington P.D."

"Where'd *they* get the address?"

Otero-Hansen shrugged. "From an anonymous caller who warned about a possible killer in the area."

Barbara looked at the contractor's sign in the front yard and then punched numbers into her cell phone. The phone rang six times before a woman answered. She hit the speaker button on the phone.

"Paul Shepherd Reclamations, emergency hotline. How may I help you?"

"This is Detective Barbara Lassiter with the Bernalillo County Sheriff's Department. Your company has a sign on a property at 127 Chaco Loop in Farmington, New Mexico. The owner's name is Franchini. Are you doing work at that location?"

"Hold on a second," the woman said. After a few seconds, she said, "Yes, that's a current job. Severe damage from a broken water pipe."

"Are the owners living in the residence while your people make repairs?"

Barbara heard tapping on a keyboard and then the woman said,

"No, they're staying in temporary quarters until the job is done."

"Can you give me their current address?"

"I don't think—"

"Ma'am, my badge number is 63267. As I said, I'm a detective with the Bernalillo County Sheriff's Office. It's a life or death situation. We're concerned for the safety of the Franchinis and are trying to locate them."

"I'm not allowed to give out that kind of information."

"Who can give me the address?"

"I would have to call my supervisor and—"

"I'll hold on this line while you call your supervisor." Barbara paused a beat and then added, "I just hope the killer who is after the Franchinis doesn't find them while I'm waiting for you and your supervisor."

"A killer."

"Yeah, lady. A killer."

"I guess I can give you the address." She went silent for a few seconds and then recited, "1456 Burro Drive." She paused again and said, "Perhaps I should give you their telephone number, too."

Barbara thanked the woman and hung up. Then she dialed the telephone number the woman had given her and, while it rang, she said to Susan, "The Franchini's moved while their home is under repair. We've been staking out an empty house."

Otero-Hansen's mouth dropped open. "Lucas will be pissed."

"He can kiss my ass," Barbara said. She cut off the call after it went unanswered.

Lucas walked up to them at that moment. "What are you girls talking about?"

No one responded.

Lucas shot them an evil look and marched off.

"Sophia, you have a car?" Barbara asked.

"I guess. Why?"

"I'm tired of doing nothing. Let's go to the Burro Drive address."

Otero-Hansen's mouth dropped open. She shook her head. "No way. I need my job."

"Then give me the keys to one of the bureau cars."

Otero-Hansen seemed unable to make a decision. She just

gaped at Barbara, But, after several seconds, she snapped her jaws closed and said, "Follow me." She led them to an unmarked car and pointed. "The keys are in the ignition. If anyone asks me, I'm going to say you must have stolen it."

"Okay. Give us five minutes, then tell Lucas about the Burro Drive house."

Otero-Hansen nodded, then said, "You're making a huge mistake."

"Whatever," Susan muttered.

Race tiptoed down the hall to the last door on the left.

The woman's screams continued, mixed with a man's shout. "Shut the hell up, you old bat." Then a sound that might have been someone being punched. Then another man yelled, "No, don't hurt her. I'll open the safe." Then another punch and a loud groan.

Race didn't like what he knew he had to do. It wasn't the smart option. But he didn't feel he had a choice. He couldn't stand outside the room while someone beat a woman to death. His pistol raised, he turned the handle on the door and slowly pushed it open. He stepped into a room lit only by a small bedside lamp. A man who stood in the middle of the room turned as he entered and fired a pistol at him.

Race felt as though he'd been clubbed with a baseball bat. His left arm, already hurting from the minor wound he'd suffered in the parking lot in Las Vegas, suddenly felt on fire as he spun around and fell face-down. The gunman stepped on Race's right hand, jerked the pistol away, and threw it across the room where it bounced off a dresser.

"Who the hell are you?" the guy shouted as he placed the muzzle of his weapon against the back of Race's head.

Race turned to face right and saw an elderly woman dressed in a nightgown on the floor, about eight feet away. Her face was covered in blood, as was the carpet beside her. She appeared to be unconscious. An elderly man dressed in pajamas lay on the carpet to the right of the woman, off to the side and slightly behind the gunman. His face was battered and bloody, but, unlike the woman, he was conscious. His eyes locked with Race's.

"You don't recognize me?" Race said.

The gunman grabbed Race's good arm and pulled him over onto his back. He squinted and seemed to study Race's face. "No, asshole, I never saw you before. Now answer my question. Who are you?"

The old man groaned, which diverted the gunman's attention for a split second, but he laughed and quickly turned his attention back to Race.

Race noticed the facial scars he'd seen before. Then he glanced down and saw the chains on the backs of the man's boots. He'd seen those chains just before he'd lost consciousness three plus years ago. "I remember *you*," Race said.

The guy snickered. "So, tell me when we met. I'd like to know before I blow your head off."

Race noticed the old man look over at the woman, close his eyes for a beat, and then look back at Race. There was a steely cast to his expression: his eyes narrowed, his jaw set. He slowly rolled to his side.

"Think back, asshole. Go back three years, three months. Remember being in Amarillo?"

The guy seemed to consider the question for a moment. "Sure. Mother and two young girls. Sweet stuff. So what?"

"You still don't recognize me?"

The guy continued to stare at Race. It took him a few seconds. "You're the husband. You came in just as we were about to leave." The man laughed. "I beat the shit out of you with a tire iron. Thought I killed you." He smiled. "Sure did a job on your face, didn't I? Nice scars."

Race felt blood run down his left arm. He felt light-headed. "You made a bad mistake, not killing me. Now you'll pay for what you did to my family."

This time, the guy laughed as though he'd just heard the funniest joke of all time. "Notice I'm the one holding the gun."

The old man rose to his knees behind the gunman.

"Killing me won't do you a bit of good. The police know you're in Farmington. They're on their way here now."

The laugh again. "So you stormed in here instead of waiting for the cops. You're full of shit. As much as I'm enjoying our conversation, I really don't have time to talk anymore. I think it's time I finished what I started in Amarillo." He laughed again.

The man's expression became gleeful. He moved his pistol to Race's forehead, just as the old man charged him from behind. The old man was built like a bowling ball and must have weighed at least two hundred pounds. He grabbed the man's gun hand as he collided with him and propelled him toward a dresser, near where Race's pistol had landed. Sickening thuds filled the room as they grappled with one another and crashed into the piece of furniture. The old man had both his hands on the other man's gun; the gunman pounded the old man's face with his free hand.

Excruciating pain shot through Race's arm as he struggled to his feet, picked up his pistol from the carpet in front of the dresser, and stuck the muzzle into the gunman's cheek. "You've got one second to let go of your weapon."

The guy groaned and released his hold on his own pistol, which the old man grabbed.

Race kept his weapon trained on the guy while he moved to the door and flipped a wall switch with the back of his right hand. Bright light flooded the room. Then he walked over to the old man who was on his back on the carpeted floor. He seemed dazed.

"Can you hear me?" Race said.

The old man shook his head, as though to clear it. "Yeah," he said. Then, "Karla. How's Karla?"

"Are you Franchini?"

The old man nodded.

"You need to lie still. I'll call the paramedics."

"Bullshit," Franchini cursed. He extended a hand to Race and offered him the pistol. Race placed his own weapon in the back of his waistband and took the gun from Franchini. The old man rolled to his knees and held onto the dresser as he stood. Race saw the intruder twitch and quickly stepped toward him. "You move and I'll shoot your ass. You got it?"

The man glared.

Then Race stepped next to Franchini. "There's a cell phone in my left jacket pocket, Mr. Franchini. Please take it out and call 9-1-1."

Franchini took the burner phone from Race's pocket and dialed the number. He gave the operator his name and address, told her that an intruder had entered his home and beaten him and his wife. He paused for a few seconds, then said, "I can't stay on the line. I have to take care of my wife." Then he cut off the call, returned the phone to Race's pocket, and removed a pillow from the bed. He placed the pillow under his wife's head. The old lady was crumpled on the floor. Blood oozed from her left temple and streamed from her nose and mouth.

"Take the case off the other pillow," Race told Franchini, "and try to stop the bleeding on your wife's head and face."

Karla Franchini moaned when her husband worked on her wounds.

"What are you going to do?" the intruder asked.

"Under any other circumstances, I'd do things to you that even you couldn't anticipate or imagine. But, since the paramedics and police are on their way here, I won't have time for that. I'll just have to shoot you."

He pointed the pistol at the man.

"No, wait. Maybe we can work something out."

Race was flabbergasted. But then he remembered there was something this guy could tell him that maybe no one else could. "What's your name?"

"Reese McCall."

"What do you do with the coins you steal?"

The guy just stared back at him.

"Last chance, asshole. Who hires you to do the robberies?"

The man's mouth dropped open. "How'd you—"

"Answer my question."

"Screw you."

Race pressed the muzzle of the weapon against the man's right shoulder and pulled the trigger. The pistol's report hurt his ears when it echoed off the walls, and almost covered the sounds of the man's screams. Almost.

Race pressed the pistol muzzle against the man's left shoulder. "Three seconds. That's all you have."

"No, wait. Wait. I'll tell you." McCall gulped and took in a slow, noisy breath. "Evan. His name is Evan."

Race pressed down harder. "Stop screwing around. What's his last name?"

The guy whimpered. "Evan McCall."

"McCall?"

"Yeah. He's my brother."

"Where can I find him?"

"Highland Village, near Dallas."

"What's his address?"

McCall blurted his brother's address.

Race checked on the elderly couple and saw that Mrs. Franchini had regained consciousness.

"Oh, Nicky," she said. "What happened?"

Franchini said, "Are you okay, honey?"

The women caressed her husband's cheek as tears flooded her eyes. "I'm fine, sweetie," she said through shuddering sobs.

"I have to get out of here," Race said. "I know it's a lot to ask, but you'd do me a huge favor if you didn't mention to anyone what I said about the robbery in Amarillo."

Franchini shot Race a weak smile. "What robbery in Amarillo?" Then he said to his wife, "This man saved our lives."

"I understand," she said and smiled weakly. "I know nothing."

The old man tried to laugh, but all that came out was a groan. He looked at Race and said, "A friend of yours called here a little while ago. Told me your name. Said you were on your way here. I suppose you'd like me to forget about that phone call."

Race smiled at the man. "That would really be helpful."

Franchini said, "It's amazing how forgetful you get as you age." Then he frowned and said, "You're bleeding."

Race looked at his arm and the blood that flowed onto the carpet.

Franchini struggled to his feet, used the bed for support, and pulled the belt from a bathrobe at the bottom of the bed. He shuffled over and tied the belt around Race's arm, above the wound.

"You should get that looked at."

Race smiled. "I can't very well go to a hospital."

Franchini nodded. "There's a guy who owes me. Got a little clinic over in Aztec. You think you can drive that far?"

Race thought about it. Did he dare take the chance of putting himself in the hands of a stranger? He realized he didn't have much choice. "Yeah, I can make it there."

Franchini gave him a name and address. "Drive straight to that location. I'll call him. He'll meet you there."

Race nodded. Then he told McCall to stand up.

McCall grunted as he rolled to his knees and stood.

Race pushed him with the pistol down the hall to the front door.

"Open it," Race ordered.

When they were a few steps from the door, on the cement walkway to the street, Race clubbed McCall on the back of his neck and kicked the back of his right leg. McCall dropped as though he'd been pole-axed. Race walked around in front of him.

"Let's work something out," McCall said.

"I'm going to shoot you three times," Race said.

McCall's eyes were like saucers.

"I just want you to understand that one bullet is for my wife, Mary, one for my daughter, Sara, and one for my daughter, Elizabeth. You'll bleed out before help arrives, and you'll be in agony until you die."

Race placed the pistol muzzle against the guy's abdomen and pulled the trigger three times. He slipped the weapon into a jacket pocket, knelt, and took a coin from a pants pocket. He wiped the coin on his shirt to eliminate prints and stuffed it into one of the abdominal wounds. McCall squealed like a wounded animal. Race repeated the process twice more, putting coins in the other two abdominal wounds.

Barbara drove the FBI vehicle at breakneck speed toward the Burro Drive location. Twice, she came close to going off the road into a ditch.

"If you don't kill us first, I suspect Lucas or Lieutenant Salas will."

Barbara was pretty certain Susan was only slightly exaggerating their situation. "You want to go in like the Marines or pussyfoot around?"

"Semper fi, baby. Semper fi."

234

"I figure we're maybe a mile out."

Race heard the noise of a high-powered engine. It sounded like a high-performance engine in a police cruiser. He fast-walked to his truck and cranked the engine. On his way out of the neighborhood, a white sedan sped past him, going toward the Franchini house. A couple minutes later, he heard multiple far-off sirens as he drove back across the river bridge. Like a good citizen, he pulled over when an ambulance, several cars with roof lights flashing, and a SWAT vehicle roared toward him.

# CHAPTER 46

Barbara watched paramedics drive away with the Franchinis. Then she and Susan moved from the street to the front of the house and observed two Farmington detectives work the scene around a body near the home's front door. One of the detectives told Farmington Police Chief Summers that he'd called the New Mexico Office of the Medical Investigator in Albuquerque to give them a heads-up that a body would be transported there.

"Good. Let's make sure that happens as quickly as possible."

"Real circus," Barbara whispered to Susan. "The dead guy looks like one of the men in the Brownell video. See the tats."

"Yeah. The good things that came out of this little road trip of ours are that it appears the last of the Three Ghouls is dead and Bruce Lucas came off looking like a dufus."

"Always smart to find the good in everything," Barbara said.

Agents Sophia Otero-Hansen and Allen Vincent exited the front door of the house and joined them. Vincent pointed at the body. "Wonder who killed him."

"Did Franchini say anything?" Susan asked.

Vincent shrugged and pointed again at the corpse. "Said a man came in shortly after this guy arrived. Told us he wore a mask, like a balaclava. Claims he and his wife would be dead if it weren't for the masked man."

"Could he give any description of the man?" Barbara asked.

Otero-Hansen said, "Franchini told us he was in a lot of pain and slipped in and out of consciousness. He couldn't tell us anything more."

"What about the wife?"

Otero-Hansen said, "Mrs. Franchini claims this asshole knocked her out and that she didn't regain consciousness until the paramedics arrived. She didn't see or hear a thing."

"They'd have a real good reason to try to protect the shooter," Susan said.

"You have to make allowances for my partner," Barbara said. "She's very cynical."

A sly smile creased Susan's lips. "Gee, what if the shooter was the reporter Lucas released a little while ago?"

"Now that would be a great ending to an otherwise shitty day."

Barbara laughed. "By the way, did anyone check out that Audi parked on the street?"

"Oh, yeah," Vincent said. "It's registered to a Farmington woman. A Katherine Luneski. The locals called her home and sent an officer there. They haven't been able to locate her."

"Or her body?" Susan said.

"Yeah," Vincent continued. "That asshole there probably murdered her for the car."

"Anything else in the vehicle?" Barbara asked.

"We found a backpack with a change of clothes, almost fifty thousand dollars in cash, and some very valuable jewelry."

"No coins?" Otero-Hansen asked.

Barbara noticed Vincent grimace and slightly shake his head at Otero-Hansen. Then he walked into the Franchini house. She looked at Otero-Hansen who turned her gaze away.

One of the Farmington detectives looked up at Otero-Hansen. "Did you say something about coins?"

Otero-Hansen suddenly seemed out of sorts. She mumbled something unintelligible and went inside the house.

Barbara moved a step toward the detective. "What about coins?"

"I've never seen anything like this." He pointed a pocket flashlight at the wounds in the dead man's torso. Something shined under the light beam.

Susan stepped up next to Barbara. "What is it?"

"Looks like coins," the detective said. "Three of them."

The second detective went down on his knees and leaned in to look more closely. He chuckled. "Like someone left a calling card."

Race opened the driver's side window despite the freezing temperature. Anything to keep him alert. He felt faint, on top of being exhausted. The bathrobe belt around his left upper arm had stopped the bleeding, but he'd lost a lot of blood before Franchini had applied the tourniquet. He steered the truck with his knees while he rubbed his face with his right hand, which gave him momentary relief from overwhelming fatigue.

After fifteen minutes on the road, he found the address Franchini had given him. He shook his head as though to clear it and squinted at the sign on the building: Atcitty Animal Clinic. He looked left and right of the building, but there was no medical clinic. He checked the address again and wondered if he'd misunderstood Franchini. Then he smiled and thought that Franchini was a pretty smart man. A veterinarian was a better option than a hospital or medical clinic. The police would more than likely call and visit those places once they discovered that some of the blood on the Franchini bedroom carpet belonged to someone other than the Franchinis and Reese McCall.

He struggled to exit the pickup truck and staggered toward the clinic's front door. A man in street clothes opened the door as he reached it.

"You'd better let me help you," the man said, as he took Race's arm.

"Nicholas Franchini sent me."

"Yeah, I know. I'm Doctor Joseph Atcitty. Let's go into my surgery."

Race attempted a laugh but all that came out was a cough. He swallowed and said, "Thank you."

Atcitty moved Race to a room with a stainless steel table, white cabinets, and a linoleum floor. A huge lamp hung over the table. He helped him onto the table and said, "You'll have to lie on your right side and bring up your knees. My usual patient is nowhere near as tall as you."

This time Race emitted a low laugh that sounded to him like more groan than laugh.

"I'll give you local anesthetic. Try to relax. I suspect you'll feel some pain."

Race nodded and closed his eyes as Atcitty cut away his jacket and shirt sleeves. He felt the man wash the wound and then inject his arm several times. Some time passed—he wasn't sure how much—before the doctor held his arm with one hand and inserted something into the bullet wound. He felt lightheaded and had an irresistible need to sleep.

The next thing Race knew, he was on the surgical room floor with a pillow under his head. It took a few seconds to realize where he was and why. He looked at his injured arm and touched the bandage around the bicep. As he attempted to sit up, Atcitty entered.

"How's the patient?"

Race succeeded in rising to a sitting position and slid against a cabinet for support. "Not too bad, Doc."

"I tried to carry you into my office, to the couch there, but you were too heavy. I couldn't leave you on the table."

"How's my arm?"

"I removed a bullet and gave you a shot to prevent infection. I'll give you some antibiotic pills, antibiotic ointment, and bandages before you leave. I'm sure there's an interesting story about all this."

Race shrugged, then moved to stand; Atcitty quickly came over and helped him to his feet.

"You should really rest."

"I'm sure you're right."

"Sounds as though you're not going to heed my advice."

"I wish I had the luxury. What time is it?"

Atcitty looked at his wristwatch. "4:35 a.m."

Race nodded. "I'd better hit the road. What do I owe you?"

Atcitty waved a hand to dismiss Race's question. "No charge."

Race tilted his head and asked, "Why'd you help me? You put yourself in jeopardy."

The doctor smiled, then he pressed his lips together and his eyes hardened. "I don't know if you're familiar with Navajo life, but family and clan are foremost in Navajo culture. Just the act of leaving the reservation can be exceedingly traumatic for us. But that's what I did. I attended UNM undergraduate school and UC Davis vet school. When I came back home to open a business, I couldn't find a bank that would finance my practice. I was discouraged and angry . . . but then I met Nicholas Franchini. He loaned me the money to get into business on an interest-free basis and gave me all his business. He has a stable of quarter horses that I take care of. Then he spread the word all over the Four Corners area that I was his veterinarian of choice. Now I have more business than I can handle and I'm interviewing for a second doctor to add to my practice. I would do anything for the Franchinis . . . including putting myself in jeopardy."

Race stepped forward and stuck out his hand. Atcitty took it and they shook. "Thanks again, Doc."

"Be careful driving. Try to get some rest as soon as you can."

"I'll do my best."

Race wasn't just tired. He felt depleted of all energy and emotion. For three years, he'd told himself that his campaign of revenge would be over when the men who murdered his family were all dead. But now there was one more man who had to pay: Evan McCall, Reese McCall's brother. And he might very well be the worst of the lot. Apparently, to accumulate valuable coins, he had coldly, without concern for innocent people, turned Reese McCall and his cronies loose to torture and murder.

After he stopped at a gas station in Bloomfield and filled the truck's tank, he used the rest room to change from the green surgical scrubs Atcitty had given him to a clean shirt, khakis, and a light zippered jacket. He removed his false beard and mustache and tossed them along with the wig he'd worn into the trash. Outside, the cold cut right through his jacket and seemed to penetrate his bones. Back behind the wheel, he decided he would charter a plane in Albuquerque to fly him to Dallas. He'd long ago established a rule of not using commercial airlines because he didn't want to be at the mercy of their rigid schedules and delays, and because he didn't want to go through security screenings.

Race drove south toward Albuquerque, but found himself dozing off. He nearly ran off the road a half-dozen times. By the time he reached Cuba, a sleepy hamlet that was essentially a speed trap in the middle of not much else, he could no longer stay awake. He found a motel that accepted cash without ID and took a room. After he set the alarm on his cell phone to 9 a.m., he kicked off his shoes, crawled under the covers, and immediately fell asleep.

The FBI contingent, along with Barbara and Susan, landed back in Albuquerque at 6:50 a.m. Lucas and Darzi, without even a thank you or a goodbye, marched off together. Vincent and Otero-Hansen shook hands with Barbara and Susan, thanked them for their help, and then took off.

Barbara and Susan retrieved their Crown Vic in the parking lot and, with Barbara behind the wheel, drove away from the airport toward Interstate 25.

"You have any questions you'd like to ask?" Barbara said.

"Ha. As many as I suspect you have."

"You go first."

"Did you see Agent Vincent's reaction when Sophia asked about coins in the backpack they found in the stolen Audi?"

"Yeah. And I saw Sophia turn red when Vincent glared at her, and again when that detective asked if she had mentioned coins."

"Little slip of the tongue. But what's the significance of her question? What's the importance of coins?"

"I don't know the answers to those questions," Barbara said, "but I suspect our vigilante was the guy who killed that S-O-B who attacked the Franchinis and probably murdered Mrs. Katz. The coins in the dead guy's wounds clarified that. He left them as calling cards."

"Too bad we don't have a clue about his name."

"Yeah. But we now know what he looks like, assuming he wasn't wearing a disguise."

"You think it was the man with the fake press credentials."

"I do. But I'm not so sure his press ID was counterfeit."

"You're giving me a headache, Babs. If his ID was real, how the heck did he get it? Betsy Jaramillo said there's no one named Phillip

Taylor at the paper."

"How the heck, indeed."

"You know, something else just hit me," Susan said. "Let's check with OMI tomorrow about the three coins."

"What's that going to tell us?"

"If the killer—*if* the shooter is our dark angel—follows his usual MO, then maybe the number of wounds in McCall and the number of coins means something."

# CHAPTER 47

After she showered and put on clean clothes, Barbara picked up Susan at her home. She then drove to Weck's Restaurant on Louisiana and ordered enchiladas with a fried egg, coffee, and an orange juice. Susan ordered hot tea and an English muffin.

"It's going to be a long day," Barbara said. "That's all you're eating?"

"Yep. Important to watch my curves." Susan smiled. "I'm thinking Bruce Lucas turned up his nose at the way I was dressed because he thought I didn't look good in my jeans."

Barbara had just taken a drink of coffee. She coughed at Susan's remark. As coffee leaked from her nose, she grabbed her napkin and tried to stifle her laughter.

Susan smiled. "What's wrong, partner? I'm serious."

"You've never been serious a day in your life. Look what you made me do. I got coffee on my white blouse."

After breakfast, Barbara drove downtown and left the car in the underground lot.

"You call Salas and tell him we're back?" Susan asked.

"No. I mean, we weren't gone that long. It's not like we missed any duty time."

They exited the elevator and entered the homicide squad room at 8:30.

"Uh, oh," Susan muttered.

"What?" Barbara asked.

"You can't feel it? It's too quiet. Something's up."

Barbara looked around the squad room and whispered, "Yeah, I see what you mean."

One of the male detectives came in from the break room with a cup of coffee in hand. When he looked at them, he grimaced and tipped his head in the direction of Salas's office. "You'd better get it over with."

"Oh, boy," Susan said.

They dropped their purses in drawers in their desks and looked at one another.

"Let's wait 'til he summons us," Susan suggested.

"Okay, but—"

Salas's high-pitched voice cut through the oppressive silence in the squad room. "Lassiter, Martinez, get your butts in here."

"Sounds like a summons to me," Susan said.

Barbara hustled toward Susan and grabbed her arm. "Please don't say anything that could be construed as sarcasm, disrespect, or humor."

Susan raised her eyebrows. "*Moi?*"

Barbara thought, *This will not be good.*

She led the way to Salas's office, knocked on the door jamb, and walked up to the lieutenant's desk.

"You wanted to see us?"

In less than a second, Salas's face turned apoplectic-red.

"When I got in here this morning I picked up the message you left on my office phone. Do I understand correctly that you two were in Farmington last night?" He coughed, which made his face redder. "With the FBI!"

Barbara opened her mouth to respond, but Salas raised a finger to stop her.

"Why didn't you call my cell? You could have asked my permission."

"It was nearly midnight, Lieutenant. I didn't want to wake you."

"Bullshit. You didn't want me to tell you not to go."

"There's that," Susan muttered.

"What was that, Martinez?"

"Nothing, Lou. Just clearing my throat."

Barbara said, "We were invited by the Bureau to go to Farmington. We tied the Flagstaff and Socorro videos together, which allowed the Feds to close in on the last of the Three Ghouls killers."

"The what?"

"Three Ghouls. The guys doing the home invasions where dozens of people have been murdered."

"So, you two just took off with the Feds, without my permission, without even a 'Lieutenant, would it be okay if we take a trip with the Federal Bureau of Investigation to go find a mass murderer'?"

"Well, I did call and—"

"You must think I'm stupid."

Salas turned his gaze on Susan and gave her a look that seemed to dare her to say something.

Barbara felt her own face go hot as she turned to look at Susan. She said a silent prayer that her partner would keep her mouth shut. For a second, she was relieved that Susan appeared to do just that. But then her heart seemed to drop into her stomach when Susan's eyes went wide and she spread her arms and tilted her head.

Salas jumped out of his chair, which turned over and crashed into a bookcase. A plant on the bookcase's top shelf fell to the floor and exploded in a mass of dirt, broken stems and leaves, and pottery shards. He jabbed a finger at Barbara, then at Susan.

"You don't work for the damned FBI; you work for the Bernalillo County Sheriff's Office." His voice rose another octave. He pointed at his chest. "You work for me."

He looked down at the mess on the floor, then back up at them.

"As of this second, you two are suspended. One week. That will hopefully give you time to get your heads screwed on right. Give me your sidearms and shields."

Barbara placed her service revolver and shield on Salas's desk, wheeled around, and walked out. She looked over her shoulder and had a sinking feeling when she saw Susan hadn't moved.

"Oh, shit," she said under her breath, and turned back to pull her partner out of Salas's office. She was just an arm's length away, when Susan stepped forward, placed her sidearm and shield on the desk, pointed at the mess on the floor, and said, "Didn't your wife give you that plant, Lieutenant?"

The veins in Salas's forehead bulged and his face turned purple. "That's two weeks, Martinez. You want to go for three?"

Susan did an about face and moved past Barbara, who followed her to their desks.

"Was it worth two weeks' pay?" Barbara asked.

"You betcha, Babs. You betcha."

Barbara returned to her desk, took her purse from a drawer, and looked at Susan.

"You ready to go?"

"Sure. But we need a ride."

"Why's that?"

"We're suspended, so we probably aren't allowed to use the department-issued vehicle."

"You recall the lieutenant saying anything about not using a car?"

"No."

"Well, there you go."

In the elevator down to the parking lot, Susan said, "You know, I was thinking about something. No one has ever found any DNA or fingerprint evidence left by the vigilante killer. The guy has always been so cautious, apparently carefully planning his murders. But I don't think he had time to plan the shooting in Farmington. Not if he's the same guy who showed up at the Chaco address impersonating a reporter."

"Yeah, but we don't know if it's the same guy."

"True. But let's say for a minute it was the same guy. If it was, he showed up at the Franchini's former house on Chaco because he thought they still lived there. Maybe it was the guy with the Press I.D. who called Farmington P.D. Then Lucas kicked him off the site and we later discovered he wasn't a reporter after all. What if he then went to the Franchini's new address? He had no time to plan much of anything. He followed the intruder into the house, confronted him, and shot him."

Barbara turned one hand palm up. "And your point is . . . ."

"My point is that he might have left behind fingerprints or hair. Maybe we could track the guy down forensically."

Barbara breathed out loudly. "I wonder if the Farmington P.D. found any trace evidence."

"Maybe Sophia knows."

Barbara handed Susan her cell phone and asked her to pull up Otero-Hansen's number in her recently called list. Susan connected with Otero-Hansen, put the cell on speaker, and asked about the crime scene processing order in Farmington.

Otero-Hansen said, "That was Farmington P.D.'s crime scene. Maybe you should call up there."

"That could be a problem," Barbara said.

"Why's that?"

"Well, Susan and I have been suspended for two weeks."

"What?"

"Yeah, our boss is pissed about the little joy ride we took with you to Farmington."

"Speaking of joy rides, Lucas was pissed off beyond all belief when he discovered you took off in a bureau vehicle."

"Oh, boy," Susan groaned.

Otero-Hansen laughed. "Darzi told Lucas to keep his mouth shut about the whole thing."

As soon as Otero-Hansen hung up, Susan called OMI and asked to speak to Martin Wulfe. She put her cell on speaker while she waited for the Chief Field Investigator to answer.

"Wulfe."

"Hey, Wulfie, it's Susan Martinez."

"I'm busy here. Unless you're calling to invite me to lunch, I don't have time to talk right now."

"Okay, Wulfie, I'll buy lunch. Just one question. How many coins were found in the wounds on that corpse transported from Farmington last night?"

"Why?"

"Come on, Wulfie. It's a simple question that deserves a simple answer."

"Well, since you're buying lunch. There were three coins inserted in the guy's abdominal wounds. One in each wound."

"Anything else placed anywhere else in or on the body?"

"Nope. Just the three coins."

"Thanks, Wulfie. Any other evidence from the crime scene?"

"Hard to believe, but we found nothing. The crime scene photographs showed blood on the carpet in the Franchini bedroom. We took samples, but, without a DNA match in the system, we have nothing to compare them to. By the time the OMI techs arrived there from Albuquerque, the whole house had been vacuumed and scrubbed clean. The carpet in the bedroom had been pulled up and disposed of. There wasn't a fingerprint in the place."

"How the hell did that happen? That's dereliction of duty."

"Farmington P.D. put an auxiliary officer on the Franchini house. Someone called him and told him he was being pulled off the site. Told him to drive out to the Navajo Irrigation Project to check on a fatal accident. The guy left the house and drove around for hours before calling in to the station to get the exact location of the accident."

"The poor schlub," Susan said.

"When are we having lunch?"

"I'll get back to you on that."

"That's about thirty-five lunches you owe me, Martinez."

"You know I'm good for them."

"Yeah, yeah."

"That was interesting," Barbara said.

Susan said, "Yeah. You know there was only one time that we're aware of when the Three Ghouls killed three people: the home invasion in Amarillo. Almost every incident involved two victims; usually elderly couples. The Flagstaff incident involved five victims. And there was one time when there were four people killed."

"What are you thinking?"

"There were three bullet wounds in McCall's abdomen and a coin placed in each of those wounds."

"Huh."

"This case has got me tied up, twisted, and beyond frustrated," Susan complained as Barbara pulled up in front of her house.

"Maybe our suspensions are a good thing. We need a break."

"To do what? You gave up drinking a while ago. Neither of us skis. Besides, I despise being cold. And the weather's not conducive to playing golf or tennis."

Barbara sniffed. "Since when do you play golf or tennis?"

Susan hunched her shoulders and spread out her arms. "Just saying. I know I'd look good in those little short skirts the women wear."

"I have something else in mind. Henry has a friend at the "U" who would like to meet you. Teaches in the Latin American Studies Department."

Susan frowned, but quickly smiled. "Latin American Studies, huh?"

"That's right."

"When?"

"How about tonight? There's a great band at Blacky's. Dinner first. Good conversation. Some dancing. Who knows where it might lead?"

"What's the guy's name?"

"You know, I forgot to ask. He'll tell you when he picks you up tonight."

For maybe the thousandth time, Kathy Luneski swore she would never take another drink as long as she lived. Her eyelids felt as though they were glued to her eyeballs and her head felt as though a jack-hammer banged away at her brain. Eyes still closed, she moved her left hand around until it fell off the side of what she guessed was a bed.

"Where the hell am I?" she muttered. She dropped one leg over the side of the bed and rolled until her feet touched the floor. She covered her mouth as a wave of nausea overwhelmed her. She couldn't decide what she needed more, to puke or to pee.

The jack-hammering began again. She covered her ears with her hands. Then she realized someone was banging at the door. She pried open her eyelids and looked around. It didn't take long to realize she was in a motel room. "How the hell did I get here?" she asked herself.

The knocking began again. "Hold your horses," she tried to shout, but her words came out through her dry throat as an unintelligible series of rasps.

She groaned like an old buffalo as she unsteadily stood and walked to the door. A peek through the peephole told her nothing. Her eyes weren't working that well. She opened the door and looked down at a diminutive woman in jeans, a blouse, and a ratty sweater.

"You want your room made up?" the woman asked.

"Where am I?" Luneski asked.

"Where are you?"

"Yeah, where the hell am I?"

"You're in room 121 at the Dew Drop Inn. Are you okay?"

Luneski pushed past the woman and looked left and right. No Audi. Then a wave of nausea hit her again and she pushed past the woman into the parking lot.

# CHAPTER 48

Evan McCall felt as though he'd overdosed on speed. It wasn't like his brother to not call him after completion of an assignment. Considering the amount of money that Reese would get from the Franchini job, it was incredible his brother hadn't already contacted him. He checked online to see if there was any news about a home invasion in Farmington, but, as yet, there was nothing.

Then his jitters turned into a massive headache when his cell phone rang and he saw the caller ID: Vitaly Orlov. For a moment, he considered ignoring the call, but he knew that would only put off dealing with the problem, and the longer Orlov had to wait to talk with him the angrier the Russian would get.

"Hello."

"You hear anything?" Orlov said in heavily-accented English. "Here" sounded like "heerre," propelled on a blast of breath.

"Nothing yet. He may not . . . acquire the goods until tonight."

"I thought you said he vould act quickly."

"Yeah. But it's a long way from where he was to where he had to go. I'll let you know the second I hear something."

"There vas news item about voman murdered near that area. Maybe your man did that."

McCall's breath caught in his chest; his lungs seemed to have stopped working. He hadn't heard about the murder, but if his brother had murdered a woman . . . . What the hell had his psycho brother done now?

"He's a professional, Mr. Orlov. He'll get the job done just like always."

"I don't like vhat I hear in your voice, McCall. You're not screwing vith me, are you?"

"Of course not. I—"

"I've paid you over million dollars in last five years. This job is biggest I've ever given you. Big bucks for you."

McCall wanted to remind the man that for every dollar Orlov had paid him, the mobster had probably received at least ten. But he didn't have the nerve.

"Give me a few hours, Mr. Orlov. I'll hear from my guy by then."

"It's 9:30. I expect to hear from you by 6 tonight." The man paused for a second, and then added, "Maybe I should come to your place? I can pick up goods from Flagstaff job and you can bring me up to date on Farmington."

"Yes, sir."

McCall heard Orlov mutter something in Russian just before he terminated the call. He stared at his cell and felt acid leak into his stomach. Orlov hadn't said anything about the two men whose bodies were discovered in a van in New Mexico. The news media had already announced the connection between those two men and the Three Ghouls, so Orlov had to know that Reese's two partners were no longer in the picture. He'd never told Orlov the names of the three men, or that his own brother headed up the crew. But the Russian did know about the horrific crimes the three had committed in conjunction with the coin robberies. He'd screamed when the news had picked up the story about the first home invasion five years ago, about how children had been assaulted and killed. But, in the end, all Orlov cared about were the rare coins and making a fortune when he, in turn, sold them to private collectors who couldn't have cared less about the coins' bloody provenance. Nor did Orlov or the collectors care that there was blood on the coins.

McCall had been horrified by what his brother had done. He'd always known there was something off about Reese. As a kid, his brother would pull wings off butterflies and torment cats and dogs in the neighborhood. But, until he tortured and murdered coin collectors and their families, he'd had no idea just how off he was. After his last conversation with Reese, he'd decided it was time to bail out of this arrangement with the Russian mobster and to sever his ties to his brother. What Reese had done tortured his mind; Orlov scared the crap out of him.

Race woke ten minutes before his alarm went off. He felt lightheaded and slightly feverish. He popped one of the pills Doctor Atcitty had given him and re-bandaged his wound. He left Cuba at 10:15 a.m. after he applied a disguise that matched his Arnold Webber identity on a New Mexico driver's license. He ate a light breakfast in a diner. With a 1:00 p.m. departure time out of the private air terminal in Albuquerque, he figured he had time to stop at his Albuquerque bank on the way.

After an hour-and-twenty-minute drive, he arrived at the bank and parked in a lot across from the entrance. He removed his briefcase from the front seat and carried it into the bank.

The entrance included two sets of doors with a small foyer between them. Race walked to the far end of the lobby where he was greeted by a young woman who he didn't recognize from his previous visits. *That's good*, he thought.

"May I help you?" she asked.

Race smiled and handed her the key to his box and his Arnold Webber photo ID. "I need to access my safety deposit box."

She barely glanced at the ID. "Of course. Please sign the log and I'll take you right into the vault." While Race signed the log, she said, "You know next month we're converting to a handprint system for entry to the vault. You'll need to come in after the first of the month so we can put your print into our system."

Race didn't like this news one bit. The last thing he wanted to do was put his hand print into a system that could be accessed by law enforcement agencies. He would have to check with the banks where he had other safety deposit boxes to see if they were about to convert their systems as well. "I'll do that," he told the woman.

It took all of three minutes after the woman used the bank's and Race's keys to open his box, place it on a table in an adjoining private booth, and leave Race on his own. He would not return to this bank again, so he removed all of the cash from the box: over five hundred thousand dollars, and stacked it in his briefcase, after he took a 9 millimeter from the case and stuck it behind his back—inside his waistband. He made certain his fleece coat covered the gun, then returned to the vault, replaced the box in its slot, and locked the safety deposit box door. He asked the woman to lock her side of the box door, thanked her, and moved toward the entrance. Outside, he moved to his pickup truck, unlocked the front passenger door, and tossed his briefcase on the front seat. He was about to step up behind the wheel when a jacked-up pickup truck pulled into the lane between the bank entrance and the parking lot. Two men leaped from the truck's front and back seats on the passenger side. Race thought he saw a third man exit the truck from the back seat on the driver's side. The two men on his side of the truck carried shotguns and wore masks.

Race shook his head. "Shit," he muttered. Out of nowhere, he remembered the saying, Timing is everything. "This is pretty shitty timing," he muttered.

He looked at the pickup truck driver whose head jerked around like a bobble head toy. Race slipped his cell phone from his jacket pocket and called 9-1-1.

"What's your emergency?"

"I'm parked outside the People's Thrift Bank on Jefferson, south of Paseo del Norte. Armed men just rushed inside the bank. There's a black pickup truck out front with a driver inside."

When the 9-1-1 operator asked for his name, Race disconnected the call. As he replaced the phone in his pocket, his heart seemed to stop. The driver had spotted him and now stared directly at him. The man suddenly pointed a huge pistol at him and fired a round through the open passenger side window of the black pickup.

As Race ducked behind his open truck door, he slammed his bandaged arm against the edge of the door. "Shit," he cursed as pain ripped through him. He expected to hear the "clunk" of the bullet strike his pickup, but the round apparently sailed past him. He pulled his gun from the back of his waistband, propped it between the door and the truck frame, aimed, and fired three shots. The man jerked sideways, then slammed forward against the pickup truck's steering wheel. The truck's horn steadily blared and the man remained still.

Race climbed inside his truck and sped away from the parking lot as three men raced out of the bank. They carried nothing but their shotguns. Race guessed the blaring truck horn had caused them to abandon their plan to rob the bank.

It was a twenty-minute drive on southbound Interstate 25 to the Albuquerque Sunport's private air terminal. It took Race almost the entire twenty minutes to calm down. He forced himself to stick to the speed limit as a caravan of police vehicles, emergency lights flashing, rushed north. He felt a flash of anguish hit his brain. So much death. Ever since Eric Matus had been killed, he'd questioned the mission they'd been on. But he segregated the sudden spasm of guilt into a corner of his brain. As much as he wanted to quit, there was still work to be done.

At the airport, he removed the Arnold Webber disguise and applied his Karl Simmons disguise to match the Texas ID. He checked the disguise in the truck's rearview mirror—dark glasses, false mustache and beard, a Beatles hair piece, and a red baseball cap. Then he slipped his 9 millimeter under the front seat, left the truck in the parking lot, and entered the terminal. He apologized for being fifteen minutes late, went through a scanner, was escorted to the jet he'd chartered, was handed a drink by an attendant on board the plane, and was asked to fasten his seat belt. The charter had cost him twenty-two thousand dollars for a round-trip flight to and from Dallas.

After takeoff, he opened Google Map on his phone and familiarized himself with the location of Evan McCall's address near Dallas and the best route to it from the airport. Then he located a pawn shop between the airport and Highland Village.

The plane landed at 4:05 p.m., Dallas time. It was bright and sunny, although very cool. Race picked up the rental car he'd reserved with a black market credit card he'd bought on the Dark Net and took State Road 114 to State Road 121, where he stopped at the pawn shop he'd identified.

"Howdy," Race said to the man behind the counter.

"How can I help you, sir?"

"You have any automatics for sale?"

"Pistols?"

"Yeah."

"I got 'em out the wazoo. Anything in particular you want?"

"A 9 millimeter with an extra magazine. I'd also like to buy a knife. Eight inch blade."

"If you want to walk out with the pistol you'll need a Texas ID."

Race pulled his wallet from a pants pocket, took out a falsified Texas driver's license from between his false California, New Mexico, and Nevada IDs, and handed it to the man.

"All right, Mr. Simmons," the man said, "let's see what we've got for you."

Race was in and out of the shop in fifteen minutes. He drove on the 35 Interstate to the Highland Village community, near Lewisville Lake. He arrived at McCall's address at 5:25 p.m.

McCall lived in a single-family, detached residence on a serpentine road packed with upper middle-class houses and plenty of expensive SUVs and luxury sedans. Spacious, immaculate lawns fronted the houses.

There were no children's toys on the lawn in front of McCall's place. Race muttered, "Damn," when he thought that he should have asked Reese McCall if his brother had a family. A wife and kids at McCall's home would seriously complicate things in ways he didn't really want to think about. He parked on the street behind McCall's block, put his weapon inside the back of his waistband, took the sheathed knife from his briefcase, and put it in his jacket pocket. Then he circled the block on foot.

Evan McCall had grown steadily more agitated as each hour passed and he hadn't heard from his brother, Reese. Every minute that took him closer to his meeting with Orlov only made him more anxious and fearful.

When 5 p.m. came and went, and he hadn't heard from his brother, McCall had begun to suspect that something was terribly wrong. He went to his computer and checked Google for Farmington news once again. What he saw this time made him frantic: *Unidentified Man Killed in Home Invasion. Local Couple Injured.* McCall read the article and, although his brother wasn't named, he knew that Reese was dead as soon as he read the Franchini name. But he was confused by the section of the article that dealt with who had killed the intruder. The shooter wasn't identified either.

McCall was certain of a few things. Once Reese's picture was in the news, someone would recognize him and notify the cops. It would be a no-brainer for the cops to then identify next of kin. That would be him. At that point, there was a strong possibility Orlov would eliminate him.

McCall quickly packed a suitcase and removed his cash, passport, and the coins from the Flagstaff caper from his wall safe. He checked his watch and saw it was 5:30. He had thirty minutes before Orlov showed up. Suitcase in one hand, he went to the front door to lock up before he went to the garage. As he raised his hand to turn the dead bolt, the doorbell rang. His heart, which already beat frenetically, suddenly seemed to hammer at the inside of his ribs as though it wanted to escape his body.

"Oh dear God," he rasped. "Orlov."

He knew he was done for. He opened the door. He breathed a sigh of relief when he saw a stranger there. "What do you want?"

Race looked at the suitcase in the man's hand. "Going somewhere?"

"What the fuck business is that of yours?"

Race shook his head, stepped forward, punched McCall in the center of his chest, and watched him drop the suitcase and fall backward to the floor. Race used a foot to push the suitcase against a wall. The man's legs moved like pistons as he tried to push away from the door, but then his legs stopped moving, and he lay flat and gasped for breath. Race searched the man for weapons, but found none.

"Why'd you have your brother murder my family?" Race demanded calmly.

"Who are you? I didn't . . . I wouldn't—"

"Oh, but you did. Your psycho brother and his friends tortured and killed dozens of men, women, and children, including my wife and daughters."

McCall still wheezed, but he tried to sit up. "They weren't supposed to hurt anyone. I told him that over and over. He wouldn't listen."

"But, even though you knew what kind of sick monster he was, you still sent him out on other jobs. Didn't you?"

"It wasn't me. I swear. It was Vitaly Orlov. He wanted the coins Reese stole. He sells them all over the world to rich collectors. He forced me to do it."

"How did he force you?"

The man babbled for a while, then said, "He threatened to kill me if I didn't cooperate."

Race looked in the man's eyes and knew he'd lied. He was suddenly dizzy. Every time he thought he'd reached the end of the vengeance game, another player popped up.

"Who's this Orlov?"

"Russian Mafia. Owns clubs in Dallas. Got all sorts of other businesses, too. Please, Mister. I was just following orders. I never wanted anyone hurt. That's the truth."

Race's mouth went sour. *I was just following orders.* The defense of cowardly, immoral people. McCall screamed when Race kicked his left thigh.

"Where can I find Orlov?"

McCall's face was twisted grotesquely as he rubbed his leg. "He's supposed to be here at 6." He actually smiled, as though he was about to be let off the hook.

"Why?"

"I have . . . coins I'm holding for him."

"What coins?"

McCall gulped and his voice broke when he said, "From a robbery in Flagstaff, Arizona."

"William Brownell," Race said in a voice tinged with sadness.

"How'd . . . ? Who are you?"

Race felt his whole body go hot with rage. His injured left arm burned with pain. But he forced himself to remain calm. "You hired your brother and his crew to steal coins, then he sent the coins to you, and you passed them on to Orlov. That's when he paid you, right?"

McCall nodded.

"How'd you know where to send your brother?"

"From Orlov."

"And how'd he know?"

"An inside guy at—"

"The appraisal company," Race mumbled under his breath.

"What?" McCall said.

"The appraisal company," he repeated.

"I don't know anything about an appraisal company. I once overheard a phone conversation Orlov had with a guy at some insurance company. I think that's where his information comes from." McCall paused a beat. "I can't be certain."

"Sonofabitch," Race muttered. It wasn't the appraiser, Sylvan Tauber, who'd fed information to this nest of rattlesnakes. It was someone in an insurance company who had access to policy information.

"Did Orlov ever mention the name of the insurance company?"

McCall chewed on his lower lip for a moment. "Maybe he said the name once." He squinted and added, "Surety something or other . . . I think."

Surety Collectors Insurance, Race thought. The company I used. The top insurer of coin collections, worldwide.

"Did Orlov mention the name of the person at the insurance company?"

McCall shook his head as though he would never stop. "No, he never did."

Race pulled out his gun and pointed it at McCall, who threw out his hands as though to protect himself. "Get your suitcase and bring it here."

McCall did as Race had ordered and limped to the foyer. He collected his suitcase and placed it on the coffee table in the living room.

"Sit down," Race ordered.

McCall moved to a wing-backed chair and sat.

"You're going to be a good boy and sit there quietly. When your friend, Orlov, arrives, you'll open the door and invite him in. You give him any reason to suspect something's wrong, I'll shoot you."

McCall nodded.

"Put the suitcase on the coffee table."

Again, McCall obeyed without hesitation.

Race unzipped the suitcase. Inside were clothes on one side, a FedEx box in the middle, and piles of cash on the other side. He looked up and glared at McCall. "Are the Brownell coins in the shipping box?"

"Yes."

"You were about to run off with the coins, weren't you? Skipping out on Orlov."

McCall briefly shook his head, but then looked down at the floor.

After he removed the FedEx box from the suitcase and placed it on the coffee table, Race closed the suitcase and dropped it behind a chair in a far corner. He sat on a straight-backed chair opposite McCall. "Tell me about Orlov."

McCall raised his head and looked at Race. His eyes bugged out. "He's a very bad dude. He and his people have taken over a lot of the rackets in Dallas. The Mexicans, the Asians, all the gangs pay him tribute. They do business only if he allows them to."

"Why did he get into rare coins?"

"It's not just coins. He's figured out that he can fence extremely valuable items, including coins, gems, paintings, and antique books."

"And, unlike drugs," Race said, "he's got no product costs except what he pays the people who steal the stuff. Plus, about all the cops and the Feds care about today is drugs and terrorists."

"If he tried to steal drugs from dealers, they'd shoot back. Private citizens are easy targets."

"Also, the people who buy the stolen goods from him aren't about to brag about how they got them, and they don't ask questions about where the goods came from."

"You got that right," McCall said. He chuckled, seemingly now relaxed in Race's presence, despite the pistol. "What Orlov told me was that coins and gems are his favorites because a small number of them can be worth a lot, and they're easy to hide and ship."

"Will he show up here alone?"

"No way. He always has a couple gorillas with him. Big, no-neck, steroid freaks. They scare the crap out of me."

Race looked at his watch: 5:53. "You stay there until Orlov shows up. Then you go to the door and let him in. Bring him here into the living room and get him to sit. Show him the box with the coins."

"What are you going to do?"

"We'll see."

"You're making a mistake messing with—"

A series of loud knocks on the front door interrupted McCall. Race stood. "Stand up," he ordered. "Go to the door."

Race followed McCall toward the front door, then peeled away into the kitchen, which was across the foyer from the living room. The curved wall that screened the kitchen from the foyer extended ten feet from the front door. Race stood behind that wall and peeked around it at McCall.

There was another loud series of knocks. McCall swayed as he stepped forward and stopped two feet from the door. "Shit," he muttered as he turned toward Race.

Race could tell from McCall's flushed face and eyes—which bounced around like ping pong balls—that the man's performance might fall short of Academy Award standards. He lost sight of McCall when he backed up around the end of the curved wall. He held his breath when the man opened the front door. If he warned Orlov, there was a good chance the house would become a bloody battlefield.

"Hel . . . hello, Mr. Orlov," McCall stammered. "Please come in."

"Vhat's the matter, McCall, you sound nervous?" a man asked in a Slavic accent.

"No, no. I'm just . . . there's a lot going on."

"You are complaining?" the Slavic accent said.

"Of course not, Mr. Orlov. I just don't want anything to fall through the cracks."

Surprisingly, McCall's voice now sounded fairly steady. Then he reappeared and limped into the living room, followed by a tall, slender man dressed in what appeared to be a very expensive silk suit. Then the broad backs of two men. Also in suits, the men looked as though they had been stuffed into their clothes.

"Something wrong with your leg?" the slender man asked.

"I bumped into a dresser," McCall explained.

Race figured the bodyguards would search the house to make certain there were no threats against their boss. Before they could turn around, he moved from behind the wall and shouted, "You two, down on the floor."

Both bodyguards reached under their jackets as they spun around.

Race moved his weapon back and forth between the two men. "Show me your hands. Down on the floor."

"Vat is this?" Orlov shouted, his Slavic accent even more pronounced. He gave McCall a menacing look.

"Shut up," Race said.

The bodyguard on the left removed his hand from under his jacket and bent as though to follow Race's instructions, to get on the floor. The other man jerked his right hand from under his jacket. Race saw the hand was full of a very large pistol and shot the bodyguard in the knee. The man fell to the floor, dropped his weapon, and grabbed his leg. He bellowed a continuous stream of what sounded like Slavic curses until Race rapped him on the side of his head with his gun. It didn't knock him out, but, other than groans, it shut him up.

Pain erupted in Race's left arm when he extended to pick up the man's weapon. He straightened and kicked the gun down the hall. He then stood behind the other bodyguard, placed the muzzle of his pistol against the man's forehead, and barked, "Remove your weapon and toss it away."

The man did as Race had ordered.

To both men, he said, "Pull up your pants legs. I want to see your ankles."

When he saw that neither man wore an ankle rig, Race sidestepped into the living room and stood where he could watch all four men.

"You're in big trouble," Orlov said, his voice full of arrogance and menace.

Race gave the Russian a sour look. "I told you to shut up." He waggled his gun at the Russian and pointed it toward a chair in the living room. "Sit down."

Orlov opened his mouth as though he was about to say something, but he clamped it shut, moved to the chair, and sat. He again looked at McCall, this time with as much venom in his look as Race had ever seen on any man's face.

Race walked behind Orlov and patted him to check for weapons. He removed a cell phone from Orlov's shirt pocket. A bulge in an inside jacket pocket proved to be a small, leather-bound, spiral notebook. Race stuffed the phone and notebook in a pants pocket as he walked back to a spot where he could watch the other men, too.

"Orlov, I've got one question for you."

The Russian turned to look at him.

"Who's your contact at the insurance company? The person who tells you about the coin collections."

Orlov jerked a look at McCall. "You told him?"

McCall was flushed and his eyes did the ping-pong thing again. He hunched his shoulders. "He had a gun on me. What was I supposed to do?"

When Orlov looked back at Race, his expression was completely absent emotion. "Go fuck yourself," he spat.

Race kept one eye on the bodyguards while he took three steps toward Orlov. The Russian glared up at him; not an ounce of fear showed in his features or body language.

"Is that your final answer?"

Orlov blurted a loud laugh. Then he smiled. "You're a dead man."

Race threw a side-kick into Orlov's chin. A loud *crack* sounded and Orlov's head bounced off the back of his chair. He sagged as though his bones had turned to dust and slid down in the chair.

Race pointed his weapon at McCall. "Come here."

McCall obeyed.

"Get down on your knees."

McCall whimpered. "Please don't. I'm sorry about your family. I—"

"Get down. NOW."

McCall knelt in front of Race, his head bowed, his arms tightly folded.

"There's a knife in my right jacket pocket. Take it out and use it to cut the draw cords off the blinds. Then tie up that asshole." Race tapped the automatic against the top of McCall's head. "Look at me."

McCall raised his head and met Race's gaze.

"If you even look like you're thinking about trying something, I'll pull this trigger without a moment's hesitation. You understand?"

McCall nodded.

McCall took out the knife, stood, and moved to a bank of windows that faced the street. He unsheathed the knife, cut the blinds cords, and brought them to where Orlov slouched in the chair. After he resheathed the knife and put it on the coffee table, he propped up Orlov, pinned his arms behind his back, and tied his wrists together.

"Now do his ankles," Race ordered.

McCall used another cord to secure the Russian's ankles. When he finished with Orlov, Race ordered him to bind the bodyguards' hands behind their backs. McCall frenetically scurried around, seemingly wanting to please Race. After he finished with the bodyguards, Race ordered McCall to return to his chair.

When Orlov regained consciousness, he shifted his jaw from side-to-side, moaned, and then mumbled as though he had a mouth full of pebbles, "You broke my jaw, you prick."

"One more time; who's your contact at the insurance company?"

Orlov grunted.

Race walked to the foyer and looked down at the bodyguard he'd shot. The man lay on his stomach. Blood had pooled on the floor by his wounded leg. "Do you know if your boss has a friend at an insurance company?"

The guy groaned.

"Keep your mouth shut," Orlov mumbled.

"So, you do know. What's his name?"

Orlov mumbled something unintelligible.

Race guessed, from their physical appearances, that the bodyguards were obsessed with physical fitness and body-building. Race decided to push that button.

"How long do you think it'll take to get that knee back in

shape?"

This time, the man whined.

"I already know the name of the company. If you don't tell me the contact's name, I'll shoot you in your other knee."

"No, don't," the wounded man pleaded.

"Then talk."

"Orlov will kill me."

"Not if he's dead."

"I overheard him mention a name. Karl Swenson."

Orlov made a noise that sounded like a growl.

Race returned to the living room and touched Orlov's jaw with the 9 millimeter. The Russian groaned, then growled again. Then to Race's amazement, the man laughed. Between his Slavic accent and broken jaw, Race had a difficult time understanding all that Orlov said. But he caught enough of it to get the gist of his words: "McCall here said he vas sorry about your family. Did his killers murder them?"

Race glared at the mobster.

"Probably tortured them, didn't they?"

"Shut your damned mouth," Race shouted.

"I vish I'd been there," Orlov said. "Vould have enjoyed myself."

Race pointed his pistol at the center of Orlov's forehead. "I told you to shut up."

Orlov looked at McCall. "Vat job vas this?" he asked. "Vat did newspapers say your men did to them?"

McCall looked as though he might collapse. He turned pale and his eyes were like saucers.

Orlov shot a look at Race that seemed to be pure evil. "Come on; tell me vat happened to your family. How many people were at your home?"

Race's eyes seemed to lose focus. Then, as though a red filter had been inserted into his corneas, the room suddenly looked awash in blood. His head ached and he felt dizzy. The pain in his left arm was now excruciating. Orlov's thick lips, bushy eyebrows, and lopsided grin seemed grotesque. Race stepped forward and shoved the barrel of the gun against the mobster's forehead. He closed his eyes for just a moment to clear his vision. When he opened them again, the grin was still on Orlov's face. He felt a wave of immense satisfaction course through him, as though his nightmares, rage, and despair of the past three years were about to lessen. He had the man behind all the pain and suffering in his gun sight.

Orlov continued to grin and then spat in Race's face.

Race pulled the trigger

Race now heard other sounds—voices and the roar of a powerful car engine. He pulled back from Orlov, moved to the front window, and cracked the blinds. A small crowd of men, women, and children had gathered on the sidewalk across the street. A police cruiser pulled up to the curb. Race looked back at McCall and knew another shot fired now would probably bring the cop storming into the house. This was Texas, after all. He clubbed McCall on the forehead with his gun and watched him collapse sideways on the couch, put the weapon in his jacket pocket, picked up the knife from the coffee table, and then ran to the rear of the house. To avoid leaving fingerprints, he used the fabric of his jacket to cover his hand as he opened the back patio door, and then sprinted across the backyard. He struggled to roll over the back wall that separated McCall's house from the one behind it, and ran along the side of that house toward the street. Race slowed as he cleared the front of the neighbor's house, put the knife in his jacket pocket, and forced himself to walk at a casual pace to his rental car. He drove off at a leisurely speed until he turned a corner. Then he hit the gas and sped away as fast as he dared to the Dallas airport.

# CHAPTER 49

Barbara and Susan had reached the half-way mark on their hike up the west side of the Sandia Mountains, when Barbara's cell phone rang. She looked at the screen and saw it was Sophia Otero-Hansen calling.

"Where are you?" Otero-Hansen asked.

"La Luz Trail. Making the most of our suspensions."

"Sounds like punishment. That's a tough climb."

"Better than having to work with Bruce Lucas."

"You know, there's something symmetrical about all three of us being in the dog house."

Barbara chuckled. "Our boss may have *acted* like an asshole, but we screwed up and deserved it. Your boss is just a pathological asshole. There's a big difference between the two of them."

"I hate it when you're right."

"So, what's going on?"

"Well, Barbara, the bank robbers we've been after are now in custody. Except for one who was shot by someone and died in the parked getaway vehicle."

"Who shot him?" Barbara asked.

"We don't know. But the bank has video cameras inside and out. We're analyzing the tapes right now."

"And you called me because . . . ."

"Because I think the shooter could be your vigilante."

Barbara tried to wrap her brain around what Sophia had just told her. "You're pulling my leg."

"Nope. I know I'm operating more on gut instinct than fact, but here's what we have. A man walked into the bank just before the robbers arrived. He went to the safety deposit vault, accessed his box, and then left with the briefcase he'd carried in. That's when he must have become aware of the robbery and decided to play Lone Ranger and save the women and children from the evil bank robbers. Someone called 9-1-1 about the robbery. I think it was your guy."

"You must have more than that," Barbara said.

"You're right. The shells from his automatic that ejected in the parking lot across from the bank entrance were 9 millimeters. That's the same caliber weapon the vigilante used in the Las Vegas incident in the lawyer's office. You remember, he shot one of the football players in the shoulder before he forced him to overdose on liquid heroin. I'll bet you forensics tells us the slug from that guy's shoulder matches the slugs we'll pull out of the getaway driver at the bank."

"Come on, Sophia. That's just conjecture. 9 millimeter pistols are some of the most common in America."

"True. But I'll bet you dinner at Marcello's that the shells came from the same pistol."

"What else?"

"Apparently, he's made five visits to his safety deposit box in the last twenty-four months. It's rented in the name Arnold Webber under a bogus Social Security number and address. We have the electronic log that shows the dates and times of his visits."

"Did the bank's security cameras catch the guy?"

"Yes, it did."

"Does the guy look like the *reporter* up in Farmington?"

Otero-Hansen paused and then said, "No." Another pause. "But he could have worn a disguise."

"Sounds like conjecture on top of conjecture, mixed with intuition. What else you got?"

"Nothing," Otero-Hansen said, "until forensics gives us something on the slugs and we finish viewing the video of the outside of the bank. "But, if my instincts are correct, your dark angel killer is in Albuquerque."

# CHAPTER 50

Susan's doorbell rang at 7 p.m. sharp. She thought, I'll be damned; a man who knows how to show up on time. She walked to her front door, looked through the peephole, and saw a forty-something, blond-haired man. His eyes looked blue; he was neither tall nor short. "Looks like a Mormon missionary," she muttered as she threw open the door.

"You got the wrong address, *amigo*."

The man's eyebrows shot upward. Then he grinned. "You're Susan Martinez, right?"

"Yeah. So what?"

"I'm your date." He stuck out a hand. "Roger Smith."

Susan didn't immediately respond. Then she finally said, "Barbara said you're in the Latin American Studies Department."

"I am." Then Roger's eyebrows arched again. "Oh, I see. You thought I would be Hispanic."

Susan felt her face heat up. Barbara had pulled a fast one on her. Barbara knew she liked her men tall, dark, muscular, and handsome. Roger was "nice-looking," but he wasn't tall or powerfully-built. And he sure as hell wasn't dark. Whether they were Hispanic had nothing to do with it. Susan shrugged. "I just assumed."

He smiled. "I hope you like flowers," he said as he handed her a mixed bouquet.

"Sure. Why don't you come in while I put them in a vase?"

Roger and Susan met Henry and Barbara at Piatanzi on Juan Tabo Boulevard. The food was delicious and the service excellent. However, conversation lagged. At least between Roger and Susan. When it came time to leave for Blacky's, Susan said to Barbara, "I need to use the ladies room." Barbara followed her.

"You like Roger?" Barbara asked as they stood in front of the mirror.

Susan jerked a look at Barbara. "He's all right."

"Maybe if you tried talking to him, you might discover you have something in common."

Susan said, "He's not really my type."

"Jeez," Barbara said. "What's wrong with him?"

Susan shrugged. "He's a little like Henry. Nerdy."

Roger left his car in Piatanzi's lot. He and Susan piled into the backseat of Henry's Saab and traveled to Tijeras Canyon. *Blacky's* potholed parking lot was packed with cars, pickups, and motorcycles. Muted rock music poured from the building. Inside, the music was deafening.

Susan took in the packed space, which had four rows of tables that ran from between a pool table in the back to a slightly raised stage behind a tiny dance floor in the front. Every stool was taken at the bar on the right, and dozens more patrons crowded behind the bar stools and along the windows in the back and around the pool table.

"We'll never find a place to sit," she said.

Henry held up a finger. "We'll see about that." He waved at and walked over to a man who stood just inside the entrance. They hugged and then the two of them came over to where Roger, Barbara, and Susan waited.

"Meet the owner of this glorious establishment. John, these are my friends." Henry introduced everyone.

"Glad you could join us tonight," John said. He nodded at two burly guys who disappeared for a moment and then returned with a small table and four chairs. The two men placed the table and chairs just off the dance floor, to the front of the stage, and then the owner said, "All yours. Enjoy."

After they took seats and draped their coats over the backs of their chairs, Henry asked, "What would you like to drink?"

Susan said, "Bourbon on the rocks."

"Make that two," Roger said.

"Pepsi for you and me?" Henry asked Barbara. She nodded. He turned and serpentined his way through the packed lounge toward the bar.

Barbara leaned into Susan. "That's another thing I like about Henry. He drinks scotch, but he always drinks what I drink when we're together. Knows I don't drink alcohol anymore."

Susan smiled.

Henry returned a few minutes later. "The waitress will bring our drinks."

The band pounded out a rendition of Wilson Pickett's *Mustang Sally*. Susan caught herself tapping her feet to the music, but stopped when Roger smiled at her and shouted, "Are you originally from New Mexico?"

Small talk, Susan thought. Wonderful. Then she heard Barbara groan. She turned to look at her and asked, "You say something?"

Barbara nodded. "Yeah. I said, 'Oh, shit, it's Leno Sanchez.'"

"Where?" Susan asked.

Barbara pointed toward the far side of the dance floor. "Over there. And I think he spotted us."

Susan had dated Sanchez off and on for six months. When she needed her libido exercised, she'd see him. Otherwise, as Barbara had said the other day, Sanchez was all brawn and no brains. How he'd ever passed the APD exam and become a cop was beyond her.

"What's wrong?" Henry asked.

"Nothing," Susan said. She watched Sanchez, dressed in motorcycle leathers and heavy-soled boots, cross from the back of the room to their table.

"*Ola*, Suzy," Sanchez shouted. He bent down and tried to kiss her on the lips, but only brushed her cheek when she turned her head.

Sanchez had positioned himself between Susan and Roger's chairs. He didn't acknowledge the others, even Barbara, who he'd known at least as long as he'd known Susan. Susan tried to see

Roger's reaction. She was embarrassed by Sanchez's rudeness, but she was also embarrassed to admit to him that she was here with someone as nerdy as Roger.

Sanchez finally nodded at Barbara, then turned back to Susan. "Who're your friends?"

Susan pointed at Henry. She shouted, "Henry Simpson, meet Leno Sanchez." She tried to see Roger, but Sanchez blocked her view. "Roger Smith is behind you," she said just as the band finished the song and announced they were taking a break.

Sanchez turned slightly and glanced down at Roger. He snorted, turned back to Susan. "What are you doing with this *pinche joto*?"

Susan's first instinct was to tell Sanchez to get lost, but she said nothing. She instantly felt badly about her cowardice; she felt even worse when she saw the disappointed look in Barbara's eyes. About to try to redeem herself, she heard Roger say, "Hey, Mr. Leno, you want to explain to me what you meant when you referred to me as a *joto*."

Sanchez smirked at Susan, then turned around and said to Roger, "*Joto, maricon*, twinkle toes, it's all one and the same."

Roger said, "So, you used the word *joto* in a derogatory sense, assuming that I am of the homosexual persuasion and therefore deserving of ridicule."

"Huh?"

"Sorry, Mr. Leno. Did I speak too quickly or was it the multi-syllabic words that threw you?"

Barbara stood. "It was obviously a mistake coming here." She grabbed Henry's hand and said, "Let's go."

Henry hesitated for a beat, but then dutifully stood.

"Leno, I want you to leave," Susan said. "Do you—?"

Roger said, "Excuse me, Susan, but Mr. Leno and I are having a conversation."

"But—"

Roger's voice dropped an octave. "Susan, I do not need your assistance." Then he said to Sanchez, "I think it would be an appropriate and gentlemanly thing for you to apologize for your rudeness and for your use of a slur against the many fine people in the homosexual community."

Sanchez laughed and said, "Fuck off, *joto*."

Susan now stood and pushed Sanchez aside. She looked at Roger. "Our ride is ready to leave," she said, and took a backward step away from the table.

Roger looked at Sanchez, then at Susan. "One moment, please, Susan." He turned back to Sanchez. "You know, it's quite interesting. Do you realize you've used a singularly Southwestern pejorative to raise suspicion about my sexuality with little awareness of the richness of the word? *Joto* actually originates from medieval Spain where it was used colloquially to refer to the jack or knave in a deck of cards. In its migration to Mexico, the word became disfigured and reformed in illiterate societies. Thus the knaves among your kind thought that, by injecting a socially disapproving sexual connotation, the word would restore its pejorative value. So now *joto* alludes to a closeted homosexual. I congratulate you on your perspicuity, but I want to correct you on one point: I am neither *joto* nor *maricon*, but you, Mr. Leno, are a *joto* in its anachronistic sense."

Sanchez stared open-mouthed at Roger as though he had dropped into Blacky's on a spaceship.

Roger picked up his coat and marched after the others to the entrance. They had just cleared the door when it was thrown open and Sanchez emerged into the freezing night. His forehead was scrunched into a confused series of tracks. "Did you just call me a *joto*?" he shouted.

"Bravo, Mr. Leno," Roger said. "Something finally sank in. Did you come out here to apologize?"

"Like hell." Then he threw a punch. His mouth opened and his eyes widened when Roger dodged his fist.

Susan stepped toward Roger. She extended her arms to pull him away, but he sloughed off her hands. Then, to Susan's surprise, Henry grabbed her arm and told her, "Stay out of this."

Susan was more than surprised to see how calm both Henry and Roger appeared. She felt she had to do something to stop the situation before Sanchez lost all control and pulverized her date. She came forward again, but Roger pointed at her and growled, "Susan, back off."

The determined, calm look she saw on Roger's face startled her.

Roger took one step toward Sanchez. "Mr. Leno, I would like to ask you a question. Did you refer to me as a *joto* because I am shorter than you are, because you outweigh me by at least fifty pounds, because I am Caucasian, or for some other reason?"

"What the fuck?" Sanchez grunted as he threw a left jab.

Roger slipped the punch and swatted Sanchez's arm.

Susan was now dumbfounded. Then she saw the bar's owner and two of his bouncers step outside. Henry intercepted them and said something to the owner. Whatever he told the guy caused him to stand and watch. She quickly turned back toward Roger just as Sanchez tried to connect with Roger's skull with a roundhouse right hook. This time, Roger caught the bigger man's arm and, using Sanchez's momentum, sent him crashing into the grill of a gigantic pickup truck parked nose-in at the entrance.

The expression she saw on Sanchez's face was pathetic. She almost felt sorry for him. But when he stood and charged at Roger, any sympathy she had dissipated. Apparently, Roger felt the same. He side-stepped Leno's charge and crunched his thigh into Leno's side as the man careened past him and flew into the cattle guard on the front of an SUV, not three feet away from where she stood. The effect of his head connecting with the metal guard made the sound of a dull bell. Sanchez was knocked cold.

Then the sound of sirens filled the night. The owner came over and said, "Henry, I think it would be a really good idea if you all called it an evening. I'll deal with Sanchez."

Henry thanked the man and said to Barbara, "You ready to go?"

She smiled. "Fine with me. The last thing I need in my file is an arrest for disorderly conduct." Barbara waved at Susan while Henry collected Roger.

Susan wanted to say something to Roger on the way back to Piatanzi's parking lot to get his car. She eyed him several times, but his attention was on the street outside his window. She'd acted badly all evening and was truly ashamed of herself. Maybe she could think of something to say when they were alone in Roger's car.

When Henry dropped them off, Susan caught Barbara's blank stare. She knew she'd treated Roger poorly, but had also embarrassed

Barbara. Probably Henry, as well.

Roger opened her door for her, then walked around the back of the car and slid behind the wheel.

They drove in silence until Roger turned onto her street. Susan took a deep breath and let it out slowly. "I'm sorry about Leno. I guess he's a bigger asshole than I already knew."

"But he *is* big, strong, and handsome," Roger said.

"What's that mean?"

"I think you know exactly what that means. I'm obviously not your type, Susan, and I'm too old to believe I can change people. You're a beautiful woman, but that's not enough for me. At my stage in life, I want a friend; someone I can trust; someone who respects me and who I can respect."

He stopped in front of her house and quickly exited the vehicle. By the time he reached her door, she'd already opened it and stepped onto the sidewalk.

Tears leaked down her cheeks. "I screwed up, Roger. I'm really sorry."

"So am I, Susan. So am I."

# CHAPTER 51

By the time Race deplaned, it was nearly 11 p.m. and bitterly-cold and windy in Albuquerque. Snow had dusted the landscape in all directions. He turtled his head down into his jacket and put his hands in his pants pockets while he walked to his parked truck. Inside the vehicle, he checked behind the front seat to make certain his briefcase was still there, then he removed his disguise as he sat in the truck and waited for it to warm up. He tried to cope with the empty feeling that had come over him in Dallas. He didn't like feeling uncertain, emotionally drained. All his life, he'd been strong—the one who everyone else leaned on. Even as a twelve-year-old, after his father died from cancer, he'd been the one his grieving mother could rely on. In the Army, he was the one the other soldiers looked up to, listened to. During his business career, the managers and employees expected him to solve problems, to set the path for the future. He'd been the bulwark for his wife and daughters. But now he felt uncertain, indecisive. He'd always, in the past, seen uncertainty and indecisiveness as something that afflicted weak people, not him.

Something had changed. Something deep inside him. At first, he thought he was just angry that he'd violated the oath he'd made to himself: to kill everyone responsible for Mary, Sara, and Elizabeth's deaths. He'd broken that oath when he let Evan McCall live. And now he contemplated putting an end to his crusade.

He considered the possibility that he'd just gotten tired of killing. God knows, he thought, I've done enough of it. But something else came to mind, and it shook him to his very core. Before he flew to Dallas, he'd planned his next moves. He would eliminate Evan McCall, then fly back to Albuquerque and drive to California to murder Sylvan Tauber, the appraiser with Holmsby Rare Coin Valuations. If he had done that, he now knew he would have murdered an innocent man. The confidence that he'd had in his mission had been shaken by that near mistake. Without any hesitation, after wiping it of fingerprints, he'd disposed of his pistol in a dumpster near the Dallas airport. That action had seemed like a crossing-the-Rubicon moment.

He shifted the truck from PARK to DRIVE, but didn't move from the parking spot. A wave of sadness rolled over him and tears sprang to his eyes. Then sobs overwhelmed him. His throat tightened and his chest felt as though a steel band tightened around it. He intoned the names of his wife and children. He thought about Eric Matus, about how he'd been responsible for his friend's death. They'd started out to avenge their families' deaths, but had moved on to something a lot bigger. Something more . . . consequential. He no longer felt angry about what Eric had done—lying to him and collecting fees from the people to whom they had brought some closure. What he had done didn't, in Race's mind, undermine all the support Eric had given him over the last three years.

Race wasn't certain how long he sat there in his truck, but as empty as he'd felt before, it now seemed as though his mind and soul were void of meaning. For years, he'd nourished his very being with a quest for revenge. Without that quest, his life now seemed empty, without purpose. He suddenly felt useless and he drove to a motel on East Central Avenue and booked a room for the night. Although he had no idea where he intended to go, he planned to hit the road in the morning. He looked around the room and remembered what Eric had said to him about the way his life had changed. One thing he decided he would do in the future was to never stay in a rundown motel if he could avoid it.

Although he didn't feel particularly hungry, he knew he should eat something. It had been hours since his last meal—breakfast in

Cuba, New Mexico. He called a pizza place and ordered a delivery. While he waited for the pizza to arrive, he booted up his computer and Googled *Farmington home invasion*. He picked a local news channel's posting. The lead-in was all about a 'mystery man'—as the news commentator put it—who had shot and killed a home invader and saved an elderly couple. FBI agents, Bruce Lucas and Sophia Otero-Hansen, were then interviewed. At one point in the interview, Agent Otero-Hansen said, "Our thanks go to Detectives Barbara Lassiter and Susan Martinez of the Bernalillo County Sheriff's Office for their assistance. The Bureau's policy is to maintain strong relationships with local law enforcement departments. This is a perfect example of how that policy pays off."

When the camera panned on Agent Lucas, his mouth looked as though he'd just sucked on a lemon.

Something bothered Race while he watched the news program. No one mentioned the fact that coin collectors had been targeted by the home invasion gang. There wasn't even a mention of Nicholas Franchini's collection being the reason that Reese McCall had targeted the man. He felt frustrated and then that frustration turned to anger. If he'd been able to identify the rare coin connection to all the home invasions, surely the FBI would have been able to do so, as well. The police reports in each robbery would surely have included information about the stolen coin collections. The police must have forwarded that information for inclusion in the NCIC database. Then an idea came to him that made him shudder: What if someone at the FBI had suppressed the information about the coins? He tried to come up with a reason for that being done, but couldn't do so.

"Damn, damn, damn," Race rasped.

As far as he'd been able to discover, the first of the home invasions dated back five years, and there had been more than a dozen since then. If the FBI had been aware of all of the crimes and had not disclosed the coin collections as the common link, the Bureau might very well have been responsible for Mary, Sara, and Elizabeth's deaths three years ago. In fact, by not warning other coin collectors, every murder and robbery since the first one might have been prevented.

Race had agreed that Jim Dunhill should inform the Worldwide Coin Collectors Association about his theory that coin collectors had been targeted by the Three Ghouls. That was unnecessary now that the last of the Three Ghouls was dead. But he wondered if the association was informed after the fact, if coin collectors all over the U.S., and the world, for that matter, might raise hell about what had been keep secret from them while murders continued to occur. He sent off an email to Dunhill and suggested he release the specific information they'd gathered two nights ago in Dunhill's shop.

Race decided to undress and try to sleep. He emptied his pockets and found the cell phone and little notebook he'd taken off Vitaly Orlov. He thumbed through the notebook pages and found names at the top of each page—one contact per page—for about fifty individuals. Below the names were phone numbers and email addresses. From the country codes and area codes shown, the names were in countries all over the world. There were no physical addresses. The pages had been arranged in alphabetical order by contact name. Below the contact information on each page were what Race assumed were transaction data, with dates and dollar amounts. He flipped back to the first page and studied the information there for a Siegfried Bauer. On October 22, five years ago, Bauer appeared to have consummated a transaction with Orlov worth seven million, eighty thousand dollars.

He went through each page and found similar entries, except, on a number of pages, there were multiple transactions. After Race read the information on a page near the back of the notebook, under the name of Farhad Zubeida, he turned to the next page and found an untitled page. In fact, the next four pages were the same—no title, just several columns on each page. The first column showed dates. The next column included dollar amounts. The third column showed what appeared to be two-to-five-letter abbreviations. He ran a finger down the column and recognized some entries as abbreviations for foreign banks. The fourth and last column listed number sequences.

Race's pulse accelerated when he realized that Orlov had written what could be bank account names and numbers. Orlov must be one of those people, he thought, who apparently loved to be able to look at his assets at any time on any day. A quick mental calculation told Race that the Russian had deposited something on the order of forty-two million dollars in the accounts.

He noted the first deposit date from five years earlier—July 17, then paged back through the notebook until he found a transaction date—July 13. By the time he'd compared the first five deposits with the transactions listed in the notebook, and had found that those transactions coincided closely with home invasions around those same dates, Race was confident that the notebook catalogued the loot from each of the robberies, the subsequent sale of the stolen items from those robberies, and the deposits of Orlov's proceeds from those sales. He wondered why there were about fifty pages of transactions and not only enough to match the number of home invasions. But then he found duplicative dates on the transaction and deposit pages. Apparently, Orlov had split up the stolen items among multiple clients.

If he could track deposits from their source to Orlov's accounts, he would have proof that the stolen goods had gone from Orlov to the individuals shown in Orlov's notebook. Because of the dollar amounts involved, the clients must be heavy-hitters. Race felt a rush of excitement over the possibility of taking down four dozen, or so, wealthy, immoral bastards who had played significant roles in the deaths of innocent people. Then he wondered if any charges could be brought against these people. They could plead ignorance about the source of the coins. Race thought about that for a minute and came to the conclusion that, even if charges couldn't be brought against the buyers, at the very least he could release their names and embarrass them.

He assumed the buyers had wire-transferred monies into Orlov's accounts. With their locations all over the globe, that would have been the only logical method of payment.

"Come on, Race, think," he chided himself.

After he paced for a few minutes, he couldn't come up with a sound way to track deposits into Orlov's account. Without passwords, he couldn't get into the bank accounts. And attempting to hack the Swiss bank's server would be difficult, at best, and could expose him to their security personnel.

"Shit," he muttered as he crossed the room for about the hundredth time. Then he remembered how angry Orlov had been when one of the bodyguards gave up Karl Swenson's name. Race researched Surety Collectors Insurance and found that the company, a subsidiary of an insurance conglomerate with nearly six hundred billion dollars in reserves, was headquartered in Kansas City, Missouri, with offices in twenty states. He wondered how Karl Swenson had covered up the losses his company must have sustained from the thefts of the coin collections. Insurance companies had intensive loss mitigation and underwriting systems. Eight digit losses over five years must have raised red flags inside Surety Collectors Insurance, despite the huge reserves of the parent company.

Race delved deeper into the *Surety* website and found a section on specialty insurance products. Under the *NUMISMATICS/ARTIFACTS* link, he discovered that the company insured over eight hundred thousand collections worldwide with total annual premiums of almost nine billion dollars. "Sonofabitch," Race whispered. "That's how Swenson covered up losses. The company insures so many collections that the losses are inconsequential to the total amount insured. And any losses could be recouped by raising insurance premiums charged to clients." Race remembered how the insurance premiums on his collection had gone up at least five percent annually. If every one of Surety's clients had experienced the same rate increases, then the incremental premium revenue to the company more than made up for any theft losses incurred.

Perhaps Swenson was the key source of information in the entire scheme. Without an insider at the insurance company providing coin collection information to Orlov, there would have been no scheme. Race's blood seemed to boil. Over the past three years, he had concentrated his hate, anger, and lust for revenge on the men who had murdered his family. But he now focused on Karl Swenson. The insurance executive, like Orlov, Evan McCall, and the Three Ghouls, was ultimately a cause of all the murders.

The rage that Race had lived with for the past three years returned. The need for revenge returned. Except his need for violence and retribution were more intense than he'd felt before.

And it was all narrowly focused on one target: Karl Swenson, the CFO of Surety Collectors Insurance.

# DAY 11

# CHAPTER 52

Barbara called Susan at 8:30 a.m. and asked, "How did things end last night?"

"Not very well."

"That's too bad. Roger's a nice guy."

"Yeah, he is."

"Uh hmm," Barbara said. "You hear anything from Leno Sanchez?"

"Why would I hear from him?" Barbara detected a hint of anger in Susan's voice.

"I don't know. Thought he might call to apologize for being an asshole."

"That's the problem with assholes; they aren't capable of apologizing for their bad behavior."

"Besides," Barbara said, "he's more than likely embarrassed about being cold-cocked by a guy as nerdy as Roger."

Susan squinted at Barbara. "That was martial arts that Roger used on Leno, wasn't it?"

"Yeah. Not bad for a Latin American Studies PhD. Henry told me Roger's taken judo lessons for years. On another subject, a little bird called me this morning. You wanna guess?"

"It's too early for twenty questions."

"Lieutenant Salas."

"What the hell did Sniffles want?"

"I think he felt badly about suspending us. I suspect he saw Sophia's interview on television."

"That was nice of her to mention us in such glowing terms. Did he revoke our suspensions?"

"Nope."

"So, what did he want?"

"Told me he'd heard that two of his detectives were involved in an altercation last night at *Blacky's*."

"And?"

"I told him he'd received bad information. That his detectives were merely observers."

"That's it?"

"No." He also said he'd heard that APD patrolman Leno Sanchez was involved in the altercation. That he was knocked cold by an unidentified man. He added that he knew Sanchez was a bully and has been disciplined before for brawling."

"All of those bits of information are accurate," Susan said.

"Apparently, the APD wants to identify the man who beat up Sanchez."

"That's not good. What did you say?"

"That I'd never lied to him and wasn't about to start now. Then I asked him to do me a personal favor and not ask you or me any more questions about the altercation that happened last night. I told him that Patrolman Sanchez was one hundred percent at fault and there was no reason to damage the reputation of a perfectly fine man."

"That's it?"

"Oh, there was one other thing he mentioned. APD suspended Leno. The reason they want to talk to the guy who knocked him out is because they would like his statement to present to a disciplinary board. They're not after Roger; just Sanchez." She paused and then added, "But they probably have more than enough evidence already without—"

Barbara's landline rang.

"Can you hold a sec? My home phone's ringing."

"Sure. Go ahead."

Barbara picked up her home phone. "Hello."

"Detective Lassiter?"

"Yes. Who's this?"

"I understand you helped the FBI on the Three Ghouls' gang."

"I asked you for your name."

"I'm sorry, but I won't give you my name. I could give you a false name, but what would be the point?"

"How'd you get this number?"

"You keep asking questions I have no intention of answering."

"What do you want?"

"What would you say if I gave you information about why each of the Three Ghouls' victims was targeted?"

"I would say that could be very interesting."

The man laughed. "I see you're a master of understatement."

Barbara put the landline and her mobile on speaker mode and put them next to one another. "I hope you can provide proof."

"Detective, answer a question for me. How would you describe your work ethic? Your partner's, too."

"What kinda game are you playing?"

"No game, Detective. I just want to be certain that if I turn information over to you you'll do more than just sit on it. What I can give you will reveal incompetence at the federal level, the reason for the home invasions, and the names of the players in a scheme that was responsible for the deaths of dozens of innocent people."

"To answer your question, my partner and I bust our asses every day. We don't know what's it's like to *sit on it*, as you so eloquently stated."

"Good."

"And why have you decided to drop this gift of a lifetime in our laps?"

"Two reasons. Your names came up on the news last night about how you and your partner made the connection between one of the men who murdered William Brownell in Flagstaff and the man who kidnapped and murdered Heather Katz. That took skill and insight."

"You said there were two reasons."

"Yeah. I want to see if you can bring justice for victims by making every person pay who had anything to do with this robbery scheme."

"How about a hint of what you're referring to?"

"Sure, Detective. After all, I plan to provide the press with some of the same information I'm about to send you." He paused a beat. "Every one of the houses targeted by the Three Ghouls had a world-class rare coin collection on the premises."

Barbara's brain sparked with the comment Sophia Otero-Hansen had made in Farmington about coins. "Sonofa—"

"What was that?" the man asked.

"Nothing. Tell me something. You seem to be concerned about justice. What if we can't bring justice for the victims when all is said and done?"

"Let's hope that's not the outcome. Someone else might try to do so."

Barbara's heart seemed to skip a beat. She took a deep breath and waited to slowly release it. "Like *you* did in Farmington for the Franchinis and in Albuquerque for the Graves? And in a lot of other places?"

There was a long hesitation on the other end of the line until the man said, "I can't even begin to understand what you're talking about, Detective. Why don't you give me your email address? I think we've talked enough."

# CHAPTER 53

Race had surmised that the mobster, Vitaly Orlov, must be, at a minimum, the subject of police investigations in Dallas. Orlov might even have been arrested at some time in the past. Race spent several hours in the early morning looking at Google postings about Orlov. He discovered a trove of information about the man, from his date of birth, to the names of his wife and children, to charities he supported, to the companies he owned, to his arrest record. He thought he might be able to use his password hacking system to enter Orlov's computer, but the only websites with which the man had any relationship were the sites for his strip clubs. There was nothing there but promotional messages about the clubs' dancers and atmosphere. The guy had done a masterful job creating a positive public persona. Even though he was in the adult entertainment business, he appeared to be nothing less than a legitimate businessman.

Then he went back to Orlov's little notebook and tried to come up with information from his bank account records. He agonized over the information there and became more frustrated by the second. He'd slammed the book down on the desk in his motel room and was about to pack up to hit the road, when an idea struck.

"How did Orlov pay Evan McCall and Karl Swenson?" Race asked himself. "What if he used one of the accounts in the notebook?" He realized the way into Orlov's accounts might be through wire transfers he'd made into McCall and Swenson's accounts. He needed to get those bank account records. McCall, according to news reports, was being treated for a severe concussion in a Dallas area hospital. That left Swenson.

Karl Swenson hadn't even attempted to sleep the night before. His mind reeled with dire thoughts about what might happen.

"Aren't you going in today?" his wife asked him.

"Goddammit, can't I take a day off without you nagging me?"

"I wasn't nagging; just asking. Are you feeling all right?"

"I'm fine."

His wife looked at him, huffed, and left the den where Swenson had been parked since early that morning.

Swenson surfed the Internet on his cell phone for current information about the murder of Vitaly Orlov in Dallas. But there was nothing new. Orlov's death meant that there were unlikely to be any more paydays coming his way. That wasn't all bad, he told himself. He'd put away a lot of money that Orlov had paid him, and, with the mobster's demise, maybe the connection between them had been severed. However, his mind was twisted around a few questions that weren't answerable without more information. What worried Swenson the most was the possibility that Orlov had left behind evidence that would prove they had communicated with one another.

"Why did I get in bed with that asshole?" Swenson said under his breath. But the answer quickly came to him. He'd never felt he'd had a choice. The business trip to Dallas. The evening in the strip club. The hour he'd spent with one of the dancers. "One little hour," he whispered. "One damned hour, and it all came down." Orlov had video of the time he'd spent with the dancer. It was a classic record of sexual depravity that had festered, unfulfilled, in a corner of Swenson's brain for decades. The stripper had teased the inclination out of his brain and encouraged him to escape the bonds of his conservative, religious upbringing. But she'd had no idea just how violent that inclination was, until he'd beaten and choked her to death.

Race learned from local news that the Albuquerque police had discovered his safety deposit box. He thought, *Thank God I emptied the box.* He tallied his cash reserves and came up with four point three million dollars. Fortunately, he'd used a different ID for each box he'd opened, so it was highly unlikely the authorities would discover his other caches. He had more than enough cash on hand to last him a lifetime.

He called a charter company at the Albuquerque Sunport and reserved a private jet for a flight to and from Kansas City, where Surety Collectors Insurance was headquartered. Where Karl Swenson lived. A call to Swenson's office had informed him the man was out for the day. Then Race called the Swenson home number.

"Hello."

"Mr. Swenson?"

"Who is this?"

"Is this Karl Swenson?"

The man hung up.

Race called back. When the man answered again, Race said, "You hang up again and I'll tell your wife and your employer what I know."

The man moaned. "What do you want?"

"Drive to the Park & Ride at 3rd and Grand. Take the 3 p.m. Main Street MAX bus southbound. Sit in the next to last seat."

"What—?"

Race hung up and went to work on a disguise—large nose, dark glasses, handlebar mustache, and a blue baseball cap. Then he drove to the airport. The flight to Kansas City took three hours. There he picked up a rental car using another credit card and ID he'd purchased on the Dark Net and made the thirty-minute drive to the corner of 74th Terrace and Broadway, at the south end of the Main Street MAX bus route. He parked his rental car and boarded the next north-bound bus. At a few minutes after 2 p.m., he left the bus at Crown Center, bought a cup of coffee and a roll at a small shop, swallowed another pain killer to try to numb the pain in his left arm, and waited for the 3 p.m. bus to arrive.

The 3 o'clock bus arrived at Crown Center at a few minutes before

3:15. There were four other people in the queue to board it. Through one of the windows, Race scanned the bus's interior. He spied Swenson at the back. Other than looking as though he hadn't shaved and appearing worried, he resembled his photograph on the Surety Collectors Insurance website.

Race boarded the bus, took a seat in the middle, on the other side of the aisle from Swenson. There were ten people on the bus and most were seated in the front half of the vehicle. Race twisted slightly in his seat and watched Swenson out of the corner of his eye. As each minute passed, Swenson seemed to become more agitated. He continually turned to look out the windows on both sides and huffed loudly. Two women who were seated near Swenson at the rear stood and moved closer to the front.

Within fifteen minutes, all but two of the other passengers had gotten off the bus. Race stood, left his seat, and moved to the rear seat, behind Swenson. The man had watched Race move toward him and then whipped around when Race sat down.

"Face forward," Race growled.

Swenson quickly obeyed. "What do you want?" he rasped.

Race poked him hard in the back of his neck. "Shut up."

As Swenson rubbed his neck, Race dropped a pen and piece of paper over Swenson's shoulder onto his lap. He said, "I want the name of the bank, the number, and the password for the account into which you deposited monies from Orlov."

"Who are you? I—"

Race smacked the man on the back of his head this time. He hit him so hard that it sounded as though someone had thumped a melon. "No more questions, asshole."

Swenson's shoulders slumped.

"Last chance, Swenson."

The man cleared his throat. "I want the original of the video."

Orlov must have blackmailed Swenson to get him to cooperate, Race realized. "I've got it here in my pocket," he lied. "You give me the information I want and you'll get the video."

"Show me the video."

This time, Race punched the back of Swenson's head, which caused the man to yelp. An elderly male passenger turned to look at Swenson. After a few seconds, the man turned away.

"Write down the information I asked for."

Swenson scribbled for a few seconds and then handed the paper and pen back over his shoulder.

"Now, please give me the video."

Race said, "Patience, asshole." He took his cell phone from his shirt pocket, placed it on his right thigh, and pulled up the website for the Swiss bank Swenson had identified and clicked on the customer service number. When the call was answered, he picked up the phone and asked for the Wire Department.

"This is Karl Swenson. Account number 634987512; password 9825640. Please give me the current balance in my account in American dollars."

After a minute, the man on the other end of the line said, "Mr. Swenson, the balance in your account as of the end of business today was one million, four hundred thirty-eight thousand, seventy-two dollars and fifty-eight cents. Is there anything else I can do to assist you?"

"Actually, there is. Would it be possible for you to email a log of all deposits into my account, including dates, amounts, and the names of the banks from which those deposits originated?"

"That would be no problem, Mr. Swenson. Would you like me to use the email account we have on record?"

"Please hold for a second," Race said. He pressed his phone against his chest and poked Swenson. "Do you have your cell phone with you?"

Swenson nodded.

"Open the email account you use to communicate with the Swiss bank."

Swenson nodded.

Race moved his phone back to his ear. "That would be fine. Thank you."

After he disconnected the call, Race put his own phone back in his shirt pocket, took Swenson's cell phone, and waited for the email to arrive from the Swiss bank.

"Are you going to give me the video?" Swenson said.

"As soon as the email comes through."

They rode in silence for five minutes, until Swenson's cell phone pinged. Race opened an email from the Swiss bank. In the message, he saw that all of the deposits to Swenson's account had come from one Cayman Island bank account: number 1113794876, titled *Romanov Enterprises*. He wrote down the account's name and number and the name of the bank on the same piece of paper on which Swenson had written his account information. After he pocketed the paper and returned Swenson's cell phone to him, Race pulled his sheathed knife from his jacket pocket, removed it from the sheath, and waited for the bus to make its last stop on the southbound route. Then he stood and stepped into the aisle next to Swenson.

The man looked up at him with a semblance of relief in his expression. His eyes were wide with anticipation. Race guessed that whatever was on the video that Swenson seemed to want very badly was so incriminating he was willing to give up almost anything—including one-and-a-half million dollars in a Swiss bank account.

Race bent over and put his face inches from Swenson's. "Why'd you do it?"

His eyes leaked tears and his voice sounded hoarse. "I didn't mean to hurt anyone." He choked for a second. "I ruined my life." After another pause, he asked, "Can I please have the video now?"

Race straightened up and glared down at the man. "I lied. I don't have the video." He moved his hand with the knife away from his leg.

In an instant, Swenson went from defeated to devastated. His body seemed to collapse from within, and he slumped in his seat as though he didn't have the strength to hold himself up. As though he was beyond despair. In that instant, Race knew that Swenson hadn't exaggerated. He *had* ruined his life. But Race also realized the man had no idea how much worse his life was about to become. Prison would be hell for someone like Swenson.

The last of the other passengers had left the bus.

"End of the line, gentlemen," the driver announced as he stepped down through the front door of the bus.

Race turned on Swenson and hit him in the head with a right hook that seemed to vibrate up Race's arm to his shoulder. After the man slumped to the floor, Race moved to the rear exit door and down to the street. As he walked to his rental car, he tossed the knife into a trash can. Then he used a burner phone to call the Kansas City FBI office and asked to speak with an agent.

"Special Agent MacAuslan."

"Agent, are you familiar with the Three Ghouls case?"

"Can I get your name, sir?"

Race said, "Why is that the first thing law enforcement people always want to know? No, you may not have my name. If you're smart, you'll listen carefully. There's a man on the Main Street MAX bus that just docked at the 74th Terrace and Broadway station. His name is Karl Swenson. He's the CFO of Surety Collectors Insurance Company. Swenson fed appraisal information on valuable coin collections to a man named Vitaly Orlov in Dallas. Orlov then hired a guy named Evan McCall, who hired the Three Ghouls to steal coin collections. In turn, Orlov sold the coins to wealthy collectors all over the world."

"Hold on, sir. I can't write that fast."

Race blurted a laugh. "Don't play games, Agent. I know you're recording this conversation and trying to trace the call. It won't do you any good. Just pay attention. Swenson has a cell phone on him. There's an email from a bank in Switzerland that will tell you how much he was paid by Orlov for the information he provided. It will also show you the account in the Cayman Islands from which Orlov's money was wired. If you contact Detective Barbara Lassiter with the Bernalillo County Sheriff's Department in Albuquerque, she can provide you with more information."

# DAY 12

# CHAPTER 54

Race returned to Albuquerque, to his motel, gathered up his things, and planned to head west. He didn't have a destination in mind. It just felt right to him to drive toward the coast. It was after midnight when he stopped in Kingman, Arizona. Before he went to bed, he tried to identify something that had aggravated him all day. There was something that felt undone about the way he'd left things. An errant thought had nibbled at his brain on the drive from Albuquerque. But the substance of whatever his memory tried to dredge up just wouldn't surface. He went to bed, resolved to work on whatever it was after his brain was rested.

The same old dream returned at some point that night to wake him. As usual, he was drenched in sweat and his head ached. He sat up and noticed a sliver of sunlight peek through a corner of the curtains. Race groaned and forced himself to get out of bed. He showered and hurriedly dried himself and dressed, then dug into his suitcase for Orlov's notebook. He turned to the page in the back with what he'd assumed was information about Orlov's bank accounts and looked down the list to the Cayman Island bank from which Orlov's wire transfers to Swenson's bank account had originated: *Cayman First Security Bank*. He placed a finger on the line and read aloud the bank's initials: CFSB. Then he ran his finger across the page to the last column . . . the column with what he'd presumed were account numbers. He went to the dresser and picked up the piece of paper on which Karl Swenson had written his account information and on which Race had written the bank account from which Orlov had wired funds to Swenson.

The number on the piece of paper read: 1113794876. But the number on the page in Orlov's notebook read: 1113794876-848259. Race scanned the other account numbers on the page and noticed something about them that hadn't resonated with him before. All of the account numbers were hyphenated, with a series of six numbers after the hyphen. Something about the final six numbers seemed odd to Race. He studied all of them for several minutes, took a five-minute break, and then returned to the notebook page. And then he saw it: in every case, the numbers after the hyphen were the same six digits as on the Cayman First Security Bank line, but in different order. The suffix to the account on the first line was 598248. The numbers after the hyphen in the second line were 248895. Every line had the same numbers in the suffix, just in different sequence.

Race felt butterflies erupt in his stomach and a chill run down his spine. He booted up his computer and opened the site for the Cayman bank, accessed the customer on-line link, and typed in the numbers 8-4-8-2-5-9.

A pop-up showed on the screen: *Welcome, Mr. Orlov. What service may we provide you today?* Below the pop-up was a list of services next to check boxes. Race clicked the cursor on CURRENT BALANCE. Within ten seconds, the screen showed that Orlov's account had over three million dollars in it.

It took an hour to query all of Orlov's accounts on-line. By the time he'd finished, he'd discovered a total of forty-two million, two hundred sixty-two thousand, nine hundred one dollars and thirty-two cents. He thought about what might happen to all that money if the Feds discovered the accounts. They'd probably confiscate it. Maybe the insurance company would sue to recoup the losses they'd paid to the estates of the Three Ghouls' victims. Or, perhaps Orlov's family would claim it all.

Then an idea came to him that seemed to be infinitely more justifiable and elegant than any of the other alternatives he'd just considered. He opened the website for a national victim's assistance group and found the organization's telephone number. He called the number and asked to speak to someone who handled contributions.

"This is Natalie Johnson. How may I assist you?"

"Miss Johnson, my name is Vitaly Orlov. I would like to make a contribution to your organization, but need wire transfer instructions so my bank can wire funds to your account."

"That's very nice of you, Mr. Orlov. But I should advise you that we only allow wire transfers into our account in an amount greater than one thousand dollars. Do you plan to make a contribution of that size or greater?"

"Greater," Race said.

"Wonderful. Would you like me to email the instructions to you, or can I give them to you now over the phone?"

"Now would be best."

During the next hour Race purged all of Orlov's accounts and transferred the money to the charitable organization.

There was other research that Race had planned to do. He felt energized as he Googled a number of Orlov's clients' names from the Russian's notebook and found, for the most part, they were respected members of finance, industry, government, and old name families from across the planet. He went through the notebook, page by page, until he found a transaction that had closed five days after Mary and his daughters had been murdered. Orlov had apparently sold the coins the Three Ghouls stole from Race to a man named Jean-Louis Rambert of Nice, France. Race studied everything he could find on the Internet about Rambert.

Race then took photos with a cell phone of every one of the client pages in Orlov's notebook and sent the photos to Detective Barbara Lassiter's email address.

The next email he sent was to Victor Graves at the *New Mexico Herald-Tribune*: This is the last time you will hear from me. I appreciate your help and hope you've found some peace. Attached is a summary of what I've learned about the five years of home invasions committed by the Three Ghouls. You might find it helpful if you decide to publish a story about those monsters. A few questions you should ask are: Why wasn't any of the information about the coin thefts released to the media? Who made the decision to withhold that information? How many of the victims of the Three Ghouls would be alive today if the coin collection link had been made public five years ago?

Race heaved a huge sigh. He suddenly felt free. As though he'd unburdened his soul by accomplishing the mission he'd started over three years ago. But then a new weight bore down on him as he thought about Eric Matus. Even the murders he'd committed—despite the vile natures of his victims—seemed to burden his conscience. Then the faces of his wife and daughters filled his mind and cleared it of any feeling of guilt. He whispered to himself, "Maybe I can atone for the evil I've done with good deeds in the future." He didn't feel convinced.

To try to clean his mind of bad thoughts, he picked up Victor Orlov's cell phone and scanned through it. Apparently, the guy didn't often use the phone or he frequently deleted most of his phone activity. There were only three names in his recent calls list. They were all Dallas numbers. When he called them, Race learned they were numbers for Orlov's strip clubs.

There were no email accounts on the phone, but there were forty-nine listings in the Contacts section. Race scrolled down through the contacts and saw that a few showed the same telephone numbers that were in the recent calls list. He continued down the list and found that many of the listings showed only first names or initials. Nothing really piqued Race's curiosity until he came to the two listings under the letter "S.": "Steve" and "S." Next to the "S" listing was the telephone number 202-555-3000. Race recognized the Washington, D.C. area code.

"Hmm," he whispered. He dialed the number using Orlov's phone and dropped his jaw when a receptionist answered, "Federal Bureau of Investigation." He terminated the call and asked himself, "Why would a criminal like Orlov have the FBI's telephone number in his contact list? And why the main number?"

He scrolled back up to the "A's" and opened each contact. Nothing. Then he opened a contact listed as SD. The telephone number for the contact also started with the D.C. area code and the same prefix in the FBI's main number. The final four numbers were 3193. Race dialed the number and got a recording that told him he had reached the extension of a man in the FBI's Criminal Investigation Division. The name meant nothing to him. After he considered what Orlov's connection to the FBI might be and couldn't come up with anything viable, he decided to send the information on to Detective Barbara Lassiter. Let her deal with it.

# CHAPTER 55

"Your friend is a wealth of information," Susan said. "His last message raises some very interesting possibilities."

"I can come up with two reasons why Sanjay Darzi's initials and telephone number would be in Orlov's cell phone," Barbara said. "Darzi's on Orlov's payroll, or Orlov's an informant for the FBI."

"Considering Orlov's connection to the Three Ghouls, I would have to say that neither possibility would be good."

Barbara nodded. "You wanna share with Sophia?"

"Sure."

"How are you enjoying your vacation?" Sophia Otero-Hansen asked as she took the chair between Barbara and Susan at a table in Yanni's on Central Avenue near the University of New Mexico.

"Ha, ha, ha," Susan said. "It's nice to see that Federal agents have a sense of humor."

Otero-Hansen patted Susan's arm. "Enjoy it while you can. You'll be back working 24/7 again before you know it."

Susan groaned.

Barbara said, "Our guy at OMI told us that Farmington P.D. left the Franchini house uncovered. Apparently, the place was sanitized."

Otero-Hansen wagged her head. "Franchini called in a professional cleaning crew."

"When the hell did he do that?" Susan said. "He was in the

hospital."

"Musta called them from his hospital bed. Claimed he didn't want his wife traumatized any more than she was already. Didn't want her to come home to blood on the carpet. He had the crew come in before the OMI techs arrived from Albuquerque."

"What about fingerprints?" Barbara asked. "The guy who killed McCall must have left prints somewhere."

"Nope. Franchini told the cleaners to wipe every inch of the place."

"It's like the old man wanted to destroy evidence," Susan said.

Otero-Hansen spread her hands. "I could see why he might want to protect the guy who saved their lives."

"Didn't the locals put up crime scene tape?" Barbara said.

Otero-Hansen laughed. "Of course. The cleaners removed that, too."

After a waitress took their order, Barbara asked, "Why'd the Bureau suppress the information about the coins?"

Otero-Hansen's face reddened. She opened her mouth but didn't say anything.

"Come on, Sophia, you can tell us."

"I don't know anything about why. All I know is that Lucas ordered us to keep our mouths shut about the coin collection link to the home invasions."

"How and why'd the Bureau keep the information out of the NCIC system?" Barbara asked.

"I have no idea."

Barbara thought Sophia looked incredibly uncomfortable. "It's a colossal blunder or someone's in the tank with the bad guys."

Otero-Hansen shrugged. Then she said, "I can agree that someone made a mistake, but I don't buy the theory that there's corruption involved."

Barbara pulled a copy of the email she'd received from the man who had earlier sent her Orlov's notebook pages. "Read that," she said.

Otero-Hansen took the sheet of paper and read it. Then she read it again. Finally, she looked up at Susan, then at Barbara and said, "Oh shit."

"How'd you get this?"

Barbara looked at Susan and then back at Otero-Hansen. "We're detectives. We're paid to uncover juicy information."

"I'll look into it," Otero-Hansen said.

"You've got forty-eight hours. If you don't bring us an explanation that isn't bullshit within that time, we're going to our boss and to the media. If there's corruption at the FBI, that's a story that must be told."

Otero-Hansen's color turned dark red. After a few seconds, she turned pale.

"I wondered why Darzi came all the way from D.C. to join your team on the trip to Farmington."

"That was curious, wasn't it?" Otero-Hansen said.

"How will you handle this information?" Susan asked. "Based on the little time we've been around your boss, I suspect that asshole would probably try to suppress any information that could harm Darzi."

"Lucas was already in trouble because of the way he handled things in Farmington. Letting that reporter go. The word is out that Darzi's retiring Lucas, but with full pension benefits. Darzi's doing the old D.C. two-step to cover his ass."

Barbara shook her head. "There's no justice."

Susan said, "At least Lucas won't be around to screw things up anymore."

They sat quietly for a minute, then Otero-Hansen asked, "Anything new on your vigilante killer?"

Barbara looked back at Susan. "You go ahead, Susan."

Susan smiled at Otero-Hansen. "We were just talking about him before you arrived. We received a phone call and email from a guy who we believe is our dark angel. He provided us with information about people involved with the Three Ghouls robberies and left us with the impression that he wanted the system to deal with them."

"You going to share that information with me."

"Maybe," Barbara said. "We'll see."

Otero-Hansen shot her a sour look.

"We've come to the conclusion the guy's a ghost," Susan said. "We'll never find him, especially now that he's stopped."

"You mean you don't think he'll do any more killing? How could you possibly know that?"

"The fact that he called us and gave us information tells me he's done.

After Otero-Hansen left the restaurant, Susan asked, "You get anywhere with that stuff our mystery man emailed?"

"Yeah. I went over most of the files. You know the people in there are rich, powerful, and influential."

"What can two little old female detectives in River City do with a bunch like that?"

Barbara smiled. "I'll put you up against the lot of them any day of the week. But we can always bring in Sophia if we need Federal clout."

"Which I think we will."

Barbara nodded.

Susan asked, "You want to get together—"

Barbara's cell phone rang. Susan waved to tell her to answer it.

"Lassiter," Barbara said into the phone.

"Detective Lassiter, this is Special Agent Chet MacAuslan in Kansas City. You have a minute to talk?"

"Hold on a second."

She muted the phone and said to Susan, "An FBI agent in Kansas City. Let's take this outside."

They exited the restaurant and walked to the corner of the building. Barbara took her phone off mute and engaged the speaker. "I'm back, Agent MacAuslan. My partner, Detective Martinez is here, too. What can we do for you?"

"I received a call from a man who suggested I contact you regarding information he provided me. Something about the Three Ghouls crew."

"This caller give you a name?"

"Nope."

Barbara met Susan's gaze and they both nodded.

"Tell you what, Agent MacAuslan, you give me what you have and we'll reciprocate."

The call with MacAuslan lasted ten minutes. Barbara signed off after she'd promised to send the man copies of the information she'd received the day before from the mysterious, unidentified caller.

"That was interesting," Susan said. "Bet that insurance company CFO in Kansas City has plenty to tell them."

"I'd love to be in on that interrogation," Barbara said.

"How about getting together tonight to go over that stuff the guy emailed us?"

"Isn't it your yoga night?"

"I got kicked out of the class. I guess I'll have to find another yoga group."

"Why?"

"I organized a revolt. You remember the guy who water-boarded me with his sweat?"

"Of course." Barbara giggled until Susan frowned at her.

"I convinced four other women in the class to complain about the guy. They all elected me to be their spokeswoman."

"Seems to me you all had something to complain about. Why were you kicked out of the class?"

"The guy was the instructor's boyfriend. She really took it personally when I told her the guy smells like spoiled beef jerky."

Barbara tilted her head and squinted at Susan. "That's all you said?"

"Well, I may have mentioned that any woman who hung around with someone who smelled as bad as he did must have a fetish for rotten meat."

"That will do it every time," Barbara said.

"Anyway, do you want to get together?"

"I can't. I have a date."

A wistful expression came to Susan's face. "Henry?"

"Yeah, and Roger's coming along, too. We're going for Chinese." Barbara paused a second. "I'd invite you to join us, but I . . . know how you are."

"What's that supposed to mean?"

Barbara swallowed the lump that had suddenly come to her throat. She'd been tempted to have this conversation with Susan for a long time, but had been fearful she might ruin their friendship.

"Come on, Barbara, what's on your mind?"

"I can understand why you'd prefer dating guys who are macho men. That's your personal preference. But treating a man badly because he doesn't look like a man off the cover of a romance novel just isn't right."

Susan's eyes narrowed and her lips tightened. "Excuse me," she said. "I spent too many years married to a man who was everything that . . . ."

"Everything that Leno Sanchez isn't?" Barbara said, finishing Susan's statement.

Susan's face reddened. She looked away.

"God forgive me for talking ill of the dead, but the only things your husband Manny had going for him were his looks and you. He lacked balls, personality, and confidence. Overall, he was just plain lacking. Guys like Leno Sanchez have all those qualities. But they're lacking where it counts: love, affection, respect, selflessness—"

This time Susan held up a hand and stopped Barbara. "Sounds like you've been practicing that speech."

"Yeah, I guess I have. I've wanted to say these things to you for a while."

Susan's eyes widened and her eyebrows arched. "I should be pissed at you."

"Because I told you how I feel?"

"No, because you held back telling me for so long."

Barbara tried to hide the surprise she felt but knew she'd been only half-successful in doing so. "Thanks for listening."

Susan smiled. Then she seemed to turn melancholy. Her eyelids lowered and the corners of her mouth turned down. Then tears fell from her eyes. "My marriage to Manny was a mess. I loved him so much when we met in school. I thought I'd died and gone to heaven the day we married. But things just seemed to go downhill from there. I've avoided getting serious about any man ever since Manny was killed."

"I understand," Barbara said. "I guess your choices are to either enter a convent or open yourself up to meeting a good man."

Susan nodded. "I guess we should take off."

"Sure," Barbara said.

Susan looked up at the sky. "Looks like the weather's finally turning for the better."

"Yeah. It's about time. The last two weeks have been miserable. Atypical Albuquerque weather."

Susan turned and stared at Barbara. She looked a little unsettled and a lot unsure of herself.

"You know, I'm the last person Roger would want to see," Susan said.

"Are you saying you'd like Roger to give you another chance?"

She blushed. "Yeah, that's what I'm saying. Do you think he would?"

"As long as you leave Bitchy Susan at home and let Sweet Susan come out and play."

"I can do that, Babs. I would really like to do that."

TWO DAYS LATER

# CHAPTER 56

Sanjay Darzi tried to display professional calm, even though his body seemed to be stoked on amphetamines. His three teams of Special Agents had gathered in the hangar at DFW Airport and were composed of FBI personnel from bureau offices from throughout the southwest. He raised a hand to get the attention of the thirty-five men and women. The people there immediately went quiet.

"You've all been briefed on our mission. Vitaly Orlov's criminal organization stretches from Texas to Louisiana on the east and to Arizona on the west. Special Action Teams will hit Orlov's non-Texas businesses simultaneously with the start of our operations here. Dallas police officers will join your teams. Each of you will supervise a squad of police officers and will raid the location on the ops order in the folder already given to you. I want you to rendezvous with your assigned police officers by 0930 hours. We will take down all locations at 1000 hours sharp." He looked over the group of agents and asked, "Any questions?"

A man at the back of the hangar raised a hand and shouted, "Do we bring all contraband and cash we confiscate back here?"

"Correct," Darzi answered. "There's a secure property room set up behind me. I'll want everything properly inventoried. All you have to do is box up whatever you find and bring it back here."

He looked over the group again. When no other questions were asked, he announced, "It's now 0842. Let's do this as quickly and painlessly as possible."

As the men and women in the hangar dispersed, Darzi waggled a finger at Special Agent-in-Charge Bruce Lucas, who walked over to him.

"You know where Orlov's home and office are?"

"Yes, sir."

"Good. We'll go to the home first."

"You think he's got cash and drugs stored there?"

"We'll soon find out."

Lucas drove a gray Chevrolet Tahoe from the tarmac outside the hangar. He swung through the industrial part of the airport and then out onto public streets. They were still a couple miles away from the Turtle Creek neighborhood of Dallas when Lucas asked, "Are cops going to join us in the search?"

Darzi shook his head. "Not necessary. I had our people evacuate Orlov's home and office early this morning. There won't be any resistance. Orlov's accountant is meeting us at the house. He'll accompany us to the man's office, too. The CPA has combinations to Orlov's safes and keys to his cabinets."

Lucas scoffed. "How'd you get the accountant to cooperate?"

"We worked out an immunity deal. He cooperates and he doesn't go to jail for thirty years on RICO charges."

Orlov's accountant was waiting for Darzi on the front steps of a palatial residence that looked as though it had twenty thousand square feet of space under a pitched slate roof. The accountant was a large, corpulent man with rheumy eyes, broken veins in his cheeks, and dark bags under his eyes. The guy had a tic in his left eyelid that twitched continuously.

"Lead the way," Darzi ordered the man.

At 1000 hours, the FBI squad leaders with their contingents of Dallas police officers stormed strip clubs, restaurants, nightclubs, and office buildings owned by Vitaly Orlov. By 1015 hours, cardboard boxes full of cash, drugs, weapons, and files were already being loaded in the backs of FBI SUVs and panel trucks. The teams had hit facilities in Dallas, Fort Worth, Plano, Flower Mound, Garland, Irving, Lewisville, and a dozen other cities around the Dallas and Fort Worth metroplex.

The teams punched holes in walls, tore up carpeting, slashed sofas and chairs, and generally made a mess of Orlov's holdings.

In Richardson, Texas, about twenty miles north of Dallas, Special Agent Daniel Duckworth supervised his squad of police officers as they packed up cash found in a cardboard box hidden behind the drywall of an office, half-a-dozen automatic rifles, and a large crate of prescription opioids. Duckworth performed a cursory sweep of the nightclub he and his squad had been assigned to and was about to order his people to load up and lock up when something caught his eye. At the end of a hallway, at the back end of the building, Duckworth noted that the exterior walls ran in a straight line but the interior walls didn't match up. At first, he assumed there might be a utility chase between the interior and exterior walls on one side of the hallway. But, after some reflection and banging on the interior wall with his fist, he decided that a little demolition work might be in order.

"Get me a sledge hammer," Duckworth called to one of his cops. When the man returned with the tool, Duckworth told him, "Make me a hole in the center of that wall."

He watched the cop slug away at the wall, creating a hole the size of a large medicine ball.

"That's good," Duckworth said. "Let me take a look."

He took a flashlight from the policeman and shone the light beam into the hole. "Well, well," he said. "What do we have here?" He reached into the hole and grabbed a canvas bag, hefted the bag from the space behind the wall, and placed it on the floor. He pulled open the drawstrings and looked inside. Duckworth snatched the bag off the floor, slung it over a shoulder, and marched to an office on the other side of the club. After he closed the office door, he laid the bag on a desk, and extracted twenty-seven DVDs in plastic containers. He then went through the stacks of DVDs, reading the grease-penciled writing on each disk. There were names on each plastic tray. He went through them one-by-one, but he didn't recognize any of the names. Until he came to the twenty-first DVD. Written on that tray in bold, black letters was the initial "S" followed by a period, and the name DARZI.

Duckworth opened the plastic tray and removed the DVD. He powered up a television and a DVD player on a credenza and inserted the disk. After five minutes of viewing, Duckworth felt his heart hammering. "Oh, shit," he exclaimed."

ONE WEEK LATER

# CHAPTER 57

The sun shone bright on Albuquerque's Old Town Plaza. It felt wonderful on her back.

"Finally warmed up," Barbara said to Susan.

"About damned time. I can't remember a February this cold." Susan looked around and smiled as she watched what appeared to be an extended Hispanic family picnic lunching in the park at the center of the plaza. An elderly couple sat in folding chairs, while three pairs of adults tried to shepherd half-a-dozen children. "I remember when my folks used to bring us down here."

"How long's it been since you lost your parents?" Barbara asked.

"Almost five years. Mom died of cancer; Dad followed her six months later. I swear he died of a broken heart." Then Susan grimaced, but quickly tried to smile at Barbara. "Thank God I have you as a partner," she said. "Other than cousins who I never see and with whom I have nothing in common, you're the only family I have."

Barbara nodded. "Same with me, partner."

"Don't you have an aunt who lives in Santa Fe? Married to a cop."

"My aunt passed away several years ago and I was never close to her anyway. When my parents died there was nothing really left that tied us together." Barbara scrunched up her face and wagged her head. "Probably should give my cousins a call some time."

"They're in Santa Fe?"

"No, they're here in Albuquerque. Their father still lives in Santa Fe."

Susan again smiled at Barbara. "You know, we're pathetic. Got cousins right here in River City and never even call them."

"Phone calls work both ways. My cousins never call me either."

Susan suddenly looked serious and said, "I can understand that, with your personality and all."

"You should talk. I'll bet—" Barbara stopped when she spotted Sophia Otero-Hansen cross Old Town Plaza from the south. She elbowed Susan seated next to her on the park bench. "Here she comes."

"Can't wait to hear her story."

"Ought to be a doozey."

Otero-Hansen stopped in front of the bench and looked down at them. "You two look like two kids at Christmas. Full of expectation."

"Don't disappoint us," Barbara said.

Barbara slid to the right to make space for Otero-Hansen.

"Thanks. I don't think I could tell you what I learned while standing. My legs are a bit shaky."

Barbara made a go-ahead gesture with her hand as Otero-Hansen sat between them.

The FBI agent took in a big breath and let it out slowly. "Would it be enough to tell you that Sanjay Darzi has been forced to retire from the Bureau, pending possible legal repercussions?"

"No. Not even close," Susan said.

"I didn't think so." She visibly swallowed, then said, "Darzi was using Orlov as a confidential informant. The Bureau and the DEA caught him moving vast amounts of cocaine eight years ago. The Feds worked out a deal with him. In return for immunity from prosecution, Orlov provided intelligence about his former drug connections. But Orlov didn't change his stripes. Instead of just dealing in narcotics, he got into the business of fencing other things."

"Like rare coins," Susan said.

Otero-Hansen nodded. "Bruce Lucas worked the first three home invasion cases. At the time, he reported to a Special Agent in Charge who reported to Darzi. Somehow, Darzi put two and two together and tied the home invasions to Orlov. Darzi realized that his CI had put him in jeopardy. He was high enough up in the FBI that he was able to scrub the NCIC system of any reference to coin collections being stolen. Every time Orlov's crew stole another collection, Darzi made certain there was no reference to the coin collection in the computer. He knew Orlov was fencing valuable coins and knew that was really the only way anyone could make a connection between Orlov and the Three Ghouls. The only references recorded in the system had to do with torture and murder."

"Why didn't Darzi shut Orlov down?" Barbara asked.

Otero-Hansen's face went red. She gulped and shook her head. "Turns out Orlov had a video library in one of his Dallas nightclubs. He was extorting people who he'd filmed doing nasty things. Last week, Darzi sent teams to Dallas to sanitize every one of Orlov's clubs, his residence, his office, and a restaurant the Russian owned. One of the teams uncovered a vault of videos. But the team leader, after viewing some of the videos, turned them over to the FBI's Office of Professional Responsibility. You see, one of them showed Sanjay Darzi in the buff with a man *and* a woman."

Barbara turned to look at Otero-Hansen. "You said Darzi retired."

"That's right."

"In other words, your story will never go public."

Otero-Hansen momentarily looked nauseous and then shrugged. "That's right. Unless you decide to tell the media. Part of my mission here today is to convince you to keep what I've told you between us girls. You will accomplish nothing by disclosing what I've told you except to undermine confidence in the Bureau."

"Maybe that's exactly what should happen," Susan said.

The nauseous look came over Otero-Hansen's face again.

"You said your mission is to try to get us to keep our mouths shut," Barbara said. "Is that on orders from Washington?"

Otero-Hansen nodded and said, "I'd really appreciate your cooperation. If I fail to get your cooperation, it won't go well for me."

"We'll get back to you on that," Barbara said.

Otero-Hansen stood, looked from Barbara to Susan, and then

walked away. Barbara watched her return to the south side of the plaza and cross the street to a car. After she entered the sedan and drove away, Barbara turned back to Susan and was surprised at the expression on her partner's face.

"What's wrong, Susan?"

Susan pointed to the bandstand in the center of the plaza.

Barbara turned her head to look where Susan pointed. "Sonofa—" she blurted as she recognized Leno Sanchez.

"That bastard must be stalking me. I thought I'd seen his car a few times, but I brushed it off as just my imagination."

Barbara stood to intercept Sanchez, who wore a stormy look. His face appeared flushed and his eyes were like small black marbles. He moved with apparent purpose. When he tried to move around her, Barbara stepped forward.

"What the hell are you doing here?" she demanded.

Sanchez seemed to look through her. He gripped her arms and shoved her backward. She hit the ground with an "oomph" and shouted, "Leno, don't do anything stupid."

But Sanchez had already moved toward Susan, who had come off the bench and advanced on him. Sanchez grabbed her by the throat with his huge left hand and swung her around. As Barbara got to her feet, she saw Susan aim a knee at Sanchez's crotch, but the man must have anticipated the kick and deflected it off his thigh. He balled his right fist and cocked it as though he was about to pummel Susan's face.

"You cost me my job, you bitch," he roared. "I thought we had something, and then you embarrass me by being seen in Blacky's with some *joto*."

Barbara rushed at Sanchez and tried to put him in a chokehold. But he tossed her off him as though she was weightless. She heard Susan gasping for breath. She jumped behind him and again tried to put him in a chokehold, but he swung his cocked arm and hit her in the chest with his elbow. The blow sent her flying. She tried to get to her feet, but stumbled and fell to her knees. The center of her chest felt as though she'd been struck with a baseball bat.

Barbara sucked in a breath, got to her feet, and pulled her .38 from her hip holster. She grasped the barrel end of the gun and swung it with full force against the back of Sanchez's head. The big man shook his head, released Susan, and slowly turned around to face Barbara. His eyes were crossed and his mouth gaped like he was a beached fish. He seemed confused. Then his eyes rolled up into his head, his legs gave way, and he collapsed onto the dirt.

The extended family that had been enjoying the unusually warm weather now gathered around Barbara and Susan and the semi-conscious Leno Sanchez.

"You got him good," one of the young women announced.

Another one said, "Man, he went down like he was a sack of bricks."

"Everything's okay here," Barbara said to the small crowd that had formed around them. "We've got it under control."

As the people walked away, one of the Hispanic women turned, pointed at Sanchez, and shouted, "Only a *pinche joto* attacks a woman."

"You hear that, Leno?" Susan said as she bent down and looked into Sanchez's glazed eyes. "Who's the *pinche joto* now?"

TWO WEEKS LATER

# CHAPTER 58

"I saw your Corvette downstairs," Barbara said. "I can't believe you finally got it back."

"Can you believe it? It's been almost three weeks."

"What did your crooked mechanic charge you to fix the thing?"

"Anything he charges is cheap. That car is a classic."

"That car is a classic piece of shit."

"What's got your panties twisted this morning?" Susan asked.

"You're not angry about the Feds taking the case from us?"

"You need to come back down to earth, partner. Did you really believe we'd ever be able to run an international investigation from little old Albuquerque, New Mexico?" Susan banged a riff on her desk with her hands. "At least your friend, Sophia, got a promotion and is heading up the whole kit and caboodle out of D.C."

"I told you she wasn't that much of a friend."

"What do you mean?"

"She's the one who made the decision to ace us out of the investigation team."

Susan's big eyes went wide. "You're kidding?"

"Nope."

"After all we did for her, including agreeing to keep our mouths shut about Sanjay Darzi?"

"Yep."

Susan said, "She probably didn't have a choice. Some big gun at the FBI more than likely told her to dump us. Besides, what could we have added at this point?"

"Eh, you're probably right. But I had visions of trips to London and Paris. Exotic places across the globe."

"Look at it this way, Babs. Sophia's got D.C., London, and Paris. We've got Martineztown and Espanola."

"Oh, that makes me feel so much better."

Susan wagged a finger at Barbara. "Before you get too morose, I had a thought last night that might elevate your spirits."

"It would have to be pretty damned spectacular to elevate *my* spirits."

"What's wrong? Is everything all right with you and Henry?"

Barbara frowned. "No. That's not it. Henry's taking care of me just fine. But even with his undivided attention to my needs, I'm still pissed and frustrated." She spread her arms. "You said you had a thought last night."

"Yep. I did some research early this morning. Called the National Personnel Records Center at the National Archives in St. Louis. Talked to a lady in the Military Records Office. Had a nice conversation with—"

"I assume this is going somewhere," Barbara interrupted.

"Okay, Miss Panties-All-Twisted-In-A-Knot, do you want to hear my story or are you going to interrupt me again?"

"Go ahead."

"What's one of the first things we usually do when a person of interest pops up in the middle of an investigation?"

"We check on his background, his family members, and his associates."

"Right. And who popped up in the middle of our vigilante killer case who we never checked on?"

Barbara leaned back in her chair and rubbed her temples. Then she recited a list of people they'd encountered during the investigation. "The families of the victims. The Graves, the Puccinis, the—"

"Cold."

"The guy and his girlfriend at the Bellagio?"

"Colder."

"One of the victims in the Las Vegas parking lot?"

"Warmer."

"Just tell me, will ya?"

"Eric Matus."

"And you called the Military Records Office . . ."

"Yeah. As I was saying before I was rudely interrupted, I had a nice conversation with a lady in St. Louis. I asked her a very simple question: What were the names of the men who served with Eric Matus on his Special Forces "A" Team?"

"Sonofagun," Barbara said. "You're thinking the vigilante is someone who served with Matus?"

"You remember we considered that Matus might be the killer when it was discovered that his talent agency was nothing but a front for who knows what?"

"Right. But when those two guys, along with Matus, were killed in the parking lot in Las Vegas, we initially wrote off Matus as the killer."

"But then we figured that wasn't probable because the Bukowski guy had been shot and there was no weapon found at the scene. Later, we assumed the killer offed Reese McCall in Farmington and Vitaly Orlov in Dallas, which obviously proved that Matus couldn't be the killer."

"So, we wrote off Matus as collateral damage and never checked to see if the killer might have been associated with Matus at some point in the past."

"Exactamundo," Susan said. "That's where we screwed up."

"You found out something from the records office?"

"There were seven guys from Matus's Special Forces "A" Team the Army shows as still alive. Six of them didn't ring any bells. But one did."

"You're killing me, Susan. Who?"

"Guy named Robert Thornton."

"Isn't that the name of—?"

"Yeah, one of the Three Ghouls' victims. He lost his wife and two daughters, and was nearly beaten to death himself when those three psychopaths broke into his home over three years ago."

"Oh shit. And he's the only one of the Three Ghouls' victims who survived an attack."

"That's right. And he had a valuable coin collection taken in the home invasion."

"He lived in Amarillo, if I recall correctly."

"He did. I called the Amarillo P.D. Talked to a Detective Forrester. He told me Thornton left Amarillo after he lost his family. Apparently the guy calls in to Forrester every few months or so to find out if there's been any progress in the case. Forrester said he got a call from the man about three weeks ago. Thornton claimed to be in Philadelphia on business. Forrester hasn't heard from him since."

"Did you do a search for Thornton?"

"I sure did. Remember when you said that the guy's a ghost. Well, he still is. There's been literally nothing transacted in his name since he sold his home and computer business in Amarillo three years ago. No credit cards. No driver's licenses. Absolutely *nada*. I called the other six members of Thornton and Matus's SF unit. None of them ever heard from Thornton or Matus after they left the service.

"I Googled the guy and found some really old stuff on him. Handsome guy. College graduate. Baseball player. Awarded a Silver Star and two Purple Hearts for service in Iraq. He was an IT superstar renowned in his industry. He could apparently make a computer sing."

"All-American all the way."

Susan grinned. "There's something else. You remember the three coins found in Reese McCall's three abdominal wounds?"

"Of course."

"Three coins for three victims. Thornton's wife and two daughters."

"It must be him," Barbara said. "You're a genius."

"Aw, shucks, Babs." Susan chuckled. "There's one more little piece of information you might be interested in."

"What's that?"

"Robert Thornton and his wife Mary were part of a theater group in Amarillo. Thornton played supporting roles as an actor in the group. His wife did all the makeup for the actors."

"I'll be damned," Barbara said. "Thornton was at the very least exposed to makeup and disguises. He's a ghost because he keeps changing his appearance."

A sour expression came over Barbara's face. "We have a name and a face. But there wasn't one piece of forensic evidence found at any of his kill sites that tie's him to a single crime. Even if we brought the guy in, short of a confession, we'd never hang a thing on him."

"And, I suspect, bringing him in is a highly unlikely event. Ghost, dark angel, or spirit warrior, Robert Thornton, I'm afraid, is out in the wind. And I'll bet that's where he stays."

"We'd better talk to Salas before we close our investigation," Barbara said.

"Yeah. Good idea. But I don't think he'll be against it."

That evening after work, Barbara ran the three blocks from her house to the Albuquerque Academy and put in an hour's jog around the school property.

She downed a bottle of water back at her place and kicked off her running shoes. Just the thought of a hot shower felt exhilarating. She crossed the den and moved toward her bedroom when her cell phone rang. She looked at the caller ID: Sophia. Wonderful. Just about the last person she wanted to talk to. But she admitted she was acting petulant and childish and answered the call.

"Hey," Barbara said.

"Hi, Barbara. How are things?"

"Good. How 'bout with you?"

"Things are good, although this Vitaly Orlov investigation is driving me mad. I can't tell you when I last exercised or had a good meal. Most of the people we're investigating are Teflon-coated. Every time I go after one of them, I get a call from the State Department, or the CIA, or the Commerce Department, or one of a dozen other agencies suggesting I back off."

Barbara sighed, suddenly happy that she and Susan didn't have to deal with Washington politics and corruption.

"Anyway, that's not why I called. I thought you might be interested in something that just came to my attention. You remember that one of the pages in Orlov's notebook had the name

Jean-Louis Rambert on it?"

"Sure. The owner of the company that manufactures chair lifts for ski resorts."

"That's the guy. Except, he's also a major arms dealer who has some very bad Middle Eastern groups on his client list. I just received a call from an agent I sent to Nice to talk with Rambert. He found the man dead in his home."

"Dead, like heart attack dead?"

"Nope. Dead, like swallowed liquid heroin dead."

Barbara took a sharp intake of breath. "You're making that up."

"No way. Did you happen to notice in the information your anonymous benefactor sent you when Rambert bought coins from Orlov?"

"Yeah. About three plus years ago. Five days after the home invasion in Amarillo, Texas. Five days after Robert Thornton was almost beaten to death. Five days after Thornton's wife and two daughters were brutally assaulted and murdered."

"Sounds as though you already suspect Thornton is your vigilante."

"Susan and I talked about just that today. We also learned that Thornton served in the Army with Eric Matus, the guy killed a few weeks ago in Las Vegas."

"We ought to be able to put Thornton away for the rest of his life. My God, he murdered more than a dozen people."

"Did he leave any evidence behind in Nice?" Barbara asked.

"No, but—"

"Do you have a clue about his whereabouts?"

"Not yet, but—"

"Neither do we." After a beat, she added, "Think about what the man has done, then tell me if there's a jury in the land that would convict him. He eliminated scumbags, including those bank robbers in Albuquerque; he brought closure to families who suffered horrendous losses; and, if it is Robert Thornton, he suffered unimaginable personal loss himself."

"Yeah, but none of that is reason to let him off the hook."

"Okay, tell you what I'll do. I'll bring the guy in and charge him with multiple counts of murder if you can find him for me. You guys have the budget to mount a national investigation; we don't. But I want to remind you of something you told me a few weeks ago. Remember when you said the Three Ghouls investigation at the FBI had gone on for years and that the careers of several agents had been ruined because of their inability to track down the gang?"

"Yeah, I remember."

"How much time do you think the Bureau would allow you to work on finding Robert Thornton before it decided you had wasted time and resources for nothing? And let's say you did find Thornton, charged him, and brought him to trial, what would the Bureau's reaction be if you couldn't prove that Thornton had broken a single law, or, if you could prove he was the vigilante killer, but a jury found him innocent?" Barbara waited for Otero-Hansen to respond, but after a few seconds of silence, she added, "And if you pursue this, Lucas's stupidity and Darzi's crimes might be revealed. That happens, you'd become persona non grata throughout your organization."

Otero-Hansen still didn't respond for several seconds. Then she finally said, "Say hello to Susan. I'll call you if I'm ever in Albuquerque."

# EPILOGUE

Septuagenarians Harry and Ruthie Galante walked between 7 and 8 p.m. every night, rain or shine. Not that it rained very often in Henderson, Nevada. But as Harry frequently said, "It sure shines a lot here in Nevada."

Their routine was to go right down their street, turn left after two blocks, and then meander on a walking trail for two miles. At the end of the trail, they'd reconnect with their street and stroll back to their ranch-style house. This was just like any other day. The same course. The same conversation about this or that neighbor. Old lady Folger and her fifty hummingbird feeders. Jock Teettle and his goddamn bulldog that crapped all over the neighborhood. The ten-year-old O'Hara twins who were already hell on wheels.

"Wait 'til they're teenagers," Harry would say every time he and Ruthie passed the O'Hara house.

Christy Ledbetter's house was four doors down from the Galante's home. Harry always sucked in his gut and stood a little straighter when they passed Christy's house. Even at seventy-six, Harry had an eye for good-looking young women. Ruthie knew this and never let it bother her. Harry could look all he wanted as long as he didn't touch. As they approached the Ledbetter house, Harry pointed at the pickup truck out front.

"I thought Christy sold that truck a few weeks back."

"She did," Ruthie said. "Angeline told me the man she sold the truck to is back here for a visit." Ruthie poked Harry with her elbow. "I guess you're shit out of luck, Harry. She's got a boyfriend."

Harry smiled at Ruthie. "She don't know what she's missing. But you could tell her all about that."

Ruthie giggled. "You're like a teenager, Harry."

"Hope the guy's nicer to her than her bum-of-a-husband was."

Ruthie took Harry's hand. "Angeline says he's real nice. Nice looking man, in a rugged sort of way. Has a beard and mustache. Must have been in an accident, though. Got a bunch of scars. Maybe a bit older than Christy. I think she said his name is Hugh Crandell."

"What's the guy do for a living?"

"I don't know. But he must have a good job. Angeline said she heard from Christy that he just got back from France on some big business deal."

THE END

# ABOUT THE AUTHOR

Prior to a long finance career, including a 16-year stint as a senior executive and board member of a NYSE-listed company, Joseph Badal served for six years as a commissioned officer in the U.S. Army in critical, highly classified positions in the U.S. and overseas, including tours of duty in Greece and Vietnam, and earned numerous military decorations.

He holds undergraduate and graduate degrees in business and graduated from the Defense Language Institute, West Coast and from Stanford University Law School's Director College.

Joe now serves on the boards of several companies.

He is the author of eleven published suspense novels and a two-time winner of the Tony Hillerman Prize for Best Fiction Book of the Year ("Ultimate Betrayal" in 2014 and "The Motive" in 2016). The Military Writers Society of America awarded Joe its Gold Medal in 2016 for "Death Ship," its Silver Medal in 2016 for "Terror Cell," and its Silver Medal in 2015 for "Evil Deeds." His "The Lone Wolf Agenda" was named the top Mystery/Thriller novel in the 2013 New Mexico/Arizona Book Awards competition.

Joe also writes a monthly blog titled *Everyday Heroes*, and has written short stories published in the "Uncommon Assassins," "Someone Wicked," and "Insidious Assassins" anthologies.

"Dark Angel," Joe's 11th novel and the second in his *Lassiter/Martinez Case Files* series, will be released on January 24, 2017.

In addition to authoring novels and short stories, Joe has written dozens of articles that have been published in various business and trade journals and is a frequent speaker at business, civic, and writers' events.

# "EVIL DEEDS"
## DANFORTH SAGA (#1)

"Evil Deeds" is the first book in the *Bob Danforth* series, which includes "Terror Cell" and "The Nostradamus Secret." In this three book series, the reader can follow the lives of Bob & Liz Danforth, and of their son, Michael, from 1971 through 2011. "Evil Deeds" begins on a sunny spring day in 1971 in a quiet Athenian suburb. Bob & Liz Danforth's morning begins just like every other morning: Breakfast together, Bob roughhousing with Michael. Then Bob leaves for his U.S. Army unit and the nightmare begins, two-year-old Michael is kidnapped.

So begins a decades-long journey that takes the Danforth family from Michael's kidnapping and Bob and Liz's efforts to rescue him, to Bob's forced separation from the Army because of his unauthorized entry into Bulgaria, to his recruitment by the CIA, to Michael's commissioning in the Army, to Michael's capture by a Serb SPETSNAZ team in Macedonia, and to Michael's eventual marriage to the daughter of the man who kidnapped him as a child. It is the stops along the journey that weave an intricate series of heart-stopping events built around complex, often diabolical characters. The reader experiences CIA espionage during the Balkans War, attempted assassinations in the United States, and the grisly exploits of a psychopathic killer.

"Evil Deeds" is an adrenaline-boosting story about revenge, love, and the triumph of good over evil.

https://amzn.com/B00LXG9QIC

# "TERROR CELL"
## DANFORTH SAGA (#2)

"Terror Cell" pits Bob Danforth, a CIA Special Ops Officer, against Greek Spring, a vicious terrorist group that has operated in Athens, Greece for three decades. Danforth's mission in the summer of 2004 is to identify one or more of the members of the terrorists in order to bring them to justice for the assassination of the CIA's Station Chief in Athens. What Danforth does not know is that Greek Spring plans a catastrophic attack against the 2004 Summer Olympic Games.

Danforth and his CIA team are hampered by years of Congressionally mandated rules that have weakened U.S. Intelligence gathering capabilities, and by indifference and obstructionism on the part of Greek authorities. His mission becomes even more difficult when he is targeted for assassination after an informant in the Greek government tells the terrorists of Danforth's presence in Greece.

In "Terror Cell," Badal weaves a tale of international intrigue, involving players from the CIA, the Greek government, and terrorists in Greece, Libya, and Iran—all within a historical context. Anyone who keeps up with current events about terrorist activities and security issues at the Athens Olympic Games will find the premise of this book gripping, terrifying, and, most of all, plausible.

"Joe Badal takes us into a tangled puzzle of intrigue and terrorism, giving readers a tense well-told tale and a page-turning mystery."
—Tony Hillerman, *New York Times* bestselling author

https://amzn.com/B00LXG9QNC

# "THE NOSTRADAMUS SECRET"
## DANFORTH SAGA (#3)

This latest historical thriller in the *Bob Danforth* series builds on Nostradamus's "lost" 58 quatrains and segues to present day. These lost quatrains have surfaced in the hands of a wealthy Iranian megalomaniac who believes his rise to world power was prophesied by Nostradamus. But he sees the United States as the principal obstacle to the achievement of his goals. So, the first step he takes is to attempt to destabilize the United States through a vicious series of terrorist attacks and assassinations.

Joseph Badal offers up another action-packed story loaded with intrigue, fascinating characters and geopolitical machinations that put the reader on the front line of present-day international conflict. You will be transported from a 16th century French monastery to the CIA, to crime scenes, to the Situation Room at the White House, to Middle Eastern battlefields.

"The Nostradamus Secret" presents non-stop action in a contemporary context that will make you wonder whether the story is fact or fiction, history or prophesy.

" 'The Nostradamus Secret' is a gripping, fast-paced story filled with truly fanatical, frightening villains bent on the destruction of the USA and the modern world. Badal's characters and the situations they find themselves in are hair-raising and believable. I couldn't put the book down. Bring on the sequel!"
—Catherine Coulter, *New York Times* bestselling author of "Double Take"

https://amzn.com/B00R3GTLVI

# "THE LONE WOLF AGENDA"
## DANFORTH SAGA (#4)

With "The Lone Wolf Agenda," Joseph Badal returns to the world of international espionage and military action thrillers and crafts a story that is as close to the real world of spies and soldiers as a reader can find. This fourth book in the *Danforth Saga* brings Bob Danforth out of retirement to hunt down lone wolf terrorists hell bent on destroying America's oil infrastructure. Badal weaves just enough technology into his story to wow even the most a-technical reader.

"The Lone Wolf Agenda" pairs Danforth with his son Michael, a senior DELTA Force officer, as they combat an OPEC-supported terrorist group allied with a Mexican drug cartel. This story is an epic adventure that will chill readers as they discover that nothing, no matter how diabolical, is impossible.

"A real page-turner in every good sense of the term. 'The Lone Wolf Agenda' came alive for me. It is utterly believable, and as tense as any spy thriller I've read in a long time."
—Michael Palmer, *New York Times* bestselling author of "Political Suicide"

https://amzn.com/B00LXG9QMI

# "DEATH SHIP"
## DANFORTH SAGA (#5)

"Death Ship" is another suspense-filled thriller in the 45-year-long journey of the Danforth family. This fifth book in the *Danforth Saga*, which includes "Evil Deeds," "Terror Cell," "The Nostradamus Secret," and "The Lone Wolf Agenda," introduces Robbie Danforth, the 15-year-old son of Michael and Miriana Danforth, and the grandson of Bob and Liz Danforth.

A leisurely cruise in the Ionian Sea turns into a nightmare event when terrorists hijack a yacht with Bob, Liz, Miriana, and Robbie aboard. Although the boat's crew, with Bob and Robbie's help, eliminate the hijackers, there is evidence that something more significant may be in the works.

The CIA and the U.S. military must identify what that might be and who is behind the threat, and must operate within a politically-corrupt environment in Washington, D.C. At the same time, they must disrupt the terrorist's financing mechanism, which involves trading in securities that are highly sensitive to terrorist events.

Michael Danforth and a team of DELTA operatives are deployed from Afghanistan to Greece to assist in identifying and thwarting the threat.

"Death Ship" is another roller coaster ride of action and suspense, where good and evil battle for supremacy and everyday heroes combat evil antagonists.

"Terror doesn't take a vacation in 'Death Ship'; instead Joseph Badal masterfully takes us on a cruise to an all too frightening, yet all too real destination. Once you step on board, you are hooked."
—Tom Avitabile, #1 Bestselling Author of "The Eighth Day" and "The Devil's Quota"

https://amzn.com/B016APTJAU

# "BORDERLINE"
## LASSITER/MARTINEZ
## CASE FILES #1

In "Borderline," Joseph Badal delivers his first mystery novel with the same punch and non-stop action found in his acclaimed thrillers.

Barbara Lassiter and Susan Martinez, two New Mexico homicide detectives, are assigned to investigate the murder of a wealthy Albuquerque socialite. They soon discover that the victim, a narcissistic borderline personality, played a lifetime game of destroying people's lives. As a result, the list of suspects in her murder is extensive.

The detectives find themselves enmeshed in a helix of possible perpetrators with opportunity, means, and motive—and soon question giving their best efforts to solve the case the more they learn about the victim's hideous past.

Their job gets tougher when the victim's psychiatrist is murdered and DVDs turn up that show the doctor had serial sexual relationships with a large number of his female patients, including the murder victim.

"Borderline" presents a fascinating cast of characters, including two heroic female detective-protagonists and a diabolical villain; a rollercoaster ride of suspense; and an ending that will surprise and shock the reader.

"Think *Cagney and Lacey*. Think *Thelma and Louise*. Think murder and mayhem—and you are in the death grip of a mystery that won't let you go until it has choked the last breath of suspense from you."
—Parris Afton Bonds, author of "Tamed the Wildest Heart" and co-founder of Romance Writers of America and cofounder of Southwest Writers Workshop

https://amzn.com/B00YZSAHI8
Available at Audible.com: http://adbl.co/1Y4WC5H

# "THE MOTIVE"
## THE CURTIS CHRONICLES: #1

In "The Motive," Joseph Badal presents the first book in his new series, *The Curtis Chronicles*. This latest addition to Badal's offering of acclaimed, best-selling thrillers delivers the same sort of action and suspense that readers have come to expect and enjoy from his previous nine novels.

Confronted with suspicious information relating to his sister Susan's supposed suicide in Honolulu, Albuquerque surgeon Matt Curtis questions whether his sister really killed herself. With the help of his sister's best friend, Renee Drummond, and his former Special Forces comrade, Esteban Maldonado, Matt investigates Susan's death. But Lonnie Jackson, the head of organized crime in Hawaii, afraid that Matt has gotten too close to the truth, sends killers after him.

This is an artfully written book that will appeal to readers who like thrillers with fully-developed characters, a big plot, and plenty of action, seasoned with friendship and romance.

"The Motive" puts the reader on a roller coaster ride of non-stop thrills and chills, propelled by realistic dialogue and a colorful cast of characters. It is another entertaining story from a master story-teller where good and evil struggle for supremacy and everyday heroes battle malevolent antagonists.

Joseph Badal's "The Motive" was awarded the Tony Hillerman Prize for Best Fiction Book at the New Mexico/Arizona Book Awards ceremony. This is Badal's second Tony Hillerman Prize, which he also received in 2014 for his stand-alone thriller, "Ultimate Betrayal."

"Sharp, fast-paced, well written."
—Meryl Sawyer, *New York Times* bestselling author of "Death's Door"

http://a.co/8VPEdhU

# "THE PYTHAGOREAN SOLUTION"
## STAND-ALONE THRILLER

The attempt to decipher a map leads to violence and death, and a decades-long sunken treasure.

When American John Hammond arrives on the Aegean island of Samos he is unaware of events that happened six decades earlier that will embroil him in death and violence and will change his life forever.

Late one night Hammond finds Petros Vangelos lying mortally wounded in an alley. Vangelos hands off a coded map, making Hammond the link to a Turkish tramp steamer that carried a fortune in gold and jewels and sank in a storm in 1945.

On board this ship, in a waterproof safe, are documents that implicate a German SS Officer in the theft of valuables from Holocaust victims and the laundering of those valuables by the Nazi's Swiss banker partner.

"Badal is a powerful writer who quickly reels you in and doesn't let go."
—Pat Frovarp & Gary Shulze, Once Upon A Crime Mystery Bookstore

https://amzn.com/B00W4JVIYC

# "ULTIMATE BETRAYAL"
## STAND-ALONE THRILLER

Inspired by actual events, "Ultimate Betrayal" is a thriller that takes the reader on an action-packed, adrenaline-boosting ride, from the streets of South Philadelphia, through the Afghanistan War, to Mafia drug smuggling, to the halls of power at the CIA and the White House.

David Hood comes from the streets of South Philadelphia, is a decorated Afghanistan War hero, builds a highly successful business, marries the woman of his dreams, and has two children he adores. But there are two ghosts in David's past. One is the guilt he carries over the death of his brother. The other is a specter that will do anything to murder him.

David has long lost the belief that good will triumph over evil. The deaths of his wife and children only reinforce that cynicism. And leave him with nothing but a bone-chilling, all-consuming need for revenge.

" 'Ultimate Betrayal' provides the ultimate in riveting reading entertainment that's as well thought out as it is thought provoking. Both a stand-out thriller and modern day morality tale. Mined from the familial territory of Harlan Coben, with the seasoned action plotting of James Rollins or Steve Berry, this is fiction of the highest order. Poignant and unrelentingly powerful."
—Jon Land, bestselling and award-winning author of "The Tenth Circle"

https://amzn.com/B00LXG9QGY

# "SHELL GAME"
## STAND-ALONE THRILLER

"Shell Game" is a financial thriller using the economic environment created by the capital markets meltdown that began in 2007 as the backdrop for a timely, dramatic, and hair-raising tale. Badal weaves an intricate and realistic story about how a family and its business are put into jeopardy through heavy-handed, arbitrary rules set down by federal banking regulators, and by the actions of a sociopath in league with a corrupt bank regulator.

Although a work of fiction, "Shell Game," through its protagonist Edward Winter, provides an understandable explanation of one of the main reasons the U.S. economy continues to languish. It is a commentary on what federal regulators are doing to the United States banking community today and, as a result, the damage they are inflicting on perfectly sound businesses and private investors across the country and on the overall U.S. economy.

"Shell Game" is inspired by actual events that have taken place as a result of poor governmental leadership and oversight, greed, corruption, stupidity, and badly conceived regulatory actions. You may be inclined to find it hard to believe what happens in this novel to both banks and bank borrowers. I encourage you to keep an open mind. "Shell Game" is a work of fiction that supports the old adage: You don't need to make this stuff up.

"Take a roller coaster ride through the maze of modern banking regulations with one of modern fiction's most terrifying sociopaths in the driver's seat. Along with its compelling, fast-paced story of a family's struggle against corruption, 'Shell Game' raises important questions about America's financial system based on well-researched facts."

—Anne Hillerman & Jean Schaumberg, WORDHARVEST

https://amzn.com/B00LXG9QFA

44371703R00192

Printed in Poland
by Amazon Fulfillment
Poland Sp. z o.o., Wrocław